FOREVER JACOB

Project New Hope

ISBN 978-1-61434-277-9

Printed in the United States of America.

BookLocker.com, Inc.
2011

First Edition

Vo Tran
yawzway.com
yawdraws@gmail.com

FOREVER JACOB

Project New Hope

Vo Tran

Special thanks to family (Thuy—for your continuous motivation),
Maryann Miller, Mrs. Doyle,
and to you—the reader.

Prologue

Her hands, blackened by a layer of dried blood mixed with dirt, were wrapped tightly around a protruding ledge nearly at eye-level. Her tight grip was the only thing keeping her balanced atop a narrow shelving of rock. With eyes sealed closed, she pressed her forehead against the back of her hands attempting to catch a much needed breath of the wickedly cold air. A warm, red fluid trickled down the entire length of her arm, soothing her velvet skin from the frosted-over surface of rock. The blood branched off into smaller streams and merged into the deep gashes of freshly open wounds all along her side, creating a chaotic assortment of red patches that stained her musty-smelling shirt.

Her feet were anchored inside a pair of knee-high boots, braced for yet another push—another exhausted effort. "Come on, Eve…" she encouraged herself. "Need to…start climbing."

She opened her eyes and exhaled, expelling a thick, nearly opaque plume of mist from her lungs which crystallized instantly in the cold air. "You…you can do this. You're almost at the top."

She bent her knees ready to push off. Her intent was pure, and her mind focused. The rest of her torn and battered body, however, disagreed and refused to respond. Before she could even attempt another effort, the muscles in her legs twitched and jerked before simply giving out. "Shit!"

Her feet slipped off of the rock shelf forcing her blunt fingernails to tear into the ledge. Her body hung suspended for a moment and then slammed into the side of the solid rock wall with a disgusting-sounding thud. Her heart pounded against her ribs causing a searing pain with every thump. Her respiration became erratic, forcing out an endless trail of mist that engulfed her entire face. Her feet dangled precariously. They were in a wild, dizzying search to find a natural crevasse, another ledge…anything within the wall to support her weight.

When a small opening was offered to her, she didn't hesitate. She buried both her boots so deep inside the opening; she could only hope that they would come loose when she needed them to.

Secure for the moment, Eve closed her eyes and took a dozen laborious breaths, pondering what could have happened. When the wild beat of her heart finally slowed, she opened her eyes and smiled slightly. She had been able to hang on. "Shit!" she said, exhausted by the sense of relief. "Shit..."

It didn't take long for the adrenaline to drain from her body. Once it did, her smile immediately became a grimace. She thought she would be used to the pain by now, but being wedged up against the sharp edges of rock, fused with the overwhelming cold, felt exactly like it did the very first time. It was mind-numbingly painful. She rested her head against her shoulder for a moment and then looked down, just in time to see the sections of the rock shelf, that had supported her fragile weight, crumble beneath her feet and fall into the chasm below.

That could have been me. "God damn, him!" She scrabbled to hang on with her fingers, as more pieces of rock fell away and plummeted downward to be swallowed by the pitch-black abyss from which she had come. "God damn artificial gravity!"

There was a brief moment of silence before the thud of rocks, colliding with the ground, rose to her level. If it was possible, it made her hate him even more. This was *his* creation, and she hated him for even giving birth to the idea. "God damn, you!" she cried. "It's all your fault. You did this to me!"

She tried to rest her head on the rock-face but bumped her chin which made her bite her lower lip. A bitter-warm, copper taste tickled her tongue. She hated the taste and immediately spit out as much of the blood as she could. The rest trickled down the side of her mouth and dripped from her chin, adding more red splotches on her shirt. "How could you do this to me?" she whispered.

Gravity, the ever-lasting nuisance, had haunted her ever since she had reached the base of the mountain—the only vantage point within this barren landscape. It tormented her each and every inch of the way up the mountain which stood tall and proud. And even now, as the final ledge separated the black sky from her reach, artificial gravity provoked her into hating him even more. Fortunately, the anger she felt toward him and his creation, strengthened her grip on the mountain's side. Artificial gravity wasn't going to take her that easily. She wouldn't allow it…She couldn't allow it. She wasn't going to become one of them…She couldn't.

She ignored the stink of oil, sweat, and blood from her shirt. She hated the smell of the oil. It was disgusting, and an odour she would never forget. She made herself look up. There were not any further reasons to look down. She moistened her dry, cracked lips and clenched her teeth in an effort to regain a bit of composure, but nothing could contain the awful moan expelled from her broken body. She winced. Flowing in unison with the biting wind, a lock of her blood-stained hair battered the side of her face. Now blood moistened her lips. She could actually taste the pain; only this time, she could not spit it back out. It was sharp and bitter.

Self pity, however, was tasteless. There was none of it for her to sink her teeth into. She would just have to swallow the ever-growing pain and continue forward.

I have no choice.

She glanced up. The final ledge—the temporary horizon line—far from the security of the ground, watched over her. She had to reach it. She had to get up and over it. From there, at the very top of the mountain, she could finally assess the situation she was facing. At the very least, she could allow her exhausted body the chance to rest.

"Come on, Eve. They're coming. They're coming for you. You can do this. Can't let them take you…"

Ignoring the lingering pain in her arms, she forced herself upward. Her right hand ached, as she grasped the ledge above. She took in a deep breath. The cold air burst inside her lungs, causing yet another whimper to be expelled into the silent night. The pain was unbearable, but she knew she had to push herself. "Okay…that's one…" The words came out in a moan. "One…more."

At a time when realistic goals required a single-minded approach, one ledge at a time, she couldn't resist the impulse to look ahead. Pain momentarily eased when she saw the mountain's summit—the end of her journey. And just above the mountain's peak, the moon was advertising itself in not so subtle ways. Using a dazzling array of finger-like glows that filtered across the ledge, it seemed as if the moon was gesturing her toward it—encouraging her forward.

The muscles in her jaw clenched, rippling the side of her face. "No more hesitating," she said, with determination. She stiffened her legs, pushing up with all her strength. She stretched her left hand up and over the ledge, beyond the crest of the mountain once thought to be so impenetrable. With one last effort, she pulled herself up and onto the mountain's summit. *Finally*!

It was a rather ugly landing, as her body rolled down a bit of incline, but style didn't matter. All she cared about was that she had finally made it. Her breath came out in a loud whoosh, as her body flattened out and came to rest. Her legs and arms flopped to her sides as if they outweighed her entire body and then remained still.

With her actions no longer dictated by the need to scale the mountainside, she could finally face the black sky. The sight took her breath away. The stark contrast between the pitch-black night and the shimmering highlights from the array of stars played tricks on her vision. Every twinkle of the millions of stars made it seem as if they were moving. As if they were alive. As if they had a heart and a soul, each with its own story to tell.

Seeing the stars brought bittersweet memories of her father, reminding her of the stories he used to tell her while they were star-gazing. Those special moments were perhaps the only times they actually shared a genuine smile with each other.

As always, her vibrant-green eyes eventually made their way to the brightest star in the sky—the North Star. "Mom..." The sight was too much for her to comprehend at the moment. It had been so long since she had seen stars—so long since she had been in hiding. She had started to think she would never see them again. A single tear escaped the corner of her eye and ran down her cheek, but she barely noticed it.

At the moment, nothing seemed to matter. She didn't care that a sharp crescent moon watched silently over her. She didn't care that the moon's glow highlighted the peaks and valleys of open wounds that stretched across the entire length of her body. She didn't care that it exposed her ragged and torn clothes that she had worn for what seemed like forever. The moon didn't care, either. It just stared with a relentless silence.

At that very moment, she did not feel like the woman who had just trekked across a destroyed Earth, braved her senses and scaled an endless mountain to escape. She wasn't the physically destroyed woman who had no idea if the final chapter of her storied life had already been written. She was simply that young girl from many moons ago looking up at the starry night next to her father. It had been a time when she still loved him and she had been sure that he loved her...

Her hand suddenly formed a tight fist and slammed into the solid rock floor. "He never loved me."

She sat absolutely still for a moment and became aware of a warm bead of fluid running from somewhere deep in her hairline that trickle down the side of her face. She immediately wiped it away with the back of her hand. The mere thought of what he had done, destroyed any sense of nostalgia that she had once treasured so deep inside. The attention she offered to the stars was now severed. Any sense of gratification that she had rightfully earned from conquering the mountain was completely eradicated. Pain that had ravished her body immediately returned. All that she could ask herself now was, "Was running away worth it?"

Running from them, running from him, nearly losing her life...was it worth it? A sudden metallic rumbling in the distance unequivocally confirmed that it was.

"Shit!" she cried. Her body became rigid. The shearing of metal, the ever so familiar clanking, tore into the silence like a streak of lightening rips into a cloud-drenched sky and was growing louder and louder.

Without the slightest hesitation, she flipped over onto her stomach and forced herself to do the unthinkable. She needed to see where the sounds were coming from. She crawled back to the edge of mountain, contradicting her efforts to this point. Trapped pockets of air from deep within her joints popped and crackled with every movement, shattering any silence not yet forfeited by the approaching sounds. "Please..." she whimpered, practically in tears. "Please...don't be there. Don't be there."

She repeated the words over and over until she reached the small incline that separated mountaintop from the threat below. She wrapped her hands around the lip of the mountainside but then hesitated. Instincts were trying to pull her over, begging her to look down, but fear and the realization of what she might see kept her timid. The din from all the clanking and squealing was now to the point of being unbearable. It tore into her ears, sank deep into her emotions, and reopened unhealed wounds.

But she knew she could no longer hide. No matter what was on the other side of the crescent, she had run out of ground. No matter if they had found her, there was no place left for her to run. But still, she had to make sure. She clung to the slightest bit of hope that the sounds could just be an echo in the far distance. Maybe they would break left instead of right, retreat instead of engage.

She sighed. Who was she trying to fool? She knew what their orders were and why they were stalking her. But she had to make sure. Even if it was just to confirm the inevitable. "Please...don't be there," she forced herself to say one last time. She pulled herself as far over the ledge as she could go, giving herself the best possible vantage point. A stream of sweat, stained with a reddish tint, trickled down her face. It did little to distract her. Every one of her senses was now being overwhelmed by the sight before her. Her whimpering of, "Oh my...god..." barely got through her lips. She was stiff with fear. Her stomach seemed to drop to the very soles of her boots and then surge back up again, threatening to exit out of her mouth. She had to blink a few times just to make sure that what she was seeing was the truth. In the end, her eyes did not lie.

The mass of mechanical beings below, stretched from one end of the horizon to the next. They were coming fast and determined, with primary orders set. They were not to return until those orders were fulfilled. And in this stage of their evolution, mechanical beings rarely failed in meeting an objective.

As Eve lay flat against the mountaintop, she became aware of a different sound—a deep, rhythmic thumping. It didn't take long for her to realize that the thumping wasn't coming from the distance. It was her heart, pounding against her ribcage. It was a painful feeling she knew too well. She pulled back from the edge. What could she do? She was trapped.

Desperate, she turned around in hopes of finding a way out. Anything would do at this moment. Her eyes were drawn to the other side of the mountaintop. It was a short distance, but one that was not even worth the effort of trying to cross. There was no protection for her there. She had made a tactical error in thinking she would find security on the mountain. If her stomach could sink any lower, or deeper, it just did. Greeting her was the sharp, false horizon line where the mountaintop cut the sky in half. There was no way down. The mountain had lured her onto its false sense of security and was not going to let her go.

The approaching sounds recaptured her attention. She heard the shearing of metal plates grinding against each other, the roaring thud of cold steel colliding with the granite Earth. Her heart no longer was the only source of pounding. The entire mountain was now trembling, sending a cold chill up the entire length of her spine. She stared at the mass of mechanical beings relentlessly moving toward her, shaking the Earth with thousands of footfalls. The entire mass looked as if it was taking the horizon with it, leaving an enormous trail of dust in its wake.

It didn't matter what direction she looked, they were coming. She glanced to the right, they were coming. She glanced to the left, they were coming. In all directions, they were coming. It was an ominous sight soon detailed enough to reveal individual parts making up the mass.

Each polished surface reflected the moon's glow and dispersed it back into the pale night. Pistons didn't need highlighting. They were distinct enough through simple yet violent motions, as they drove themselves deep into form-fitting chambers. Gears were well-defined on their own, as they rotated in a blurred mess, propelling angular limbs forward.

They were so noisy, so disgustingly loud that she could hear nothing when she let out a sigh. She surrendered. Her body slumped even further down, nearly collapsing over itself from the hip. Her face became as rigid as the rock she was perched on. She sat there in complete silence, feeling betrayed. She knew very well who had sent them. She knew who had given them the order. And by doing so, meant that he still wanted her, maybe even loved her. Why else would he have them go after her? But she couldn't call this love. Not when all she could feel was pain.

The stars, and the way the moonlight caressed the night with no real sense of urgency, were all so beautiful. If the ones below hadn't found her, this would have been a perfect place to lie down and allow time to pass by. Unfortunately, the mountain's height would only delay their progress. They would make it up to her soon. She could already smell the pungent, sourness of their surfaces and hear the random, metallic voices calling out to her. She was down to her final option—one that she had hoped would never offer itself to her.

She knew what had to be done.

Her hand slipped down alongside her left boot and stopped when it was met by a slender buckle. A long-running seam was stitched all along the side of the boot with golden-brown strapping. Resting on the top half was a flap that was secured by an elliptical button. She allowed her hand to rest for a moment, hoping for something to happen that might just be enough to coax her hand away. The metallic voices directing orders from below, and the first blue beam searching for her, would simply not allow this.

"Damn it," she cried. With her breath held, she twisted the button and unlocked the buckle. She flipped over the small flap revealing an antique revolver—a dirty bronze weapon. It was rusted but had just enough reflective surfaces left to absorb most of the moon's glow. She then wrapped her hand around the cold handle. With a slight twitch of her wrist, she pulled the revolver from its holster and allowed her arm to fall to her side. Determined, she looked down to check the progress of her enemies.

The smell of raw metal was intoxicating. The mechanical beings were now so close, she could see their body parts sharpened to fine points. The shape of their limbs matched the peaks and valleys of the wounds that had been inflicted all over her body. They had caused her the pain and were undoubtedly ready to finish what they had been sent out to do. She could not let this happen. She raised her hand, and the moon's glow was allowed to send its highlights along the revolver's defined surface. She glanced at the barrel. Engraved into its length, on the left side, were the words, *Love, Always and Forever, Daddy.*

"You never did," she whispered.

Eve ran her finger along the entire length of the barrel. It was cold to the touch. Her fingers stopped at the blunt end of the barrel. With a flick of her wrist, she snapped the gun open, allowing the muzzle to point downward. Instantly, the cylinder ejected from the side and rested in an open, inviting stance. Six chambers now stared at her. Five were empty and darken by their own cast shadow. The final chamber held a bullet. This was all she needed to see. She rotated the cylinder so the blocked chamber was one click from the very top. Taking in a deep breath, she then cocked her hand, snapping the cylinder and barrel back into place.

She wasn't sure if *she* had caused it but the horrific sounds had suddenly stopped. Unfortunately, they were immediately replaced by a dizzying array of blue beams that ran up the side of the mountain and danced around in a feverish search to pinpoint her location. She squinted when the blue beams hit her face and defused the greens of her eyes into a pale grey.

They had found her. The time was now.

She grimaced, as she staggered to her feet. Her broken body did not allow her to stand very tall but enough to afford her a new vantage point, one that also meant she was no longer concealed behind any part of the mountain. She looked down and was met by an eerie silence. Every now and then, the silence was briefly disrupted by the offensiveness of metal parts adjusting themselves or pistons blowing off stored energy.

They watched. Thousands of them. Mechanical beings, just like her father. The distinctly round highlights coming from the lenses of their eyes were focused directly on her, piecing right through her. They were waiting. For what, she did not know. But just then, one of them turned and spoke into their shoulder-mounted speakers. He was the largest one of them all.

"We found her, sir. Awaiting further orders."

Whatever those orders were, she wasn't going to let them commence. She raised her hand and pressed the open end of the barrel against her temple. The entire mass below suddenly reeled back. She had caught their attention for all the wrong reasons. It made her happy in a way, knowing that she still had at least some sort of control over her own fate—one that they could not take from her. Sweat pooled around the tip of the barrel before trailing down the side of her face.

Her thumb slowly reached up and pulled back the small, triangular hammer until it locked in place and remained still. Trembling from the combination of anxiety and fear, her index finger inched its way toward the trigger.

A deep breath followed.

Strangely, because of the adrenaline flowing through her body, the air she was breathing in suddenly seemed warm. The thick stream of condensation that was released from her lungs, confirmed that the air was still bitter cold. Not as cold as the end of the barrel that was now imprinting its circular shape onto her temple.

As she took one final glance down below, she couldn't help but think of the irony presenting itself to her. Gears, bolts, and cold steel would not stop until her fate was sealed. Now, here she was with gears, bolts, and cold steel pressed up against her temple with the exact same intent. Either by the awaiting or the immediate, her fate would be determined by parts—metal—man-made. It was inevitable. Her index finger twitched, as it locked down onto the trigger. Her eyes slowly closed until finally the moon's glow, the starry night's sky, and the overwhelming fear was nothing more than a thought. She bit down on her lip and whispered. "So this is it. This is how it ends…"

Chapter One

"Pin-bot?" Grace called, from inside the light-voided room. "Pin-bot, are you in there?"

Her calls went unanswered. Not a sound, not even a *beep*. "That's weird. I thought I heard something in here."

She postured up, lazily resting her hands on her broad hips. A low buzzing sound radiated from her eyes, as they focused and then refocused. Internal lenses protruded in and out and rotated left to right in attempts to adjust to the low light she was blanketed in. Unfortunately, her night vision did not want to work at the moment, so a quick blink disabled the normally useful function.

Perhaps the night vision no longer worked or simply required a simple upgrade.

"Like that's going to happen," she muttered. Fortunately, there was an alternative way of bringing light into the room. It just required a little more effort on her part. She sighed and then began to make her way to the far end of the room.

With each step, she was mindful of where her feet ended up. The small clanking sound let her know that the bottom of her feet had made metal-on-metal contact with the floor, and not something else. She blamed the lack of light when ever her foot *did* snag onto something other than the floor. It was the perfect excuse. "Damn it!" she complained, as sensors within the surfaces of her plating detected the minor collisions. "What's going on here? Why are these objects floating around everywhere?"

Finally, she made it to the end of the room with no external damage done to her metal casing. At least, she hoped not. A thin sliver of light, from a small seam in the wall, cut a straight line across her face. It shimmered against her polished surfaces and reflected back onto the walls but was temporarily disrupted, as she reached up. She sank her fingers inside the seam and tore open the pair of metal shutters. Natural light poured into the room, filling it from corner to corner. Nothing was left untouched by its intense brilliance.

Grace scanned the entire room. Immediately visible were the millions of dust particles, roaming freely in every direction and in a hurry to get nowhere. They were successful in interrupting the natural light that was surging through the single window, but not nearly enough to conceal the majority of the room.

She let out another windless sigh. No matter how many times she had been in this room, no matter how many times she pondered what a little bit of creativity could do, it always looked awful.

Four simple walls had their continuity broken by a large entryway which predictably had no door, only a few tired hinges—remnants of a once sturdy barrier between the room and the hallway. Deep-brown patches of rust stained all of the eroded cracks on the surrounding walls. Rows of rivets and screws that at one time lined up in flawless symmetry with each other, now protruded from every corner joint, sagging in unison with the buckling metal frame. Above were scalloped plates fused together to form the ceiling which looked impressive at first but failed to live up to that first impression due the haphazard application of small plates that had been used to cover many holes, most likely due to rust.

There was very little furniture in the room, but that was probably the only design choice she had made. A small table, cornered by a pair of flimsy chairs, had supporting legs that had been welded, re-welded and then welded again. She wasn't distracted by these unsightly flaws, however. She had seen them so many times she had grown accustomed to their rather unattractive qualities. What the light had brought to her attention today, however, forced her to reel back so much so that she needed to brace herself against the wall with one hand. She shook her head at the disgusting sight. "Look at this mess!" she cried, sweeping her other hand through the air from one end of the room to the next.

Boxes and their contents were scattered everywhere, floating precariously at knee level. The few items that she had bumped up against were still spinning uncontrollably in air. As the objects swirled around her, they were reflected off the brilliant chrome surface of her head, failing only when they skimmed across the slightest of indentations—blemishes.

Grace was not able to see her own reflection which was for the best. A single mess of this magnitude was more than she could handle at the moment. She pushed off of the wall and forced herself back into the heart of the room, this time, easily weaving around the floating items with the aid of the light.

She stopped and stood there, now with both hands weighing down her hips. She shook her head again. The nearly invisible motors controlling her upper lip retracted, causing it to curl. Nearly every single box in the room had been opened. Their contents were scattered everywhere, floating in every direction. They looked as if they had been clumsily searched through and then obviously left that way. She sighed, dropping her hands to her sides. The slight shift in weight was enough to force a loud creak in the weak, metal floor. "How many times do I have to tell him?" she said, walking over to the wall closest to the entrance way.

A quick peek out into the hallway justified her disappointment. She pointed out into the hallway at the meticulously positioned rows of boxes punctuated by green LED lights. "See? That's what's it supposed to look like." She looked back into the room. "This? This isn't how Pin-bot and I left it, now is it?" she asked, expecting some sort of response.

The mess could only offer her a mocking stare. One of the items, a very basic model of the moon, even rose a bit higher. Although she knew the movement was quite coincidental, she still took it as a sign of disrespect. She had seen enough. Comparing the hallway with the room had not been the reason why she'd walked over to this particular wall. It was the simple switch that was mounted at shoulder-level. “Magnets on,” she said, as if reciting it for the hundredth time. “Magnets on!”

She flicked the switch. Her knees instantly buckled, as the added pressure increased her weight. She had already been magnetized as suggested by the small, green LED lights on her heels and the fact that she was grounded when everything else in the room was floating. Increasing the magnetization of the room gave her an always surprising tug that required a bit of readjusting.

At once, all the boxes, their contents, and everything that wasn't bolted down fell to the floor. Every object let out a distinct ping-ping…ping, as they eventually settled into a more permanent position. Metal against metal always sounded this way. She had no concerns about damaging any of the boxes or items, as all of them were constructed out of metal—a common theme throughout the entire room.

With the room now magnetized and her new weight stabilized, Grace let go of the switch. All of the items were now concentrated at floor level. “A bit better” she said, before letting loose a loathsome sigh. Who was she fooling? It would be a long and tiresome task to bring this room out of its unruliness, something she wasn't too keen on doing at the moment, at least, not without a little help from Pin-bot, her trusty helper-bot, where ever she may be.

However, at that moment, Grace wasn't overly concerned about the mess itself but the one who had created it. Like Pin-bot, he was nowhere to be seen, but she knew exactly where to find him.

Carefully, she stepped over an empty cylindrical can with the inscription *Pure Blend* on its side. It was the final remnant of the mess separating the room from the adjacent hallway. As with the rest of the mess, she exerted no effort to pick up the can. Offering attention to one, but not to the whole, would be bias on her part, something even an unsightly mess did not deserve. She left the can undisturbed and forfeited herself to the hallway's grasp. Seeing the order, she smiled. Her weight returned to normal, suggesting that the hallway wasn't magnetized. Further confirming this was the ample staining of green illumination, caused by the hundreds of LED lights on nearly every object in the area. Here, every object had its own source of grounding. The most common form being simple integrating. Magnets were infused into the actual material, or, as evident from the shelves lining the walls, metal bolts were anchoring them in place.

The hallway was immaculate. Unlike the previous room, this was how rooms were supposed to look, Grace proudly noted. Every box was stacked neatly, with an almost obsessive amount of care. Not even a millimetre offset, in any direction, could be found separating any corner of each box. Most of them were closed off at the moment, concealing all of their contents, but more importantly, not allowing them to spill out.

A stranger looking at the boxes would not know if they were in the early stages of being topped off or if they were in the process of being emptied. It was impossible to know if these boxes were aiding in a future relocation or conceding to a recent move in. Shelves did their best to stay true with the walls but sagged in a few places along their length, probably because of the rust that had weakened the walls. Regardless, the simple alignment of shelves did their job and held their contents in place and out of the way. At the end of the hallway, where Grace's attention was focused, was a steep, vertical stairway leading into absolute darkness. “He has to be up there,” she said.

Slowly, she made her way down the hall. Although tidy beyond even her own standards, the hallway was rather narrow and even sunken inward in sections. Only a couple steps in and she had to cross her arms over her breast-plate to avoid rubbing up against the boxes. In places, she even had to walk sideways in order to navigate the claustrophobic channel.

She stopped for nothing. Resting on one of the boxes was a simple metal plate. It was a plaque, with *First Place: Category First Generation* engraved onto its surface. She didn’t give it a second look. Further down the hallway, her shoulder nearly grazed the rounded handle of a mighty trophy with the inscription *First Place: Assignment 101052* engraved onto its surface. Again, she did not stop. She came across a small medallion hanging from a chain with the title *First place: Assignment 022251* inscribed inside its outer perimeter. Such impressive achievements, but none was given more than a passing glance. She walked by all of them and was finally facing the daunting staircase that seemed to stare down at her with a menacing smile. It did not intimidate her. She had climbed these steps so many times in the past that its evil-looking smile looked more like a smirk to her. She placed her foot on the first step but immediately took it back. Her attention was diverted by a single boot hovering in the air at knee-level just to the side of her.

Her mouth tightened and shifted to one side. She planted her feet and let out a disappointing sigh while parting her legs about shoulder width apart. Both hands came up and rested on her hips. “Not again...” she mumbled. “How many times do I have to tell him?” She glanced over to the other end of the hall which was sealed off by a heavy door. There, the matching boot, grounded and absorbed by a green glow from the heel, stared back at her. “You see? Look at that. That’s what it’s supposed to look like.”

She turned her attention back toward the other boot. “Why can’t he do this to both of them?” She bent down, easily snatching up the suspended boot by its thick strapping. “Will you look at this?”

A thick, dry layer of mud engulfed most of the boot’s heel and sole.

“Disgusting,” she cried, chipping away at the mud with her hand. Once free of the Earthy residue, a red LED light flashed with blinding annoyance in the heel. “How many times do I have to tell him? Magnets on. Magnets on!” A quick flick of the switch returned the red LED light to its more calming green state. With a sudden whoosh, her upper body was dragged downward, as the boot became magnetized and one with the metal floor. She simply let go, allowing the boot to anchor itself with a loud thud. “There! Was that so difficult?”

A long trip back down the hall would be needed in order to partner the boots, but that could wait. For now, she simply coaxed the boot aside with the side of her foot. The size difference of her foot against the boot was so dramatic she had to smile. When she looked back up, she noted that the stairway seemed to be smiling too, exposing its jagged teeth-like steps. *At least it wasn't laughing*.

With a sigh, she placed her hand onto the rickety banister to help support her weight and began the laborious climb. Every day it seemed to get harder.

The light that had been barely generous in the hall began to subside even further with each step Grace took, and each step taken, buckled the metal supports underneath her weight. The rusted walls struggled to sustain the adjacent railing which bit into its weakened surface. It was obvious to any observer that at least some attempts had been made to cover up the wall's unsightly fragility.

Faded pictures were bolted onto the wall's crumbly surface at intervals of four or five steps. Rust had trickled down where the bolts had been driven into the walls, threatening to spill onto the pictures themselves. In a few places, it was evident, by the white outlines on the wall's brownish tones, that some of the pictures had either fallen off or had been taken down over the years. The ones that remained depicted a substantial progression in evolution. On the left side, and always the left side, was an older male who stood tall and proud with small patches of rust all around. Standing always to the right of him was a female who looked much younger. It was Grace. A slightly newer version of her, with fewer dents on her surfaces and an almost perfect sheen all around. Between them was a box full of parts consisting of limbs, plating, wires, and all sorts of unrecognizable metallic junk. Partially concealed behind the pair was a strange looking container that appeared to be filled with some sort of liquid.

To anyone viewing the pictures, the natural progression of time passing was obvious. The box holding the assortment of parts became emptier. It wasn't until the twentieth step up, and the second last picture in the progression, that a small, metallic boy appeared at the pair's side, minus essential details like arms and facial features.

It was a perfect preview for the final picture.

There, standing next to her was a completely constructed boy with arms, legs, face, and all. Bright-blue eyes were barely visible due to the picture's fading material. Surprisingly, the older male was absent from this picture, as was the smile on Grace's face which had been so dominate and consistent throughout the other photographs. At the moment, this final picture was significant for her because it meant that she was now on the final step of the staircase. This was the end of her short but laborious journey.

A single light source sheared its way into the darkness. It was coming from the lone doorway now standing tall in front of her. With bolts on one side and rusted rivets around the entire perimeter, the door had an impressive stance. The escaping light cut a perfectly vertical line along her face. She reached out and latched her hand onto the door's handle and then paused.

She did not open it. Instead, she placed her other hand on the door itself and pressed her head right up against it. She could detect the coldness resonating off of the door's metal surface. Her head shifted back and forth until it was in-line with the seam where the door met with the wall. Her ear-well twisted and then broke open into three separate chambers. Quietly, she listened. A small voice could be heard beyond the door. This was the reason she was hesitating. "What's going on in there?" she whispered.

* * *

Comfortable was not a word that Jacob would use to describe his room—more like cramped. Three of the four corners were buried behind dozens of trophies scattered throughout room. Each one varied in size and shape, but one feature remained consistent. Either the inscriptions *First Place* or *First Generation* was somewhere to be found on their surface. The rest of the room was lit by a weak glow creeping through cracks of the lone metal shutter on one of the walls. Light was evident outside but was purposely kept from fully illuminating the room. There was still enough of it to highlight each trophy, creating a dazzling display to rupture the room's tranquillity, yet not enough to distract him. Possibly because there were just so many of them.

Jacob, sitting precariously on the edge of a metal chair with his back toward the main door to the room, barely able to get his chest-plate over the edge of a generous looking desk, was the owner of each one of those trophies.

From every angle, Jacob was rather simple looking. His anterior was crafted out of a dull, chrome outer shell, snapped together in various places and polished to a fine off-white gloss. Unfortunately, most was concealed behind the desk. His visible posterior was not much different from the front, although it was far less streamlined. Bolts and thick relief cuts were reserved for this side only, mainly to give his front an overall sleeker appearance. The back of his head was only thing on his back that hadn't been blemished by junction points. A thick, heavy plate, lacking any sort of bolt holes, covered that area, and there were no hints of rust all around.

Short, stubby limbs, with a couple of wires sprouting out from the joints, were balanced flawlessly with his small, unblemished face. His eyes glowed a vibrant-blue. Both were twisting and turning in their huge sockets, intense and focused. Underlining them was a dark array of vents all down the side of his cheeks. Right now, they were in their closed position, but the joints on either side of the thin coverings suggested that they could open when need be. His mouth was a small slit in the metal and was currently tight in concentration. A thin seam dipped from the corner of his mouth all the way across his face, stopping at a pair of disproportionate screws on his head. They were massive in size, engulfing the better half of his head. It was difficult to imagine what such large screws were holding in place. They were unattractive, but not enough to disrupt his overall youthful appearance. Even with some minor changes and alterations over time, he still looked like the boy depicted in pictures lining the walls of the staircase. He was the next logical progression. An evolution of where the final picture had ended.

Nestled in the very corner of the slightly tilted desk was a round miniature model of the Earth. It was brown in colour and impaled by a short pole to keep it from rolling off the desk. It was also allowed to pivot and rotate on its centre axis, though currently, it was motionless, keeping true to its real life counterpart. Partnered next to it was a smaller model depicting the moon. It had a dusty grey complexion, with small indentations covering most of its surface and an enormous chunk missing from one side. Again, true to its real life counterpart. The moon model was strung in place by a thin piece of wire, allowing it to hover realistically close to the Earth.

Every object in the room, as well as the room itself, was constructed out of the familiar material—metal. The dull-grey colour a sharp contrast to the brownish-green plant Jacob had in his grasp.

His stubby hands, which consisted of nothing more than curved sections of metal to form a "*C*", griped clumsily onto the dried, barky stem. "Okay, wait here," he said in a voice soft and mild. He gently placed the plant down on the desk and used a regular bolt to anchor it down. With his hands now free, he reached into a desk drawer and pulled out a microscope and then secured it down in front of him. "There. Let's see what you *really* look like."

He pried loose the transparent glass slides that would house the sample. He flicked the bolt to one side. Instantly, the plant lifted and floated off the desk. "Oh, no you don't!" His hands snapped at the air, completely missing the plant. It took a few tries, but eventually, Jacob was able to clamp his hand onto the plant's stem.

"Beep-get-away?" a muffled, high-pitched voice called out from the other side of the room.

Jacob turned his head toward the closet, the other closed off door in the room, where the noise had come from. "Nope, I got it," he replied, "but it almost got away." Jacob looked back at the plant and smiled. "But I'm just too quick for you, aren't I? You're not getting away from me that easy. Took me forever to find you."

Despite the fact that his hands were so awkward looking and his movements so clumsy, he was surprisingly delicate with the plant. He held onto it and angled it inside of his grasp, as he scanned its texture and form. Then in an instant, he purposely snapped off the green, leafy section without any hesitation. "There we are. That should be all we need from you."

He secured the rest of the plant down on the desk with the aid of the bolt and then gently placed the section of leaf between the transparent slides. A bit of persuasion was needed to insert the slide back into the microscope's holding bay, but eventually it gave in to the firm taps it was receiving from Jacob's hand. "Okay, let's see what you look like."

Jacob switched on the microscope. He pressed his eye tight against the eyepiece and began rotating the dial a quarter turn clockwise, resulting in a distinct click. Which each turn, the scope's magnification increased. The second to last click brought it to nearly maximum intensity.

The blue glow in Jacob's eyes also intensified, as he tried to make sense of what he was now looking at. His eyes suddenly changed from blue to a pure white, and the trio of smaller pupils surrounding the main pupil were now visible. They twisted, turned and focused directly into the eyepiece of the microscope. What Jacob saw, caused him to fall silent. The vents on his cheeks broke open and then collapsed, broke open again only to collapse once more. Moments went by, but nothing was heard.

"Beep?" the tinny-sounding voice from the closet called out. Jacob didn't reply. "Beep-beep-anything?" it repeated.

Jacob finally pulled away from the microscope and looked toward the closet. "It's amazing!" he said ecstatically.

"Beep?"

"All these things," he explained, "there are millions of them. They're dividing into sections." He smiled. "Then dividing again and again…slowly but they're dividing alright."

"Beep-are-they?"

"I don't know exactly. Let me get a better look." Jacob needed to twist the microscope's dial one more time to fully maximize its power, in hopes to see even more detail. As he reached for the dial, a sudden gust of wind pushed the shutters on the window open, releasing a blinding wall of light into the room.

The light surged into Jacob's eyes, forcing him back and away from the microscope. "Damn it!" he cried, as his eyes attempted to adjust themselves. He then blurted out, "*299!*" for some odd reason. The light was distracting, intensified by the reflection off of dozens trophies. Jacob needed those shutters closed. "Pin-bot!" he called out, using a hand to shield the delicate lenses of his eyes.

"Beep?"

"Hey, Pin-bot! Can you close the shutters?"

There was a brief pause before the reply of, "Beep-can't," filtered through the small crack between the wall and the closet door.

"What do you mean, you can't?"

"Beep-broken…"

"Oh....right," Jacob said slightly embarrassed. "I forgot. Fine...I'll get them."

He slid off his chair and walked over to the window. Once there, he glanced outside. The light turned his complexion solid-white. "Forecast…sunny all day, every day, all the time," he playfully announced. "Same as always."

His attention immediately shifted to moon. It was getting closer he noticed. He scanned the detailed surface, observing the brilliant contrast of each crater. It made him proud that he had been able to capture all of that detail onto the miniature model that sat on his desk. Since he could name each and every crater on the moon's surface, there was no need to give it any more of his attention. He reached out and closed the shutters, instantly eliminating all the light in the room and then hurried back to the desk. The desk, the microscope, and most of the room were now blanketed in darkness. For Jacob, this was not a problem. With a simple blink and a jerk of his head, he enabled his night vision. The blues of his eyes intensified. He was now able to see everything as clearly as if the room was alive with light.

Without even sitting, he pressed his face up against the microscope's eyepiece. Silence filled the room, as he adjusted the dial. A single click clockwise brought the microscope to full strength, but it made no difference. "Hey! What's going on?" Jacob turned the dial counter-clockwise, but the results were the same. "I don't get it. Something's not right."

"Beep?"

"I don't know. They…they stopped dividing."

"Beep-on?"

"Hold on, let me make sure." Jacob took his eyes off the eyepiece and scanned the side of the microscope. "Yeah, it's still on."

"Beep-strange."

Jacob nodded. "Yeah…that *is* strange. Really strange. Why would they all of a sudden stop? I didn't do anything, did I?" There were no responding *beeps* this time. "Strange," Jacob repeated.

The door to the room suddenly opened, and Grace stepped in. "What is?"

Jacob reeled back. "Grace!" He immediately ripped the microscope off of the desk and concealed it behind his back.

She gave him a piercing stare.

Jacob lowered his head. "Sorry. I mean…Mom…"

"Better," Jacob's mom said. A quick glance around the room made her throw both hands out to the side in an exaggerated pose. "Why is it so dark in here?"

"It's not dark," Jacob replied, scanning the room with little effort.

"That's because you have night vision."

"So do you."

"True. But mine hasn't worked for ages."

Jacob snickered. "Time for an upgrade?"

She gave him a bit of an awkward glance. "Like that's ever going to happen."

Grace walked over to the window. Barely opening the shutters more than a crack, she peeked out and let out a deep sigh.

"What's wrong?"

"Closer by the day," she muttered.

"Oh…the moon."

"Yes. It's the closest it's ever been. Any day now," she softly said. With that, she broke open the shutters as far as they could go, drowning the room in light.

"Mom!" Jacob cried, throwing his arm across his face. "What are you doing?"

"Bringing some light into here. I don't know how you can work without any light."

"Damn it," Jacob cried. "*300.*" He jerked his head back and blinked, disabling his night vision. His mom instantly threw her hands onto her hips.

"How many times do I have to tell you not to use that word?"

As Grace approached the desk, Jacob repositioned himself, making sure he was always facing her. "Including this time or not including this time?" Jacob asked, with a grin.

"I knew I should have deleted that word from your hard-drive," she said. Each step brought her closer and closer to Jacob which in return made him more and more uncomfortable.

"Uh…where you going?" Jacob asked.

Grace stopped. "I'm not going anywhere. Why?"

Jacob shrugged and shifted away from her.

Curious, she stood on her toes and leaned to the left and then to the right, trying to figure out what was making him so evasive. Whenever she looked left, Jacob shifted his body to the left. When she looked right, he shifted right. It was obvious that Jacob was attempting to hide something, yet she knew how hard it was for him to hide anything from her since he stood no higher than her breast-plate. Fortunately, for Jacob, she temporarily lost interest when the plant on his desk caught her attention.

She picked it up. "What is this?"

"What?"

Grace twisted and rolled the stem between her fingers, something Jacob would have trouble doing with his stubby hands.

"Oh, that…" Jacob said.

A genuine smile crossed Grace's face, as she studied the plant's organic structure. She pulled it close to her face, scanning its texture, its form, and its non-metallic materials. "Thought I'd never see one of these again," she whispered.

Jacob reeled back. "You know what it is?"

She laughed. "Of course. It's a plant. They used to grow all over the place. This one's rather simple. There used to be much more complex ones. Ones with twisting stems, bright colours. And much larger ones with thousands of leaves sticking out from the top."

"Really?"

"Yes. Really." She gently placed the plant back on the desk and rolled the bolt over it so it couldn't float away. "Where did you find it?"

"Outside. Behind our house." Jacob shifted his weight back and forth. "Well, not *exactly* behind the house. I had to climb that big old dirt hill to get it. Got my boots all dirty."

Both the plates over Grace's eyes lifted as high as they could go. "Yes, I noticed."

Jacob pulled one of his hands free, from behind his back, and brushed the dust off his leg. "Still got some on me."

That's when Grace noticed the microscope he was concealing from her. "What do you have there?"

Not even allowing Jacob the chance to reply, she yanked the microscope from his grasp.

"Hey, what are you doing?" Jacob reached out and tried to retrieve the microscope, but he couldn't get beyond his mom's outstretched arm. "Hey! Stop! That's mine!"

"Just taking a look. Relax." Grace pressed her eye against the eyepiece and observed.

Jacob backed off. "You won't see anything. Whatever was happening before, it stopped doing it."

"Are you sure?"

"Yeah, why?"

"It looks to me like something's going on in here."

"What?" Jacob jumped up and down, attempting to drag his mom's arm down to his level. "Let me see! Let me see!"

"Oh, look, they're breaking apart...or something..."

"Yeah, that's what was happening before. Let me see! Mom, let me see!"

"Okay-okay. Relax." Grace lowered the microscope.

Jacob wrenched it out of her hands and pressed his face against the eyepiece. He was quiet, as he adjusted the intensity.

"So? Am I right?"

"Amazing! They're dividing again!"

"See? I told you."

Jacob pulled away from the eyepiece. His attention was immediately drawn to the window and the light surging in. He made a gesture that, if he had fingers, might have been a snap. "So that's why."

"What do you mean?"

"Oh...uh...nothing," Jacob said smiling. "You wouldn't understand anyway."

Grace's mouth angled down sharply. "Oh...is that right?"

"Yup. Trust me, Mom. None of this will interest you."

Grace backed off, as if offended by Jacob's unjustified claims. "So what's your interest in it? You're not planning another experiment are you? You know how much I don't like you experimenting on things." Both of her hands returned to her hips. "You *do* remember what happened last time, don't you?"

Jacob placed the microscope back onto the desk and then stood with his arms folded behind him. The plates over his eyes shifted up ever so slightly. Slowly, they both turned their attention to a large, covered up hole in the wall next to the desk. It had only been recently covered over with a thin piece of sheet metal, but a small breeze could still be detected around its perimeter. Jacob stepped in front of it. "That's was one big hole," he said, embarrassed.

"Big?" Grace said, with the plating above her eyes raised even higher than Jacob's. "You were one explosion away from taking down the entire house."

Jacob gave the wall a frustrated kick, pinging his metal foot against the metal sheet and then shrugged it off. “Yeah, but *that* experiment won me first place. In case you forgot, I'll show you the trophy.”

He was about to run off to somehow find a single trophy out of dozens but was held back by a stiff arm.

“No, it’s quite alright. I know exactly which trophy it is.”

“The first place one?”

Grace giggled. “They’re all first places.” She reached down and patted Jacob on the shoulder. “Just—” She paused, looked at the plant and then sighed. “Please, Jacob, whatever you’re planning on doing to this plant…do it outside.”

“But it’s only a plant. It’s harmless.”

“Trust me on this one, Jacob.”

Both of Jacob arms flopped down to his side, a simple form of surrender. “Okay-okay. I promise.” Jacob leaned into the desk and then looked at his mom. “Umm…so?”

“So…what?”

“I did the calculations but can’t seem to figure it out.” Jacob tilted his head to one side. “Why are you up here? Did I forget to do something?”

Grace immediately cocked her head toward the door to the room. Jacob didn't understand and just shrugged.

“Downstairs,” she said.

“Downstairs?”

“The room next to the hallway.”

“Yeah? What about it?”

Grace gave him a hard stare. “The mess?”

Jacob frowned and lowered his head. “Oh…that…” He timidly shifted his weight around, as he stuck the tip of his foot on the floor and rotated his leg from the hip. “I was going to clean it. Honest.”

A half smile from Jacob did little to convince her.

“And when was that going to happen?”

“You know…just after—”

“Just after *I* finish cleaning it up for you?”

Jacob’s half smile turned into a full grin. “Yes?”

Grace shook her head, ignoring Jacob's subtle act of disrespect. “What were you looking for down there anyway?”

Jacob pointed at the microscope.

“You made that mess just for that?”

“Well, I found it, didn’t I?”

“Did you have to go through all those boxes? I mean, every single one of them is opened. And why did you have to demagnetize the entire room? You know how much I hate it when things are floating around. I can’t be running around, pulling things off of the ceiling.” She sighed. “Even worse is when they float outside. Remember your boot?”

Jacob huffed. “Yes, I remember. Why do you keep reminding me?”

"Because it took a lot of effort to get it back. That's why I don't like you demagnetizing the room. You never end up cleaning after yourself."

"But by my calculations, it was quicker for me to demagnetize the room and have all the things float out of the boxes so I can see where everything is, instead of going through each box one at a time. It was more efficient that way."

Grace crossed her arms over her breast-plate, obviously not impressed by his excuse.

Jacob frowned. "The switch is too high. Even *you* can barely reach it."

"I can reach it."

"Okay. You can, but I can't."

"How did you turn it off, then?"

"I stood on one of the boxes."

"Those aren't meant to be used as a stepping stool."

"But I wouldn't have to go looking for my things if they weren't in boxes," Jacob said. "Don't know why we had to move out here in the first place."

"That's not an excuse, Jacob."

"But it's true, it's it? I still don't even know where most of my stuff is. If we hadn't moved out here, my stuff wouldn't be in boxes. And I wouldn't have made that mess."

Grace shifted her weight from one leg to the other. What Jacob was saying may very well be true. Still, it didn't excuse him for the mess he had created. His CPU knew better than that.

Jacob turned and started to walk toward the door, barely even picking up his feet, as they scrapped against the metal floor.

"Wait. Where you going?" his mom asked.

Jacob turned, throwing both arms out to the side. "To clean up the mess!"

"No...no-no-no!" Grace grabbed Jacob by the arm and pulled him back to her side. "It's fine. Pin-bot and I can do it tomorrow." She scanned the room. "Where is she? Been looking all over for her."

Jacob's posture suddenly stiffened. "Oh...uh..."

"Never mind. She must be in my room." Grace tugged at his arm. "Come now, time to recharge."

"What? Recharge? But I'm barely—" Jacob looked down at his chest-plate.

Centred in a gap and enclosed by two opposing plates were twelve glowing bars next to a large round orb—his hard-drive, where he stored information. The top four bars were green, the next four were orange, and the last four were red. The one at the very bottom was flashing rhythmically.

"Empty!" Jacob cried out, surprised to see the red lights.

"Yes, Jacob. Empty, as in running low, no more energy, about to shut down—"

"I know that."

"Then you know that it's time to recharge. Come now."

"Can't it wait just—"

"No! Time to recharge." Knowing very well that Jacob would try to put up a fight, as he did every single time his indicator flashed red, Grace forcefully dragged him to the end of the room.

Waiting patiently for them was a sturdy looking charger that could have been mistaken for one of the trophies. It shared the same rounded corners, though it was nowhere nearly as reflective. A single cord flowed from its base but was not connected to the outlet in the wall at the moment.

"Come on, Jacob," Grace said. "One of these days you might stop fighting this."

Jacob struggled, but he was no match for the size and strength of his mom. As she applied pressure, he had no choice but to shuffle along or end up on the floor. "Mom! Why can't I stay running a little bit longer? I know how to recharge myself."

"I don't think so. The last time you tried, you set the machine too high, and you were hyper for days. Now come on."

Jacob chuckled. "Yeah, I remember that."

"It isn't funny. You turned the house upside down. Pin-bot and I spent the entire week cleaning up the mess you made."

"That was a long time ago. I know better now."

Her eyes widened. "It was just the other day!"

"Okay, but I still know better now. Please, can't I stay running a little longer? I was about to restart my experi—" Jacob stopped abruptly when his mom released her hold. He looked up at her with wide eyes, realizing his mistake. "Oh…uh…never mind," he mumbled.

"Experiment? That's what you were going to say, weren't you?"

Jacob offered his mom a nervous smile. "Uh…not really an experiment like the others. I don't think this one will cause any more holes in the wall." He paused and recalculated. "Well, I'm fairly sure it won't."

Grace shook her head, exhausted from repeating herself. "I'm going to pretend I didn't hear that. Any experiments you might be thinking about will be done outside." She placed her hands on the back of Jacob and continued her forceful guidance toward the charger. "Come on, let's go. You're almost empty. You need to be fully recharged for your big day tomorrow."

"Tomorrow? Big day? Why, what's going on?"

"Don't tell me that you already forgotten?"

"No," Jacob turned to look at her, "but it's not *that* big of a day."

"Oh, don't be silly." Grace stopped next to the charger. "It's going to be a huge day. You're going to need a full charge for this one. *A full charge!*"

"Yes, I heard you the first time."

Jacob's head jerked back, as Grace lifted him off the floor and placed him inside the charger. Both his feet snapped neatly into the reserved slots in the charger's base. A pair of tabs popped up and locked him in place. Jacob had become quiet, as his mom fiddled around making sure every one of his limbs was secure. Eventually, the silence became awkward. Jacob had to say something.

"It's not *that* big of a deal," he repeated.

"Of course it is. It's not every day you start at a new school."

Jacob sighed. "I guess…"

His mom was now on her knees, face-to-face with Jacob. "I thought you'd be excited about going to a new school."

Jacob shook his head. "I liked my old school."

Grace pushed his torso firm against the back of the charger's supporting spines. "We can't go back there now. It's closed down for good. You know that, Jacob."

"I know. I used to go there, remember?"

His comment was met by a cold stare. He felt a purposely firm tug on his arm.

"No need to be rude."

"I wasn't trying to be," Jacob mumbled.

"It can be fun to go to a new school. You'll get to make new friends—"

"New friends? But I don't want new friends. I miss my old friends." Jacob's slit of a mouth turned down in a pout. "I don't know why they had to be reassigned already. It's not even time for us to leave yet."

"They were all from *sector 128*," Grace said in a tone of voice that indicated she had said this before, too many times. "Everyone from sector *128* to *360* was reassigned. Not much we can do about it. Just be happy that we got out of that sector when we did."

"But he hasn't even told us when we would be leaving. Why do they have to be dormant already?"

"I don't know. And they may have to stay that way for some time."

"Really? Like how long?"

"I'm not sure. Could be weeks, months, even years. Only he knows for sure. He *is* the Mayor and all."

Jacob managed to pull his arm free and slammed it against the charger's side with a loud thud. "Some answer."

His mom stood up. "Look, Jacob, all I know is that we're in sector *333* now. We're the last ones here, so it won't be long before we're also assigned. Just be happy that we're still here, and not in those pods."

"How convenient."

Grace knelt down again to look him in the eye. "At least you're still able to go to school…a new school." He didn't respond, so she shook her head and whispered, "I just hope it'll be a long time before we get reassigned." A firm push of her hand snapped one of Jacob's arms into the charger's port. "I think you'll like it there."

"Where? The pods? Not likely."

"No, silly, your new school."

"If we're going to be reassigned any day now, what's the point of going to school? I mean, I'd probably learn more at home doing my own experiments."

"Experiments?" Grace glanced up at him.

"I know, I know. Do them outside. I'm just saying. What's the point of starting over at a new school?"

"Like I said, our reassignment could be any day or long time from now. Either way, I'd rather you be at school right up until it happens." She turned her face and whispered, "And he'll get the chance meet you again."

She wasn't quiet enough, however.

"Meet who?"

"Oh, uh...new friends," she said, attempting to mask her vocal pondering. "You'll get to meet new friends." She quickly secured Jacob's other arm into the charger and then got back to her feet. "They'll all be in your class. Second generations, third generations, even fourth generations. Since it's the only school left, all the classes will be held together."

"Oh, good! I can't wait until they all start making fun of me," Jacob didn't hide the sarcastic tone.

Grace crossed her arms over her breast-plate and frowned, not knowing what he meant by that. "Why would they make fun of you? Your CPU is probably a lot more advanced than most of them." She did a quick scanning of Jacob's room. "I mean, look at all these trophies. And that's only half of them. The other half is still back at our old place. If they make fun of you because your CPU is more advanced than theirs, then—"

"They won't make fun of me because of that." Jacob pulled his arm out from out of the charger's port and raised it up. "It'll be because of this."

Grace stared at Jacob's short, stubby arm but only for a brief moment before grabbing hold of it. Jacob fought to keep it extended but was easily overpowered. She placed it back into the charger's port and secured it back into place.

"Short limbs aren't a reason to make fun of someone," she said.

"But they will. They always do," he whispered. "I hate third gens..." His voice became more animated. "I hate fourth gens..." He then shouted, "I hate them all!" His voice then subsided back to a whisper. "And sometimes—"

His mom had her arms folded over her breast-plate again and was staring down at him, impatiently waiting for him to continue. "And sometimes what?"

Not wanting to make eye contact with her, Jacob lowered his head and then looked away. "Fifth generations," he mumbled.

His mom's hands slowly slid downward until they were at her hips. She titled her fifth generation head. "I certainly hope you don't mean that."

Jacob postured up as best he could while being held in the charger's tight grip. "Sorry, Mom. I didn't mean it," he softly said. "I...I'm just—" He sighed. "How much longer do I have to be a first generation? I hate being a first generation. I hate not being able to do anything with these limbs."

"Oh, Jacob," his mom said, her voice soft with sympathy. "You can do anything. All these trophies prove it."

"It's not that." Jacob looked down and scanned his simplistic body. "I mean, I want be able to at least...I want to be able to do normal things like...you know...pick up stuff without having them drop out of my hands. And climb up the stairs, outside my room, without having to use my hands. I want to do normal things." He looked up at his mom. The once vibrant-blue glow in his eyes had dimmed. "I want become a second generation. Or even better, a third generation."

Grace stood silent. She understood his desire and sympathized with his position but knew this wasn't the best time to be making such a dramatic request. Her arms fell to her sides and she simply said, "We'll have to wait and see."

"That's what you always say. I've been a first generation for like...*forever*."

"That's all I can say, Jacob. We'll have to wait and see."

Jacob frowned, metal ridges forming in the plates above his eyes. Knowing that he wouldn't get anything else from her, he remained silent.

Grace walked around the charger, reached down and pushed the plug into the wall. An array of LED lights flashed brilliantly from the top of the charger. The lights changed from solid orange to a rhythmically flashing green almost immediately. The charger was now in standby mode. "Okay. You've been up and running long enough," Grace said, backing away.

"Wait!" Jacob called out.

"What? What is it?"

Jacob scanned his room, searching for something, anything, to delay the inevitable. Not seeing anything that would help his purpose, he quietly surrendered and mumbled, "Nothing."

Fortunately for Jacob, his mom suddenly turned her attention away from him and was walking to the other side of the room.

"I almost forgot," she said.

Jacob saw she was headed for the closet. "Umm...forgot what?" he asked, a quiver of nervousness in his voice.

Grace did not reply. She just kept advancing toward the closet which for some reason, caused Jacob to tense up with each one of her steps.

"Uh, Mom? Where you going?" Locked firmly in place, and not receiving a reply from his mom, Jacob resorted to his last option. He simply shouted, "Mom!"

Grace stopped in front of the closet door. The plates over her eyes lowered with suspicion. "Calm down, Jacob. Just need a quick look inside."

She wrapped her hand around the door's handle.

"Just warning you," Jacob murmured. "You're not going to like what you see in there."

"Why not?"

Jacob looked away.

What's he hiding from me? Without hesitating, Grace ripped open the closet door and looked inside. A hush fell over the room, as she braced for whatever Jacob was referring to, but nothing was immediately apparent. Her eyes scanned left to right, and she was surprised that nothing inside the closet seemed out of the ordinary. Staring at her were sets of Jacob's metal plating in various colours, hung neatly on a metal rod. There was nothing strange about that, especially considering that she was the one who had hung the plating in there. Grace looked up, scanning the upper level of the closet. A few boxes were resting on a shelf above the metal rod. These were hardly interesting enough to warrant Jacob's apprehensiveness. She glanced over her shoulder at him.

He quickly looked away, as if unwilling to make eye-contact with her, but she still saw the odd twist to his mouth and the furrows in his plating. This only fed her curiosity and gave her even more reason to continue her search. She brought her attention back inside the closet and scanned it even more intently. It wasn't until her eyes were lowered to the floor that she finally saw what Jacob had been hiding. She reeled back, clasping her hands together. "Jacob!" she cried.

Jacob lowered his head even further. "I told you," he mumbled.

Grace dropped to her knees.

Tucked in the corner of the closet, but clearly not out of sight, was an orb or more accurately, two halves of an orb. The top half had a pair of protruding flaps on each side. Nestled inside those flaps was an array of small, triangular blades that were merged in the center to form turbines, possibly allowing the entire orb the luxury of flight. The bottom half had a larger turbine on the back and two stubby arms on the front that when retracted, returned the orb to a fully rounded shape. Also on the front was a large, black screen with indications of small, red LED lights hidden below the surface. Both opposing halves of the orb were facing each other, held loosely together by a tangled mess of wires and circuits. Obviously, it had been tampered with, and the weak attempt at shoving its parts into the back of the closet, where no one would see it, had failed.

Jacob's mom picked up both halves of the orb. "What's this?" she yelled, turning and facing Jacob. She was in complete shock at the moment. "Is this…is this?" She couldn't believe what she was seeing. Wires from the orbs were spilling over her hands. "Is this…Pin-bot?"

With his head still lowered, Jacob replied, "Why don't you just ask her?" He tried to smile but couldn't. "She's still on at the moment."

Grace looked down at the orb. The black screen suddenly lit up with glowing red dots and began to *beep*. This startled Grace, nearly causing her to drop the pieces of the orb. "Pin-bot!" she cried. "You…you were on all this time?"

"Beep-beep," Pin-bot replied.

Without hesitating, Jacob's mom reached around and flicked the switch on Pin-bot's back, completely disabling her. The red dots on Pin-bot's face faded to black.

"Hey! What did you do that for?" Jacob cried, lifting his head.

"What did you do to her?" Grace angrily replied, holding the two sections of Pin-bot in front of her.

Jacob shrugged. "I just…you know…I...I just wanted to make her better."

"How many times have I told you not to alter her?"

"Six," Jacob replied. "Well, seven if you include this time."

"Okay, seven times. Seven times! I've told you not to alter her seven times!"

"Not alter." Jacob countered, matching the tone in his mom's voice. "Modify. I was doing some modifications."

"Modifications?" Grace turned back to the closet and gently placed the disabled Pin-bot onto the floor where she basically became a pile of spare parts. That's how Grace thought of her at the moment. Then she turned to Jacob. "What modifications are we talking about?"

"I just wanted to make her better."

"Better? How are you going to make her better? She does everything perfectly."

"Not everything. I wanted to give her a real voice. No more 'beep-beep-beep'." Jacob shrugged. "I thought it would be good if she could talk, like us."

Grace sighed. Although it seemed more destructive than beneficial, she knew that Jacob's intentions toward Pin-bot were only positive. "You know she has an adaptive CPU. She has the ability to learn," Grace calmly explained.

"Yes. I know that. I've known this since...well, since we got her."

"Then you must already know that she'll eventually learn how to speak. Just like us."

"But it was taking so long. With an adaptive CPU, she should be able to talk by now. I want to hear her speak—now."

"Just give her some time, Jacob. It won't be much longer."

"Okay...okay..."

Grace reached up and touched a small dent on the top of her head. "You know, I was looking all over for her the past few of days. She could have helped me clean up around house. And even that mess you made earlier."

"I know, and I'm sorry. I wouldn't have taken her apart if I knew you needed her right this moment."

"Well...I guess I don't need her *right* this moment. I'm sure I'll be fine without her. I just miss the funny *beeps* she makes whenever I give her a new order."

Jacob snickered. "Yeah, she does *beep* a lot."

"Just put her back together, okay? And no more modifications or whatever you call it."

"Okay, fine. I'll put Pin-bot back together, as soon as I get back from school."

Grace suddenly reeled back. "School? Oh, damn it, I almost forgot." She immediately turned back and faced the closet again.

"You know, you shouldn't use that word," Jacob said, wanting to wiggle his hand back and forth, but he couldn't.

"Oh, hush up, before I forget again."

"Forget about what?"

"I forgot that you need to dress the part." She began flipping through the various sets of metal plating hung neatly inside the closet.

"Dress the part? What do you mean dress the part? Mom?" Jacob received no reply. "Mom!"

"Hold on, Jacob." Grace skimmed through the layers of plating. A gentle humming accompanied her actions.

"Mom! Dress the part for what? Mom, are you even listening to me?"

After several long minutes, Grace finally turned back around, holding a bright-red chest-plate. "For the first day of school," she announced, with a big smile. "How's this one?" She reached over her shoulder and pulled out a pair of matching shoulder-plates. "Oh, aren't they so adorable?"

Jacob narrowed his eyes. "Adorable?"

"I like these one," Grace said.

Obviously.

Grace held the plates out. "You should definitely wear these for your first day at school."

Jacob winced at the amount of red his eyes were forced to absorb. "I wore that to my first day of school at my old school," he said. "The one that's closed down, remember?"

"Oh..." his mom murmured, paying more attention to the plating than to Jacob.

"If they were a darker red, I wouldn't mind, but those are so—" Jacob suddenly found himself talking to the back of his mom again, while she foraged through the closet. "Mom!" Jacob called out. "Why do I have to dress differently anyway? It's not really even my first day of school. It's more of a transfer. I wouldn't even have to leave my old school if it weren't for that stupid Mayor."

Jacob's eyes suddenly widened, as his mom faced him again, this time holding up a completely different set of plating. As with the red plating, the ones now in her hands were equally as bright and distracting.

"How about this one?" Grace asked, again with an exaggerated smile running across her face.

Jacob sighed. "Mom, were you even listening to me?"

"Yes," she replied, but her attention was clearly still focused on the plating. "How about blue? You like blue, don't you?"

Jacob pressed the back of his head against the charger. "Blue? I don't like blue. I hate blue!"

"But blue is just as adorable as red," she said, sounding like she wanted to give the plating a great big hug.

Jacob shook his head. "Blue is not adorable, Mom. It's worse than red. Let me pick out something when I'm done recharging."

"How about yellow, then? Yellow's always a nice colour to be seen in. It matches the sun."

"Yellow? Yellow's worse than blue." Jacob moaned. "Come on, will you get out of my closet? Please?"

Jacob's pleas went unheard as usual. Grace tended to ignore him when she was intent on picking out the right colour of plating, and today was no different. It didn't seem like she was going to heed any of Jacob's request until she finally found the right plating. She turned to the closet and again started flipping through the selection of plating.

"Okay, what about green?" She instantly changed her mind. "Orange? Or what about—"

"Mom!" Jacob yelled. "My batteries are going be completely drained by the time you find something."

Grace glanced over her shoulder and then started hanging the plating that she had picked out back on the metal rod in the closet. "Oh…sorry, Jacob. Forgot about your batteries." She closed the closet door and hastily made her way back to the charger. "I got a little bit excited, that's all. I'll let you pick out whatever you want to wear." She paused and glanced back at the closet. "Although I must say, red will look so absolutely perfect on—"

"Will you stop?"

"Okay-okay. Sorry, Jacob. I just wanted to make sure you look good for…well, you know…your first day."

Jacob attempted a sigh, but nothing came out. He had no energy left. The energy he had used to fend off his mom's almost ridiculous admiration for that red plating had drained his battery to the point where he could barely finish his own thoughts. He didn't even have the energy to speak clearly. His words were coming out in a stutter. "Just…just let me pick out something…on…my own. Okay?"

"Okay, Jacob. You've evolved enough…I guess. I'll let you pick out whatever you want."

With that, Grace flicked the charger's switch from idle to on. Jacob's head jolted back, as the surge of energy flowed through this tiny body. After a boisterous series of rhythmic clicks, to indicate that charging was underway, the charger settled into a constant, quiet hum. A cold sting tickled Jacob's metal lining while a warming sensation wrapped around his inner wiring. Jacob was now regaining energy, but ironically, his body went into a state of inertia, making it motionless. The bright-blue of his eyes faded, and his body became limp.

Grace stated to walk away when Jacob called out, "Wait…"

"Yes, Jacob?"

"Can…can you close…bright…" Jacob's head flopped down toward his chest-plate.

"What's that?"

"Too bright…can you close…window?"

"Oh...too much light." Grace finally understood what he was saying. "Okay, Jacob, I'll get it for you."

Grace walked over to the window and closed the shutters, letting the room return to the previous shadowy darkness. Because she had no night vision, she had to wait by the window until her eyes adjusted, then she might be able to make her way to the door. She could still see the slight glow of blue from Jacob's eyes but knew it was just a matter of time before they faded completely. Perhaps if she waited just a few moments, she could open the shutters again and would then have enough light to cross the room without crashing into something.

Jacob let out one final murmur before the blue glow in his eyes changed to white and then to nothing. His shoulders slumped over. Jacob was now dormant. Grace immediately pulled the shutters back open and allowed the light back into the room. “Rest well, Jacob,” she whispered.

Chapter Two

A low hum radiated from deep within Jacob's chest, and his hard-drive erupted from dormancy. With each passing moment, it would spin faster and more intensely, at the same time becoming quieter. A mere instant later, it could no longer be heard. A simple chime indicated that his hard-drive was now spinning at ideal revolutions. Jacob was now fully recharged. He lifted his head from where it was resting on his chest-plate, causing the vents on his cheeks to collapse. His eyes widened through metallic shutters. The strong, blue glow diffused by the surprising amount of light surging into the room. He immediately turned his head to one side, wincing. "Damn it, *301*!" he cried.

The lenses in his eyes twisted and turned but weren't quick enough to adjust to the light. He was forced to yank his arm from the charger and hold it against his face, shielding his eyes from the intense light.

The rays of sunlight were persistent, however. They found their way through the gaps of Jacob's stubby appendages and cut a line directly across his face. But the light didn't stop there. Every corner of the room was engulfed. Illumination crept up the walls and basked the shimmering surfaces of trophies with nearly blinding-white radiance. Although Jacob was fortunate enough to have night vision function, at this very moment, he wished he had some sort of "light vision".

That would be useful.

"I should try and invent something like that," he moaned. For now, it was merely a passing thought, one that he would surely keep somewhere on the very outer edges of his hard-drive, where the least important information was stored.

The lenses in Jacob's eyes finally found the ideal adjustment levels, and he lowered his arm. He looked over to the lone window where the sight-rupturing light was pouring in.

"That's strange. I thought I asked her to close those shutters." The plates over his eyes lowered. "I mean...I think I did...didn't I?"

He wanted to be sure. "Let me check." The glow in his eyes dimmed, replaced by a blank stare. The hum of his hard-drive became louder, as it increased its speed. From a small internal speaker, concealed behind his chest-plate, he played back the recoding from the moment just before his mom started the charger and he became dormant. There was a crackle and then a bit of distortion before the playback commenced. When it finally did, Jacob heard his voice, "Too bright...can you close...window?"

Distortion interrupted the playback just as Jacob's mom readied her reply. A loud crackle and a few hisses concluded the playback. The hum from Jacob's hard-drive quieted and then returned to normal speeds. A few blinks wiped the blank stare from his eyes, allowing the blue to fill in the circular gaps. "I must have shut down," Jacob said.

It was normal for all of Jacob's primary functions to slow down or even become fully disabled while recharging. It was simply a way of reserving the last of his energy in order to keep his most vital functions running. Recordings were not one of those vital functions.

Jacob wished he could hear what her response had been. His had been a harmless request, and he didn't think she had completely ignored him. So why were the shutters open? Maybe she had returned to the room only a short while ago and opened them.

Whether or not his conclusions were accurate, one thing still remained; the nuisance in the form of the light was still all around him. And another nuisance had been added; the annoying click*s* being blurted out by the charger that he was still trapped inside.

Click…click-click…click…click-click…This was the charger's way of indicating that it had done its job.

But did it have to be so annoying?

Jacob didn't need the machine to make that awful noise to know whether or not he was fully recharged. A quick glance down toward his chest-plate easily revealed the indicator lights. They were a solid green and on the tenth bar.

Click…click-click…click…click-click…The charger continued to cry.

"Okay, okay!" Jacob yelled. "I hear you. Fully charge!"

Normally, a full charge would take anywhere from a couple hours to half a day, depending on factors such as generation type and battery cell size. At least half that time, usually toward the end of a recharging process, was reserved for a transition period. During this time, the battery cells would circulate all the newly restored energy throughout the complex array of wiring that connected limbs to joints and joints to limbs. While in this transition period, sensors would switch to standby mode and if need be, could be enabled, though never to their maximum efficiency. Vision sensors, for example, were limited to detecting simple motions, rather than depth and detail.

Fortunately, for Jacob, this transition period had come and gone, and he was now full of energy. He wanted out. He scanned the room from wall to wall, corner to corner. Something wasn't right, he noticed. His mom should be up here by now.

Normally, even before the hum of his hard-drive would commence, she would be by his side, ready to end the annoying click…click-clicks, and more importantly, pull him free from the charger's absolute grip. She was nowhere in sight, however. The only thing by Jacob's side was the blinding light, although to be fair, light was pretty much everywhere at the moment.

"Mom?" he yelled. "Mom, you there?" There was no reply. "Hey! I'm ready to get out now!" He tightened his lips and waited for a reply. Nothing. "Mom?" he whimpered. "Are you…there?"

Minus the charger's clicks, the room was silent. Unable to do much, Jacob was desperate. He called out to the only other one who could possibly help. “Pin-bot? Hey, Pin-bot! Can you help me get out of this thing?” Already knowing the outcome of his calls, he sighed. “Oh, yeah,” he whimpered, not exactly feeling fully recharged at the moment, “I forgot.”

Jacob was starting to wish that he had heeded his mom’s request not to “modify” Pin-bot. He wished that she was on at the moment. Her beeps would be encouraging or at the very least, they would drown out the annoying sounds from the charger.

“Oh, shut up!” Jacob yelled, giving the charger a smack with his hand. “Trust me. I want out as much as you want me out.”

He had never tried to get out of the charger by himself, but he was getting desperate. He hated having to be in the machine in the first place, and every added minute of being connected, just added to his frustration. He called out one last time. “Mom! Are you there? Where are you?” There was no reply. “Ah, forget it,” Jacob said, throwing his hand down.

Click…click-click…

“Damn it! That’s it!” Jacob yelled. “*302*!” He twisted his entire upper body and then leaned to one side so he could look behind the machine. There, he noticed that the plug was still snug against the wall and needed to be pulled out in order to properly shut down the charger, finally ending its irritating cries. In such a limiting position, however, it didn’t seem as though Jacob would be able to reach it. He had to try, at least. “How difficult can it be?”

Jacob pulled his arm away from his side and reached out. He let out a long and strenuous grunt. “Stupid…first generation arms,” he complained. “Come…on. Just…a little… further…”

He could almost feel the cord with the tip of his stubby hands, but he couldn't get a firm hold on it. The plug was still tightly secure against the wall. Desperate, he slapped at the cord, hoping the vibration would dislodge the plug. It didn’t even budge. He pulled himself back upright. “Damn it, *303*!”

Jacob had every right to be upset. He was fully charged, but he wasn’t able to do a single thing.

“Useless first generation body!” Out of options, Jacob’s attention went back to the door. He wanted to call out to his mom again, but would she even hear him? He did a quick calculation and decided not to waste his efforts. He sighed. “I can’t call for her every single time I need something,” he said. “I need to start doing things for myself.”

He raised both of his stubby hands in front of his face and scanned them. If his hands were just a little bit bigger, he might be able to pull out the plug. But they weren’t. And unless he received the upgrade, he had been requesting, they will always be first generation hands, connected to a first generation body. He didn't understand why his requests for an upgrade were always dismissed, but maybe it had something to do with him always having to call for his mom whenever he needed anything. “I have to prove that I’m ready to be more than just a first generation,” he decided aloud. “I have to prove that I’m responsible enough for an upgrade.”

"Okay, plug," Jacob said, grimacing. "You're coming out of that wall. I don't know how but you're coming out."

Calculations, and possibly solutions, began to overwhelm him. But in the end, the only thing Jacob could come up with was rather simple. "Maybe if I just..."

He pressed his body against the side of the charger just to test its stability. He felt a bit of give. "Hey, this *might* work!" He shifted from side-to-side, bumping shoulders against the charger's blunt edges. For the most part, the charger remained stable. Jacob thought it must be bolted down, but he remained persistent, and it eventually paid off. With each shift of his body, he felt the base of the charger lift, though gentle at first.

"Guess it isn't bolted down," he said. Back and forth he leaned, lifting the base of the charger further and further off of the floor. "Hey, it's working."

The entire room looked as if it was on a pendulum, but, of course, it was actually Jacob who was tipping back and forth. "It's working! It's working! It's work—" Jacob's eyes suddenly widened. "Uh-oh!" he cried.

In his excitement, he had built up too much momentum. The charger, with him trapped inside, was tipping over, well beyond the point of no return. "Oh, no..." Jacob moaned, as he felt the charger going over. He could see the details on the floor, as the charger fell. He threw his arms over his face, bracing himself for the impact.

The charger slammed into the floor, rattling the room with a deafening boom, followed by an assortment of crumpling squeaks and hideous squeals. They were the sounds one would expect to hear when a large, metal object, like the charger, buckled the weakened metal surface of the floor. The charger then rolled back and forth a few times before settling into the new horizontal position. Silence immediately followed.

Fortunately, for Jacob, the impact had dislodged his legs from the machine's base, and he was finally set free. He was still grounded, however. "Well...not according to my calculations," he admitted, his voice still jittery from the accident, "and certainly not the way Mom would do it, but at least I'm out."

He glanced up at the door and waited, expecting to hear her clumping her way up the stairs. But maybe she hadn't heard the loud crash, although how she hadn't was beyond him. To his relief, the door remained closed. "Good," he said, pushing only his upper body off of the floor. Then he glanced at the charger, wanting to determine its condition. If he had somehow broken it...He didn't even want to consider how mad his mom would be and what the consequences for him would be. There was a huge dent on the top of it as well as a few scratches. "Uh-oh. Hope it still—"

Click...Click-Click...

"Still works...unfortunately."

The sound was met with a mixture of relief and disappointment. Jacob was glad the machine had not broken so he wouldn't get in trouble. But he also hated having to be trapped in it for several hours at a time and wished he could have a reprieve. He looked over toward the wall. The cord and its plug were still where he had last seen them, and they were still staring at him with their silent mockery. He reached over and with one valiant swipe, ripped the plug out from the wall and then threw it down on the floor. The charger whirled a few times before fading, finally taking with it the annoying clicks.

"And never come back!" Jacob said and then quickly amended. "A least, not until I need another charging"

He resumed his assessment of the charger's condition, sliding his hand over the machine's surface. His hand went along smoothly at first, until abruptly falling deep within the newly formed dent. "Mom's not going to like this," he said.

Jacob placed both hands against the floor and used them to push off. One last effort was needed before he could finally stagger to his feet. For the first time ever, Jacob stood tall and mighty over the charger. He enjoyed the sensation of being dominating for a few moments and then placed his hands on hips, mimicking his mom's familiar stance. "I should probably try and pick this thing up before Mom comes up here and sees what I did. But how?"

With his CPU performing the necessary calculations, Jacob came to a quick and unsatisfactory conclusion. With his first generation limbs, he would never be able to get the charger back upright. It was bigger than him by far, and his stubby hands could not even get a grip on the slick surface of the machine. As much as he dreaded his mom's reaction, he realized he was just going to have to wait for her to put the machine back where it belonged. He shrugged. "She'll find out sooner or later."

With the charger no longer the focal point, Jacob turned his attention to himself. He scanned his entire body. "Arm's okay," he said, twisting it from side-to-side. "Just a few scratches."

He lifted his legs, alternating one at a time and then rotated them at the hip. "Legs look okay. Just a small dent."

He then rotated his entire upper body from left to right and even gave his head a few shakes, temporarily scrambling his vision. "Everything still works," he confirmed. This would normally be a good sign. Surprisingly, however, Jacob slumped over and said, "Damn. *304*."

It had just occurred to Jacob that a broken joint or a damaged limb might have been useful in his requests for an upgrade. A broken joint would need to be replaced. *Or upgraded.*

A few small scratches and dents, like the ones he had just obtained, would not be enough to warrant such a request.

"Just my luck. A charger falls on top of me, and all I get are a few scratches." He did perk up slightly when he realized what standing next to the machine actually meant. "But I *did* get out all by myself. That shows some responsibility doesn't it? Won't that count for something?"

Although there might not be a trophy to show for it, Jacob was certainly proud of his accomplishment. "Hey, maybe Mom will finally see that I'm actually evolving! Maybe she'll even say, 'Jacob! I'm so proud of you! Let's get you that upgrade. A full upgrade with new arms, legs, hard-drive, *and* CPU'." He slumped over. "Yeah. Like she would ever say that."

Jacob finally decided that he had given the prospects of a potential upgrade enough of his attention. It was time to get ready to go to school, even though he was dreading that prospect. He walked over to his closet but stopped short. Hung neatly, and obviously deliberately on the closet's door handle, was the complete set of bright-red plating that his mom had been so keen on earlier. Everything was there; chest-plates, shoulder-plates, forearm-plates, even a crotch-plate. They were arranged so neatly in place, so obsessively in ascending order, that he could practically jump right in and be fitted in mere moments.

Jacob stepped closer and sighed. "Oh, Mom..." he murmured. He thought she had told him he could pick out his own plates. Didn't she? He decided to check. The plates over his eyes suddenly lowered, and the glow of his eyes faded. The hum of his hard-drive became louder, as it increased its speed.

"I'll let you pick out whatever you want to wear..." the recorded voice of Jacob's mom recited from his internal speaker. His hard-drive immediately quieted down, and the glow returned to his eyes.

"So she *did* say I could choose my own." Jacob ripped open the closet door. "Fine, I will!"

When Jacob looked inside, he was shocked. The metal bar, that normally held his many sets of plating, was bare. "Hey! What happened?"

He could see that the rest of his plating was resting on the very top shelf above the metal bar. His mom must have thrown them up there while he was recharging. The shelf was at least three feet over Jacob's head. There was no way to reach it or the plates it held. The metal bar was only a foot below the shelf, but Jacob couldn't clamp his hands around the metal bar even if he tried. "Stupid first generation limbs," he mumbled.

He was beginning to think that maybe he should keep that phrase on the very tip of his hard-drive, considering how often he was using it lately.

To get at the plating, Jacob's only other option was to demagnetize the entire room, but that would mean a trip toward the ceiling. And without Pin-bot around, Jacob might be floating up there for a while. He couldn't count on his mom to come to his rescue. She wasn't even there when he had called out to her a few moments ago. Again, Jacob slumped over. It was this lowly position that afforded him the vantage point needed to see deep inside the closet. He noticed the familiar mound of disorganized parts scattered in the corner. The out of reach plating suddenly became insignificant.

"Pin-bot!" Jacob cried, dropping to his knees.

Wires were coming out from every seam of the dismantled orb halves, but this wasn't of great concern to Jacob. He knew what each part was and where they all fit inside each another. He reached down, picked up both sections, and flicked the small switch from behind the lower half. As the orb powered on, it shook Jacob's hand with a sudden jolt. The front half of the orb released a dazzling array of solid-white LED lights, illuminating the smooth, dark, glassy surface. The lights blinked a couple times before becoming fixated on Jacob. Jacob knew Pin-bot was confirming identification. Once that was completed, Pin-bot let out a series of high-pitched beeps, and the white LED lights transformed into a pair of red heart shapes.

Recognizing Pin-bot's sign of affection, Jacob smiled and then brought the two sections closer to his face. “Hi, Pin-bot. I'm happy to see you, too. Sorry for what happened earlier. Mom didn't mean to turn you off like that. I think you just scared her.”

Pin-bot's eyes returned to their normal oval shapes. “Beep-beep-scared?” she asked.

“No, not me,” Jacob replied, fully understanding Pin-bot's broken speech. “I knew you were already in pieces. Mom didn't. She's not used to seeing you this way.” Jacob shook his head. “Wow, Mom was really upset with me. I told her that you wanted to learn how to speak, but she didn't really understand. She hated seeing you in pieces.”

The little helper-bot started wiggling around in Jacob's hands, almost like she was trying to see herself. “Beep-beep-broken?” she said.

“Yeah, sorry, Pin-bot. You're still in pieces. I didn't have time to put you back together before my batteries went out.”

Pin-bot spun the blades of her turbines, but this resulted in nothing more than a very low hum. “Beep-beep-fly?” she asked.

“No,” Jacob replied. “You won't be able to fly until I reconnect the wires from your main turbine.”

Pin-bot then broke open at the very bottom, revealing a pair of neatly concealed hands. They struggled to even twitch. “Beep?”

“Sorry, Pin-bot. Had to disable both your arms. If not, they would have pitched me when I finally put you back together.”

Pin-bot's eyes suddenly flattened out and angled downward in a familiar expression of anger. “Beep-beep-not-working?” she cried out.

“Sorry, Pin-bot. Nothing really works right now. I had to disconnect almost everything. Don't be mad. I'll put you back together, I promise.”

Pin-bot's eyes returned to red ovals. “Beep-beep,” she said in her normal tone.

“It's okay. I'd be upset too if I was in pieces.” Jacob sighed. “I'll fix you later. I need to get ready.”

“Beep?”

Jacob frowned before mumbling, “First day of school.”

“Beep-beep-school?”

“Yeah. First day,” Jacob said with little enthusiasm. “I can tell you already that it's not going to be very pleasant.”

“Beep-beep-not-happy?”

“Happy? No, not exactly. They'll make fun of me. I'm sure of it.”

Pin-bot's eyes thinned out and then angled downward. “Beep-not-friends!”

“I know. Trust me, I know. I don't want to go, but I have no choice. Mom won't let me stay home.”

“Beep-beep.”

"No need to be sorry. I guess it's better than being…you know...dormant like everyone else."

"Peep-beep-pieces." Pin-bot said, her eyes now in the shape of crescents, displaying a funny face.

Jacob giggled. "Yeah, you're right, Pin-bot. Anything's better than being in pieces. I guess I can't complain. Anyway, I need to get going. Mom's probably wondering what I'm doing up here. She must be waiting downstairs."

Pin-bot's eyes turned into hearts. "Beep-beep-good-day," she said.

"I'll try, but no promises." Jacob pressed his face against the side of Pin-bot smooth, outer surface. "Sorry to have to do this, Pin-bot, but all your beeping will probably scare Mom again."

Pin-bot did her best to shift back and forth in agreement, but her movements were limited to a few unorthodox wiggles.

"I'll see you in a bit," Jacob said.

"Beep-beep."

Jacob reached down and flicked the switch on her back. The pair of heart-shaped LED lights morphed into flat lines before fading out completely. Jacob gently placed the mangled halves of Pin-bot on the floor and then got back up on his feet. He was met face-to-face with the bright-red plating still hanging from the closet door handle. "I hate red."

* * *

A pile of cans with the inscription *Artificial Blend* stretched all the way to the ceiling, casting its shadow over the pathetic stack of cans labelled *Pure Blend.* The difference in quantity was enough to make Grace shake her head in dismay. As usual, her hands were on her hips.

"Not sure what we're going to do when this pile runs out. But I guess we'll find out soon enough." She grabbed two cans from the smaller pile and one from the much larger pile and then walked over to the table in the heart of the brightly lit room. She deposited one can of each brand on the table's rusted surface and then continued on toward the end of the room. Waiting for her on the counter was a small, metal box with a handle on top and two tabs in the front.

"Two cans a day," she recited. "Make sure he gets two cans a day. That will keep him going." She placed the second can of *Pure Blend* inside the metal box and then fastened it closed using the small tabs on the front. At that exact moment, her eyes detected movement in the hallway just beyond the entrance to the room. She turned to see who it was and was shocked to see Jacob not only out of the charger but also completely dressed. Even though he was still in the dim hallway, she could see that he wore the red plating that she had purposely left out for him. She had started picking out his plating after he had dressed himself one day and came down the stairs with plates of different colours and the crotch-plate snapped onto his chest. It was a rather embarrassing sight to say the least.

Grace stood silently, expecting Jacob to make his way over to her.

Jacob, however, didn't even seem to notice her. He walked into the smaller room, off the kitchen, and stopped short. It was the very same room that had contained the mess that he had created while searching for his microscope, but to his surprise, there was no mess to be found. "Hey, I thought she said there was a mess."

"Jacob!" his mom called out. "In the kitchen. Let's go!"

Jacob turned around and walked toward the doorway to the kitchen. "I thought you said there was a mess."

"There *was* a mess, but no need to worry. I cleaned it up."

Jacob entered the kitchen to find his mom standing at the counter, his lunch box in front of her. "You cleaned it up?" he said astounded.

His mom simply nodded.

"But when?"

"Right after I put you inside the charger."

"Didn't you need a recharge?" It was at that moment that Jacob noticed the orange light casting a small glow below his mom's breast-plate. It was her battery indicator. "You're at orange, Mom. That's almost red."

"I should be okay, for now. I'll recharge when I get back from driving you to school."

"Don't you feel drained? I know I start feeling a bit weird when my indicators hit orange."

"Not really. I *do* have an eight cell battery, so I can hold a charge much longer than you." A frown appeared over half of her face. "Well, not as long as I used to," she murmured.

"Eight cells? Wow, really? How many do I have?"

"One."

Jacob's frown looked very much like his mom's, though his took up his entire face. "Just one?"

"Yes, just one. That's all you need at the moment. As long as you recharge yourself, your body doesn't need anything more than a one-cell battery right now."

Because it's a lousy first generation.

Grace gestured to the table which supported a pair of cans on its metal surface. "Have a seat and take a drink. It'll help keep your internal parts running."

Jacob noticed that his usual can of *Pure Blend* was already opened for him. "Okay-okay. I'm going."

As Jacob walked, a loose shoulder-plate rattled, and his mom moved quickly toward him. He glanced over his shoulder. "Uh, Mom? You're following me?"

"Just need to see something, Jacob."

Jacob stopped. "See what?"

Grace reached over, applied a heavy grip onto Jacob's shoulder-plate and forcefully snapped it into place. Jacob nearly toppled over just from the force that his mom had applied.

"Mom!" He pushed her hand away and scanned his shoulder-plate to see what she had done.

"It was loose," she said, "but it's fine now."

Jacob looked up at her and noticed that she had a ridiculous looking smile on her face. "I thought I had everything on right this time."

"No-no…you did." Grace shrugged. "Except…well, that one little piece. But it's okay now. It looks good. *You* did just fine. I'm so proud of you."

Jacob's eyes widened. "Proud? Really?"

"Yes, very proud."

"Proud enough for that upgrade? 'Second Generation Jacob'. Doesn't that sound good?"

The smile instantly disappeared from her face. "We'll have to wait and see."

Jacob's hands flopped down to his sides, and he slumped over with disappointment. "You always say that."

"And I always mean it. Upgrades are difficult to find these days."

"Don't think it's *that* hard to find an arm or two or even a leg."

"Oh, I think it is," Jacob's mom countered. "There aren't as many options as you think. Be happy with what you have."

Jacob dropped his weight onto one of the chairs and then frowned. "Happy with his body? I don't think so."

"It'll have to do for now. Everything still works. No damage at all. It should last you for a while.

"So damage would warrant an upgrade?"

"Possibly."

"Damn, *304*," Jacob whispered. "Wish my charger had done some more damage."

Grace turned to go back to the counter and then stopped and faced him again. "Before I forget. What was that loud noise I heard from your room earlier?"

Jacob looked at his mom, eyes wide. "Oh…uh…that?"

"Yes, *that*. It was loud. What happened?"

"It was…uh…well…it was nothing. I just dropped something. No big deal. Just…" He glanced into the hallway and could see the steps leading up toward his room. "Just…stay out of my room until I get back." He grinned. "Please?"

"Why?" she asked, now more suspicious than ever. "What am I going to find up there?"

"Everything's there," Jacob replied.

He wasn't exactly lying. Everything *was* there, just not in the exact position that she might have remembered.

"Okay, then," Grace said. "Drink up. We need to get going soon."

Not paying attention to what he was doing, Jacob reached out to pick up his drink again. His "*C*" shaped hand might not be useful for a lot of things but it worked well for holding the cylindrical form of a can…most of the time. "Mom, did you stay in my room after I was in the charger?"

"Why?"

"The window shutters were open again. The light was everywhere."

"Don't I always open them? I don't know how you can do anything without light."

"Night vision, remember? Unlike yours, mine still works."

Grace didn't even crack a smile.

"And what about these?" Jacob asked, pointing at the red plates snapped onto various locations around his body. "These were hanging on my closet door. And you said I could pick out my own."

"I thought you would decide on the red ones." Grace smiled, tightening the motors behind her face. "Aren't they adorable?"

"No."

"Oh...I thought you said you liked them." Grace shrugged. "Well, you should have picked another one from the closet. You have a lot to choose from."

"I was going to, but you threw the rest on the top shelf." Jacob brought the can to his mouth. "How was I supposed to—"

His mom suddenly ripped the can out of his hand.

"Mom!" Jacob cried. "What are you doing? I was drinking that."

"Sorry. You picked up the wrong can." Grace replaced the *Artificial Blend* with *Pure Blend*. "This one's yours."

Jacob scanned the can that was now inside his firm hold. Everything was exactly the same as before, except, of course, the inscription. "Oh, you're right." He puckered up his lips and then drank. Most of the *Pure Blend* disappeared into his mouth and funnelled down deep into the many channels and wires throughout his simplistic body. A small stream of the clear fluid trickled down his chin and dripped onto this chest-plate.

"Are you even drinking any?" Grace said, bending down at the knees and wiping Jacob's chest-plate with her hand.

Jacob pulled the *Pure Blend* away from his mouth. "Let me finish, Mom. I'll clean up once I'm finished."

"Just keep drinking. It's easier this way."

Jacob tried bringing the can to his mouth again, but his mom's head was in his way. He had no choice but to wait. As she leaned in to clean his chest-plate, he could see the back of his mom's head. What he saw stunned him.

Just above one of Grace's ear-wells, a patch of small bubbles had formed on her metallic surface, with deep-red and brown flakes breaching through.

This was a familiar sight to Jacob. He had seen this formation inside and outside of his house so many times before. Just never on his mom. His eyes widened "Rust!" he cried.

"Really?" Grace stepped back quickly and began feeling around at the back of her head.

"Ear," Jacob said. "Near your ear."

Grace finally located the bumps that Jacob was referring to. She fell silent. She was as shocked as Jacob was. This was the first time either of them had noticed rust on her. She'd accumulated a few dents and scratches through the years. But never rust. Imperfections had always been voided on her surfaces.

"I mean…I think it's rust," Jacob said, trying to sound like the idea didn't bother him. "I mean…it could be something else. Dirt, maybe?"

His mom smirked. "Trust me, Jacob, I'm clean." She removed her hand from the back of her head, looked at it and sighed. "No, it's rust." Then she calmly reached for the can of *Artificial Blend* on the table. "I'll just have a little drink."

Jacob was surprised by his mom's composure. He thought that her reaction would be a little more dramatic. Rust was a serious matter. It was the first signs of decay. The next logical step after decay…was complete shut down. Jacob just looked at her with a blank stare.

"What's wrong, Jacob?"

"Well…it's just…I thought you'd be a bit upset having rust."

His mom shook her head. "Not at all."

"Really?"

"Yes. It's natural. We'll all rust eventually. Time is our only enemy, and it looks like it's found me."

Jacob looked away. "I…I guess so…"

Sensing his need for some reassurance, Jacob's mom took a step toward him. "No need to worry. It's going be a while before this small patch spreads to the rest of my body. And as for you, well…" she smiled, "you won't see any rust on your body for a long time."

"So...no need to worry? For either of us?"

"The only thing you need to worry about is finishing your can of *Pure Blend*."

"Oh...right." Jacob shook the can and heard the sloshing of liquid. "There's still a lot left. I can't drink all of this right now."

"Drink as much as you can. You can save the rest for later. And remember, there's another full can in your lunchbox. Drink them both today, please."

"Two cans a day," Jacob said, watching his mom drink *Artificial Blend*. "How come I'm never allowed to drink what you drink?"

His mom pulled the can away from her mouth and placed it on the table just out of Jacob's reach. "You won't like it."

"Can I try some?"

"You won't like it," Grace repeated.

"How will I ever know I won't like it if I never try it?" Jacob put his can down on the table and pushed it toward his mom. "Here, I'll trade you. Some for some."

Grace grabbed her *Artificial Blend*, raised it to her mouth and quickly sipped every last drop. "Too late," she said, slamming the empty can onto the table. "Besides, you won't—"

"Like it." Jacob sank back into his chair. "I knew you were going to say that."

"Then why did you ask?"

"Hoping you might change your answer."

"When was the last time that ever happened?" she asked, walking over the counter.

"Never?"

"Exactly."

"I hate being right," Jacob murmured.

"Okay, no more time to waste. Let's go."

Jacob slid out of his chair. "But I'm not done yet."

Grace grabbed the half empty can from his hand, sealed the opening with the integrated tab and then placed it inside his lunchbox. "Remember to drink the rest of it," she said, handing Jacob the box.

Jacob reached out. His mom instinctively let go when she felt the pressure of Jacob's hand taking over. Unfortunately, Jacob had not yet eased his hand into the slot underneath the handle, and the lunchbox fell to the floor with a thud.

"Jacob!"

He stood there. He was as surprised as she was. "It slipped!"

Jacob bent down, attempting to pick up the lunchbox but struggled to grasp the angular form with his stubby hands. It took three attempts before the box was securely in his grasp.

Watching Jacob struggling to do such a simple task made Grace feel bad for him...almost. She hadn't really noticed before what her stubbornness about the upgrade cost him, but there wasn't much she could do. As she had said many times before, an upgrade would have to have to wait.

"Sorry," Jacob said, looking up at his mom with his bright-blue eyes. "I didn't mean to drop it."

"And I didn't mean to yell, Jacob. Just be more careful, okay?"

"I'll try." *Not easy with these first generation limbs*

"That's all I can ask for," she said, smiling. "Come on, let's get going."

They walked to the end of the hall and stopped in front of a heavy door. On the floor were two pairs of boots, one larger than the other.

"Clean and more importantly magnetized," Grace announced, cocking her head toward Jacob's pair.

"Oh...yeah," Jacob said, noticing the sheen. "Thanks. It won't happen again."

"I sure hope not. You remember what happened the last time?"

"Yeah-yeah, one floated away," Jacob replied. He struggled to put on his boots.

Grace reached down to help Jacob with his boots. Pulling so hard nearly tipped him off balanced. "We're lucky that boot landed on the moon and not any further," she said. "We're also lucky that we had so much help getting it back."

Jacob grimaced at the pressure his mom was applying to his poor feet. "Good thing, too. They're my favourite pair."

"They're your *only* pair."

He shrugged. "Then I guess I should take better care of them."

"I've been telling you that ever since we got them."

"Are you done yet, Mom? I just need my boots on, not permanently attached to my leg."

"No need to be smart, Jacob." She let him go. "There. Done."

"I wasn't trying to be smart," Jacob said. "Trust me. If I was trying to be smart, I would replied using only 'Is' and 'Os'."

Grace stared blankly at him.

Jacob giggled. "It's that old language we used to use, remember? What's wrong, Mom? Can't you decode anymore?"

Grace rolled her eyes. She slipped her feet inside her own boots without any difficulty.

"Don't worry," Jacob said, with a smile. "If you ever need anything decoded, just leave it to me. I can decode practically everything. All I need is a 'thank-you' afterward."

"You should thank *me* for installing that function inside of you," his mom countered.

The plates over Jacob's eyes lowered, and the confident smile was wiped off his face. "Oh, yeah…right. Thanks."

Grace smiled. "Alright, let's go."

Grace and Jacob paused outside of their house, adjusting their vision because of the strong illumination. Pupils shifted from one angle to the next, adjusting to allow only the right amount of natural sunlight to come through. Grace's eyes were first to stabilize.

"Another bright and sunny day," she said, as the light bounced off of her reflective exterior and radiated back into the open air.

It took a while longer before Jacob's vision finally readjusted. When it did, he still used his hand to shield his sensitive eyes from the sun's intensity. "It's always sunny." he said. "Has there ever been a time when it wasn't sunny?"

Grace stepped down from the metal porch and began making her way along the metal walkway, with Jacob following. "Actually, there was," she replied.

Jacob nearly lost his stride. He wasn't expecting a reply from her, at least, not an honest one. "There was?" he said.

"Yes, of course. The sun wasn't always in the same spot all of the time, like it is now."

"Wait…you mean it used to move?" Jacob snickered. "Yeah, Mom. The sun used to move."

"No, not the sun, Jacob. I mean, it did appear as if the sun *was* moving, but actually, it was the Earth that was moving." She glanced back at Jacob. "Rotating, to be exact."

Grace continued walking until she was beside a lone car parked in the metal driveway. Jacob, however, had to stop and recalculate what his mom had just told him. He looked up at the sun. His eyes immediately adjusted to the brilliant view. A sharp halo around the sun's circular formation was completely contrasted by the moon's shadow casting over a good portion of the Earth just below it. The sun and the moon were in perfect harmony at the moment.

"So…the Earth used to move…I mean, rotate and not the sun?" Jacob recited, wanting to make sure he had heard correctly.

"That's right." Grace latched her hand onto the car's door handle. It took her a few tries before she could pry open the stubborn, rust-eroded door.

Jacob was not convinced. He could not comprehend the notion of something so significant in size being able to move on its own. "But how?" he asked.

"It's a long story."

"Sounds like an interesting one, too."

"Oh, it is, Jacob. It's just as interesting as the story behind that." Grace pointed at one of the most dominating objects in the sky.

"The moon? What about it?"

"It was never this close."

Jacob began making his way over to the car. "But I already knew about the moon. It's getting closer. It always has been. I've been telling you that for a long time now, but you never listen."

"I always listen."

"Really?" Jacob said unconvinced. "Well, then, listen to this. I did some calculations, and I think when the moon finally hits the Earth, we'll—"

"Alright, let's go," Jacob's mom said, quickly opening the door. She positioned herself inside the car and slammed the door shut.

"See?" Jacob said, now standing all by himself, "She never listens."

He made his way around to the passenger-side of the car. He couldn't open it because of his stubby hands, so while he waited for his mom to open the door for him, he looked around at the barren landscape.

His house, the only house in this particular sector that was currently occupied, was the only thing keeping the surroundings from being an absolute void. All the other houses had been abandoned long ago and were left barely standing. Most of them had fallen victim to neglect and were sinking deeper and deeper into the ground, their foundations threatening to become one with the Earth. The only other structures that remained constant were rows upon rows of metal poles. Their bases were anchored deep inside the Earth, while the rest of them towered high into the sky. A few of them were toppled over and covered in rust, making them consistent with the rest of the drab scenery. The ones fortunate enough to still be standing were joined together by thick, steel tubing at the very top of each pole. Jacob had always wondered what those were. He wondered why the poles had been meticulously placed in sections where the Earth was bare of metal coverings and why there was an odd whooshing sound coming from the steel tubing. He then wondered why he had never bothered asking anyone. *Maybe I should.*

Jacob felt a bump against his arm, as the car door moved…slightly. His mom was able to reclaim his attention with her forceful banging on the car's door. Jacob peeked inside through the window, the glass mottled with some kind of glaze. He couldn't help but notice the patches of rust that covered most of the car's surface with only a few spots still resilient enough to offer back his own reflection. The rust was thick around the hinges, making it difficult for his mom to open the door.

"Hold on, Jacob," his mom called out, her voice muffled inside the car's interior. "I've...almost... got it."

Jacob helped the best that he could by wedging his hand into the seam of the door. He gave one mighty tug before it finally gave way.

"Damn thing," his mom cried out.

Jacob jumped into the seat, placed the lunchbox under his feet and then slammed the door shut. It was much easier to close than to open. He then looked over at this mom, a bit surprised. "You've been using that word more than ever, lately."

"I know. I shouldn't. But this damn thing...sometimes it just..." Grace let the sentence fade and stuck her finger inside a slot next to the steering wheel and began cranking the ignition. A horrible sound fired off every time she turned her finger. She shook her head.

"Time for a new one?" Jacob asked, grinning.

"I wish. But this could very well be the last car we'll ever own."

A few more turns of her finger resulted in the same horrific bellowing of mechanical parts grinding together.

"It is a piece of junk," Jacob said.

Grace gave a little chuckle, nodded and then resumed her efforts to start the car.

Finally, after the seventh turn of her finger, the car decided that it was time to forfeit its stubborn ways and allow the engine to start. Surprisingly, after the guttural roars and the dramatic display of unwillingness, the sound the engine produced was rather tame. It was next to silent, just an initial whirl followed by a more consistent hum.

Jacob giggled. "It's alive!"

"Yes, and let's hope it stays alive this time." Grace flicked a switch, and the car lifted to float a few inches off the ground. Positive charged magnets at the bottom of the car pushed off the positive metal lining on the driveway with opposing force, allowing it to hover. The car was now ready to drive.

Not being grounded allowed for a smooth transition from parked to complete motion, and the current status would remain this way until the car was turned off, essentially becoming grounded again. Leave it to the operator, however, to break this basic string of commands.

Grace released her foot off of the brake, and the car lunged out from the driveway and onto the main, metal-coated road.

Jacob was jerked violently against his seat. "Mom! This the first time you driven? You nearly ripped my head from its socket."

"Sorry," his mom said, with an apologetic grin. "Metal foot."

Luckily for them, there was no traffic to get in their way...or out of her way.

"At least we're not on wheels," Grace said, attempting to somehow justify her wild approach to driving.

"Wheels?"

"You know, round, disc-shaped objects with a soft outer lining—"

"I know what wheels are, Mom. I just don't know what you meant by being on them?"

"That's how we used to get around."

Jacob could barely comprehend something so absurd. "Wheels to get around with?"

First, it was the Earth moving and then it was the moon. Now his mom had the audacity to tell him that wheels were once used as a means of transportation? Jacob didn't even want to finish his thoughts. He turned his body on an angle, away from his mom, away from her silly claims and calculated silently to himself. *She had to be making some of this stuff up.*

* * *

They had been driving for what seemed like forever. It was so quiet inside the car, Jacob could hear the low hum of the engine while he stared mindlessly through the car's blotched window. He was not feeling very talkative at the moment. How could he be? Not only was he on his way to a new school, one in which he never really agreed upon but the reflected scenery rolling across his window was depressing. A lonely stretch of shattered dunes, lifeless hills and what was nothing more than rubble flew by, as the car moved along. Every so often, the drab scenery reflections, rolling off the window, would be interrupted by the jutting remains of a once tall and mighty building now reduced to an eye sore.

The building currently overshadowing the car was at least twenty stories tall. Jacob confirmed this by counting each of the levels. His CPU was that quick. He even took into account that the lower level, the foundation, must have been buried deep within the ground. Possibly two stories deep in order to anchor the rest of the building and keep it from floating off into the sky. A heavy build-up of rust painted all the walls, beams, and the underlying structure of the building in dark-red ochre. Even the thickest of the metal walls were consumed by the rust in places and then spit out as massive holes. Light tunnelled its way into all the imperfections and busted out the other side, cutting a straight, glowing edge in every direction.

On the other side of the car, Grace, wondered what was going through Jacob's CPU. Was he worried about school? Or was he just mindlessly watching the world, what was left of it, pass them by? To break the silent monotony she said, "You're awfully quiet."

"Just watching," Jacob said, glancing over his shoulder at his mom. "Still have to get used to how quiet everything is around here. "It was never like this at our old place." Jacob suddenly sank a bit deeper into his seat and whispered, "At least, not until everyone was reassigned. Thanks to the Mayor."

"I'm just glad we moved out here when we did. Otherwise, we would have been the ones lying dormant right now."

"I don't even want to think about that," Jacob replied, returning his attention back outside the window.

They drove on in silence for a few more minutes, then Jacob noticed more of those poles with the steel tubing standing tall in an area of the ground that was not covered in metal. It was a perfect time for him to ask.

"Hey, Mom? Do you have any idea what those things are?"

Grace laughed. "You've never been outside the house?"

"Of course I have."

"You've never heard the whooshing sounds?"

"I always hear the whooshing sounds. But what is it exactly?"

"Notice how those poles are always placed in areas where there is no metal lining the ground?"

Jacob nodded.

"Magnets don't work without metal."

Obviously, Mom. Jacob wisely kept that thought to himself.

"Ever wondered why you've never floated away when you're not standing on metal? You know...when you're underneath the poles?"

Grace waited, allowing Jacob to come to his own conclusions.

"Artificial gravity!" Jacob said. "But how?"

"Simple. It's just a current of air flowing down from those tubing. It's what's pushing everything back toward the ground." Grace could hear the buzzing from Jacob's hard-drive, as the newly acquired information was being recorded and stored.

"I never knew that," Jacob admitted.

"Now you know, and hopefully you'll never forget."

"I never forget...most of the time," he said, with a simple grin. "So why not use magnets everywhere? It's stronger than air currents, isn't it?"

"For magnets to work, you need something for them to stick to."

"Yes. Metal. I know that, Mom."

"Exactly. And there isn't much of it around here anymore. Earth's dry. That's why we're forced to use air. It's even used inside buildings and homes, but it's too subtle to even detect. It's also in the ground."

"The ground?"

"Yes, Jacob. Above the Earth, through those tubes, the air is being forced downward. Pushing to create artificial gravity. Below the Earth, tubing is buried underground and air is being sucked through. Pulling to creating artificial gravity. But it's only reserved to a few confined areas. There are not enough resources to cover the entire Earth." She tilted her head. "I'm surprised it still works. Not many things here on Earth work these days."

Jacob glanced out the window to see a few more of the poles pass by, only this time, all of them were toppled over. Their bases were eroded by rust. "Yeah, I noticed," he said.

As they drove deeper into the city, more and more buildings came into view. Rust did not shy away from any of their surfaces. It claimed every bent over sign and every abandoned car littering the streets. In areas, the rust was so dominate its brownish colour blended perfectly with the Earth's crust, making it difficult to separate building from dirt.

Even the road that Grace and Jacob were driving over was not immune to the ravages of the corrosion. Every so often, patches of the road would disappear and would be replaced by rust. When they drove over these sections, the car's magnets would struggle, causing them to jerk from side-to-side.

"Mom!"

"Sorry, Jacob. It's not my driving this time. Blame it on the road."

Jacob shook his head. "Guess that's why the Mayor wants to leave this place so badly."

"Why's that?"

Jacob gestured out the window. "Isn't it obvious? All of this. It's all falling apart. Earth's falling apart."

Grace nodded and then asked, "So? How do you feel about that?"

Jacob's only response was to shrug.

"There once was a time when everything had a sheen to it," she said. "It's now either dull or breaking down. You're right, Jacob. That is why the Mayor wants to leave this place. New hope elsewhere."

"I just don't understand how it got this way. Why didn't the Mayor do anything about it when he still had the chance?"

"I don't know. I think he tried," Grace said, lifting one shoulder in a shrug. "He thought he knew what he was doing…"

"Well, he didn't do a good job of it."

Grace snickered. "No, he didn't, did he?"

Jacob turned to look out the window again. "Earth looks really bad right now, but there has to be a way to bring it back. Didn't you say Earth was once covered by plants?"

"Yes...yes it was. Unfortunately, any possibility of returning the Earth to the way it once was isn't really going to happen."

"I know, I know. I'm just saying. Instead of the Mayor going through with his plans, whatever they may be, wouldn't it be better if we stayed here and tried to at least bring Earth back to where it once was?"

"That would be nice. It really would, but there's not a whole lot we can do. There aren't many of us left on this Earth. And the ones who are still around are either dormant or in bad shape."

"I'm not," Jacob said, with a proud smile.

Grace reached over and patted him on the shoulder. "No, of course not." She reached up and tapped the side of her head where Jacob had noticed the patch of rust earlier. "But most of us are."

Jacob lowered his head. "Oh..."

"*That* doesn't help our cause, either." Grace pointed out the window at the moon that overwhelmed even the tallest of buildings. "Didn't you say it'll make contact with Earth soon?"

"If my calculations are right," Jacob replied.

"I'm sure they are. That's just another reason, or excuse, for the Mayor to want to leave."

Jacob's voice weakened. "It's a *good* reason to leave. The impact is going to be severe, according to my calculations."

Jacob's comment was enough to silence the pair for the time being. It gave them both a chance to calculate to themselves.

Soon, they approached their final destination in the heart of the last occupied sector on Earth. Here, there were more buildings flashing by the window, but Jacob didn't pay them any attention. His focus was on a pair of second generation beings heading to one of the buildings.

"Look at those second generations," he said. "They…they look so much bigger than me."

"I'm sure they're not that much bigger. They just look that way because of the distortion from the window."

"I've calculated that into the equation, Mom. Trust me, they're bigger than me."

"Well...they might be," she replied, trying her best to drown out Jacob's lack of confidence, "but you never know. There might be other students who are your size and generation."

Just as the words left her mouth, a small group of second and third generation beings walked by. Each one was bigger than the first pair.

Jacob glanced over at his mom with both plates over his eyes lowered. The vents on his cheeks flipped open. "They don't look my size. Let's face it, Mom, I'll be the smallest one in my class as usual."

"Then you'll just have to do what I used to."

"Hide?"

"No. Once you're inside the classroom, find the seat furthest to the back. Less chance of becoming a distraction."

That's it? That's the only bit of encouragement she could come up with? "Yeah…I'll…uh… keep that in mind," Jacob mumbled.

Jacob noticed that the groups of beings got larger and larger until they eventually formed into one large, single mass. He realized this must mean that he and his mom were getting closer to the school. Jacob's sensors began to feel cold and heavy. He sank down into his seat.

"No point in hiding," Grace said. "They can still see you."

"They can?" Jacob sank even further down into the seat, as far as he could go. "How about now?"

His feet now touched the car's undercarriage which he had never felt before. He remained in this awkward position even as his sensors detected the car's sudden stop. He glanced up at his mom but didn't move. The blue glow in his eyes dimmed.

"Well…Jacob," Grace said, before pausing for a moment.

Jacob knew what she was going to say next. "Let me guess. We're here?"

"Yes, Jacob. We're here."

Jacob still didn't move. He wasn't ready to forfeit his cowardly stance.

"Time for you to go, Jacob." Grace reached down and physically pulled Jacob back onto his seat. "Come on, it's not going to be *that* bad."

Keeping his profile as low as he could, Jacob cautiously looked up and out the window. He was shocked when he saw the massive building off to the side of where they were parked. "What...what is this place? Doesn't look like any school that I've ever been in."

"It's definitely a school. Well...not always. There have been a few changes made to it."

"Like what?"

"Nothing that you need to be concerned about." Grace reached down and picked up Jacob's metal lunchbox. "Remember to drink both the cans inside. You need them."

Jacob took the lunchbox from her outstretched hand and pressed it snugly against his chest-plate. "Thanks."

"No need to thank me now. I'm sure you'll be doing that when I pick you up after school."

"Doubt it," Jacob whispered.

Grace reached over and pushed open the door. Mindless chattering from outside immediately surged inside the car. "Okay, Jacob. Out you go."

"Now?"

"Yes, now. Go on."

Jacob peeked out. Second, third, and even fourth generations were all converging outside the school's massive, sculpted door. None of them seem to have even noticed Jacob or the car he was hiding inside, but that did little to persuade him to get out.

Grace gave Jacob a couple of pats on the shoulder, though, they were not for reassurance. She was trying to coax him to move. Jacob finally got the idea and slowly slid sideways off his seat and out the door. He landed as gently as he could on the metal curbing adjacent to the sidewalk so as to not draw any unwanted attention. He took two steps forward but made sure he was still within an arm's length of the car, which in his case, wasn't very far. "Where am I supposed to go once I get inside?"

"Through the main door, and keep going straight, then walk around the statue until you get to room *332*."

"Statue? What statue?"

"You'll see. Oh, and say, 'Hi' to the Professor for me."

The car lifted off the ground, sending Jacob a couple of steps back. One of his stumpy boots snagged onto the curb, and he fell to the ground with a loud thud. The laughs commencing all around him quickly brought him back up to his feet.

"See, Mom!" Jacob cried. "They're already laughing at me!"

Grace held the car in a hover. "You can't really blame them, Jacob. You fell. That's always funny."

Jacob frowned.

"Sorry, Jacob. I'm only teasing. See you in a bit."

The car silently pulled away from the curb. The gust of residual wind, given off by the car's simple engine, pushed Jacob further along the sidewalk. In an instant, his mom was gone, and he was on his own.

Jacob stood with his back facing the school, hands clasping his lunchbox against his chest-plate. He knew that from this angle, judgements, stares, and laughs from others could not reach him. If they did, at least he wouldn't have to challenge them straight on. There were no sensors on his back, only protective plating, something he wished he had all over his body right now.

He could hear snatches of random chattering. *Are they talking about me? I hope they're not talking about me.* He tried to increase his audio input to make out what they were talking about, but it was at its max, and the only way he would hear would be to go closer and face them. But he didn't want to do that. And the more the chattering increased, the more his assumptions ran out of control. *They are! They have to be. What else could they be talking about?*

He heard a burst of laughter behind him. *That's it!* He disabled his hearing sensors, muting out all the sounds. *Good. Now I don't have to hear them laughing at me.* He could just imagine what they were saying. "Look at that first generation," he said in a whinny voice. "Look at his short arms, look at his short legs. Look, he barely stands higher than our knees."

Jacob sighed and then looked down the road where the horizon had taken his mom away from him. There was nothing but a thin, hazy line that stretched from one end of the sky to the next. She wouldn't be back for a while. The vents on his cheeks opened and remained open for longer than usual. *Might as well get this over with.* He closed his eyes. *Okay…you can do this, Jacob. They'll laugh, but in the end, your CPU is more advanced.*

Then he had a thought that made him grin. They wouldn't laugh at him if he showed them the trophies he'd won. He'd just bring one…That idea was cut short when he realized there was no way he could carry one of the large trophies to school. They were all as big as he was. He shook his head. "Damn first generation limbs. *305.*"

Jacob continued to stand with his back to the school for several minutes and then realized he would have to turn around sooner or later. He started to turn, giving himself a pep talk, "Just ignore them. Go inside. Get to class, and before you know it, it will be over. Then Mom will be waiting outside, ready to take you back home. Back home to Pin-bot. Back home to your room. Back home to your microscope with the plant inside. Everything will be good again."

Maybe it was because of all the time he spent pondering the positives but by the Jacob was facing the school, there was no one left to send negative thoughts his way. Jacob's eyes opened, and he was more than surprised—he was embarrassed. They had all gone inside, leaving Jacob and his quick assumptions on their own. He immediately enabled his hearing sensors. *Okay…maybe not out here, but I'm sure they'll make fun of me once I get inside…I think.* The grip on his lunchbox eased, and Jacob took a few steps forward.

The building he was advancing on was enormous. Its daunting shadow stretched far and had enough bulk to drape over Jacob, creating a cooling shield from the relentless sun. Even with his neck angled so far back that it nearly locked up, Jacob could not see the very top of the building. Its foundation consisted mainly of rock, a substance not commonly used in current structures. The exterior walls, however, were constructed using more common materials. They were caged off by ugly metal grading, with twisted rebar that looked like they were unsure of which direction they were going. The connecting slabs of sheet metal were complete with a fresh coating of rust. Like all the surrounding buildings, this one's mighty stance would eventually be reclaimed by the Earth from which it had come.

Now standing before Jacob was an impressive staircase. It reminded Jacob of the staircase leading up to his room at home, although this one was at least three times the size. If the staircase at home grinned at Jacob every time he was at its base, this one was letting out a bellowing laugh. He stopped in front of the first step, what he thought of as its mouth. It stood parallel to his hips. "Glad everyone's inside now and not out here to see this." he said. "This isn't going to be pretty, that's for sure."

He threw his lunchbox up and onto the first step and then reached up with his stubby limbs and pulled himself up. The vents on his cheek opened and let out an exhausting sigh, as he stood on the first step. They let out an even longer, more dejected sigh when Jacob realized that this was only the first of twelve. "Ah, damn it!" he cried. "*306.*"

After what seemed like an eternity, Jacob finally reached the top. A series of freshly obtained scratches on the surfaces of his arms and legs testified to the long and hard-fought battle to get there.

"Finally," Jacob said, relieved. "I hate stairs."

He was now completely out of the sunlight and deep inside the school's shadow. This allowed the indicator lights on his chest-plate to become more prevalent. He noticed that a full green bar had disappeared. "Wow! It took one full bar just to get up these stairs?" He picked up his lunchbox and began walking. "I really need an upgrade."

In front of Jacob was a tall and sturdy-looking door. Metal, of course, with rust all along its edges, but the center was clean and gleaming. It had a single ringed handle that he gripped and pulled. The forced he applied ripped the handle out of his grip, flinging his arm back. And the door remained closed. "Damn, *307*. Trying to be tough, huh? Alright, have it your way."

He dropped his lunchbox, reached out with both hands and clamped onto the handle, ready to throw his entire weight into his efforts. Then he noticed the direction of the hinges. If he was capable of it, he would have blushed with embarrassment. He let go of the handle, placed only one hand against the door and pushed. The door eased open without much of a fight. "Room full of trophies and I don't even know how to *push* open a door," Jacob muttered.

The scraping of the door's hinges echoed deep inside the building and then faded sharply. Jacob stepped inside just as the last of his classmates disappeared into the room at the end of the hallway. The door slammed shut behind him with a mighty thump. It took a moment or two for Jacob's vision to adjust to the lack of light in the hall, so he stood until it did and then headed in the direction the other students had gone. He guessed that was the classroom. Although dim, there was enough light filtering through the cracks in the ceilings that Jacob did not need to enable his night vision. He could easily see the rows of doors on each side of the long hallway. He looked at each door, as he walked by, but none of them had evidence of light seeping through their seams, suggesting that there was nothing or no one on the other side. Jacob walked deeper into the sterile hallway, keeping mainly to the left, though it wasn't entirely necessary, as both sides of the hall were mirrored exactly, door for door, detail for detail. Each step he took released an unwanted echo. He tried to be quieter, but the sound of metal striking metal was never easily dampened. The only real way to stop the sound would be to stop walking, which Jacob suddenly did. Not because of the noise but because of what now towered over him.

"Wow!" Jacob said, in absolute awe. There it was. The statue that his mom had told him about.

The statue rose from the floor and peaked at the ceiling. It was constructed out of a brilliant looking metal, a kind Jacob had never seen before. The statue was so shiny, so flawless, so...golden. It was kept in immaculate condition and made the trophies in Jacob's room look dull in comparison. Jacob walked up to the statue's base and craned his neck to see the whole thing. It was the image of a man, larger than life. His heavy jaw-line, constructed from multiple plates, and deep sunken lenses for eyes were enough to intimate anyone, let alone an insignificant first generation, such as Jacob.

The grand statue's pose was as equally impressive as it was exaggerated. Pinned underneath one of his feet was a disproportionate depiction of the Earth. One hand was on his hip with the other pointed toward the ceiling. Jacob didn't have the slightest idea where or what he was pointing to. It didn't matter. Jacob felt so small and insignificant standing next to the giant.

"He looks important. Wonder who he is." At that moment, something made Jacob's hard-drive skip a revolution. It let out a small click. The plates over Jacob's eyes lowered. "He looks...familiar." *But how was this even possible?* Jacob was almost positive that he had never seen this man up until now. *He didn't even know if it depicted a real person.*

The clanking of his boots returned, as Jacob walked around the mighty statue and continued forward. The final room at the end of the hall not only had a thick stream of natural light billowing out but Jacob could hear the same noisy chattering he'd heard outside. He slowed his pace, noticing the second to the last door in the hallway. It was numbered *333* and looked different from the other doors. Rust did not cling on its surface like the other doors. It looked much heavier and was reinforced with thick plating all around its edges. And it had a massive lock sealing it shut. "Wonder what's hiding inside."

Much like the man depicted in the statue, the reason this door was so different would have to remain a mystery. Jacob stopped just shy of the final room in the hallway. A large *332* was engraved on the frame above the door. "Well…this is it." Jacob whispered, using the same pale tone that he had been using since the exact moment that his mom had stopped the car.

Jacob pressed his face against the gap between the door and the frame and peeked inside the room. "Wow…there's so many of them." His eyes began their instinctive scanning motions, sweeping from one corner of the room to the next.

Second, third, and fourth generations crowded the room. Most were busy talking in large groups that were concentrated toward the far wall which had at least a dozen windows allowing the light to filter in. Others sat quietly in rows of desks, occupying themselves with past assignments. Jacob counted at least fifty students, but there could be more. He wasn't going to stand there and count each one. "No first generations...I knew I'd be the only one." His main concern now was to enter the room without being noticed.

A whirring from his hard-drive drew his attention, then the recorded voice of his mom played back, "Find the seat furthest to the back. Less chance of becoming distraction."

"Good idea, Mom," Jacob said, opening the door and stepping in.

Nobody seemed to pay any attention to Jacob, as he quietly slipped through the doorway and into the classroom. He moved in a half-crouch so he would be as small as possible which wasn't hard to do considering his short stature. He held his lunchbox well away from his chest-plate so it wouldn't clang against it. He crept deeper and deeper into the room, keeping close to the wall, almost clinging to it. He tip-toed across row after row of desks that all looked to be reserved. Their tops were either laden with personal contents or their chairs had been pushed out suggesting someone had claimed the desk. There was a single desk right in the very front of the room, which didn't look occupied, but Jacob didn't even consider it.

Jacob made his way clear to the back of the room without even a single stare pointed in his direction. *Nice work.* An empty desk and chair was his reward. It was easily the most inviting desk in the room. He pulled the chair out from under the desk, careful not to scrap its feet across the metal floor. "Success," he whispered. He lowered himself onto the chair and stowed away his lunchbox beneath the desk. "You did good, Jacob. You did real good," he whispered.

Unfortunately, his self proclaimed victory was short lived.

A loud screech screamed out next to him, and Jacob felt a heavy, yet surprisingly cushioned tap against at his left shoulder.

"Hey, One Bolt. You're in my seat," a high-pitched voice said.

Jacob intended just a quick glance over his shoulder but couldn't keep from staring. Behind him was an odd looking being. Bulky, confusing…just plain messy. He was either a third generation or possibly even a fourth.

Jacob couldn't tell from the mix-and-match parts forming his body. The strangest part about him was his left arm. The one on the right was normal, with a hand and fingers, but the other arm, the one that had tapped Jacob's shoulder, wasn't an arm at all. It was a massive wheel, connected to his shoulder by thick plating that could be called an upper arm. But that wasn't the only wheel. Instead of legs, he had wheels on both sides of his base which kept him upright. And as far Jacob could tell, there was another spare wheel attached to his back. He could just see the edges of a rim and spokes sticking out on either side. The rubber surrounding each rim was worn-down, nearly tread-less, though oddly enough, sections were shimmering from the light.

"Wheels...You...you have wheels..."

"Yeah, wheels. You have a problem with that?"

Jacob shook his head and looked away. "No, I just—"

"Just what?"

"Nothing..."

"Then stop staring." He stuck his left arm out and then revved the wheel, sending a thick plume of white smoke into Jacob's face. "Go on, move it. Find yourself another desk. This one's mine."

"Okay!" Jacob raised a hand to fan away the smoke. "Sorry, I didn't know this seat was taken."

He picked up his lunchbox and moved away from the desk. *Wow, I never met anyone so rude.* As Jacob walked, he could hear the one with wheels reclaim his chair with a loud thud. Fortunately, for Jacob, there was another empty desk nearby.

"Ha! Who do you think you are? That seat's taken," the one with the wheels cried out. "All the seats back here at taken. Take the one up front. No one wants it. It's all yours."

Jacob frowned. "Yeah, thanks a lot," he whispered. *And what's this "One Bolt" he keeps calling me?*

Jacob's options were severely limited. Either take the lone desk up front or continue to be hassled by the annoying one with the wheels. Either way, Jacob was surely to arouse unwanted attention at any moment now. He kept his head down, as he walked to the front of the room, hoping to make it to the desk without another incident. He was almost there, when an old man ran across the room toward him, a smile stretched across his entire rust-engulfed face. He was somehow able to pinpoint Jacob from the rest of the class. The pistons in his legs squealed and popped from the rust and obvious lack of lubrication, as he knelt down in front of Jacob. He reached out, grabbed Jacob's arm with this thin, frail hand and began shaking it.

"You're Jacob!" he cried.

"Yes, sir. I'm Jac—"

"Brilliant." The old man threw both his arms into the air. "Absolutely brilliant!" He lowered himself even further, so his face was only an inch away from Jacob's. "I knew you were Jacob," he whispered. "I could just tell."

For no reason that Jacob could think of, the man suddenly reached out and latched both his hands onto Jacob's shoulders and then forcefully began turning him around, studying him with each revolution. "Let's see what we have here. Ah, yes...plate's still there. Wires where they should be. Bolts all in the right locations..."

As Jacob was being spun around, he took note of the man's details. He was clearly many generations older than Jacob. Rust had saturated nearly every part of him. Many of the bolts holding his surfaces together were either stripped away, replaced by the wrong size bolts, or missing entirely, leaving gaping holes that allowed Jacob to see all the way to the other side. Wires were completely exposed through dented seams. Some had been tied off, while others just dangled freely from adjoining limbs.

Jacob had never seen anyone like him before. It was as if he was wearing time on his exterior, with each patch of rust representing a different generation. Jacob was mesmerized, although he realized that his staring might have come off as being rude. "It not polite to stare," his mom would say.

The old man had turned Jacob completely around one final time but continued to study his facial details, the vents on his cheeks in particular. "Good," the old man said. "Everything still works."

Why wouldn't I still work?

Growing uncomfortable, Jacob's planted his feet so the strange old man could not turn him again.

The man must have sensed Jacob's discomfort. "Oh...sorry," he said, realizing how awkward his greeting must have been for Jacob. "Forgive me, I didn't mean to be so intrusive."

Jacob nodded to acknowledge the apology. "I didn't mean to stare, either, sir. I...I've just never seen someone so..."

The old man laughed. "There's no need for *you* to be formal, Jacob. Just call me Professor Smith."

"Yes, sir...I mean, Professor Smith. Sorry for staring."

"That's quite alright, Jacob. I know I'm not as shiny and new as I used to be..."

Jacob's eyes widened. "You...you were new at one time?" Jacob shook his head. "I'm sorry, I...I didn't mean that."

"No, no, Jacob. It's fine. Age is experience, so I don't apologize for being old. Like most of us, I've changed over the years...but *you*?" He shook his head in amazement. "My goodness, you haven't changed one bit."

"I...I haven't?"

The professor reached out and gently pressed open the vents on Jacob's cheeks and then allowed them to close on their own. "Not at all. She did a good job at maintaining you. Not a single hint of rust."

"Uh...who, sir?"

"Grace, of course."

Jacob reeled back. "Mom?"

Again, Professor Smith laughed. "You're still calling her that, I see."

Okay, this is getting beyond weird. "Yes, sir. I'm not allowed to call her anything else. Especially Grace. She doesn't like that for some reason."

"Keeping true to her words. Good for her."

Jacob had no idea what this strange man was referring to. He shrugged his shoulders. "Well…anyway, sir, she told me to say, 'Hi' to you for her."

"Indeed. I'm sure she'll get the opportunity to tell me that face-to-face." Professor Smith scanned the room. "Well, Jacob, it looks to me like you're having trouble finding a place to sit?"

Jacob glanced around the room using only his eyes. "All the desks are taken, sir. I wanted to sit in the back but—"

"No-no-no-no," the professor said, shaking his head. "You don't want to sit back there, Jacob." He winked. "That's where I keep the most annoying ones."

Jacob giggled. *That was so true.*

The professor stood upright, the action accompanied by the loud squealing and cracking from his joints. "I knew you were coming today, so I made sure I had a place reserved just for you. It's the best seat in the room."

Professor Smith latched his hand around Jacob's arm and escorted him to the front of the room. By now, most of those in the classroom had directed their attention to the commotion, caused by Professor Smith and Jacob. Jacob kept his head straightforward, deflecting as many stares away from him as he could, though a few of them managed to slip through his guard. When the professor finally stopped, he and Jacob were, of course, next to the desk that Jacob wanted no part of.

"Just for you," The professor said, with a genuine smile. "I even had one of the students polish it and buff it."

"Oh…you…you...did?" Jacob said, unable to return the smile. "Uh…thanks a lot, sir." He looked up at the professor. "But, sir, do I *have* to sit here?"

The professor grabbed the lunchbox from Jacob's hand and placed it under the desk. "Of course not, Jacob."

Jacob smiled. "Really?"

"That's right. Because right now, there's something we have to do first."

The desk was just a temporary stop. Professor Smith escorted Jacob all the way to the front of the class.

"Sir?" Jacob said, attempting to pull his arm free. "Professor Smith!"

"It's okay, Jacob. Nothing to worry about. I just want to introduce you to the rest of the class."

Jacob felt his limbs go limp. *Oh, no...Just what I didn't want.*

The professor finally released his tight hold on Jacob's arm, only to place a heavy hand on Jacob shoulder. Then he called out, "Alright, everyone, settle down. Settle down, everyone! Back to your seats. We're about to begin."

One by one, the students did as they were told. Chair legs squealed against the metal floor, as they were pulled out from under each desk. Soon, everyone was comfortably in place. As expected, all eyes were now on Jacob who felt his joints beginning to seize from the lack of lubrication. Chattering subsided to just a few murmurs, and Professor Smith spoke over the low hums.

"It's definitely a pleasure to see each and every one of you again. Looks like everyone made it in this time." He scanned the room, stopping at the very back where he focused on the one with the wheels. "I'm glad to see some of you actually decided to show up."

Jacob realized to whom the professor was referring when he saw the one with the wheels shrug.

"Today is a very special day," Professor Smith said to the entire class. "Not only are we treated with another gloriously sunny day on this beautiful Earth of ours but we also have someone very special here today."

The vents on Jacob's cheeks opened and then collapsed in an instant. There was no escaping the stares this time.

"I am very proud to introduce the newest member to our class." The professor turned and motioned to Jacob, as if he wanted him to speak.

The entire class stared silently at Jacob.

Jacob tuned to the professor. "Uh...what do you want me to do, sir?" he whispered.

"Introduce yourself to the class. They're all watching you."

I see that.

Wishing he didn't have to, Jacob turned and scanned the room. The awkward, almost terrifying silence was making his sensors leap from their highest peak and then back to their lowest of lows in an instant. It seemed like every eye in the room was piecing right through him and he couldn't take it any longer. He adjusted his vision so that everyone in the room was slightly blurred. Now he could avoid making direct eye contact with any of them.

The silence was finally pushed aside by the one furthest to the back of room. "Look, it's a first generation," shouted the one with the wheels. "Are you sure you're in the right class? Stand up. We can barely see you!"

The remarks triggered an eruption of uncontrollable laughter from the class. Jacob felt his joints stiffen. The invisible amour of confidence Jacob had tried to achieve, by avoiding eye contact, cracked at the seams and crumpled to the floor from the sheer weight of embarrassment. As he scanned the room, with his head lowered, he was a bit surprised to see that not everyone was laughing at him.

Sitting in one corner was the most brilliant mechanical being Jacob had ever seen. Even with his vision slightly blurred, he found her stunning, and he immediately allowed his vision to refocus. He needed to register her finest details.

She seemed to be holding herself apart from the rest of the class, facing the window and staring out as if there was something of great interest outside. The light seeping through the glass grazed her glossy-white casing, causing a sheen unlike anything Jacob had ever seen. It enhanced the sleek, smooth curves of her body and highlighted the nearly invisible seams flowing from one limb to the next. Jacob was delighted when she turned from the window and he could see her face. He locked eyes with her for a moment and then quickly had to look away.

Having a hard-drive to store information was a unique feature, and Jacob was glad that he had one. Even though they had only looked at each other for an instant, Jacob was able to record what he had just seen. *I've never seen such vibrant-green eyes before.* He wanted to see them again but was too timid to look her way.

The comments from the class increased in volume, so Professor Smith raised one arm and called out, "Quiet, everyone! Settle down! And you..." he pointed to the one with the wheels. "Remember, you're back there for a reason."

The one with the wheels just shrugged.

Gradually, the class quieted, and order was restored.

"Okay," Professor Smith said. "This is Jacob, and yes, as it was so rudely mentioned, he is a first generation."

"Ha! I knew it." The one with the wheels yelled out.

"Quiet!"

"Sorry, sir."

"Jacob used to attend school in sector..." A single plate lowered over Professor Smith's eye, and he reached up and tapped his finger against his chin. He glanced down at Jacob. "Sector *333*, I believe it was?"

"Yes, sir."

Professor Smith threw his hands in the air. "Did you hear that? Sector *333*! The same school that has beaten us at just about every contest, project, and assignment."

The buzz of conversation started again, as everyone realized who it was that was standing in front of the classroom. Jacob noticed that even the one with wheels was surprised at the announcement. He and Jacob made eye contact for the first time, though Jacob was quick to look away. Vibrant-green eyes were one thing, a cold stare from the one with wheels, was another.

"That's right," Professor Smith said. "Jacob is a first generation, and yet, he was able to beat our entire school at every single contest. He alone." He looked down at Jacob. "I bet you have a room full of trophies."

"A room and a house full," Jacob replied, finding composure in talking about something he could be proud of.

"And I'm one-hundred-percent positive that all of them have *First Place* somewhere."

Remembering what his mom had said about not being too boastful, Jacob kept his reply to a simple, "Yes sir."

Professor Smith nodded and then turned his attention to the class. "Students, one and all, listen. There might not be many days left for us on this beautiful place we call Earth. But the burden of time should not. and will not, be held against us." He paused and tilted his head down toward Jacob and smiled, "Especially now that our presence has been graced by such brilliancy."

"Brilliancy? Who? Me?" Jacob whispered, pointing blindly at himself.

"Absolutely."

Professor Smith began slapping his hands together in what Jacob recognized as clapping. He seemed to want the class to follow his lead. "Someone like Jacob comes by once in a sun's lifetime. Let's hear it for him!"

The majority of the students did something that Jacob never expected to see. They erupted into a loud, animated bout of applause. The plates over Jacob's eye could not have shifted up any higher. They nearly locked in place, opening his eyes to almost ridiculous proportions.

"See, Jacob?" Professor Smith said, looking down at Jacob with a large grin. "As I said. Nothing to worry about."

Jacob smiled in return. He wasn't sure why he was getting all this attention or if he even deserved any of it, but the positive attention was so much better than the laughs and jeers he expected. "Thank you, sir."

"No need to. This was all for you, because of you."

"But why?"

"You'll see, my son. You'll see."

Jacob found that response a little strange. But a lot of strange things were being said, or not said, lately. His mom had been doing that for weeks.

"There's no need to complicate things right now, Jacob," the professor said. "You will have plenty of opportunities to use your calculations for more important things. I sure you'll be doing just that in the upcoming days."

Still wondering what the professor was talking about, Jacob just stood there. Professor Smith finally had to coax him to his desk. "Nothing more up here. Go on, Jacob, back to your desk. The first lesson is about to start."

A gentle push steered Jacob toward the desk he had been dreading ever since he had first seen it. Now, it wasn't so bad. Before he sat down, another ripple of applause swept the room. Jacob glanced around, and when his gaze reached the back of the room, he noted that the one with the wheels wasn't applauding. Was it because of some tension left over from their abrupt introduction? Was it just because clapping was impossible with that massive wheel arm? Either way, Jacob wasn't about to let him spoil his mood. Now comfortable in his seat, he took a quick peek over his shoulder, toward the corner of the room where the girl sat. She smiled at him. He turned away, though unlike the last time their eyes had met, Jacob now found himself brimming with confidence. *I guess this new school isn't so bad after all.*

* * *

There was no wonder why the sheen on Grace's hips had faded. Whenever she was exasperated, her hands would instinctively rest against her hips. This stance was becoming more and more frequent, as Jacob evolved, and as she stood in front of the fallen charger, she assumed the familiar pose.

"So…this is how he got out? That's what the loud noise was."

A series of beeps quickly followed. Pin-bot, or more accurately, the messy remnants of her, were scattered across Jacob's desk.

"Did you even see him get out?" Grace asked, shifting her weight from one side to the other. "How did he manage to tip it over?"

"Beep-beep-turned-off," Pin-bot replied.

"You were what?" Grace asked.

Grace had never really understood much of what Pin-bot had to say. Ever since she had taken the helper-bot, or "Pin-bot", as Jacob eventually renamed her, out of the box, every reply or comment coming from her just sounded like random beeps with an occasional word or two tacked on at the end.

"Beep-beep-off!" Pin-bot yelled, using a higher frequency. Her eyes straighten out and then angled downward.

"Okay-okay, no need to shout. I got it. You were *turned off*. Sorry, I forgot."

"Beep-beep," Pin-bot replied in a normal pitch.

Grace sighed. "So…what do you think, Pin-bot? Keep it his way or pick it up?"

"Beep?"

"Should I pick up the charger or let Jacob do it?"

Pin-bot attempted to shrug, using the flaps on the very top of her head, but they were trapped up against the wall next to the desk. Even if she could, Grace didn't give her a chance to reply.

"Of course I'll do it," Grace said, dropping her hands to the sides, revealing the dull patches on her hips. "I always do."

She bent down and wrapped her hands around the charger's crown and tipped it back up to its usual position. She took a step back and pondered. "Everyone wants to evolve so quickly, Pin-bot, but they never stop to ask themselves if they should."

"Beep-beep-evolve?"

"You?" Grace replied, making her way to the desk. "I think Jacob wanted you to evolve."

She picked up both halves of Pin-bot, attempting to shove a few of the many exposed wires back inside the seams. They simply fell back out. "I told him not to, though. I much rather have you the way you are. Besides, you'll evolve on your own, Pin-bot. We all do." Grace gently placed the two halves of Pin-bot back on the desk. "Sorry, Pin-bot. I don't have the slightest idea what part goes where."

"Beep-beep-good-at-fixing," Pin-bot pointed out.

It took a second, but Grace finally realized that Pin-bot was referring to her past, when she was good at fixing things. She forced a smile. "Yes, I was good at that sort of thing a long time ago, but I had to record over most of that data. What I have stored away isn't enough to get you back together in one piece. Sorry, Pin-bot. He took you apart, he'll have to put you back together."

"Beep-beep."

"Okay, then. Time to turn you off." Grace reached back and flicked the switch on Pin-bot's back, allowing the red dots of her eyes to fade to white and then to nothing.

There was no reason for Grace to store Pin-bot back inside the closet. Jacob would eventually have to repair her, and he usually did all of his work on his desk. So she set the pieces to one side of the desktop and turned to leave. Then she noticed something odd. Held down by a bolt, right next to Pin-bot's motionless body, was the small plant. Sunlight was being sheared off by the nearby microscope, drenching the plant in shadow. "You don't belong here."

Grace picked it up and walked to the window. A simple push from her hand secured the shutter against the wall, allowing the light to fill the room. She put the plant down on the windowsill, allowing the light to wash over it. "Don't know why he always closes the shutters. You *and* Jacob both need light."

* * *

Never influenced by the time of day, the sun's rays struck with the exact same intensity at the exact same location everyday…all day. The flat courtyard behind the school was awash in the glow, with only a few small places having the advantage of a hard-edged shadow cast by the school building. The students were taking their mid-day break, sitting at the many tables scattered across metal-lined perimeter of the courtyard.

Jacob needed this short break. He was still trying to sort out the various reactions the other students had toward him, as well as what the professor had said. Fortunately, he was no longer burdened by the need to find a seat furthest to the back this time. While he still wasn't a part of them yet, he was a bit more comfortable with the other students. Stares from his classmates were no longer received with defensive gratitude. Still, Jacob sat alone with his lunchbox propped high on the table. As he sipped the half empty can of *Pure Blend*, a steady stream of classmates flowed by his table, each offering a simple nod or a genuine smile his way. All except for the one with wheels.

Jacob was convinced, however, that the thick line of tension between him and the one with the wheels was strung together by a unique situation. Their introduction to each other wasn't exactly a *tip of the head, followed by a smile*. They had obviously started off on the wrong foot. "Or wheel," Jacob said out loud, with a smirk.

Sitting three rows back from Jacob, the odd being was sending the most unfriendly stares his way. Jacob wasn't sure why. Certainly the animosity over the desk should have worn off by now, and Jacob was positive that he didn't steal his seat this time. Whatever the reasons may be, Jacob wasn't going to allow the one with wheels or his stares to spoil a perfectly good mood. He was pleased that the rest of his classmates appreciated him for who he was internally, and not by the first generation body he was unfortunately encased in. He set his can of *Pure Blend* down on the table beside his lunchbox and then scanned his hands. He rotated them, observing their simple construction.

"Maybe I don't need an upgrade after all," he said, confidently. He reached out and picked up his can of *Pure Blend*, but his stubby hand failed to grip onto the can's simple curvature. It slipped out of his grasp, bounced off the table and then rolled underneath it. "Damn it! *308.*" *Too much confidence.*

He immediately looked around to make sure no one had seen his little accident. There was no better way of killing off any positive perception about one's self than with plain clumsiness. Fortunately, for Jacob, his classmates were all too busy enjoying their time outside of the classroom to even notice. Well, most of them. The one with the wheels was still staring at Jacob. Jacob just shrugged it off. He was beginning to become immune to the mindless stares.

He peeked under the table and found the can resting next to one of the table's legs. It had rolled far enough out of his reach that he would have to bend down in order to retrieve it. Jacob briefly disappeared out of sight. When he emerged, he was face-to-face with the one with the green eyes. The can of *Pure Blend* nearly slipped out of his hand for a second time.

Since she was standing so close, Jacob could not look away without appearing rude. Neither did he want to look away. Her eyes were mesmerizing, not only because of the unique colour but also because they were so large they took up most of the upper part of her face. Light was attracted to her at the perfect angle, making it seem as though she was surrounded by a halo.

How convenient.

She smiled at Jacob and he nearly fell out of his chair.

"*Pure Blend*," she said, in the softest voice he had ever heard.

"Excuse me?" Jacob mechanically replied.

She pointed at the can in Jacob's hand, soon to be sent underneath the table again if he didn't tighten his grip. "*Pure Blend*," she repeated.

Jacob looked at the can. "Oh...yeah...*Pure Blend*," he said, with an obvious jitter to his voice. "How...how did you know?"

Her smile didn't fade. "It says so right on the can."

"Oh...yeah. Right." He laughed. *How embarrassing.*

"It's my favourite."

"Really? Mine too." Jacob reached out and offered the can to her. "Would you like some? I have another one, so it's no problem."

"No, thank-you. I have some of my own."

Jacob set the can down on the table. Then came the awkward silence that he knew would eventually find its way into the conversation. He looked at her and smiled, she did the same. His eyes were wide on all sides, much like hers, though his was obviously forced while hers were completely natural.

"You're the new one, right?" she asked, finally breaking the silence.

"Who me?" Jacob wanted to slap himself in the face. *Who else would she be talking to?* "Uh…yes. It…it's my first day here."

"How's it been so far?"

"Better now." *Much better now*, he wanted to say.

"That's good." She offered her hand to Jacob. "Hope..."

Jacob scanned her unblemished hand and immediately noticed that she had proper fingers—something he could only wish for. He held back. He wasn't sure if she would want to touch a stubby, first generation hand. Yet, Jacob couldn't allow her gesture of friendship go unaccepted. It would be a perfect way to ruin a near flawless introduction so far. He reached out, nudged her hand with his and then quickly retracted it, tucking it back behind him. *Oh, well, better than nothing.*

She just stood there with a strange expression, and Jacob realized she was waiting for something. He finally realized that in the confusion over the handshake, he'd forgotten what she had said. "I'm sorry. I didn't hear what you said before."

"Hope."

"Hope? Hope for what?"

She giggled. "No, not that, silly. That's my name."

Jacob lowered the plates over his eyes. "Hope? Really?"

"Yes. I know. It's a funny name—"

"No." Jacob smiled. "It's not funny. It's a nice name. I never met anyone with that name before."

"It was a name given to me by my—"

Suddenly, a loud screech tore through the entire courtyard. It originated a few tables back, and the one with wheels came screaming toward them, covering the distance in a mere instant. His large wheel arm was out in front with the wheel pressed firmly against the ground, twisting and turning, steering him toward the pair. He finally pulled to a halt next to Jacob and Hope, sending a plume of white smoke billowing toward the sky. He wrapped his massive arm around Jacob's shoulder. The heat and smell of burning rubber was immediately evident.

"Jacob, the one and only. So nice to make your acquaintance."

Jacob shook his head. The guy made it sound like some kind of title. *The one and only? What was he up to?* He tried to pull out of the grasp on his shoulder. If the smell of burnt rubber wasn't enough to endure, he had to contend with the disgustingly dense aroma of grease and oil permeating off of the one with the wheel's bulky, chaotic mass.

"Just Jacob is fine," Jacob said.

"Ah, don't be so modest. We all heard what the professor said about you." He turned and faced Hope. "Well, well, well, if it isn't Hope. You're looking good as usual. New plating I presume?"

"Yes, it is." Hope quickly reached up and tried to cover the left side of her breast-plate. She wasn't quick enough, however. Jacob noticed the indicator light on her breast-plate blinking orange.

"Yeah, it figures. Everyone is reduced to rust and scrounging for used parts..." he looked over at Jacob and mumbled, "and here she is, with shiny new plating—" He cocked his head back and took a good look at Jacob's nearly flawless casing. "Huh? Am I missing something here? Were they handing out new parts and nobody told me?"

Jacob didn't know how to respond to that, so he just shrugged.

"Nice to see you too, Wheeler," Hope said.

Jacob couldn't help himself. He blurted, "Wheeler?"

"Yeah, that's right. Wheeler's what they call me. You have a problem with that?"

Jacob simply looked away.

"That's what I thought," Wheeler said in a tone that was close to a snarl. Then he turned his attention back to Hope. "Are you going to join us or are you just going to stand there looking shiny?"

"Sorry," Hope said, "I can't stay."

Although Jacob didn't show it, he was completely disappointed by her decision. He couldn't blame her, however. If it was possible to free himself from Wheeler's strong grip, he would also leave. *Such an annoyance. No wonder the professor makes him sit at the back of the class.*

"A pity," Wheeler said. "I would have brought over a chair for you."

Jacob knew that Wheeler was being sarcastic. He could sense a line of tension between Wheeler and Hope. This wasn't exactly surprising. An annoyance, such as Wheeler, always seemed to have an unlimited supply of line.

"So...what are you waiting for?" Wheeler asked.

"Just wanted to say, 'Hi' to Jacob," Hope said. "No need to be rude. I'll be out of both of your way soon enough."

"It's no problem," Jacob said. "You could stay."

"No," Wheeler said, tightening his grip around Jacob's shoulder. "You heard her. She has to go."

Jacob remembered the indicator on Hope's breast-plate. It was unusual to require a recharge this early in the day, though it wasn't completely unheard of. Sometimes a full charge wasn't possible, depending on the situation. "Recharge?"

Hope shook her head. "That's not what the light is for," she said, removing her hand from the left side of her breast-plate to fully reveal the orange indicator.

If it wasn't indicating battery levels, what else could it possibly be for?

"Yes, yes, whatever," Wheeler said. "If you're not going to join us, Hope..."

"Okay-okay, I'm leaving," Hope said, just as the ground beneath them began to tremble.

The trio turned their attention to the far wall. A massive shadow crept out from behind it.

"Uh-oh. Here comes trouble," Wheeler said, poking Jacob's side with his elbow.

The largest being Jacob had ever seen emerged from behind the wall and made his way over to the trio. It was no wonder why his shadow took a moment or two to completely reveal itself. He was enormous. Each one of his steps were accompanied by a loud hiss, as massive pistons pulled out from chambers attached to his legs and upper body and then ended in a ground-shaking thud, as they returned to their compressed position. It only took a few strides for him to cover the distance to the table. He stood beside Hope, like a mountain next to a pebble. If Hope stood her tallest, she might have reached the upper part of his hips. But only with the tips of her antennas that stretched a couple inches above the top of her head. The massive mechanical being's shadow eradicated the back-light that had given Hope her radiant glow.

Jacob didn't know who he was, but his harden exterior, deep dents, and impressive stance made him want to dive underneath the table. Wheeler, however, didn't seem as easily intimidated.

"Well, well, well," Wheeler said, "if it isn't Brute." He nudged Jacob and grinned. "Thought I heard clanking. Must be the loose screws."

Brute lowered himself. The twin pistons that attached his upper body to his lower half hissed with such force, it snapped the air around them, distorting it. The dark-red, almost black glow of his eyes scanned the diminutive first generation perched silently on his chair. Jacob wanted to pull back, but his entire body was stiff with apprehension. He was relieved when Wheeler spoke up again, attracting Brute's attention. Maybe it wasn't so bad having an annoyance around.

"Shouldn't you be digging a hole somewhere?" Wheeler said, with a smirk. "Or moving rocks...or whatever dirty job you're assigned to?"

Although Brute was looking directly at Jacob and Wheeler, he acted as though they were nothing more than minor distractions, ones that he could get rid of with a mere flick of his hand. "Training wheels and a simple generation. Shouldn't be around these two," Brute said, addressing Hope with his deep, metallic voice. "You might catch a virus."

Although viruses were now extinct, they were, at one time, fatal. Now the term could be used as a form of mockery, and Jacob wondered at the animosity of this giant.

"Now, now, Brute," Hope said, playing the unwilling role of *peacekeeper*. "They're my friends."

"Yeah, Brute," Wheeler said. "Calm down. You'll pop another screw in your head. It's not like you have a lot of screws left up there to spare."

Wheeler looked over at Jacob with a smile on his face, but with Brute so close to him, Jacob wasn't about to return the smile. Brute could squash Jacob with one finger.

Brute clenched his jaw, grunted, and leaned in closer to the pair, immediately wiping the smile from Wheeler's face. Wheeler even used Jacob as a shield by ducking behind him.

"Hey!" Jacob cried, not wanting to be caught between the pair.

Whatever Brute had intended, his plan was interrupted by a buzz that indicated an incoming call on the transmitter fused to his massive shoulder. He pulled away from the pair and pushed a button on the transmitter. He listened for a moment and then said, "Yes, sir. She's standing next to me." Another short pause, then he said, "Yes, sir. On our way." Brute pushed the button to end the transmission and glanced down at Hope. "Time to go, Hope. Your father's waiting."

He reached down and grabbed Hope by the hand and started leading her away. Her entire forearm disappeared inside Brute's grip.

"It was nice meeting you, Jacob," Hope said.

Jacob raised his hand and waved. It didn't take long before Brute and Hope were gone from his sight. He didn't realize it but his hand was still in the air, now waving at nothing.

Wheeler pulled himself out from behind Jacob, drove in a complete circle and then parked behind the table. He dusted his shoulders off, seemingly regaining all of the confidence he had before Brute showed up. "About time they left."

"Where'd they go?" Jacob asked.

"Ah…I don't know," Wheeler replied, not sounding very interested. "She's always leaving with Brute. Why else do you think he would come to the school? To learn? Ha!"

Jacob looked at Wheeler with a blank stare. He didn't know what Wheeler meant by that.

Wheeler sighed. "Big pistons and bolts..." He paused to tap the side of his head. "But not much going on up there."

"He's not very intelligent?"

"Ha! Let's just say, if he was to ever to be taken apart and used for spare parts, his CPU would be the last thing to go."

"Why did he take Hope away? Isn't there still another half a day of school left?"

"Ah, don't worry about her. Like I said, that lump of carbon always comes by and takes her. I don't ask…she doesn't tell. It's easier this way." Wheeler rolled forward and back a couple times, getting himself comfortable. "By the way, One Bolt, thanks for backing me up."

Jacob cocked his head back. "What?"

"When Brute was in front of us. I was speaking for the both of us, One Bolt."

Jacob shrugged. *There was that name again.* "I wasn't the one making fun of him. And why do you keep calling me that?"

"What? 'One Bolt'?"

"Yeah. My name is Jacob. 'The one and only'. Remember?"

"Yeah-yeah, I know. But I like One Bolt better."

"Why? What does that even mean?"

Wheeler chuckled. "Look at you." He revved his wheels, pushed away from the table and then drove around Jacob a few times. With each pass, Wheeler either poked Jacob's side or prodded his back. During his last pass, he even grabbed Jacob's arm, examined it and then allowed it to flop back down. "Look at you," he repeated, parking beside Jacob. "Looks like you were put together using…I don't know…one bolt?"

"Oh, yeah? Well…I know why they call you Wheeler." Jacob stood up, walked around Wheeler a few times while scanning each and every part of him. Jacob noticed the odd, mismatched plating fused to various parts of Wheeler's exterior, the long antennae attached to the top of his head, and the columns of indicator lights on his chest-plate blinking a bright orange at the moment. In the end, however, what Jacob could never seem to pull his attention away from were the wheels. Jacob sat back down. "Your wheels. That's why they call you Wheeler."

"Wow." Wheeler raised his hands in the air and waved them around. "It's true! It's true! His CPU is advanced. The one and only, Jacob, has an advanced CPU!" He reached over and tapped Jacob's head. "What do you have in there? Some sort of super CPU?"

"Stop it." Jacob pushed Wheeler back.

"No, seriously," Wheeler said, his voice now in a more composed tone. "What do you have up there, One Bolt? Must be pretty damn powerful if you're winning all those assignments the professor talked about."

"I don't know," Jacob said.

"Come on, One Bolt, you must know."

"No, I don't. And stop calling me that."

"How many calculations per minute?"

"What?"

"Clock speed…how fast can you compute?"

"What does that mean?"

"Single core, dual core? What? What do you have up there?"

"Whatever!"

"Why won't you tell me?"

"Because I don't know." Jacob admitted. "Stop asking me. Why are you even here? There are plenty of seats out here. I didn't steal this one from you this time."

"Oh…about that," Wheeler said, in a surprisingly humbled voice. "Sorry. I wasn't trying to be rude. The professor makes me sit back there."

"He told me about that. Why does he do that?"

Wheeler shrugged. "I don't know. To keep an eye on me, I guess." He reached back, flicked his antennae and then mumbled, "It's not like he needs to."

Jacob grabbed his can of *Pure Blend* from the table. "Is it because you're so annoying?"

Wheeler rolled his eyes and then noticed the can in Jacob's hand. "Hey, what do you have there?"

Jacob pulled the can away from his mouth. "What? This?"

"No, your other hand." Wheeler gave a little shake of his head. "Yes. That."

"*Pure Blend*…my favourite."

"*Pure Blend*?" Wheeler leaned back so quickly, he almost toppled over, but his brakes were firmly compressed and held. "But…but I thought …" He cocked his head at Jacob. "How much do you have?"

Jacob reached over and opened his lunchbox. "Another full can in here. Why? What do you drink?"

Wheeler had to blink a few times in order to refocus. A flap over a small compartment on his base opened. He reached down and from it pulled out a can. "*Artificial Blend*," he said. "Only the best." He cracked opened the top of the can, brought it to his mouth and then took a few messy gulps. A thick stream of dark fluid drizzled down the side of his face. He slammed the can down onto the table and repeated, "Only the best!"

"I wouldn't know. I've never tried it."

"What do you mean you never tried it? Everyone's tried it. What's your excuse?"

"Well…" Jacob shrugged, "my mom. She won't let me."

"Ha! Your mom?" Wheeler began looking around the courtyard, as if scanning for someone. "Your mom… Tall, slender…kind of shiny?"

"Yeah." Jacob couldn't resist the impulse to look around, too. "How did you know?"

Wheeler turned back to Jacob. "Just a guess." Wheeler placed his can of *Artificial Blend* onto the table. "Well, if tall, slender, and kind of shiny is your mom then she's not around, One Bolt." He then gave the can a little nudge, pushing it closer to Jacob. "Go on. Take a sip."

Jacob stared at the can next to his *Pure Blend*. He had always wanted to try it, but his mom would always insist he wouldn't like it. Now here he was, with a can of *Artificial Blend* staring him in the face and his mom nowhere in sight.

"Go on," Wheeler said. "I'm not going to tell anyone, especially your mom."

"Okay-okay. I'll take a sip if you take a sip of mine."

Wheeler chuckled. "What's so special about your stuff? It can't be any better than mine."

"Just try it. I'm sure you'll like it."

"Ha! Doubt it."

"Okay. How about this. We both take a sip at the same time?"

Wheeler nodded. "No problem here."

In unison, they reached out and grabbed the opposing cans, raised them their mouths and took a sip. Jacob's eyes widened. Wheeler's eyes widened. They slammed the cans down on to the table and spat out the liquid.

"Yuck!" Jacob cried, cleaning the dark fluid from his mouth.

"How can you drink that stuff?" Wheeler said, scraping the clear residue from his mouth with his hand and then pushing the can back toward Jacob. "Feels like my mouth is going to rust."

"It's a whole lot better than yours," Jacob replied, taking a sip of his *Pure Blend* to get rid of the bitter after-taste from the *Artificial Blend*.

Gradually, smiles crept across their faces, and then they both began to laugh.

"Didn't think it was going to taste that terrible," Wheeler said.

"Yeah, guess my mom was right."

The line of tension strung between the pair might not have been completely severed, but for now, at least, there was a bit of give. A siren sounded, and the other students in the courtyard started gathering their things and getting up.

Jacob glanced at Wheeler. "Time to get back to class?"

"Yeah, looks like it," Wheeler said.

Jacob took one last swallow of his *Pure Blend*, emptying the can and then placed it inside his lunchbox. Before he could close it up, Wheeler grabbed onto his arm. "That other can's still full, right?"

"Yeah, why?"

"Oh…no reason." He began to rev his wheels. "Well, I guess I'll see you tomorrow, then."

"What? Tomorrow?"

"Yeah, you heard me."

"But we still have half a day left."

"No, *you* have half a day left, One Bolt. Me? I have to get going."

"Going? Where? And stop calling me that."

Wheeler shrugged. "Got things to do, One Bolt."

"Recharge?" Jacob asked, pointing at the orange indicator light on Wheeler's chest.

"That's not a battery indicator."

"Then what is it?"

"Never mind." Instead of driving away from Jacob, Wheeler did the opposite. He rolled right up beside him and said firmly, "Oh, and about Hope…I saw the way you were looking at her, One Bolt. Don't think I didn't notice."

"What do you mean?" As soon as he asked the question, he knew he wasn't fooling Wheeler.

"Sorry to have to say this, One Bolt, but she's not your type. Trust me on this. I mean, look at her." Wheeler picked up Jacob's arm. "Now look at you. Maybe after an upgrade or something"

Jacob pulled his arm out from Wheeler's grip. There was an awkward silence before Wheeler gave his wheels another rev.

"Sorry, One Bolt. I have to go. We'll talk more tomorrow." Before Wheeler pushed off from the table, he suddenly reached into Jacob's open lunchbox and snatched the full can of *Pure Blend*. "Mind if I borrow this?"

"Hey! Wait! I need it!"

Wheeler spun around, placed his wheel arm onto the ground and was out of reach before Jacob could even move. "I'll bring you back another can tomorrow," Wheeler said, using his wheel arm to steer himself in and out of the crowd. "Promise!"

"Wheeler! Wait! But...but I thought...I thought you didn't even like *Pure Blend*!" There was no point in yelling. Wheeler was gone. The dust trail Wheeler had left behind hung in the courtyard while Jacob closed up his lunchbox and made his way back inside the school. Another half a day left, but the class was minus two completely contrasting personalities.

* * *

Grace eased her foot off of the acceleration pedal and allowed the car to slow down. The gentle hum of the engine fell silent, as she guided the car parallel to the curb, next to Jacob. He was waiting for her in the exact same location, in the exact same position, as when she had last seen him that morning. He stood with his lunchbox clenched tightly against his chest, his expression unreadable. She sighed. She had not had the chance to recharge her batteries, and she wasn't sure if she had enough energy to deal with any complaining.

She reached for the door and pried it open. Jacob leaped inside the car, tossed his lunchbox down into the undercarriage beneath the seat and then made himself comfortable. Grace wasn't expecting to see him so animated. Usually by this time of the day, his energy level would be dropping. She glanced at his indicators. They were at orange, one stage before the cautionary red. Red indicators meant the loss of body functionality was not far off and then the inevitable—temporary shut down.

"I'd better get you home before your indicator changes to red," Grace said.

Jacob looked down. "Oh, I didn't notice."

"You do seem to have a lot of energy. Normally you're practically falling over when you're at orange."

Jacob shrugged. "Just happy to be going home, I guess."

"Then I won't keep us waiting." Grace's foot pressed down on the accelerator, and the car pulled away from the curb.

They drove for a few minutes in silence, then Jacob said, "So?"

Grace echoed the word and the tone.

"Aren't you going to ask me about how my day went?"

Grace shifted her weight to one side, expecting the worse. "Was it as bad you expected?"

Jacob smiled. "No, Mom. It was rather...interesting."

"Interesting good or interesting bad?"

"Interesting good. Better than I expected."

Grace was relieved. "That's good to hear, Jacob. Do you want to tell me about it?"

Jacob readied his hard-drive. There was a lot of information he needed to pull from it, most importantly, the part right around the time when he noticed a pair of brilliant, green eyes. His hard-drive stopped right at that exact point. "There was this girl who sat next to the window," Jacob began. "She was so—"

"Did you meet Professor Smith?"

"Professor Smith?" Jacob said, quietly snickering. "Yeah, did I ever. He nearly pulled my arm out from the socket."

"How was he?"

"Old."

"No, I meant, *how is he doing*?"

"Oh...fine, I guess. Other than a lot of rust, he seems fine. He seems to remember you for some reason."

Jacob's mom laughed. "And so he should. I was a student of his."

"Really? You?"

"Yes."

"Wow! That must have been a long...long time ago," Jacob joked.

Grace's laugh disappeared. "Anyway...I assume he was happy to see you?"

"You can say that again. Throughout the entire day, he kept checking up on me, asking how I was feeling and if I drank both cans. He even wanted to make sure that all of my parts were working. And he kept doing this over and over again." Jacob glanced over at his mom and raised one of the plates over his eye. "In a way, he's a lot like you, Mom. Only older, much older."

Grace wasn't sure if this was a compliment or not, but she smiled anyway. "He's probably just happy to have a new student in his class. The way things are right now, you're probably going to be his last."

"It was nice meeting him," Jacob admitted. "He definitely made me feel like part of the class." *They would probably still be laughing at me if it weren't for him.*

"Sounds like he hasn't changed at all."

"But I wanted to tell you about someone else." Jacob's tone suddenly softened. "She had the brightest, green eyes I've ever seen and—"

"Were you able to find the back of the class?"

"Huh?"

"The advice I gave you. Were you able to find the seat furthest to the back of the room?"

"Oh...that," Jacob said, having to pause his hard-drive once again. "I almost did. I managed to get right to the back of the room, but the desk was taken by this really weird and annoying one named Wheeler."

"Wheels?"

"No, Wheeler."

There was a slight tilt on her mouth when she heard the odd name. "My goodness, what kind of name is that? *Why* would anyone have a name like that?"

"Because of his wheels..."

Grace looked over at Jacob with barely any movement in her face. "Wheels? You mean, like we talked about earlier?"

"Exactly. He has wheels everywhere. Four in total. One on his arm, two on his base, and even a spare one on his back." Jacob noticed a blank look on his mom's face. It was the exact same expression he would have whenever he needed to retrieve information from his hard-drive. *Wonder why she needed to consult with her hard-drive at this moment.* "Are you okay, Mom?"

Grace blinked a few times, relinquishing her expressionless stare. "Oh…fine. It's just been a long time since I've seen wheels. Anyway, you were telling me that you met someone else? Green eyes or something like that?"

"Yes, there *was* someone else." Jacob let his hard-drive spin, and the tone of his voice softened once again. He sunk deep into his seat and sighed. "I've never seen anything like it before. She had the most amazing green eyes I've ever seen."

"She?"

"Yes," Jacob said, staring off into the sky through the windshield. "And she had no blemishes at all. And so shiny. Even more-so than you."

His mom smirked. "Well…does *she* have a name? Or should I call her 'perfection'?"

"If you want to," Jacob replied, with a wide grin. "She was close to it."

Grace sighed. "Are you going to tell me or not?"

"Hope," Jacob finally said. The soft tone Jacob had used allowed her name to float across the interior of the car.

It hit his mom with full force. Grace's hand slipped off of the steering wheel, causing the car to jerk. "Sorry, Jacob. Did you say '*Hope*'?"

Jacob could see his mom's posture stiffen in her seat. He thought he knew the reason for it. "I know, I know. It's a weird name…"

"No…no-no…" Jacob's mom said, shaking her head. "It's not that…"

Grace was now staring out of the car's window with an almost blank look on her face. Jacob became alarmed. "Mom? What's the matter?"

Grace refocused her attention on Jacob. "Did you talk to her?"

Jacob noticed that her tone wasn't exactly a curious one—it was more of a cautious one, so he matched the tone. "For a bit."

"About what?"

"Nothing really. We were only able to say, 'Hi' to each other."

"That's all?"

"Well, she had to leave—"

"To go where?"

"I don't know. I didn't —"

"Did she know who you were?"

Jacob had enough of his mom's suspicious questioning. "The professor did introduce me to the class. Why all the questions, Mom?"

"Oh…sorry, Jacob." She pointed at the indicator on her breast-plate. "Didn't get a full charge. CPU's not completely functioning. You know how cranky I can get when that happens."

Jacob laughed. "Yeah, I know."

"She sounds…nice."

"She is." He sighed and then glanced over at his mom to see her indicator was at red. "Thought you were going drop me off and then go back home to get a full charge?"

"I was...but there were a few things I had to do around the house. Barely got my foot inside the charger, and the next thing you know, it was time to pick you up. Don't worry, Jacob, I'll get a full charge eventually." She pressed down on the accelerator until it was all the way to the floor. "Oh, that reminds me. There's someone waiting for you when you get home."

"Really? Who?"

"You'll see. She's on your desk at the moment."

* * *

Excited to be almost reconstructed, Pin-bot began shifting her body from left to right. Jacob immediately retracted the screwdriver in his hand, not wanting to accidentally poke her with it.

"Pin-bot, careful! I'm not done putting you together yet." Jacob flattened his hand against Pin-bot, pinning her against the desk in an upright position so he could work on her unfinished side. Carefully, he began to crank the screwdriver clockwise. Each full turn resulted in a satisfying click.

"As I was saying," Jacob said, continuing to recite nearly everything he had told his mom in the car, "her eyes were so green, her smile was perfect...everything about her was perfect. Can't wait to go back tomorrow and see her again."

"Beep-beep-Pin-bot-perfect?"

Jacob ignored Pin-bot, concentrating on the delicate rotation of the screwdriver until he heard a final click. He put the screwdriver down, snapped the small tab behind Pin-bot closed, smiled and said, "Done!" Jacob lifted his hand off of Pin-bot and took a step back.

Pin-bot immediately spun around. The flaps on each side of her upper top half opened, revealing her small turbine engines. They began to whirl with a near silent hum, lifting her off the desk and into the air. Jacob watched proudly, as she examined herself. The larger turbine on the bottom half of Pin-bot pivoted back and forth, steering her from left to right. The front portion of her casing-plate opened, and a pair of clamp-like hands extended out. They opened and closed a few times before retracting, allowing her shape to be streamlined again. Pin-bot let out a satisfying *beep*. She was now back in working order. Jacob guessed that she was happy to be more than a pile of scraps, stowed away inside a dark closet. He smiled, waiting for some sign of gratitude from Pin-bot. Instead, her eyes flattened out and she lunged at him. She collided against his head with a loud thud.

Jacob stumbled back. "*Hey*! What was that for?"

Pin-bot levelled off and began assaulting Jacob with a string of random, high-pitched beeps. This wasn't exactly the "thank-you" Jacob was expecting or deserved. He reached out and grabbed onto Pin-bot before she could butt him on the head again.

"Whoa…relax, Pin-bot!"

Although Pin-bot's angry beeping seemed chaotic, Jacob had no problem understanding her and finally understood her actions.

"Pin-bot, there is no need to be jealous of Hope. I barely even talked to her." He felt Pin-bot's turbines ease up. Then he remembered what Wheeler had told him earlier, just before he had left the courtyard. He frowned. "I…I'm not even her type." *Maybe after an upgrade.*

"Beep-beep?"

"Of course, Pin-bot. You'll always be my favourite."

Pin-bot's eyes expanded to their usual ovals, finally allowing Jacob to set her free. She flew over and gently nudged her smooth surface against Jacob's face. The shape of her eyes morphed into a pair of large hearts, as she let out a quintet of apologetic beeps.

"It's okay, Pin-bot. Just…no more butting me, okay?"

Pin-bot backed away. She wasn't about to promise anything.

"Okay?" Jacob said, in a firmer tone.

"Beep…"

"Maybe? What do you mean, 'maybe'?"

Pin-bot looked away. With her simple CPU, how could she predict the future?

"Ah…I guess that's better than nothing. Anyway, we better get this place cleaned up before Mom comes up."

"Beep-beep-messy."

"Yeah, I know. It took a lot of tools to put you back together. Let's get to it."

It wasn't long before tools were stowed in drawers, and the top of the desk was cleared of everything except two screws. Although initially proud of his work, Jacob was suddenly turned off by it. "Where did these come from?"

Jacob and Pin-bot looked at each other, neither of them had an answer.

"Uh-oh. These aren't from you, are they, Pin-bot?" Before she could reply, Jacob smacked the side of the desk. "Damn it, *309*! I might have forgotten to put them in somewhere."

Pin-bot wasn't ready, or willing, to discredit Jacob's work. She knew how long it took him to piece her back together and didn't want him to feel ashamed of his accomplishments. That would be a form of disloyalty, something she wasn't programmed to do. Once again, she tested all her functions. She spun around in circles, finally stopping when she was facing Jacob again. She then tilted from side-to-side, opened and closed her hands, even strung together a line of evenly pitched beeps just to be sure. Everything seemed to be in working order. She opened and closed the flaps on the top portion of her body in a shrugging motion. "Beep-beep-feel-okay."

"Really? Are you sure? I mean…these screws must have come from you. They're the right size." Jacob bent over and gave them a closer look. "And the right shape."

"Beep-beep-feel-fine," Pin-bot repeated.

Jacob paused so that he could calculate the situation. *If Pin-bot is working and not complaining then surely she must be fine.* "If you're certain everything's working…then I guess these are extras. No use for them now."

Jacob picked up one of the screws…at least, he attempted to. It fell through his stubby fingers and back onto the desktop. "Damn it, *310*."

Seeing this, Pin-bot immediately lowered herself and did what she was programmed to do—assist. She picked the screws with her tiny hands without any problems and then dropped them into Jacob's open hand. Again, the screws fell through the seams of Jacob's hands. This time, they rolled off of the desk.

"Beep-sorry!"

"Not your fault, Pin-bot. It's these stupid first generation hands." Jacob looked beside the desk and saw that the screws had landed inside a metal box that stood about chest high to him. He didn't recognize the box. "Hey, where did this come from?"

"Beep-beep-Grace," Pin-bot said.

"She put this in here? Guess she was moving things around while I was at school." Jacob sighed. "She's always doing something. Good thing she has an eight-celled battery." *Wish I had the same.*

He pressed his upper body against the edge of the box, reached in and began searching for the pair of screws. The box was full of junk, from tools, to broken parts. All were constructed out of metal, of course. Pin-bot hovered over top of Jacob, wanting to help but was too late.

"It's okay," Jacob said. "I think I found—" His hands stopped their search. They detected something at the very bottom of the box. Something usual—not made out of metal. He clamped his hand around the object and pulled it out. It was soft and cylindrical. He held it up so Pin-bot could see it clearly. "What…what is this?"

"Beep-don't know."

Upon closer inspection, Jacob noticed that the object actually consisted of a half a dozen sheets made of a material Jacob hardly saw anymore. They were all rolled together to form a tube. He placed it on the desk and with Pin-bot's help, unrolled it. She grabbed one end, held it secure, while Jacob pulled the other end until it was flat.

"They're pages." Jacob ran his hand through the entire pile, fanning apart the edges of each page. He was careful, as the material was well into the process of deteriorating. As Jacob scanned each page, he noticed that there was something inscribed on each of them. It was written in a language he had never seen before...at least, he didn't think he had. The majority of the pages were completely stained by dark patches which meant that some of the inscriptions were lost forever.

"Beep-beep-decode?"

"Hold on," Jacob replied. "Let me try. I'm sure I can."

He flipped through every page, scanning as much of the inscriptions as he could and then stored it onto his hard-drive. "There," he said, scanning and recording the last page. "Let's see if I can decode all of this."

The glow in Jacob's eyes turned from blue to pale white. His hard-drive spun at its maximum velocity, as he began decoding. The inscriptions of the pages read:

-Everyone tells you that life changes the moment your first born arrives. They weren't lying. I can't believe I'm saying this but…becoming a father is the greatest thing that's ever happened to me…Have to put getting married to Sarah a close second, otherwise she'd kill me. Daughter is so beautiful. Born on the eve of New Year 's Day…a perfect name. Got to hold Eve for most of the day, as Sarah rested. Went home for a bit. Didn't manage to do any work. Prototypes will have to wait. I'M A NEW FATHER, AND I LOVE IT! Will go back to the hospital first thing in the morning. Hold Eve and then kiss Sarah for sacrificing 9 months.

-Took a break from building my prototypes just in time. Witnessed Eve take her first steps. I nearly cried…proud father syndrome. Wonder what her first words will be. Wonder if Sarah and I will be around to become grandparents. She's growing up so fast. Blink and we'll miss it. That's why I spend most of the night with my eyes open.

-I took Eve into the hospital to see her mom. She was so happy to see her. Nothing better than being held by mommy. Sarah's going to be there for at least a few days. Doctors don't know what's wrong with her. Damn doctors. My wife's life is in their hands and they have the nerve to tell me to go home, rest and then come back tomorrow. This is my damn wife they're talking about. This is Eve's mom. Same shit for the past 3 months. I hope there's nothing wrong with her. Eve's 2 years old now. Mommy and baby shouldn't be away from each other this long. I'll take Eve to see her again first thing in the morning. I'm sure mommy misses baby…baby misses mommy…hubby misses wifey…

-Been a while since my last entry. Wasn't sure if I was going to do this again. I still see Eve crying in her room. Sarah passed away New Year's eve. How ironic. She should be celebrating her birthday, but now, this day will always be linked with her mother's death. It's been well over a week, and Eve still hasn't recovered. I held Sarah's hand right until the very end. Told Sarah that I loved her. Promised her that I would protect Eve with my life—whatever happens, I would protect her. I get upset when I think about the promise Sarah made to me. She promised that we'd be together...forever.

-Is it wrong for me to think this way? Any sane man would count the days when their daughter becomes woman, when that woman becomes a mother. But me? I'm beginning to dread them. Each day brings her closer to the inevitable. How can anyone explain the process of life to me and tell me that it's fair? We all die. No matter how good we are in life. I know eventually that my Eve will die. It's not fair. Something so pure and innocent, so

strong…taken away…by time. Humans are so weak. Cancer took my wife, but I promise, it won't take anyone else that I care about.

Maybe there's a way to stop all of this…

-I find it difficult to manage work and Eve. I'm trying. God damn it, I'm trying! I want her to grow up knowing that I did everything I could for her. That's why I have to work. I have to create them. Life will be so much easier for her when she's older. I know she's upset with me right now. Another promise I made to Eve…another promise broken. Finally got the prototypes completed and they are in the final stages before mass production. Should be happy, but I'm not. Not when daughter tells you, "You spend more time with your work than with me". Still have many projects overdue, but they will have to wait. Another broken promise and I'm sure I won't be able to patch things over with her. Eve loved laying outside at night and staring up at the sky. I think we should go camping. It's been a long time since we looked up in the sky together and saw the stars

-Received highest honours for my work. My creations are a success. Industrial grade models are selling quicker than we can build them. Customer grade models soon to be released. Time divided, however. Such high demands meant no time for proper testing. Few minor glitches were found…mostly software virus. Nothing serious so far, but they'll need to be fixed. Also secretly working on advanced prototypes. Artificial intelligence built right in. If time permits, I may even add in personalities, something my first models were lacking. This should make them more human-like. Personalities. Wonder who I can use...

The glow in Jacob's eyes returned to their usual blue, and his hard-drive slowed. He looked over at Pin-bot with both plates over his eyes raised. "What…what does all that mean?"

It was absurd for him to be asking Pin-bot. If Jacob couldn't make sense of what was on the pages, how would Pin-bot? Her CPU wasn't capable of dealing with such calculations. She opened and closed the flaps on the upper half of her body, a gesture that qualified as a shrug.

"I mean…I decoded everything perfectly. I know a lot of it is covered by all this dried, black stuff, but it shouldn't be this difficult for me to put the pieces together." For the first time that Jacob could remember, his CPU seemed…ordinary.

The door to his room suddenly came open. Jacob's mom stepped inside the room carrying another box. "Why's it always dark in here?"

Jacob watched silently, as she walked to his desk and then dropped the box next to the other one. It landed with a loud thud, and the contents rattled.

"I'm sorry to have to do this, Jacob, but we're out of room downstairs. I'll have to keep these up here for now. But don't worry. It's just junk. I'll get rid of it soon enough." She stood up straight and noticed a fully reconstructed Pin-bot hovering a few feet away from her. "I see you finally got Pin-bot up and running again." She gave Pin-bot a gentle tap with her finger, and the little robot offered a pair of crescent eyes.

"Yup. She's up and running…maybe even better than before."

"Prefect. And not a moment too soon. I can use her help around the house."

Grace started to walk toward the window, where Jacob was sure she would open the shutters. That's what she did every time she came into his room. But she stopped after only taking a couple of steps. She saw the pages on the desk. "Where did you get these?" she said sharply.

Jacob stumbled back, surprised at her reaction. He wasn't exactly hiding the pages from her. "What? These?"

"Yes, where did you find them?"

Grace took a step toward Jacob. He took a step back. She reached out, but Jacob snatched up the pages and retracted his arm, holding them behind his back. He wasn't sure why she was so intent on taking them away from him.

"Give them to me!" Grace demanded.

"What are they?"

"Jacob!" She took another swipe at Jacob, but he stepped out of her reach.

"Tell me what they are and then I'll give them back to you."

"They're not important. Give them to me!"

"They must be important if you want them back so badly."

Grace had enough of Jacob's games. She grabbed him by the shoulder and then pulled his arm around and took the pages.

"It's okay," Jacob said, backing off. "Go ahead, take them. I've already recorded them to my hard-drive. I even decoded everything."

Jacob's mom rolled the pages up and buried them inside one of the seams along her side. "You…you decoded it?"

Jacob nodded. "Yup, almost everything."

"And? What did they say?"

Jacob shrugged. "I didn't understand it. The words don't make a lot of sense. Who wrote it?" He looked at his mom, hoping she would clear up the confusion, but she didn't say anything. "You must know."

"No…I'm not able to decode them. That wasn't a function I was equipped with. Besides," she began to make her way toward the charger, "he's not important anymore."

"Who isn't?"

"The one who wrote the pages."

Jacob watched, as his mom placed the charger's plug into the wall. The charger's LED lights blinked, signalling that it was now in standby mode.

"Come over here, Jacob. It's time for you to recharge."

"But, Mom, I still want to know more about those pages. Who wrote it? What do they mean?"

"Some other time." Grace tucked the pages even deeper into her side, further feeding Jacob's suspicions. "Right now, you need to recharge. You need to be ready for another day of school."

"School?" He smiled. Suddenly, the pages were no longer interesting. Jacob hurried over to his mom without any more argument. There was even a bounce in his steps, something that his mom had never seen while his indicators were flashing red.

"Looks like someone's excited to get back to school."

"That's right. Things to do…friends to see."

Green eyes or wheel?

Jacob stepped into the charger, and then he noticed Pin-bot over by the window. "Wait, you're not going to open them, are you?"

"Open what?"

"The shutters. Why is Pin-bot hovering over there?"

"Calm down, Jacob. She's over there because I don't need her over here."

"She's not going to open the shutters?"

"No."

"Good," Jacob said. "And keep them closed, Pin-bot."

"I don't know why you hate the light so much," Grace said.

"It distorts my vision. I have to keep readjusting my eyes."

"Your eyes are the exactly the same as everyone else's, Jacob. I don't see them complaining."

Jacob looked around the room. "Uh…Mom? Who are you talking about?"

"No one." Grace snapped Jacob's leg in place, and he was now secure. "There you go. Ready for a full recharge." She reached around the back of the charger.

"Wait, Mom?"

"Yes," Grace said, resting her hand on the switch.

"I wore red already. I don't want them seeing me wearing red again. Can I pick out my own plating once I'm done recharging?"

There was a slight hesitation before his mom finally said, "Yes, of course you can."

She started to flick the switch to activate the charger but hesitated and then bent down so she was eye-to-eye with Jacob. "Before I leave, I have to tell you something, Jacob. In case I forget."

"Sure. I'm not going anywhere."

There was a long, awkward pause before Grace finally said, "Friends are always nice to have but sometimes, there are those that you might not want to get too close to."

Because he was running out of energy, the plates over Jacob's eyes began to lower. But he channelled what little energy he had toward listening. He wasn't sure what his mom meant by what she was saying, so he didn't respond.

"What I'm trying to say is, not everyone is who, or what, they seem. I just don't want you to get hurt, Jacob, that's all."

Jacob's mouth tilted downward. His CPU had stalled. It was an odd feeling. "Well, uh…okay…I guess…"

"You'll understand what I mean, eventually, Jacob."

I sure hope so.

Grace stood up and finally flicked the switch. "Charge well."

"Yeah…you too, Mom…"

Soon, the glow of Jacob's eyes faded. His head flopped down toward his chest-plate. Jacob had entered his dormant state. Grace stood behind the charger, patiently waiting for this moment, as she would every time Jacob entered the charger. She reached down and pushed open the vents on Jacob's cheeks, making sure they remained opened and then gestured over to Pin-bot, who followed Grace's instructions and butted opened the window shutters. Light filled the room.

With the shutters pulled apart, Grace noticed the plant that she had placed on the window sill. It was clearly thriving from its new location. It was being soaked in the light, as was Jacob at the moment. She gestured over to Pin-bot. "Alright, let's go, Pin-bot," she said. "He needs his rest."

"Beep-beep."

Chapter Three

Eve let her finger slip off of the trigger, and she pulled the revolver away from her temple. The hollow muzzle left a circular imprint against her delicate skin.

Why? Why should I end it this way?

Taking her own life, with the aid of something mechanical, would bring no gratification. It wouldn't be a true return to her birthplace. Earth created her, Earth nurtured her. It kept her alive when others attempted to take her. No mechanical object will ever take her. She threw the revolver over the side of the mountain. It clanged against the rocky protrusions multiple times before landing in the heart of the massive gathering below. Mechanical beings surrounded the familiar object, obviously fascinated by it.

"Take it," Eve said, watching from her skyline perch. "It's a thing. Just like you. You're all the same. Created for death and destruction."

Blue beams, shot from below, washed over her. They wanted her. They were under orders to retrieve her, and they would stop at nothing to carry out those orders. The front line opened fire. Their shoulder-mounted cannons erupted with blinding-white muzzle flashes. Smoke climbed its way up the mountain side.

Eve stumbled back but did not retreat. She knew their offensive was not directed at her. That wouldn't be true to their orders. Instead, pieces of the mountain were sheared off. Explosions ripped through the hard rock as if it were clumps of dry dirt. They were trying to retrieve her, and destroying any obstacle in their path was the only way they knew how.

Such simple minds. Would they ever evolve?

A small section of the mountain crumpled beneath Eve's feet, and something hit her in the face. She keeled over but maintained her balance. She could taste the blood in her mouth before it poured out. The cannons grew silent. The attack immediately ceased. Perhaps they finally realized that they had inflicted damage to her.

"Didn't know you cared," Eve moaned. She straightened and then stumbled the few steps needed to bring her adjacent to the edge of the mountain. She cautiously peered over and saw the side of the mountain she had recently scaled. The ledges and toeholds she had used to come up no longer existed. Only unwarranted destruction remained. There was no way down now. She was completely trapped. "Bastards."

Their blue beams converged onto her again, forming an almost solid path from her all the way to the bottom. The glow in their eyes carried on far and wide, making it seem as though the open sky was reflecting down on a calm, restful ocean. Eve knew what an ocean looked like. Her father had shown her pictures.

"You want me so bad?" Eve called out. "As you wish!"

She took a step closer to the edge. The entire gathering below reeled back, as if a harsh breeze had swept across the surface of that imaginary ocean, disrupting its once calm integrity. "I was created from the Earth," Eve said. "And I will die from the Earth!"

She took in a deep breath, sent one final gaze up to the stars...then jumped.

Wind snapped, snarled, and bit at her skin. The texture of the mountain looked so smooth as it blurred by her. The ground was getting closer. Individual glows from mechanical eyes below soon converged as one. "This is it," Eve whispered, closing her eyes. "This is how it ends."

* * *

A loud thud.

Pin-bot let out a series of cautionary *beeps,* as her twin turbine engines stuttered, dipping her entire body up and down in an erratic little dance. She had managed to find refuge next to the wall, narrowly escaping Jacob's inelegant escape from the charger. This was the first time she had ever witnessed his method of getting out of the machine, but Jacob was getting accustomed to picking himself off of the floor, with this charger by his feet.

Click...click-click...

"That damn plug," Jacob said, "*311*. Get that, will you, Pin-bot?"

Pin-bot lowered herself, clamped her hands onto the charger's plug and yanked it from the wall. Her eyes transformed into crescents. Another order, as simple as it was, completed. The charger whined for a brief moment before the sound faded away.

"Thanks, Pin-bot."

Pin-bot flew over and hovered by Jacob's side, scanning nearly every part of him. Assisting Jacob was her primary functions, but his well-being was also a priority. "Beep-beep-okay?" she asked.

Jacob raised his arms and rotated them around. "Fine."

It did not seem that way to Pin-bot. She noticed quite a few scratches on Jacob's once pristine exterior.

"Oh, these? They're from yesterday. Most of them are. Nothing a simple upgrade couldn't fix, isn't that right, Pin-bot?"

He grinned at Pin-bot and nudged her with his elbow, but she just hovered in place. One of the enhancements Jacob had promised Pin-bot was the addition of subtle humour. She had always been able to detect it, but she just never had the capacity to react to it. Obviously that was still true.

"Ah...never mind." Jacob turned his attention to the fallen charger. He sighed and placed his hands on his hips, mimicking his mom. "Think she'll notice?" he asked, with a tilt of the mouth.

Pin-bot rotated toward Jacob and then back toward the charger. She might not have been equipped with the most advanced CPU but even she could see the large dent on the charger's surface. It made the one next to it even more pronounced.

"Mom's not going to like that," Jacob admitted.

Pin-bot swivelled back and forth in agreement.

Jacob removed his hands from his waist and threw them in the air. "Stupid light must have gotten into my eyes. Couldn't stick the landing."

"Beep-beep-close-shutters?" Pin-bot asked.

"Mom said was going to keep them closed. Why did she open them again?" Jacob began his short trek toward the window.

"Beep-beep-didn't-open," Pin-bot said.

"Then who did?" Jacob grabbed one side of the shutter to pull it closed but paused when he didn't hear a reply from Pin-bot. He glanced back at her. She had backed into the corner of the room, her eyes angled upwards. She was quivering.

"Pin-bot? It…it was you?"

"Beep…"

Jacob cocked his head back. "But...but why?"

"Beep-beep-orders."

"But I wanted them closed. Why did Mom's orders override mine?"

Pin-bot slowly began inching closer and closer to the door. The question was too complicated for her to calculate. She was programmed to follow orders from both Jacob *and* Grace. It just so happened that Grace had given her orders right after Jacob's, so the last order was the one she would respond to. She wasn't sure how to explain this to Jacob. Instead, she opened the door and simply disappeared down the staircase. In her simple mind, she wouldn't have to answer the question, if Jacob wasn't able to find her.

"Pin-bot!" Jacob called out. "Pin-bot! Wait, get back here. I'm not mad at you!" He sighed. "I just hate all of this light."

As Jacob slammed the shutter back against the window, plunging the entire room in darkness, the plant that he had left on the desk lifted off of the window sill and floated in front him. He reached out and grabbed it by the stem. "Hey! How did this get over here?"

A blink of his eyes and a cock of his head enabled his night vision. As he turned the plant around, he noticed how green and vibrant it had become. Many of its leaves had a sheen to them, while the stem bounced back when he flicked at it with his hand. Jacob turned his attention to the window. "The light…Just like when I was looking at it under the microscope. Those tiny things that I saw under the microscope must be dividing like crazy right now."

He pulled open the shutter and gently placed the plant back onto the sill. "I'll get a better look at you when I get back. Got to go to school."

It wasn't too long ago when the thought of school made Jacob lower his head. Now he couldn't wait to get there. *Better get going.* He made his way over to the closet. To his surprise, there was a set of plating already hanging from the closet's door handle. He blinked his eyes and cocked his head back, disabling his night vision. It was the red plating. *But she said I could pick my own this time.*

He swung open the closet door expecting to see a large selection of plating he could choose from, but instead, he faced an empty closet. Jacob stumbled back. "What! Where…where are they? Where's all my plating? They're all…gone!"

Jacob knew who was responsible for opening the window shutters, she had admitted to it, but stripping his closet of all his plating? Had Pin-bot done that, too?

No. She would have no reason to do that which only left one other possibility. He slammed the closet door closed, ripped the red plating from the handle and charged out of his room yelling, "Mom!"

* * *

Grace, in her customary pose, with hands on her hips, stood in front of the dwindling pile of *Pure Blend*…if it could even be called a pile. She wished that the piles were reversed—that the *Artificial Blend*, reaching for the ceiling, was the *Pure Blend*. For Jacob's sake, of course. She grabbed two cans, reducing the "pile" even further. She wasn't sure what was going to happen when she used up all of the cans. It was best that she didn't even think about that. *When it happens, it happens*. That might not be the best perspective with which to look at things, but with no options available to her, it was the most realistic. She walked over to the end of the room, not even bothering with own can of *Artificial Blend* this time. She could go days without it, unlike Jacob and his *Pure Blend*. As she dropped the cans onto the counter, she recited, "Two cans a day…every day."

It was as if this phrase had burnt a permanent dimple onto her hard-drive. She couldn't go a day without repeating it to herself or more importantly, to Jacob. She knew that something this important required repetition, and, as annoying as it was at times, it was the best way of making him remember...at least, she hoped. She reached underneath the counter and retrieved Jacob's lunchbox. There was a rattling and clanking sound, as the lunchbox's contents rolled around inside.

"Beep!"

The lunchbox slipped out of Grace's hand and fell onto the counter. "Pin-bot! My goodness! I didn't even hear you."

"Beep-beep-help?"

"Sorry, what was that?"

"Beep-beep-help!" Pin-bot repeated.

"Oh…no, I'm fine. Just need to pack these cans and then I'm done."

Pin-bot hovered in place, a pleading expression in her large, round eyes.

"Oh, alright," Grace said, surrendering to the silent request. "You can fetch me a can of *Artificial Blend*."

"Beep-Jacob?" Pin-bot asked, perking up.

"No, not for Jacob. It's for me. I only inject *Artificial Blend* into Jacob when he's dormant."

Pin-bot did not know what that meant, but she didn't care. She was just happy to help. She made her way to the mountainous pile of *Artificial Blend* and retrieved a can from the very peak.

"By the way, Pin-bot, did you hear a loud noise coming from upstairs? Was it what I think it was?"

Pin-bot hovered at the far end of the room. She wasn't sure what to do. She didn't know if she should tell Grace the truth, as it would obviously upset Jacob, but if she lied, one of her basic functions would be overridden.

"Pin-bot?" Grace said, hands on her hips.

"Beep-don't-remember."

Pin-bot was the perfect assistant, but not a very good liar. Her turbines began to stutter, as her hands trembled to the point where they could no longer grip the can. It slipped out of her grasp and fell to the floor.

"So...I guess I'll be the one picking up the charger again," Grace confirmed.

"Beep-help! Beep-beep-help!" Helping was her way of apologizing.

Grace laughed. "No, it's quite alright, Pin-bot. I did it before, I can do it again. What you *can* do is go upstairs and get Jacob. It's almost time to leave for school. Let him know that I left a set of plating for him to wear."

Pin-bot didn't even get the chance to swivel her lower turbine engine before Jacob stepped into the room, snapping a shoulder-plate in place. "I saw them."

It was the same plate that was loose the previous day, Grace recalled. This time, it looked to be securely in place. *He remembered. Good for him.*

Jacob stayed close to the doorway. "You said I was allowed to pick out my own. I recorded it this time."

Grace placed her finger on the edge of her mouth. "I did?"

"Yes, you did." Jacob looked over at the corner to the room. "You remember, don't you, Pin-bot?"

Again, Pin-bot was placed in an awkward situation. Her simple-functioning CPU was quick this time, however. She turned around and faced the wall. To her, she didn't have to reply if she wasn't looking straight at them.

"What's wrong with her?" Jacob said, with a shrug.

"I don't know," his mom replied. "But I believe you. Both of you."

Pin-bot turned back, but only at a minimal forty-five degrees.

"There aren't any plates in my closet. Where are they?"

"I put them in some boxes."

"Why?"

"I was going to clean them. It's been a while since I cleaned them."

Jacob cocked his head. "Clean them? But they weren't dirty!"

"They were a little dusty. And some were a bit scuffed up. I was going polish them up for you."

"They're fine the way they are, Mom. I don't need them shined or polished or whatever it is you're going to do with them."

"Okay…okay. Fine, I'll leave them the way they are."

"The way I like them," Jacob said. He scanned the entire room. "So…where are they?"

"I told you already. They're in one of those boxes." Grace pointed toward the hallway.

Jacob leaned back, angling himself in-line with the hallway. Boxes were everywhere. It was impossible for him to tell which boxes held his plating unless…"I'll have to demagnetize the entire hallway."

"No! No-no-no. I'll find them and bring them up to your room," Grace said. "Don't need another mess. Besides, you're already wearing the ones I picked out."

"Didn't have much choice."

"They're so adorable—"

"Mom! Not again!"

"Okay-okay…Sorry." She noticed the indicator lights on Jacob's chest-plate. "So…full charge. How are you feeling at the moment?"

"Okay, but…" Jacob looked down at his chest-plate to see the green light flashing, "even though the indicator is green, I just don't feel like it's green. It's like I didn't get a full charge or something." Jacob reached up and caressed the back of his head. "Feels like I'm only at yellow…or even orange…not quite red."

Jacob's mom hurried over to Jacob's side and lowered to one knee. "Let me see." She pushed Jacob's hand away and began feeling around at the back of his head.

Jacob stood there confused and rather uncomfortable. "Mom?"

She ignored him and continued her examination.

"Mom! What are you doing?" He began squirming.

Pin-bot flew over and joined in. She hovered over Jacob's head, scanning it from left to right. Her extended arms were scraping against Jacob's head every time she made a pass over him.

Jacob flailed his arms. "Stop that! Just stop it! Both of you!"

"Jacob, hold still," his mom ordered. "Let me see what's wrong."

"There's nothing wrong with me." Jacob jumped back, prying himself away from them. He frowned at his mom and then at Pin-bot. "Damn it, *312*! Your circuits loose or something?"

Grace rose to her feet. "Don't say that, Jacob."

"Well, you're both acting crazy."

"I just…I just wanted to make sure everything's running smoothly."

"And everything *is.* I was probably just upset about having to wear red again. I hate red."

"That's it, then? Everything's running smoothly?"

"I think so."

"You're positive?" Grace walked back toward the counter. "Because you know, Jacob, I was the one who put you together. I'll know if something's wrong."

"Positive."

She hesitated for a moment, but eventually she said, "Well…okay. If you're absolutely positive..."

"I'm absolutely positive!"

"Okay, Jacob. Calm down. I just wanted to be sure."

Pin-bot also backed away, though her retreat was mainly due to the piercing stare Jacob was giving her.

"Okay. Since everything is fine, I guess we should get going."

"Yes, finally," Jacob mumbled.

Grace opened the lunchbox, ready to refill it with two full cans of *Pure Blend* when suddenly, she turned around and yelled, "Jacob? What's this?"

Jacob stood there, wide-eyed. "Uh…what's what?"

"This!" Jacob's mom pulled out the single, empty can of *Pure Blend* that had been tucked away inside the lunchbox.

One of the plates over Jacob's eyes lowered. "Umm…an empty can. What does it look like?"

"Don't get smart."

"Well, it is, isn't it?"

"Where's the other one?"

Uh-oh…Wheeler. "Umm…I'm not exactly sure. I might have left it at school or in the courtyard…or—"

"You *did* finish it, right?"

Jacob shrugged. "I forget. Lots of things happened that day."

Grace sighed. "Jacob…two cans a day—"

"Every day," Jacob recited. "I know, I know. You keep telling me that."

"And I mean it. It's important, Jacob."

"Okay. I will!" Jacob made sure that his mom's back was turned when he glanced over to the few cans of *Pure Blend* remaining on the counter. Once they run out, he wouldn't have to hear her say that boring phrase again. "Finally!"

He didn't realize he had said that out loud until his mom walked over and handed him his lunchbox. "Finally, what?"

"Nothing. We should get going."

Pin-bot followed closely behind the pair, as they walked toward the main door.

"While we're gone," Grace said, looking back at Pin-bot and smiling, "take care of the place. No swinging from the ceilings."

Pin-bot hovered in place. *How is that even possible?*

Jacob shook his head at his mom. "No humour, remember?"

"Oh…right."

* * *

There wasn't much to look at during the quiet car ride to the school. Other than the blinding sun, the only other thing in the sky was the moon. It wasn't hard to miss. Even if you weren't looking directly at it, it was still able to make its presence felt with its dense shadow alone. It crept across the

Earth, burying anything that had been touched by the sun. The moon was the closest it had ever been to the Earth. It was so close that for the first time ever, Grace was able to see the rows upon rows of enormous anchor points on its dimly-lit shadow side. The size of a 500 story building, each anchor point was made from slabs of metal with giant ringed-loops at the end. A few of them still had a link or two of chain still attached through these ringed-loops. The diameter of each link suggested that these chains had once been attached to something of enormous size.

Grace wondered if Jacob even noticed them. She couldn't recall seeing them on the scale model that he had made of the moon, and Jacob was fairly accurate when it came to finer details. He had even accounted for, and recreated, each and every crater scarring the moon's surface to their exact size and location. Even the missing chunk, cutting the moon's girth by a quarter, had been painstakingly recreated. If his scale model was missing the anchor points, it was most likely due to the fact that the moon was simply facing the other direction when Jacob had began constructing his model.

"Wish there was a way of stopping it," Jacob said, opening a can of *Pure Blend* and taking a sip.

Guess the moon was on Jacob's mind, as well.

"The moon?" Grace asked, just to be sure.

"Yeah. I mean, there probably isn't but..." Jacob paused and then sank into his seat.

"What is it?"

The vents on Jacob's cheeks opened, and he sighed. "It's just that...you know...I wouldn't mind staying."

Grace glanced down at him. The plates over her eyes were raised. "You would?"

"Yeah. I like Earth. It's the only place I know."

"Didn't realize you like it so much here," Grace said, trying to hide her smile. She wasn't doing a very good job of it. Jacob easily detected it.

"It's too bad we have to leave." Jacob shoved his elbow against his lap and rested his chin inside his open hand. "Just wish there was a way of stopping the moon...you know...push it away or even better...destroy it—get rid of it completely."

"It's funny that you mentioned it, Jacob, because that's exactly what happened."

Jacob's face slipped off of his hand. "What do you mean?"

"Project Retaliation."

"Project Retaliation? What's that?"

Grace pointed directly at the moon, more accurately, at the large chunk missing from its face. "He did exactly that. He tried to destroy it."

"Who? The Mayor?"

Grace nodded.

Jacob sighed. "Lucky guess."

"He thought it would work. But in the end, there weren't enough resources. The effort barely made a dent."

"What exactly did he do?"

"I wasn't there when it happened, so I don't know everything. I was told by a few who actually saw it that the Mayor used some sort of cannon. It fired three times at the moon. Two missed. The last was a direct hit...sort of."

Jacob pointed out the obvious with a simple gesture. "Sort of? But the moon's still up there. I guess it didn't work."

Grace laughed. "Project Retaliation, or plan *B*, failed miserably. That's the main reason the Mayor went straight to plan *C*.

"What's plan *C*?"

"Something he refers to as 'Project New Hope'."

Jacob pressed his back against his seat. "Project New Hope? Wait... isn't that just—"

"Exactly, Jacob. That's where we are today."

Jacob couldn't help but release a sarcastic laugh. "The Mayor doesn't seem very tenacious."

Grace cocked her head back and blinked a couple times. "Tenacious? That's a pretty big word, Jacob. Where did you learn that from?"

"I don't remember. Guess I picked it up from somewhere." He tapped the side of his head. "Probably this advanced CPU I have up here."

"Well, Jacob, if your CPU is so advanced, what would *you* have done if you were the Mayor?"

"I don't understand. Why ask me?"

"It's simple, Jacob. What would you do to extend your time here on Earth?"

"Are you asking what I would do to *save Earth* from the moon?"

"More importantly...save us. When the moon hits, it will be the end of us all."

There was a long pause, as Jacob began his calculations. Grace noticed that the pause was longer than usual. Then when Jacob was finished, she was disappointed when he merely shrugged.

"I...I don't know, Mom. That's a bit too advanced for me."

"Nothing?"

"The moon is on its way, like it or not. It's just too bad that it had to come to this. I'm sure it could have been prevented... somehow, but it's too late now." Jacob looked up at his mom, and she noticed that the glow of his eyes had paled to nearly white. "Sorry, Mom. I know you expect me to have an answer for everything. This one's just too complex, even for me."

Grace forced a smile. "It's okay, Jacob. Like I said, time is our only enemy. It's just too bad that we don't have much of it left." She gave him a firm pat on his shoulder and asked, "You sure you're okay?"

"What do you mean?"

"You remember. Something about not feeling completely recharged?"

Jacob waved it off. "I'm fine. Feeling a bit better ever since I got in the car." He took one final sip of the *Pure Blend*. "Probably just needed to get out of the house."

Grace grabbed the empty can from Jacob and stashed it inside his lunchbox, next to the full one. "Make sure you drink the other one."

"I know, I know. Two cans a day," Jacob recited. "You tell me that every day. Why is it so important?"

"Just want to make sure every part of you is running properly." She gave Jacob a wink. "You'll tell me if something is wrong, won't you?"

"You mean, like a broken limb, loose screw…disconnected wire?"

"I was thinking more internally."

"Internally? Why would you need to know what happens to me internally?"

"Isn't it obvious, Jacob? So we can fix it."

"What would 'fixing' involve? An upgrade?"

Grace glanced at Jacob using only the corner of her eyes. "What are you getting at?"

"Just want to know if 'fixing' involved an upgrade."

There was a short pause before she replied, "Yes…possibly."

The internal motors in the very back of Jacob's face tightened. "Is that so…" he said, grinning.

Jacob suddenly reached up, pressed his hand against his head, while his other hand flailed about. "My...head! Something's...wrong…Sensors overheating…need fixing. Need...upgrade!"

Grace laughed.

Jacob's hands flopped back into his lap. His shoulders slumped forward. "Didn't work, did it?"

"Not even close."

Shortly after Jacob's rather pathetic attempt to get his mom to agree to an upgrade, they drew close to the school. Looking out the window, Jacob noticed an impressive gathering outside. There were so many in the crowd, some of them were spilling out onto the road, and Grace was not able to park their car at the same spot she had used the previous day. She had no choice but to simply stop the car in the middle of the road. Luckily, there wasn't any traffic to be concerned about.

"Look at them all." She leaned over Jacob's lap to look out the passenger- side window.

"Looks like everyone is out here," Jacob said. "Damn, *313*!"

"I'll pretend I didn't hear that."

"Sorry…Think we're early?"

"No, we can't be. There's no lock on the main door. Locks on the *side* door, but that's an exit only…"

"Huh? How do you know?" Jacob asked, surprised.

"I just do," Grace replied, still staring at the crowd. "They didn't mention anything about some special event to you yesterday?"

Jacob shook his head. "Nothing."

Jacob reached over, pulled the car's door handle and created a small seam where door met quarter panel. Noisy chattering from the assembled crowd spilled inside the car's interior. Jacob reached over and grabbed his lunchbox.

"Where are you going?"

"To class," Jacob said, slightly shocked at his mom's question. He shoved the door the rest of the way open and began lowering himself out of the car. "Where else?"

"Should I follow you? Maybe I should follow you. At least to see what's going on?"

A firm, outstretched arm from Jacob kept his mom seated. "If it's important, I'll tell you everything that happens when you pick me up later."

"Well, look at you," Grace said, with a smirk. "Could barely get you out of the car the other day. Now you can't wait to get rid of me."

Jacob tried to mimic his mom's usual pose but with the lunchbox occupying one hand, he was only able to get one hand on his waist. "I didn't say that, Mom."

"I was just teasing," she said, smiling. She reached over and grabbed the door's handle, ready to close it, but Jacob had yet to move out of the way.

Rather than backing up, Jacob surprised Grace by sticking his head inside the car. The plates over his eyes were lowered. "Mom, you told me about plan *B*, Project Retaliation, and plan *C*, Project New Hope..." the corner of his mouth angled downward, "but what was plan *A*?"

"Plan *A*?"

"Yes. There had to be a plan *A*. What was it?"

He's not ready to know about Project Redemption. Although time wasn't doing any of them any favours at the moment, now wasn't the best time to tell him. Grace tightened her grip on the door's handle and pulled. Jacob jumped out of the way, just as the door closed. Muffled inside the car's interior, Jacob's mom said, "Sorry, Jacob. I think I hear Pin-bot calling me."

The car lifted off the road and sped off.

Jacob kept his eyes on the car until it was swallowed by the horizon. He reached up and scratched the side of his head. "But Pin-bot doesn't have any way of communicating remotely." Jacob wondered why his mom would avoid his question. It seemed harmless. *Oh, well. Another mystery to be stored away until later.*

The crowd gathered outside of the school had grown considerably. None of Jacob's classmates, however, seemed interested in him, unlike the previous day which was why he was stuck staring at their backsides. He wanted to yell out, "*Hey, remember me? The one with all the trophies...the one you gave a round of applause to,*" but he knew better than that. He wasn't *that* conceited, though he was getting a bit desperate. He scanned from one end of the crowd to the next. It was basically an impenetrable wall. *Wonder why everyone's out here. Something must be going on.* Not able to see much from his current position, Jacob decided to start walking. He thought that eventually he would find a weak spot in the crowd where he could finally force a path to the front door of the school. Jacob barely completed half a dozen steps when he heard someone calling out to him.

"One Bolt! Hey, One Bolt!"

Jacob stopped and looked around, finally spotting the annoyance. "Wheeler," Jacob mumbled. Of course it was Wheeler. The smell of burnt rubber, the screeching from his wheels, and the annoying calls of, "One Bolt". Who else could it be?

Wheeler burst out from the crowd and drove toward Jacob, using his wheel arm to steer. Once by Jacob's side, Wheeler threw his massive wheel arm over Jacob's shoulder. Jacob winced at the awful, bitter smell of burnt rubber.

"Hey, didn't you hear me calling you?"

"I heard you," Jacob said, "but that's not my name, so stop calling me that."

"Why? Did you get a few more bolts installed since the last time I saw you?"

"What? No."

"Well, then…One Bolt it is."

Jacob began walking.

"Hey, wait." Wheeler tightened his hold on Jacob and successfully pulled him back. "Where are you going?"

"Trying to get around them." Jacob pointed at the crowd. "I want to know what's going on."

Wheeler snickered. "Ha! Weren't you listening to the professor a few days ago?"

Jacob just stared.

"Oh…right, you're new here."

"Is something happening that I don't know about?"

Wheeler reached over and grabbed Jacob's arm. "That's an understatement. Here, get on. I'll show you."

Jacob scanned Wheeler from top to bottom but could not quite understand what he meant when he said, "Get on".

"What are you waiting for, One Bolt? Get on!"

"Okay, fine," Jacob said, "But what am I supposed to get on? I don't see anything."

Wheeler reached back, picked Jacob up off the ground and then placed him on the small ledge protruding from the back of his lower base. "Hang on," he ordered.

"Hang on? Hang on to what?"

"To anything!" Wheeler revved his wheels, dropped his wheel arm out in front of him and then drove straight into the crowd. Jacob had no choice but to go along for the ride.

When Wheeler had told Jacob to hang on, he was certain that he didn't say, "Wrap your arms around my face."

"One Bolt!" Wheeler yelled. "You're covering my eyes! I can't see where I'm going!" He reached up and shifted Jacob's hands down slightly. At least now, he could see the ones he was colliding into.

"Sorry!" Jacob held on tightly, trying to brace himself so Wheeler's maddening pace wouldn't make him fall off. Everything around him was a blur.

"Out of the way! Come on, move aside. Make way!" Using his wheel arm to steer, Wheeler was twisting and turning his way through the confusing maze of metallic limbs.

Jacob felt his lunchbox slam into the very same limbs and was shouting out apologies right and left. He heard a wretched squeal, as his the corner of his lunchbox scraped someone's side. "Uh-oh…that's going to leave a mark…Sorry…"

Finally, to Jacob's relief, the pair burst through the final layer of limbs and body parts and were now right at the front of the crowd. Jacob stumbled off of Wheeler's base, his vision temporarily scrambled. Wheeler was quick to wrap his wheel arm around Jacob's shoulder again, unintentionally offering him the smell of burnt rubber.

"You see, One Bolt?" Wheeler said. "Sometimes you just have to force your way through. It's not pretty…but then, neither am I."

You can say that again. Jacob waved his arms back and forth, trying to get lubricant back into the joints. He regained his vision by shaking his head. "But next time, how about forcing our way through a little slower? Think I lost a bolt back there."

Wheeler laughed. "I might have to call you 'No Bolt' from now on."

"I prefer Jacob."

"One Bolt it is."

Jacob sighed and looked around. Not having the crowd in front afforded him a clear view of the massive staircase leading up to the school's main door. There was a large podium at the very edge of the final step which hadn't been there the previous day. Standing like a silent sentry beside the door was a familiar being. Tall, red eyes, and not a single concave surface on his body. "What's he doing here?" Jacob asked.

"Who? Brute?" Wheeler shrugged. "Don't know."

"Don't know, or don't care?"

"Either way…"

That went nowhere rather quickly. Other than Brute and the podium, Jacob noticed nothing out of the ordinary. "Okay, so we're now at the front—"

"Wow. Clever. That CPU of yours must be overheating right now."

Jacob glanced at Wheeler's wheels and smirked. "Aren't you tired of just *standing* here?"

Wheeler rolled his eyes. "Yeah…good one, One Bolt. Anyway..."

"Well, now that we are at the front, what do we do?"

"Who do you think you are, One Bolt? We wait, like everyone else."

"Wait? Wait for what?"

"Not what…who."

"Who, then?"

Wheeler pointed up at the school's main door that had opened a crack. "There…look! Here he comes now." Wheeler reached over, grabbed Jacob's arm and placed it against his bulky chest. “Hold me back, One Bolt. I don’t want to be doing anything crazy.”

A bit too late for that.

The chattering from the crowd quickly turned to murmurs and then to nothing. Jacob realized that whoever was about to walk through the door, must be someone of great importance. What else could have justified the crowd and Wheeler’s reaction? The door to the school crept open. A sharp crackle of rusted hinges ripped into the silence. Brute stepped aside, allowing the door to spread to its very limits. It had to in order to accommodate the enormous figure who stepped out from the shadows of the hallway. He moved in heavy, measured steps, and only a few were needed to bring him to the edge of the staircase. He stopped in front of the podium, allowing the light to pour over his impressive stance.

The crowd let out a collective gasp. Wheeler simply sighed. As for Jacob…all he could do was stand silent and unmoving. He watched intently, as the massive figure looked down from his podium, scanning each and every one of the insignificant individuals making up the crowd. Something about him was so familiar. The sunken eyes, the massive plates forming a heavy jaw-line. Jacob had to adjust his vision a couple times to be perfectly sure. When his hard-drive finally caught up to his assumptions, Jacob whispered over to Wheeler, “Hey, I know him…”

Wheeler sneered. “Obviously, One Bolt. His statue is the first thing you see when you enter the school.”

“The statue? That...that's him?”

“Who else?”

Jacob looked over at Wheeler and contorted his face. “Who is he? He looks…I don’t know…important.”

“Ha! You don’t know?” Wheeler shook his head. “Thought you’d know who the Mayor is by now.”

Jacob’s attention snapped back toward the podium. Both his eyes burst open to the point where they almost locked. “That…that’s the Mayor?”

“The one and only.”

“Hey, I thought I was the one and only?”

“You wish, One Bolt. Not when he’s around.”

Jacob needed a moment or two to study the Mayor. *So that’s him—the one who made Earth the way it is.* He was the one who had reassigned nearly everyone Jacob had known into a dormant state. Jacob felt Wheeler sticking his elbow into his side.

“Not as shiny as his statue, is he, One Bolt?” Wheeler joked.

“No. Not exactly.”

“Ha! Not even close. The statue is flawless. He’s not.”

Jacob glanced over at Wheeler and noticed the smirk on his face.

“What do you think? Impressed?”

“Impressed? With the Mayor?” Jacob did another full scan of the Mayor. The shadow being cast by the school could not hide the Mayor’s impressive stature. Massive pistons protruded from every corner of his body, and twin gears were mounted on opposing sides of his massive shoulders. Even with a few strides distancing the pair, Jacob realized that the Mayor was the only one around who made Brute look unimpressive. He looked back at Wheeler and replied, “Yes. I'm impressed.”

Wheeler shook his head. “Not me. I mean, look at him…waving and smiling to the crowd. What a fake.”

Jacob scanned back at the crowd. Wherever the Mayor directed his waves, that particular section of crowd would smile back at him. “They seem to disagree with you.”

“Ah, what do they know? The Mayor has a hold on them, and they’re obviously not even trying to struggle their way out. It’s those damn speeches he gives. They’re so addicting.”

“What speeches?”

“Quiet. I think he’s about to make another one. Don’t let him get to you, One Bolt,” Wheeler warned. “Listen but try not to record.”

“Sure.” *Whatever that meant.*

The Mayor lowered his hand, while tightening his invisible grasp on his admirers below. One last scanning of the crowd assured him that their attention was completely his. The Mayor pressed his enormous upper body against the podium and then straightened his posture.

“My fellow mechanical beings,” the Mayor began, in a voice at least one pitch lower than Brute’s, “I honour you with my presence on this glorious day. As you all know, Earth is on its final breath. We have evolved from it, peaked from it, and now, we have outgrown it. Our time here has expired. Earth can no longer, and will no longer, sustain us. Our evolution, however, has not reached its true potential. We are strong. We must embrace our strength.”

The Mayor backed away from the podium and reached one hand toward the sky in a pose that mimicked the statue inside the school, flawlessly. “Our future is amongst the stars.”

Jacob looked up, but all he saw was a sky saturated by the sun’s ambiance and the moon’s influence. *What are stars?*

The Mayor returned to the podium. “Many have already taken the first step. As for the rest of you, the time is near. The rest of the pods will soon be ready. And when the day finally arrives…when we lift off away from this Earth, away from our weakness, our future will welcome us with an open embrace. Enjoy your final days here on Earth, for soon, it will no longer exist. Earth will fade but we? We will continue on.”

The Mayor concluded his speech with a simple gesture of his hand. The massive gears on opposing shoulders bit down violently against each other in order to bring his heavy arm above his chest. The crowd erupted in a frenzied bout of applause. It was much louder and more animated than the one they had given to Jacob the previous day. Though the crowd seemed to have taken everything the Mayor had proposed and welcomed it, Wheeler obviously wasn’t as easily impressed. Jacob had noted that Wheeler had been agitated throughout the speech.

"That's it? That's his plans for us?" Wheeler stared at Jacob with a nearly blank look on his face.

"Doesn't sound like much of a plan," Jacob added.

"Of course not! He has no idea what he's doing. Just like Project Redemption…just like Project Retaliation…just like Project—"

"Wait, what was that? Project Redemption?" Could that be plan *A* that his mom shied away from talking about earlier?

"You heard me. Project Redemption."

"I heard. What is that, exactly?"

"What do you think, One Bolt? The reason why we're in this mess in the first place. The reason why Earth is nothing more than a dead rock."

"What exactly did he—"

"Someone should ask him." Wheeler tightened the motors in his mouth, giving his face a hard look. "Go on. You do it. Go right up to him, and ask him what his specific plans are. Where does he exactly plan on taking us? I bet he won't have an answer."

"Why me? Why don't *you* go ask him?"

Wheeler stumbled back. "What? Are you serious, One Bolt? Me? Face-to-face with the Mayor? I'd rather delete myself."

"I'm guessing you dislike the Mayor?"

Wheeler sighed. "That CPU of yours, One Bolt. You're going to burn it out one of these days with your delightful insights. Come on. Let's get to class. My sensors are on overload at the moment."

Wheeler revved his wheels and then pulled at Jacob's arm, but to his surprise, Jacob did not bulge. "Hey, you coming or what, One Bolt?" He glanced over at Jacob and noticed that his attention had been forfeited elsewhere. "One Bolt?"

Wheeler raised his wheel arm and waved it up and down in front of Jacob's face, attempting to get his attention. He even revved his wheel, releasing a white line of smoke right into Jacob's face. *Nothing*. Wheeler decided to adjust his sights so that they angled directly in-line to where Jacob was staring. That's when he noticed her. "Oh-no. Here comes trouble." Wheeler tugged at Jacob's arm with a sense of urgency. He had Jacob's arm fully extended. "Come on, One Bolt, we got to go. Now!"

"In a minute," Jacob finally replied.

"No, right now! Let's go!" Wheeler's pleads were all for nothing.

Hope stopped in front of pair, and Jacob found her green eyes and wide smile a nice distraction. She nodded in Wheeler's direction and said, "Wheeler…"

Wheeler sighed and mumbled, "Hope…you're looking good as always."

Hope then focused her attention on Jacob, the real reason why she had made her way over. "Hello, Jacob. How are you?"

Jacob smiled. "I...I'm…going good, Hope." He shook his head. "I mean, doing good. And yourself?"

"This isn't going to be pretty," Wheeler mumbled.

"Much better now that I'm here," Hope said. "Are you two heading to class?"

"Yes," Wheeler announced, as he tightened his hold on Jacob's arm.

"Oh...you are?" There was a hint of disappointment in Hope's voice.

Jacob began pulling his arm from side-to-side, attempting to free himself from Wheeler's tight grip. "Why, Hope?" he asked. "Is there something we can do for you?"

"I really wanted you to meet someone." Although it didn't seem possible, Hope's smile grew bolder. "Someone very special."

"Who?"

"You'll see. This way. Follow me."

Wheeler drove between the pair. "That's really nice of you, Hope, but Jacob and I really should be getting back to class. You know how the professor gets when we're late."

Hope clasped both her hands together in front of her breast-plate. Her eyes opened to their fullest, causing even Wheeler to stumble back. "Please? It won't take long. I promise."

Wheeler shook his head. "Sorry, Hope, but Jacob and I have to get going. Maybe next time."

"But there might not be a next time." She stared at Jacob, raising the plates over her eyes as high as they could go.

It was now all up to Jacob to decide. He looked over at Wheeler, who had a rigid stance, compressed upper lip, and a horrible stench of oil mixed with rubber.

"One Bolt!" Wheeler ordered. "Let's go already!"

Jacob then looked over at Hope. There was a pleading expression in her green eyes that was hard to resist.

"It won't take long. I promise." Hope smiled at Jacob, who immediately made his decision.

He looked over at Wheeler. "I'll meet you in class."

"Thanks, Jacob." Hope grabbed Jacob's hand and pulled him free from Wheeler's grasp.

Wheeler could only watch, as Jacob and Hope ran off together. He sighed. "Shiny exterior...wish I had it."

They made their way around the far side of the school. Standing on the other side was Brute. Hope stopped. Jacob nearly fell backwards.

"Brute?" Jacob whimpered, with wide-eyes. "We're meeting Brute?" *I hope not.* Their first meeting had been less than formal, and Jacob wasn't keen on repeating it.

"No, it's not Brute," Hope said.

That was a relief to Jacob, although they were still too close to the massive mound of immovable parts for his comfort. Jacob felt exactly the way he did during their first meeting, and if there was a table within reach, he would certainly be underneath it this time.

Hope tapped on Brute's leg, and he turned. Twin pistons hissed, as he lowered himself to her level. Jacob wished he could retreat back behind the school, and if it was possible, even further, but Hope had a firm grip on him. Brute looked at Jacob, his beady-red eyes piercing right through him. Jacob was glad when Hope stepped between them and asked, "Is he still here?"

"Yes. In the courtyard." Brute's voice was hard and had a metallic clang to it that reverberated. "I will see you to him."

"Great," Hope said, smiling back at Jacob.

As with the previous time when he was caught in Brute's overwhelming stare, Jacob couldn't offer a smile back.

Brute lead them through the courtyard, the very same one where Hope had introduced herself to Jacob for the first time. The conversation was still a recent save to his hard-drive and quite possibly would never be erased. They continued on until they were at the very end of the courtyard. Already, Jacob could see an enormous figure, slightly bent over with his back turned to them. Brute motioned for Hope and Jacob to stop, but he continued forward, walking up next to the figure.

For Jacob, seeing Brute standing taller than the figure wasn't unusual. Brute was taller than anyone he had ever seen. He had to blink a few times, however, the moment the figure straightened. Jacob had considered Brute as the most impressive being he had ever seen, but now he had to change that. The figure towered over Brute, who had to lift his head in order to speak to him. Jacob was absolutely sure the pistons in Brute's neck were not accustomed to that sort of exertion.

Brute signalled to Hope and Jacob to come forward, as the tall figure turned to face them. Immediately, Jacob noticed the sunken eyes and the massive jaw-line.

"The... the Mayor..." Jacob mumbled.

"Yes, the Mayor," Hope said, "but I just call him Dad."

Jacob took a step back. "Dad? Did... did you say... Dad?"

Hope simply smiled and nodded.

Jacob wanted to ask one more time, just to be sure he had heard her correctly, but Brute interrupted with a formal announcement. "Sir. Hope and a simple generation are here to see you."

The Mayor's legs recoiled and opened at the knee joint. Huge pistons on both legs burst from their chambers, lifting the Mayor's upper body even higher. Brute stepped back. Even his massive bearing was not enough to let him see anything beyond the Mayor's shoulders. A single step allowed the Mayor to completely drape Jacob from head to boots in a cold, greyish-blue shadow. Jacob pulled his neck back as far as it could go. He felt one of the motors in his neck vibrate. He was silenced by the impressive figure and took note of some of the Mayor's finer details.

A pair of gears on his upper thigh shifted clock-wise with each of his movements. These drove the intertwining smaller gears into a rotational frenzy. Pistons protruded from his back and were so massive, they reached over his shoulders and draped their shadows all the way up and around to his enormous chest-plate. Unlike his distant observations from earlier, Jacob could now see distinct rust formations consuming the seams running across the majority of the Mayor's body. A good section of his face had also succumbed to rust. It was clear that any sort of cover-up would surely result in more damage, as bolts had nothing to anchor onto.

Guess even he wasn't able to escape rust's influence. It made Jacob ponder why Hope looked so flawless when her own dad was clearly far from it.

The Mayor kept his eyes squarely on the diminutive, first generation. He grinned, and in a deep, grinding voice said, "Very loyal worker, Brute is but not programmed with the best of manners." He reached out and offered his enormous hand to Jacob. The simple gesture made Jacob stumble back. It's not often that Jacob had a hand the size of his entire head shoved directly in his face. "It's quite the honour to finally meet you. Jacob, is it?"

Jacob sensors pulsated, and he felt cold all around. It was the same feeling he had when he was up in front of the class. Nerves, plain and simple.

"Go ahead," Hope said.

Jacob stuttered, "Um…yes. My name is Jacob. Very…nice to meet you… sir." He extended his arm, and the Mayor immediately grabbed onto it. Jacob's entire arm, from hand to elbow joint, was engulfed inside the Mayor's grasp. Jacob just stood there. It was up to the Mayor to commence the shaking motion, as Jacob would have never been able gain any momentum with his insignificant limbs. The Mayor began to shake Jacob's arm. Jacob's entire body nearly lifted off the ground, while the Mayor's wrist merely shifted up and down.

"Please, just call me 'Mayor' like the rest of them." Mercifully, the Mayor finally let go of Jacob's hand.

Jacob sensors let out a chime. It was a simple warning telling him that a specific body part had been under an unbelievable amount of pressure a moment ago. Jacob quickly disabled the warning and smiled to cover his embarrassment. "Yes, sir. I mean…Mayor."

The Mayor took a step back so that he could see something other than the top of Jacob's head. "Hope has told me a lot about you. In fact, you were the only thing she could talk about when she got back from class yesterday."

Jacob glanced over at Hope, wide-eyed. "Re-really?"

"I'm certain she mentioned who I was," the Mayor said.

"Oh…uh…not exactly." Jacob shifted his weight back and forth, attempting to find a comfortable place to stand without having to crane his neck. This wasn't easy with the Mayor standing right in front of him. "I didn't even know that you were…you know…the Mayor. Or her dad."

The Mayor looked at Hope. "Oh, I'm sure she must have mentioned something to you, since she is aware of my importance. I am the Mayor, as everyone knows."

"We didn't talk for long, Dad," Hope explained. "Brute came and got me before we got the chance to say more than, 'Hello'."

"That's not important," the Mayor said. "What's important is that I finally get the chance to meet you. Hope told me all about the trophies. So...you're the selfish one who's been winning all of my contests."

Jacob took a step back. "Oh...I'm sorry, sir. I wasn't trying to be selfish. I'll return all the trophies if you want."

The Mayor laughed. It was a deep, terrifying laugh that nearly caused Jacob to stumble over his feet, as he tried to step back even more. "No need to be modest, young one. Those contests were created as a simple way to gauge the intelligence of our current population." *A simple way of categorizing what I'm working with.* The Mayor lowered himself as close as he could to Jacob, without trying to be threatening. It wasn't exactly working. Jacob was backing away from him. The pistons in the Mayor's legs collapsed with a deep thud. "Did not expect that only *one* would be able to solve all of them. Especially a first generation."

Jacob tried to smile, but it came off looking pathetic, as only one corner of his mouth had enough confidence to lift higher than horizontal.

The pistons in the Mayor's legs expended once more, allowing him to rise back to his normal height. The popping and grinding resonating from his joints and pistons sounded like thunder had been stored inside each chamber and was now erupting. "We can use someone like you in our future," he said.

Exactly what future was that? Maybe it was time for Jacob to find out. At least, for Wheeler's sake. "Our future?" Jacob said.

"Our future is the only thing that is certain now." The Mayor's voice took on a tone that sounded like he was reciting words that had been permanently etched onto his hard-drive. "Earth can no longer sustain us. Our future is amongst the stars." He pointed up toward the sky, again, mimicking the statue.

Jacob looked up and scanned the sky again, hoping that being in the courtyard would give him a better perspective, but as expected, he saw nothing but a blank canvas. "Um...what exactly is up there?"

The Mayor's arm lowered, and it collided harshly against his side. "Our future," he insisted. "A future away from here. Away from Earth. A future that will sustain us." The stare he was offering to Jacob turned into a piercing one. "We will become strong once again. Our evolution may have begun on this pathetic rock but it will not end here."

"Why, sir? I think Earth still has potential."

"Potential?" The Mayor snickered. "No, young one, potential died with the Earth a long time ago." He pointed proudly at the scar on the moon. "You see that? That's what happens when you seek potential."

Why would the Mayor use the moon as an example? The moon was still up in the sky, as dominate as ever.

"Earth is dead," The Mayor repeated, in a hard voice. "*They* are dead. We are the peak of their evolution. They are weak." He pumped his fist into the air. "We are strong and will continue to be strong!"

Not understanding why the Mayor had suddenly become so agitated, Jacob looked over to Hope and shrugged. Hope shook her head and smiled. “Don’t worry,” she whispered. “He always gets like this when he talks about humans.”

Both of the plates over Jacob’s eyes shifted downward. “Humans?” This was the first time he had ever heard the word.

“Yes, humans,” the Mayor said, with a look of disgust on his face. “They had their chance.”

“Chance at what, sir?”

The Mayor looked away. Jacob noticed a small ripple run across the Mayor's hinged jaw. There was no need for the Mayor to explain himself any further. He was the Mayor, after all, and he did not have the time to waste on someone as insignificant as a first generation. “All you need to know is that our future awaits.”

“I know that, sir, but—”

“Time for you to head back to class,” the Mayor advised, surprisingly calm.

Jacob looked at Hope and whispered, “I didn’t mean to make him mad.”

Hope smiled. “It’s okay. He’s always like this.”

Jacob looked up at the Mayor one last time. “It...it was nice meeting you...sir.” He grabbed his lunchbox and began backing away. “Hope, are you coming too?”

“She knows the way,” the Mayor said. “Go on. Run along now.”

Jacob recognized the tone of dismissal. His mom used it all the time. But he didn't understand why the Mayor had so suddenly ended the conversation. If Hope had even an inkling of why, she didn't reveal anything in the smile she offered Jacob before he turned and sped off through the courtyard and around the school, his lunchbox clanging loudly against his leg the entire time.

Hope turned to her dad. “If you wanted to scare him, all you had to do was show him your mean face. You’re good at doing that.”

“Nonsense. If he was scared, he wouldn’t have questioned my plans.”

Hope sighed. “You and your plans.”

“It’s our future.”

“Yes, I know that, Dad. You keep reminding me.”

Lowering himself, the Mayor reached out and grabbed Hope’s hand. Most of her arm was swallowed in his surprisingly gentle grip. “It’s not just important for our kind. It’s important for us. We need to survive, and we can’t have anyone questioning our reasoning. You know this, Hope.”

Again, Hope sighed. “I...I know that, Dad.” She pulled her hand from the Mayor’s grip. “I...I need to get going. I need to get to class.”

The Mayor stood tall, drenching Hope in his shadow. “Today wasn’t a school day for you, Hope.”

“I know that. I just want to see if the professor assigned anything new. It shouldn’t take long.”

The Mayor hesitated. He was well aware of the orange indicator light on Hope's breast-plate but decided to let her go anyway.

Brute stepped forward, ready to bring her back but was stopped by the Mayor's outstretched arm.

"She'll be fine," the Mayor assured. "She knows her way back."

"Sir, her indicator's orange."

"She should be back before anything happens."

They watched, as Hope disappeared from their sights.

"And that first generation she was with, sir?"

The Mayor eased the motors behind his protruding forehead, allowing the plates above his eyes to fall. "He's harmless. Just another pod to be filled." He turned and faced Brute. "Besides, we still have much work to do."

"The pods, sir?"

"I have the others working on pods. I need you for something else...something more significant. As I recall, you worked on Project Retaliation, did you not?"

"Project Retaliation? Yes, sir. But...that was a long time ago. It failed to meet the objective."

As the Mayor began to walk off, he glanced up at the giant section missing from the moon—the scar he had inflicted onto it. "Time to get it back up and running," he said. "And this time...it won't fail."

* * *

Jacob pushed open the door to the classroom and stood there for a moment. He had arrived right in the middle of Professor Smith's daily announcements and did not want to interrupt, but the professor glanced over anyway. *Must have heard the clanking of my lunchbox.* "Sorry," Jacob said.

"It's quite alright." Professor Smith waved Jacob into the classroom.

Jacob peeled himself away from the door frame and walked toward his desk. Although he had made amends with the others in the classroom, there was still something unsettling about being the last one to enter a room full of inquisitive stares. Especially when one of those stares was intense enough to find its way to him from the very back of the room. Wheeler. *Understandable.* But Jacob ignored it this time. He slid his lunchbox underneath the desk, sat in his chair and then made himself comfortable.

"Okay, where were we?" Professor Smith said. "Ah, yes. I was saying that our visit from the Mayor needs to be taken seriously. Our time on Earth has nearly reached its final conclusion. Once the moon makes impact, it will take with it Earth's final breath."

Jacob sighed.

Professor Smith began to pace back and forth with a lowered head. "But can you blame the Mayor for his decision?" the professor asked.

Jacob knew what Wheeler's reply would be. His would probably be the same now that he had been face-to-face with the Mayor.

"Our kind can no longer sustain ourselves here on Earth," Professor Smith continued. "Earth can no longer sustain us. Time is now our enemy."

That's exactly what Mom has been saying. Strange how two minds thought alike. But to be fair, during times like these, surely everyone was thinking the exact same thing. *Time is the enemy, and it has no real weaknesses.*

"I don't know how long it will be before the moon finally touches Earth." Professor Smith suddenly lifted his head, and to Jacob's surprise, he offered the entire class a smile. "But we should not dwell on our future. We should enjoy our present. Embrace what we have left. That's why I've decided to do something special for our very last assignment." Professor Smith stopped pacing and faced the classroom. "It's your choice."

Everyone in the class looked at each other.

"That's right. This assignment, our last assignment, is completely your choice. You decide a project you would like to do."

There was a collective gasp throughout the class. Even Jacob found the notion of choosing his own project rather exciting.

"Because time is no longer something we can afford to squander, I want to make sure everyone has the chance to complete their assignment. That's why I've decided that this final assignment will be completed not as individuals but as pairs. That's right, class. I want everyone to find a partner." Professor Smith motioned for the class to form pairs. "Hurry, everyone, find a partner so we can begin!"

Desks and chairs squealed, as they were pushed together. One by one, each student found someone to pair with until almost all were partnered, except for Jacob. It wasn't as if he didn't want a partner for this assignment, she just hadn't come through the door yet. *Where could she be?* It shouldn't have taken this long to trek across the courtyard and then up the stairs.

Professor Smith approached Jacob. "Looks like you two are partners, then?"

Jacob snapped his head back. "Excuse me, sir?"

Professor Smith gestured to Jacob's side, but it was the sudden smell of oil and burnt rubber that made Jacob finally realized who the professor was referring to.

"Yes, we are," Wheeler said, placing his wheel arm around Jacob's shoulder.

Jacob didn't even get the chance to reject the offer.

"Perfect." Professor Smith nodded and then quickly walked toward the other side of the room. "Two great minds working together. Wish they still handed out trophies..."

By now, the professor was on the other side of the room, too far for Jacob to call him back. Wheeler pulled Jacob closer to him. "So? Partners?"

"Do I have a choice?"

"Not anymore."

Jacob sighed. "Yeah, I thought so."

"Ah…it'll be great. Trust me, One Bolt. I have plans for us." He looked at Jacob with a face-engulfing grin. "Big plans!"

"Really…and what are they?" Jacob definitely did not share the same enthusiasm.

"I'll tell you later. First, I have something for you." Wheeler reached into the compartment inside his lower base and pulled out a can. "I never break a promise." He slammed the can onto Jacob's desk. "I said I'd bring you back a can, so here you go."

Jacob looked at the can, read the inscription on it and then exchanged stares with Wheeler.

"So? Are you going to thank me or what, One Bolt?"

"I would if it was *Pure Blend*. What am I going to do with *Artificial Blend*?"

"That's all I have."

"What am I supposed to do with it? I don't drink it. Remember?"

Wheeler retrieved the can and then grabbed Jacob's lunchbox that had been stowed away under the desk and placed the can inside. "Take it. I have plenty more."

"So do I." Jacob grabbed his lunchbox and closed it, although not before Wheeler caught a glimpse of the *Pure Blend* inside. "I guess I'll give it to my mom," Jacob said, tucking the box back beneath the desk.

"Fine with me."

An awkward silence followed. Wheeler was again staring at Jacob in the same way he had been when Jacob had entered the classroom. "Thanks, One Bolt." Wheeler said, sarcasm heavy in his voice.

"For what?"

Wheeler snickered. "For what, he says...For leaving me earlier! I guess if I was shiny and had a pretty face—"

"Trust me. You don't."

"Don't worry. I'm not mad at you. In fact, I want to know what happened. You did meet him, didn't you?"

"Who?"

"Who, he says. The Mayor, One Bolt. Who else?"

"Hope's dad?"

"Hope's dad…the Mayor…whatever you want to call him. Did you meet him?"

Jacob nodded.

Wheeler moved in closer. Their faces were practically touching. "And?"

Feeling a bit uncomfortable with Wheeler being so close, Jacob leaned to one side, creating some much needed space. "And what?"

Wheeler backed off. "Stop stalling, One Bolt. What was he like? Did you ask him about his plans for us? Come on, give me something here."

"Okay-okay…calm down. I did ask about Project New Hope…sort of."

"What do you mean, sort of?"

"He got a bit upset with me for asking."

"Ha! I knew it. I knew he'd get upset. I'd be upset too if I destroyed the Earth and had no real backup plans." Wheeler shook his head. "Stupid Mayor."

Jacob smirked. "So...you don't like him?"

"Like him?" Wheeler slammed his hand against the desk. "For what he's done to us? Ha! I'd rather delete myself than like him. If I could, I would delete him and everything he cares about."

So this was the reason, Jacob finally realized. This was why Wheeler had so much animosity toward Hope. Wheeler's hatred of the Mayor must have filtered down to Hope. *But Hope is nothing like her dad. They don't even look the same.*

"Enough about the Mayor. My joints are getting all tense just thinking about him. Let's talk about this assignment. I have something special planned for the two of us. Ready for it?"

"Do I have a choice?"

"Come on, One Bolt. Serious."

"Okay-okay. Serious. What is it?"

Wheeler paused for a brief moment, possibly to gather himself.

Jacob watched Wheeler's face transform into an expression of concentration. *Whatever he had planned, it must have been well thought out.*

"This is the end all of assignments," Wheeler explained. "It'll make all the trophies you've ever won pale in comparison." He began waving his hand out in front of him. "It'll make—"

"Just get on with it, will you?"

"Okay, fine. But first, I need to ask you something, One Bolt." He stared at Jacob with one eye nearly closed. "Do you know who created us?"

Jacob felt the plates over his eyes drop. "Of course I do. My mom."

Wheeler laughed. "Ha! His mom, he says!"

"What? I'm right, aren't I? She did create me, I'm sure of this."

"Not who *built* us. I don't mean who bolted arms together, screwed on plating, tunnelled in wiring. I said 'create', One Bolt. What I'm asking is, do you know who *created* us?"

Jacob sat back in his chair. If it wasn't his mom, as Wheeler tried to explain, Jacob was interested to know who it was, then. He stared blankly at Wheeler.

"Humans," Wheeler said. "Humans created us."

Jacob's posture stiffened. There was that word again. *What were they? Who were they?* Without the Mayor standing over him, maybe he would get an answer this time. "Did you say, 'Human'?"

"Yeah, humans."

Jacob just gave Wheeler a blank stare.

Wheeler sighed. He had to dig deep inside his hard-drive to retrieve the information. "Multi-celled organisms with the ability to evolve, adapt, and reproduce," he recited. "Any of this sound familiar?"

Jacob shrugged.

Wheeler slapped the side of his head. "Maybe I picked the wrong partner."

"No…wait! I'm sure I heard of them before. Humans…humans..." Jacob's stare went blank again, but this time, it was because he was attempting to consolidate with his hard-drive. When his stare returned to normal, he simply shook his head. "Can't find anything about humans. But I should know about them, shouldn't I?"

Wheeler shrugged.

"What are they, exactly?"

"I just told you, One Bolt. They were the ones who created us. They created the first mechanical beings."

"Where are they now? I don't think I've seen one before."

"Of course not. They're extinct!"

Another blank stare from Jacob.

"It means they're gone! No more! Get it?"

"They disappeared?"

"Sort of. They evolved into us."

"They were mechanical, like us?"

"No-no. Nothing like us. Sure, they eventually became like us, but that's because things happened along the way. We're the final stage in their evolution. Their origins…their beginnings...were very different from ours. It's too bad you were built when you were, One Bolt. I heard that there was one left not too long ago."

Jacob began waving his hand out in front of him. "Wait. You mean they all shut down?"

"If you can call it that. From what I understand, the last one *died* not too long ago." Wheeler shifted his weight to one side, as did the corner of his mouth. "Well, sort of. Let's just say their extinction was helped along."

"By who?"

"Use your CPU, One Bolt. It's not hard to figure out."

Jacob thought for a moment and then said, "The…Mayor?"

"Of course it was the Mayor. Project Redemption."

"Project Redemption?" *Plan A!* "Tell me more about Project Redemption."

"Not now, One Bolt. Later, I promise. Let's just stay with humans for now."

Jacob's hard-drive began to hum. All this talk about humans was all so new to him. It was best that he record all of the information being thrown in his direction. "Okay, so let me get this straight. Humans created us…"

"Right."

"We evolved from them…"

"Right."

"Now they're all gone…"

"Wow, that CPU of yours—"

"Uh...where are you going with this, exactly?" Jacob asked, his hard-drive temporarily decreasing its speed.

"That takes us up to where we are now," Wheeler explained. "You and I, me and you..." Wheeler paused and moved in so close to Jacob that he could count the rivets in his face by looking at his reflection on Jacob's casing. "Wow, I really need to buff out those scratches below my eyes..." he said, touching his face.

"Get on with it!"

"Okay-okay, One Bolt. We're going to bring them back."

Silence crept between the pair. For Wheeler, his contribution to the silence was on purpose. He wanted to allow Jacob a chance to take it all in. For Jacob, however, the silence was because he was stunned.

Bring them back? Humans? Jacob's only real question was, why? The glow in his eyes stuttered. Jacob had to admit, he could not come up with any answers.

"One Bolt?" Wheeler waved his hand in front of Jacob's face. "Hey, One Bolt, you still there? One Bolt, talk to me!"

The glow in Jacob's eyes stabilized. "Bring them back?"

"Yes, bring them back. Recreate them. You don't listen very well, do you?"

"You mean, build them?"

"No! No! No!" Wheeler burst into a short bout of laughter. "Build them, he says. Yeah, good one. Weren't you even listening to me? You don't build humans." Wheeler reached out, grabbed Jacob's arm and then immediately let go, allowing it to flop back down. "You just can't bolt on an arm, screw on a leg and expect them to work. They're humans. You don't build them. You have to grow them."

"Huh?"

Wheeler shook head. "I have so much to teach you, One Bolt."

Jacob allowed his hard-drive to spin. "I'm listening."

Wheeler suddenly turned from Jacob and looked at the entrance to the classroom. "Oh, no. Not again."

"What? What is it?" Jacob couldn't see around Wheeler's bulk.

"Hope..." Wheeler replied.

"Hope? Hope for what?"

"That Hope!" Wheeler leaned to one side, allowing Jacob a clear view of the doorway.

"Oh...Hope..."

Wheeler noticed the ridiculous smile on Jacob's face. "Exactly! We'll talk more about this later. For now..." He placed a finger on his mouth, "this is between you and me. Got it?"

Jacob seemed more interested in Hope, who had made her way over to the professor.

"One Bolt! Are you listening?"

"Yeah-yeah, sure..."

Wheeler sighed. "Great..."

After a brief exchange of words, Professor Smith escorted Hope to their desk. "Sorry to interrupt you," he said.

"No… it's quite alright, sir," Jacob said.

"Well, we *were* in the middle of something," Wheeler added.

"The assignment I presume?" Professor Smith asked.

Wheeler shrugged. "We were getting there, until… you know… we were kindly interrupted."

"Again, my apologies. And I hate to do this since it appears you were well underway planning your project," Professor Smith said.

"But you will anyway." Wheeler mumbled.

"One your classmates is left without a partner."

"Let me guess," Wheeler said. "Hope?"

"I assume it won't be problem?"

"I'm sure it will—"

Jacob shoved his elbow into Wheeler's side. "No, sir! Not at all."

Before Wheeler could object, the professor clasped his hands together and said, "Brilliant! Three minds together as one. This may very well be the best assignment ever turned in. I guess everything's settled, then. The two…" he shook his head, "I mean, the three of you continue doing what you were doing. I'll be back to check on your progress."

"Thanks, sir," Wheeler said, using the tone Jacob had come to recognize as sarcasm.

The professor walked off, and Hope offered a small smile.

"Sorry. I know you'd rather not have me—"

"No… no-no!" Jacob stood and waved a hand to offer his chair to her. "It's perfectly fine. Really. Like Professor Smith said, three minds are better than one."

"Thank you, Jacob." Hope sat down and looked at Wheeler, who was staring at her with flattened eyes.

Wheeler did not understand why every time he and Jacob had something going, Hope would suddenly show up. It was getting to be rather annoying. "Comfy?"

"Yes." She smiled at him. "Quite."

Although Jacob was now chair-less, it was for a good cause. The smile Hope had offered him more than compensated for the sacrifice of a simple chair. Except now, with no other empty seats nearby, Jacob was left standing.

"You just going stand there?" Wheeler asked.

Jacob shrugged.

"Wait here," Wheeler said in a huff. He revved his wheels and then took off toward the back of the room.

Seconds later, Wheeler returned with a chair in hand. "Here," he said, dropping it next to Jacob. "Take it."

Jacob looked at the chair which looked familiar. Dark wheel marks stained the entire surface. It was definitely Wheeler's. "Don't you need this?"

Wheeler gestured down to his base, pointing out the obvious. "Does it look like I need a chair?"

It was true. Wheeler had no use for a chair, as his wheels were what kept him upright.

"So wait," Jacob said, lowering the plate over his eye, "isn't this the chair you kicked me out of the other day?"

"Yeah. The very one,"

"If you didn't need it, why did you kick me out of it?"

Wheeler looked over at Hope with a smirk on his face. "I need a place to rest my wheel arm. It's heavy."

"You can just set it on the floor," Hope suggested.

"Or I can just use a chair," Wheeler snapped back.

"Okay, calm down." Jacob pushed the chair as close to Hope as he could without making her feel too uncomfortable and then sat down.

"Comfy?" Wheeler asked.

Both Jacob and Hope smiled and then in unison said, "Quite!"

Wheeler slapped the side of his face and sighed. He began mumbling to himself, so Hope leaned closer to Jacob and whispered, "Sorry about my dad. He gets that way sometimes."

"Oh...it's okay," Jacob replied.

"I'm sure he likes you. He's just very particular about his plans."

"Alright, alright! Enough with all this small talk," Wheeler said. "Let's get back to work." He revved his wheels and then drove to the other side of the desk, wedging himself between Hope and Jacob. "This is our last assignment, so no more wasting time."

"I agree," Jacob said.

"I agree too," Hope said. "Have you two decided on a project? What is it going to be about?"

"Yes," Jacob replied. "Wheeler and I were just talking about it. We had this great idea of bringing back—"

"Effects of rust on metal surfaces," Wheeler said.

Jacob and Hope glanced at one another. Both had the same perplexed look on their faces. Then Jacob looked at Wheeler and frowned. "Effects of rust on metal surfaces? But I thought you wanted to—"

"That's the assignment," Wheeler said, cutting Jacob off one more time. "The effects of rust. How it affects metal surfaces. That's our assignment. Our assignment will be about rust!"

"Rust?"

"That's right. Rust!"

Hope wasn't sure of what was going on between the two, but the drama playing out in front of her was quite entertaining. She just sat back and enjoyed the show.

"But that's easy," Jacob said. "Everyone knows what happens when rust forms on metal."

"Yeah, well, there are still a lot of experiments we can do."

"Like what?"

"You know...like going around and finding samples. All sorts of things."

"Go around...looking for rust?"

Wheeler glanced over his shoulder and whispered, "Speaking of rust..."

Professor Smith walked over, stopping next to the unintentional leader of the group. “Well-well.” Professor Smith smiled. “It certainly looks like we've all settled in nicely.”

“Yeah, well...looks can be deceiving,” Wheeler replied.

“We're fine,” Hope said.

“Good. Very good,” Professor Smith said. “I'm willing to guess that the three of you will have something astonishing to tell me about? This is the final assignment, after all.”

“We sure have. The effects of rust on metal surfaces,” Wheeler announced.

Professor Smith had to take a step back. He looked at Jacob who shrugged his shoulders and then at Hope who did the same. Finally, he glanced back at Wheeler who was grinning. “Effects of rust...on metal surfaces?”

“Yes, sir,” Wheeler replied. “You did say this assignment could be about anything.”

“Well...yes...indeed I did,” Professor Smith said. “It...it just doesn't seem all that innovative and challenging. Especially with...” he used his finger and counted, “one, two...three of you.”

“Oh, but it is. We have to do experiments, take samples. It's actually quite a lot of work.”

The Professor had no choice but to back off. His CPU might have been worn down since it had been installed, ages ago, but it was still efficient enough that he remembered giving the class the freedom of choice for this assignment. It was too late for him to change his mind. “Well...okay,” he said, sounding more disappointed than anything. “I'm sure it'll turn out just fine. Just thought...you know, the three of you might do something that would improve our current situation.”

“Oh, without a doubt,” Wheeler said, with a proud look on his face. “Rust is always a problem. It's practically everywhere. Quite ugly at times.”

“Thanks...” Professor Smith covered one of the rusted patches on his face with his hand. “Do you really want your assignment to be about rust? Are you sure there aren't other things the three of you might want to explore? Other problems to solve?”

Wheeler shook his head. “No, sir.”

“Oh...okay, then.” Professor Smith sighed. “Work hard...I guess...”

The trio remained quiet until the professor made his way to the far side of the room to talk to other students.

“He didn't seem too happy,” Hope said.

“No, he didn't,” Jacob agreed. He turned to Wheeler. “What's this about rust? What about...” he cocked his head, hoping that Wheeler remembered the discussion they had, “you know?”

Wheeler shook his head. “I don't know what you're talking about, One Bolt. Let's not waste anymore time. We should get started.”

“Okay, fine,” Jacob said. “Where do we begin? Should Hope and I go and gather samples?”

"I'm okay with that," Hope said.

"Oh, I'm sure you two would like that," Wheeler said, in that familiar sarcastic tone. "But we don't need those just yet."

"Then what are we supposed to do?"

"Just hold on, One Bolt. We have to think this through. We have to take our time and do this right." Wheeler glanced over and quickly scanned the indicator on the left side of Hope's breast-plate. It was orange which meant it would soon be red, and Hope would have to leave. "Just don't rush things, One Bolt..."

"I'm not. And for the last time, stop calling me One Bolt!"

"That's an odd name," Hope said.

"Yes, it is," Jacob replied. "He made it up, not me."

"How did you come up with One Bolt?" Hope asked Wheeler.

Jacob reached up and covered Wheeler's mouth before he had the chance to explain. "I prefer Jacob."

"Yes, so do I," Hope said.

"Relax," Wheeler said, pushing Jacob's hand away from his mouth. "You're going to blow a fuse before we even get this assignment started."

Wheeler glanced at Hope's indicator again, just as it turned to red. He pointed at it. "Will you look at that? Red! Doesn't that mean you have to be getting somewhere, Hope?"

Hope leaped off of her chair. "You're right! I wasn't even paying attention. Thanks, Wheeler."

"Not a problem. That's what I'm here for." Wheeler gave Jacob a big smile.

Jacob was not paying any attention to him at the moment. He stood up and stepped closer to Hope. "Time to recharge? Already?"

"Not exactly. But I need to get going." She gave Jacob her usual smile and then rushed toward the door. "Sorry, you two," she shouted back. "You'll probably have to start the assignment without me. I'll see you tomorrow."

"Yeah-yeah," Wheeler said, not even looking in her direction.

Jacob had barely brought his hand toward his face to wave, when Hope slipped out the door and out of sight. "Bye, Hope..."

At least Wheeler seemed happy now. "Yup...that Hope," he said, "shiny on the outside, mysterious on the inside."

Jacob glanced over his shoulder and noticed that Wheeler was still smiling. "What do you mean by that?"

"Nothing, One Bolt. Just wondering why she's always leaving in the middle of class."

Jacob recalled what had happened the previous day. "Yeah, but you left early, too. Only difference is, you're nowhere near as shiny."

"Such negativity."

"It's true."

Wheeler gave Jacob a wave of his hand. "Have a seat, One Bolt. She's gone for the rest of the day. It'll give us a chance to finally get on with our assignment." Seeing as how Jacob was still standing, Wheeler forcefully dragged him down to his seat.

"Hey, damn it! You could have broken something."

"You shouldn't say that word."

"*314*," Jacob added.

"What?"

"*314*. Don't worry. It's just a number count for every time I use that word."

Wheeler rolled his eyes. "Okay..." *And they tell me that I'm weird.* He then drove himself closer to Jacob. "Anyway, let's get this assignment started."

"Wait, what about Hope? She's part of our team now. We're not going to start without her, are we?"

"Come on, One Bolt. You know damn well we can start this without her."

"*315*."

"Hey, I'm not the one counting. Besides, she said we can start without her. Play it back from your hard-drive. You'll hear it."

"I heard her." Jacob shrugged. "Then...I guess we can start on our own. I mean, it's not a very complicated topic to begin with."

"Not *this* project."

"Huh?"

"Come on, One Bolt," Wheeler cried, shaking his head. "Effects of rust on metal surfaces? That's so..." he glanced down at Jacob, "first generation..."

Jacob rolled his eyes and sighed. "Well...there *are* some things that we still don't know about rust."

"Like what? How it eats away at metal and then sends it back into the Earth?" Wheeler raised his hands in the air. "We did it! We solved the mysteries of rust!" He then glanced at Jacob with one plate over his eye lowered. "That *is* how it works, right?"

"Quiet down, you two!" Professor Smith called out.

Wheeler moved in closer to Jacob and whispered. "Come on, One Bolt. We both know you're more advanced than this. Rust was just a way to cover up our real plans. Humans, remember?"

"Why are you hiding this from Professor Smith and Hope?"

"Because they don't *need* to know. This is between you and me."

"I don't know," Jacob said. "I mean, hiding this from Professor Smith *and* Hope? Trying to bring back humans? Are any of these things even possible?"

"The first part is easy. We just keep telling the professor and Hope what we just said. During class we just act like we are working on the rust project. We can have Hope draw up pretty diagrams, gather samples...whatever. In the end, we'll get a good grade and all is well. But in the mean time, you and I will work on Forever Yaw without them even knowing."

Jacob leaned back. "Wait, what was that? Forever what?"

"Forever Yaw. The name of this secret assignment."

"Who or what is a *Yaw*?"

Wheeler seemed a bit hesitant in replying. "Just...you know...a name..."

"Whose name?"

Wheeler mumbled, "My name."

"*Your* name?" Jacob laughed. "Your real name is *Yaw*?"

"Stop it."

"And you're making fun of me?"

"Stop it! Just stop it!" Wheeler turned away.

"Okay…okay," Jacob said, allowing Wheeler to turn back. "But why is it…" Jacob snickered, "Forever Yaw? What about me? I thought you want me to work on it, too."

"Ha! Forever One Bolt? I don't think so."

"It's better than Forever—"

"Will you forget the name, One Bolt! It's not important. What's important is that I have your promise."

"What promise?"

"That you'll help me with his project."

Jacob looked away. "I don't know. Seems like a lot of work."

"But it'll pay off. Trust me on this. You want to stay on Earth, don't you?"

Jacob looked back in Wheeler's direction. "Of course I do. I never wanted to leave. But what does that have to with anything?"

"That's all I needed to know," Wheeler said, with a satisfied nod.

Although Wheeler seemed content at the moment, Jacob had plenty of empty space on his hard-drive that needed to be filled, primarily with answers about Wheeler's proposed Project Yaw. But before he could formulate a question, Professor Smith stopped in front of the pair. "How is the project planning coming?"

"Good, sir," Wheeler said.

Professor Smith gave Jacob a quick glance. "Everything's working out okay?"

"Yes, sir," Jacob replied.

"Brilliant!" The professor then shifted his attention to Wheeler. "Came back to let you know what time it is."

"Oh…right," Wheeler said. "Thanks, sir."

Jacob noticed Wheeler's mood change all of a sudden. It went from enthusiastic to dull. He wasn't sure why.

"Well, then," Professor Smith said, "I need to step out of the classroom for a moment or two. Do either of you need anything before I go?"

"No, sir," Jacob said. "Nothing that I can think of."

"Wheeler?" The professor asked, with a slight tilt of the head.

"No, sir," Wheeler replied. "I should be okay."

"Great. I'll be right back, then." The professor turned and quickly made his way out the room.

"Why did he remind us of what time it is?" Jacob asked Wheeler.

Wheeler waved it off. "Ah, don't worry about it." He tapped the side of his head. "Professor's got a lot rust up there. Things don't work as well as they used to." Wheeler abruptly changed the subject. "Anyway, One Bolt, I need to ask you something."

"What now?"

"Relax. I just want to know where you live. I'm guessing you're not around here. I see someone dropping you off in front of the school each day."

"That's my mom. We have to drive to get here from sector 333."

"Sector *333*? That far, huh?"

"Yeah, it's far. Can't walk it. Why do you ask?"

"Oh, no reason."

"Where do you live?"

"Pretty far from here, also. You know where the sun completely fades?"

"The other side of Earth?" Jacob said. "I've heard about it, but I've never been there."

"I should take you there sometime."

"Really? When?" Jacob could barely conceal his excitement at the prospect. He had always wanted to see what was on that other side, but his mom refused every request to take him there.

Wheeler's antenna twitched. "Oh...you know. Whenever," he said, suddenly uninterested. He pushed away from the desk. "Listen, One Bolt. We'll talk more about all of this later."

"Where? In the courtyard?"

"No, later. I have to get going."

"Going? Going where?"

"Don't worry about me. Just remember everything we talked about." As Wheeler revved his wheels, Jacob noticed him glancing down at his lunchbox. "Hey, you're not going to drink that can that I brought for you, are you, One Bolt?"

"*Artificial Blend*? No, but—"

Wheeler grabbed the lunchbox, ripped it open and grabbed one of the cans. "Good! Then you won't mind if I borrow it." He left the lunchbox on the desk, spun around and then drove toward the door. When Jacob looked into his lunchbox, he saw that Wheeler had taken the can of *Pure Blend*.

"Hey, wait," Jacob yelled, standing up. "You took the wrong one!"

"I know." Wheeler yelled back, as he disappeared through the door. "I'll bring another one back for you. Promise!"

"But you don't even like..."

The screeching from Wheeler faded to nothing.

Jacob sighed and sat back down. Just as he finished closing his lunchbox, the professor walked back into the room. He stopped in front of Jacob and noticed the practically empty desk.

"He's gone," Jacob said.

It didn't even seem to brother the professor one bit. "I know."

* * *

Jacob sat alone in front of his desk, inside his trophy-filled room. Light from the exposed window claimed every corner of the cramped space. It was unusual for Jacob to have the shutters open to allow the light in, but this time, he had a reason. Jacob pulled his face away from the microscope's eyepiece. "That's what it is," Jacob said. "The light is what causes those little circle things to divide even faster."

He removed the clear slides containing the small section of leaf out from the microscope's holding bay and held it against the light. "What are these tiny things anyway? And why doesn't metal have them?" He placed the slides down on the desk, picked up the plant with one hand and secured a half empty can of *Pure Blend* in the other. He brought the plant up to eye level and studied it, while taking a sip of *Pure Blend.* As he turned the plant to let the light touch it all around, Jacob noted how free flowing and non-mechanical the plant was. Everything around him was of metal—hard, with edges and linear angles, making the plant seem so uniquely out of place.

It must have been odd to live on an Earth full of these things.

Jacob took another sip of his drink. *Then again, it might have actually been pretty neat.* His mouth flattened, and the vents on his cheeks opened, allowing him to sigh deeply. *Too bad it will never be that way ever again.*

Jacob pulled open one of the desk drawers and gently placed the plant inside. "Don't worry. I won't close it." He made sure that there was enough light being allowed inside the drawer, since he now realized how much the plant seemed to benefit from it. "Guess that means that I'll have to keep the window open from now on."

I hate the light. It hurts my eyes.

Jacob took another swallow of his drink, and, as he went to set the can down on the desk, it slipped out of his hand. "Ah, damn it, *315*!"

The remaining *Pure Blend* spilled out from the top of the can and splashed across the slides. "Stupid first generation limbs."

Jacob tipped the can upright and then picked up the slides. *Pure Blend* had seeped through the two clear pieces and soaked the small section of leaf that had placed between them. *That's just great.* He waved his arm a few times, hoping the air would dry out the center of the slide. "Hope it still works," he said, placing the slides back inside the microscope's holding bay. He pressed his eye against the eyepiece, turned the scope one click clockwise and observed. Jacob nearly fell out of his chair.

"Amazing!" Not only were the tiny structures still working, they were dividing more frantically than ever. The plant was thriving off of the *Pure Blend,* in the same way it had from the light. Jacob pulled his eye away from the microscope and stared at the empty can on the desk. "First light, and now this? What's in this stuff?" Jacob placed his eye against the eyepiece again. One look just wasn't enough. Not only were the tiny structures still dividing but each division was being accompanied by a strange thump-clank...thump-clank...

Jacob pulled his eye away from the microscope and sat back in his chair. "That can't be right." The noise obviously wasn't coming from the microscope. He swivelled around to face the door.

Thump-clank...thump-clank...The sound was resonating from outside of his room. "Mom, is that you?" There was no reply, just the same thump-clank...thump-clank...Jacob got up and made his was over to the door.

"Mom," he said, sharpening the tone in his voice. "What are you doing out there?"

Thump-clank…thump-clank…

Why isn't she answering? Maybe his mom had another box in her hands, ready to be dumped off inside his room. *Better open the door for her, then.* As Jacob reached out, the door suddenly swung open and grazed the tip of his shoulder-plate.

Wheeler rolled into his room, and Jacob finally realized what the noise was. The thump was Wheeler's wheel arm landing on each step, while the clank was him pulling the rest of his bulk onto the step. Twenty times, Jacob counted, for each of the twenty steps making up the staircase leading to his room.

"Stairs," Wheeler moaned, leaning against the door frame. "I hate stairs."

"I know what you mean. I hate them too."

"Why? You have legs to climb with. Try climbing stairs using wheels."

Jacob paused and calculated. *Yeah, I guess would be a bit difficult*. "Glad I don't have wheels," he murmured.

"What was that?"

"Nothing."

"Hey, I saw your mom outside. Tall, slender, and sort of shiny, just like you told me...but you never told me she was *that* shiny."

"Huh? What do you mean?"

"You know. Bolts in all the right places. Gears rotating all in sync..." He raised the plates over his eyes a couple times while grinning.

"Get out of here!" Jacob cried in disgust. "That's my mom you're talking about!"

"I'm only teasing, One Bolt. Besides, she was too busy to even notice me drive inside."

"Busy? Doing what?"

"I don't know. Cleaning a bunch of plating or something."

Jacob reeled back. "What? She's cleaning them? I told her not to clean them!"

"At least it'll give you more options." Wheeler used his finger and flicked the red plating that Jacob was still wearing. "I mean, I wasn't going to say anything, One Bolt but red?" He snickered. "Red doesn't look good on you."

"I know, I know. I hate it, too."

"Then why wear it?"

"It's a long story."

"And a boring one, I'm sure."

Jacob sighed. "Anyway...what are you doing here?"

Wheeler reached inside the compartment on his base and pulled out a can. "Here, One Bolt, just like I promised."

Jacob took the can from Wheeler's hand. "*Artificial Blend*? Again?"

"It's all I have."

"Where's the *Pure Blend* that you took from me?"

"All gone."

"Gone? But I thought you didn't—"

Wheeler grabbed the can back from Jacob's hand. "Look, do you want it or not?"

"Of course not. I have a mountain-sized pile of them downstairs. And besides, I don't even like it."

"Fine. I'll keep it, then." Wheeler placed the can back in the compartment inside his base. Pushing Jacob aside, he then invited himself into the room. "Thought I would at least get a 'thank you' for my efforts," he mumbled. "But no. 'It's not my brand. I have mountain-size pile'..." Wheeler stopped in the heart of the room. His ramblings immediately ceased. With Jacob out of the way, Wheeler had the chance to view the room in its entirely. Wall-engulfing trophies were starved for attention, and Wheeler was content on feeding their request. They called out to him with their blinding highlights, caused by the light surging through the window. "Will you look at these!"

"All first places," Jacob said, with a huge smile.

Wheeler had to see for himself. He drove over to one of the trophies and scanned the inscription. "First place..." he said, running his hand along its smooth surface. Right below was the inscription *Assignment 051773*. "Create a model of the Earth and moon...Yeah, I remember that one." He moved on to the next trophy. "First place." Below that was the inscription *Assignment 091775*. "Harness the sun's light," Wheeler recited, shaking his head. "Didn't hand that one in," he whispered. He moved on to the next trophy, and, as predicted, it was another first place. "They all say first place."

"Didn't I just tell you that?" Jacob made his way over to Wheeler and gave him a poke to the side using his elbow. "Are you impressed?"

Wheeler tilted his head. "For a first generation?"

"Ah, don't start with that first generation thing again." Jacob walked over to his desk.

Wheeler met up with him. "I didn't mean it a bad way, One Bolt. What I meant was..." Wheeler offered Jacob a forced smile, "...as a first generation, you did good."

"Yeah...Thanks...I guess."

"No, really, you did good." Wheeler spotted *Assignment 051773* on Jacob's desk. He gave both the moon and Earth models a gentle nudge with his hand. "Nearly perfect."

"Almost. I created the moon model while it was still pretty far from here."

"I noticed. You're missing a few details, but it's not bad."

Jacob nearly threw himself onto the desk in order to look closely at the moon model. "What? Really? Where?"

"It's no big deal. Like you said, the moon was probably still high in the sky. I'm impressed that you managed to get the big hole missing from its side."

Jacob gently turned the moon on its axis. "It was the first thing I modelled."

"Well, you won first place. That's all that matters." Wheeler took his attention away from the models only to notice the microscope sitting on the desk. "What are you looking at?"

"All the craters," Jacob replied. "I might have missed a few."

"Not that." Wheeler pulled the microscope. "I meant in here."

"Oh…that." Jacob crossed both arms over his chest-plate. "Go ahead. See for yourself."

Wheeler placed his eye against the microscope's eyepiece. Almost immediately, he pushed away and yelled, "What? You've already started?"

Jacob stepped back. "What?"

"Forever Yaw! You've already started?"

"What are you talking about?"

"Forever Yaw! These cells!" Wheeler gave Jacob a firm stare. "Humans!"

Jacob took a quick peek inside the eyepiece and then looked back up at Wheeler with a blank stare. "What?"

"Humans, remember? I told you this already. Humans are made up of cells. Exactly what you have going on in here," Wheeler said, tapping the side of the microscope.

"Those things that are dividing are cells?"

"Yeah. The building blocks of life. Those are what humans consist of. Sort of like us with metal."

"But…but how?"

"They just do, One Bolt. No need for a long scientific explanation right now." Wheeler looked around the room. "Where did you get this sample? Better yet, *how* did you get this sample?"

Jacob took the plant out of the desk drawer and gently handed it to Wheeler. "I took a small sample from this. My mom told me that it's a plant. There used to be a lot of them on Earth."

Wheeler scanned each section of the strange-looking object. He observed the organic shape and was astonished at nearly every aspect of it. "Weird...but oddly fascinating."

"I'm guessing you've never seen anything like it before?"

Wheeler shook his head. "Never. Where on Earth did you find it?"

"Behind my house. It was sticking out from underneath the dirt. That's the only one I was able to find."

Wheeler took another look through the microscope's eyepiece. "So this plant thing contains cells too?" he mumbled. "I would have never guessed."

A strange beep suddenly sounded off from somewhere deep inside Wheeler's chest.

"What was that?" Jacob asked.

"What?"

"You didn't hear that beeping noise? It sounded like it came from inside you."

"Oh…that… it's nothing."

"Didn't sound like nothing," Jacob whispered. He reached out and grabbed the plant from Wheeler. "Don't mean to be rude, but they're hard to find." Jacob placed the plant back in the drawer but did not close it. "Need to keep the light on it."

"Why?"

"I don't know. For some reason the light makes the cells divide even quicker."

"It…it does?"

"Yup."

Another beep resonated from Wheeler's chest.

"Okay, now I know you heard that one." Jacob leaned over and peeked through the seam of Wheeler's chest-plate. He noticed orange indicator lights just below the surface. "Your batteries low?"

"It's nothing," Wheeler said, turning away from Jacob.

"Doesn't look or sound like nothing. Do you need to recharge?"

"I said, no!"

"Okay…okay. Just asking. Thought the drive out here might have drained your batteries."

"I'm fine, One Bolt! Can we just stay on topic?"

Jacob backed off. "Okay…fine." He leaned back against the desk. "So…regarding Forever Yaw…I still hate that name..."

"Forget the name!"

"Okay-okay. On the way home from school, I did some calculations—"

"Oh, no…Doubts…I knew it." He crossed his arm over his chest. "Go on, One Bolt. What is it?"

"Here, let me show you." Jacob walked over to the window, making sure that Wheeler followed. They stopped in front of the window and looked outside. There was a long pause, followed by mindless calculations, all strung together by a bout of complete silence. "I don't know if we have enough time to complete our project."

"Oh…right…" Wheeler finally said." The moon…"

"Changes our plans, doesn't it?"

Wheeler pushed away from the window. "Completely forgot about it."

"How could you? I mean, it's the only thing in the sky…well, it and the sun."

"Guess I got all excited about the prospects of…you know…Forever Yaw." He glanced over at Jacob. "Yeah-yeah…you hate the name."

They both turned their backs on the moon and leaned against the window frame.

Jacob shrugged and said, "You do know it's going to hit Earth, right?"

"Of course I do. You're not the only one who can calculate, you know."

"Well, I'm just saying. It might be sooner than later."

"How soon?"

"I don't know, exactly."

"Great. The most advanced CPU ever and he doesn't know."

"All I know is that it'll happen, so that doesn't leave lot of time for whatever you have planned." A brief moment of silence went by before Jacob asked, "How long does it take to…you know…build a human?"

"Build?"

"You know what I mean."

Wheeler shrugged. "I don't know. I thought you might with that advanced CPU of yours."

Jacob pushed away from the window and began pacing back and forth. "I don't know everything. Not with my current CPU. If I got an upgrade maybe. But my mom keeps telling me to wait and see."

"Wait for what?" Wheeler asked, joining Jacob.

"I have no idea. But that's what she keeps telling me."

"We don't have time to wait and see about anything. If we're going to do this, we have to do it now."

"But the moon—"

"Forget about the moon, One Bolt. Yeah, I see it. It's out there. It's going to hit. We'll just have to work twice as fast."

"Maybe three times."

"Or four, or five. It's doesn't matter. Our main priority right now is Forever Yaw…recreating humans."

Jacob stopped pacing. He placed both his hands on his hips. "See…that's what I don't understand. This whole 'human' thing. Exactly why are we trying to recreate them again? Why are they so important?"

"You want to stay here on Earth, don't you?"

"Of course."

"And you don't want to go with the Mayor on his *Quest for New Hope* or whatever he calls it, right?"

"No. I mean, I don't even think *he* knows where he wants to take us."

"Of course not."

"But what does all of this have to do with humans?"

"Okay...okay. Try to follow me, One Bolt." Wheeler spoke as clearly as he could. "Humans created us a long time ago. Now they're extinct. All of them. And now, with the help of our friend, the Mayor, you and I...our kind, are the ones who are going to become extinct."

Jacob lowered his head.

"Depressing, I know."

"So how will it help us to recreate the humans?"

"Okay, try to stay with me, One Bolt. We're a moon's collision away from joining the humans. So the way I see it…humans created us. They made us who we are. They made as strong at one time. So they can create us again. Then we can evolve and become as strong as we once were."

"So *that's* what…" The glow in Jacob's eyes suddenly flashed a brilliant white, nearly engulfing each lens. "…Forever Yaw is all about."

"Humans created us, but now they're gone. And for them to create us again, we need to bring them back. Recreate the ones who created us," Wheeler said, nodding.

"Recreate the ones who created us," Jacob repeated. The hum of his hard-drive could be heard rumbling within his chest-plate. *It might just work. Wheeler may look weird, reek of oil and rubber but his plan might actually work.* "And if it works, we might not have to leave Earth at all," Jacob said, wide-eyed.

"Nope. Never."

"And the Mayor will—"

"Whoa, whoa...I have to stop you right there, One Bolt. The Mayor can't know about this."

"All I was going to say was—"

"Nope. Sorry, One Bolt. We have to keep Forever Yaw away from him. In fact, no one outside of this room needs to know."

"Not even—"

"No one. Not the Mayor, not Hope."

"Hope?"

"Especially Hope. Her dad's the one who got us into this mess in the first place. Can you imagine what he would say, or do, if he found out that we're trying to bring back humans? The Mayor! The one who resorted to Project Redemption in order to get rid of them?"

"Project Redemption? I keep hearing that. What was it, exactly?"

"Forget about it. It's done. It's the past. What's important is that we work on the future. *Our* future." Wheeler placed his finger against Jacob's mouth. "And no one needs to know about it except me and you. Not even your mom."

"My...my mom?"

"Don't worry, One Bolt. Once Forever Yaw is complete, I'll let you be the first to tell her. But in the mean time..." Wheeler removed his finger from Jacob's mouth and placed it against his own mouth.

"I got it."

The door of Jacob's room suddenly swung open.

"Got what?" Jacob's mom said, inviting herself inside. In her hand was a can of *Pure Blend.* "Oh. I didn't know someone was in here with you, Jacob."

"Mom, Wheeler. Wheeler, Mom."

Wheeler drove over and stopped in front of Grace. "Ms. Jacob. It's a pleasure meeting you. Please, call me Yaw." He grabbed Grace's hand and pressed it against his mouth.

"Oh, my," Grace said. "How formal."

Jacob cringed. *Formal?* This was the same one who was calling him "One Bolt".

"Nice to meet you, Yaw. Please, call me Grace."

"Can I call you Grace?" Jacob asked.

"No." Grace gave Jacob the can of *Pure Blend.* "Here, I want you to drink this."

Wheeler watched with wide-eyes, as Jacob took the can.

"I do apologize, Yaw," Grace said. "If I knew you were up here, I would have brought some *Artificial Blend* for you."

"That's quite alright, Ms. Jacob."

"He brought his own," Jacob said. "He doesn't like *Pure Blend.*" Jacob smirked. "Do you, Wheeler?"

"That is correct, Jacob."

Jacob? What happened to One Bolt?

"Are you sure, Yaw?" Grace asked. "We have plenty."

"Yes, Ms. Jacob. But thank-you for your offer."

"Grace. Call me, Grace."

"That wouldn't feel right..." He let the sentence fade when he saw her staring at his set of wheels. "Ms. Jacob? Is something wrong?"

Grace waved her hand. "Oh! I'm sorry, Yaw. I didn't mean to stare. It's just...I haven't seen wheels in a long time. I guess that's why they call you Wheeler."

Wheeler nodded.

Grace noticed something oddly familiar with Wheeler's wheels, but she could not understand why.

"My mom says she used to have a car with wheels and drove around in it."

"Really?" Wheeler said. "Well, I can assure you, Ms. Jacob, these wheels did not come from a car...at least, I don't think they did."

"I'm curious, Yaw," Grace said. "Back when I had a car with wheels, there was still natural gravity everywhere. How are you able to keep yourself magnetized these days?"

Wheeler lifted his massive wheel arm up in the air. "Embedded metal studs."

"Clever."

"It was either that or bye-bye Wheeler." Wheeler suddenly felt the antennae on his back twitch. "Which reminds me..." He grabbed Grace's hand again and placed it against his mouth. "I have certainly enjoyed your company, Ms. Jacob, but I have to be on my way."

"But didn't you just get here?"

"That is correct. And I do apologize for leaving so abruptly, but I have prior engagements that I must keep."

"Do you need a ride?"

"That's quite alright, but thank-you for asking."

"You sure?" Jacob asked. "I thought you lived somewhere where the sun fades. Sounds far."

"Yes, Jacob, but I can manage." Wheeler drove over to the door and then paused to look back at Jacob. "Remember what we talked about."

"Yeah-yeah, I recorded everything."

Wheeler then turned his attention to Grace. "Ms. Jacob, it's been a pleasure." As he bent over to give her a little bow, his wheels started to roll backwards.

"Wait... Yaw!" Grace yelled.

Thump-clank-clank-thump... clank-clank!

The awful sound went on for at least twenty more times before ending with a single, loud thud.

Jacob and his mom raced over to the top of the staircase and looked down. Wheeler had already pulled himself off the floor and was back upright.

From where they were standing, they heard Wheeler mumbling, “Damn stairs. I hate stairs.”

“Me, too,” Jacob yelled.

Wheeler looked up. “Oh…I do apologize for the clumsiness. The wheels are in need of a good greasing.”

“Are you okay?” Grace asked.

“No damage that can’t be patched up.” Wheeler put his wheel arm down on the floor and then sped off toward the front door. “I’ll just let myself out.” Wheeler pushed on the handle, but the door did not open.

“Pull,” Grace said.

“Oh…*pull,*” Wheeler said. The door opened with one single pull.

“I make that mistake myself sometimes,” Grace said.

“No, you don’t,” Jacob said which resulted in an elbow to the side from his mom.

“Thanks again,” Wheeler called out, as he sped out the door and out of sight.

“Wow,” Grace said. “He's weird.

Jacob took a sip of his *Pure Blend* and replied, “You have no idea.”

Chapter Four

Eve knew everything her father was telling her wasn't true, but she didn't care. How often did she get the opportunity to be with him? It was just nice to be by his side. They reclined next to each other, looking up at the black sky that was drenched with stars—smiles never even attempting to leave their faces. Her father pointed up at one of the constellations. They both knew what the constellation was, but it was the stories that he created that made being out in the wind and cold all worthwhile. His finger overlapped the last star in the grouping.

"See that, Eve? That's the dragon's tail. The knight would run up its tail, all the way across its back and then free the princess from its mighty jaws."

"Did they escape, Daddy?"

"Of course they did, Eve. And they lived happily ever after."

"Well, if that's a dragon and that is its tail, why is it called the Little Dipper?"

Her father scratched his head. "Well, Eve...it's because of...because it dips..." He looked over at her and chuckled. "Because the dragon's owner is named Dipper?"

They both shared something that they both thought didn't exist anymore—genuine laughter.

The silent night cast itself over the pair once more. Eve inched closer to her father and then wrapped her arm around him. Though her future was uncertain, that fact lacked any sort of meaning at a time like this. During the difficult times they were going through, it was nearly impossible for anyone to find such peaceful seclusion, and she treasured these stolen moments with her father. Even the small patch of grass felt soft and inviting beneath her.

"And that?" Eve asked, pointing to the next constellation.

"The one that looks like an hour glass?"

"Yes, that one, Daddy."

"That one represents time. Whenever you look up at it and hope for something, time will stand still until you get what you hoped for." He looked over at her. "That's why you never stop hoping."

Although he sounded serious this time, Eve couldn't help but laugh. "Really? So why is it called Orion?"

"It was the name of that dragon?"

They laughed, but as usual, the merriment was short-lived. Their eyes eventually were drawn to the brightest star in the sky. They knew it as the North Star, and it was the one star that Eve didn't question her father about. He had told her that it was her mother, Sarah, looking down at them.

Eve's father hoped the star would always shine brightly and watch over Eve, protecting her when he wasn't around.

Eve hoped the star reminded her father that they were once a family…that they still were a family.

"I know the future of mankind is in doubt, but I want you to always remember something, Eve. I'll always love you, no matter what happens. That's why I have to do what I do. It'll make life better…for the both of us."

Eve fell quiet, the way she always did when he father talked about "work".

Eve's father stared up at the star he thought of as Sarah. He loved looking at stars but never wanted to look up and see Eve shining down on him.

Eve closed her eyes. She wanted to tell her dad that she loved him but didn't want to have to conclude by asking, "But for how long?"

* * *

The hum of the car's simple engine was the only sound heard inside the car, as Grace drove Jacob to school. Grace assumed that it was the fact that Jacob was wearing red plates for the third consecutive day that was keeping him scrunched on the other side of the car, silent. She sighed.

"I put them all back inside your closet. White, blue, yellow…they're all there. I even cleaned them for you, just like you asked me to."

Drab scenery, stained by the moon's growing presence, rolled by Jacob's window in a dull blur. "But I never asked you to clean them, Mom."

"Oh? I thought you did."

"No. I didn't. And even if I did, you forgot to bring up the clips. How am supposed to attached the plates onto myself without the clips?" Jacob raised his arm in the air and then immediately threw it back down, angrily. "I hate red!"

"But it looks so adorable—"

"Mom!" Jacob turned away. He obviously didn't agree with her, and she should have known this by now.

"I honestly don't know what happened," Grace said. "I thought I had asked Pin-bot to bring the plates up to your room *with* the clips. All I heard from her were a bunch of random beeps, so I assumed she did." She sighed again. "That Pin-bot…Can't understand what she's saying half the time."

"That's why I wanted to modify her," Jacob explained. "I wanted to give her a voice. No more beep-beep. But you didn't want me to."

"She has an adaptive CPU, Jacob. I know it's simple at times, but she'll learn how to speak, eventually."

"It's taking forever. Maybe I can adjust a few things—"

"No! No more modifying her. Please!" Jacob's mom shook her head. "I don't even know what model number she is."

"Model number? What does that have to do with anything?"

Grace faced Jacob and gave him a stern look. "Just don't! I'll get her to bring up the clips when I get back home. And it won't be a moment too soon.

It looks like you'll need new plating to cover up all of those new scratches. How did you get those anyway?"

Jacob turned away, attempting to hide the blemishes along his arms, but there were far too many to conceal from prying eyes. "Not sure what you're referring to," he said.

"I may be old, Jacob, but I'm not blind."

I know you're old, Mom, but I never said that you were blind.

"Were they caused by that loud sound I keep hearing from your room every time you're finished recharging?"

Jacob forced a smile across his face. "Oh…I didn't think you heard that."

"Of course I do. Who do you think has to pick up the charger every time?"

Jacob replaced his smile with a look of innocence. "But I'm getting better at it. I got out this time with only two scratches." He stuck his arm out in plain view. "See? Only two!"

Grace reached out and ran her fingers across Jacob's arm, feeling the depth of the scratches. They were merely surface deep, not exactly critical but enough to concern her. "We might have to buff them out."

Jacob retracted his arm. "No, we don't. I'll just cover them up with my other plating…once I get the clips back."

"Yes, good idea," Grace said, placing her hand back on the steering wheel. "You know, Jacob, those scratches you got, from trying to get out of the charger, could have been avoided altogether."

Jacob did the calculations. With his first generation limbs and the charger's firm grip, the conclusion was straightforward. "Impossible!"

"Not at all. You see, Jacob." Grace glanced at him for a moment. "I know you want to evolve and do things on your own, but it's okay to ask for help. That's what Pin-bot and I are here for." Grace checked the road in front of them. "Take advantage of the help while you can. We won't be around forever…I won't be around forever."

Jacob snickered. "What do you mean, you won't be around forever? Why not?"

Grace reached up and tapped the small patch of rust just behind her ear, the one that Jacob had so humbly pointed out to her a few days ago.

Jacob sighed. "Oh…right…rust…"

"Like it or not, Jacob, rust will eventually find its way onto everything. And Earth will reclaim everything that was once hers." Grace could hear the loud hum radiating from Jacob's hard-drive, as it spun violently, attempting to make sense of the rather confusing information she was offering to him.

"So…you're going away?" Jacob said softly.

Grace offered Jacob a smile, but it didn't seem like he was accepting the reassurance she put behind it. "Not for a long time," she said.

"But you will?"

"We all will…eventually. That's the way it goes."

"Even me?"

"Yes, Jacob, even you."

Jacob turned sharply and stared out the passenger's side window. "Doesn't seem fair."

"Not initially. But you have to remember something, Jacob. We all came from the Earth at one time. Isn't it fair that once we shut down that we should return to where we came from? I mean, if I borrowed something from your room, isn't if fair that I return it after I'm done using it?"

"Didn't you *borrow* my plating-clips and forget to bring them back?"

"Serious, Jacob. Please?"

The vents on Jacob's cheeks opened, and he let out a long sigh. "Yeah, I guess you're right, Mom. It's only fair."

Grace patted Jacob on the head. "Nothing to worry about. It will be a long time before the Earth reclaims either of us. So in the meantime, if help is offered to you, Jacob, please accept it."

Jacob quickly did some calculations. "But that's also why I need to start doing things for myself. I have to learn to do things myself for when...you know..." he paused, as if uncertain how to continue. "...the Earth reclaims you before me." Jacob shook his head. "Sorry, Mom...I know you don't want to hear that."

Surprisingly, Grace smiled. "No, Jacob. You're right." Grace didn't want to admit it, but her CPU was advanced enough for her to know that her return to the Earth would commence well before Jacob's. Everything she kept on her hard-drive seemed to revolve around Jacob lately, so the thought of not being around to see him evolve was difficult for her to accept.

"So? How do I get out of the charger on my own without causing any scratches? I've tried. It's impossible."

"Once the charger is on, and running, you fall into a dormant state, but not all parts of you are dormant. Some parts are still active, even if you don't know it. I have to lock you in place, otherwise you'd fall out."

"Really?"

"Yes. You did fall out once while recharging. Fortunately, Pin-bot was there to alert me so I could get you back in."

"Yeah, I'm glad she's around." Jacob waited for his mom to continue, but oddly, she remained quiet. "Mom?"

Grace glanced over. "Yes?"

"Well?"

"Well, what?"

"Aren't you going to tell me the rest? How do I get out?"

"What more is there to say? I just told you everything you needed to know."

"I...I don't understand. You mean...Pin-bot has to help me?"

"No, Jacob. Just look down."

Jacob did just that but saw nothing but his feet and the under carriage of the car. "Down? At what? What am I supposed to be looking at?"

Grace giggled. "Not now. When you're in the charger. Look down, and you'll see the tabs. They are what lock your feet in place when you're inside.

Just release them, and you'll get out with no more scratches. And I won't have to pick up the machine every time."

The plates over Jacob's eyes lowered, while the motors behind his face tightened. "Release the tabs? That's it?"

"That's it."

Jacob raised his arm and observed the scratches that didn't need to be there. "Wow, that sounds easy enough," he admitted. "So I could have prevented all of these?"

She nodded.

Jacob glanced over to his mom with a mischievous smile. "Well, then…guess the only way to remove these scratches is with an upgrade."

Grace only stared at him.

"Yeah-yeah. Wait and see," Jacob mumbled. "I knew you were going to say that."

"You're learning," his mom joked. "Besides, Jacob, your other plates will cover up most of those scratches."

"And they will give me the chance to get out of these red ones. Even Wheeler hates red."

"Yaw?"

Jacob snickered.

"What's so funny?"

"Nothing. Just think it's a funny name."

"That's not very nice."

Jacob threw his hands out to the side. "But, Mom, he calls me '*One Bolt*'."

Grace snickered. "One…Bolt? What is One Bolt?"

"It's not funny."

"Sorry, Jacob. What's One Bolt?"

Jacob waved it off. "Nothing. Never mind. It's a stupid name. Just call me Jacob, like always."

"Okay…*Jacob*."

"Better."

Before Jacob could even turn away, Grace abruptly added, "That reminds me, what was Yaw doing at our house yesterday? What were the two of you talking about? I heard you mentioning Forever…something."

Jacob suddenly felt heavy in his seat. He couldn't tell her. Wheeler had been adamant about telling anyone about Forever Yaw. Jacob propped up his lunchbox, wedging it tightly between himself and his mom, as if it could somehow keep mom's suspicions on the other side of the car. "N-Nothing, really," he said, with a slight jitter in his voice.

"So…he drove all that way to talk to you about nothing? Seems like a big waste of time."

Jacob slapped his forehead. "Oh…I forgot. You're right. We *were* talking about something. Just an assignment that Professor Smith wants us to do."

"Oh? An assignment? I guess he has one final assignment left in him."

"It's a good one, too. We were allowed to choose the topic, and we got to pick partners."

Grace glanced over at Jacob. "And you picked Yaw?"

Jacob sighed. "Not exactly."

"What is your assignment about? I bet it'll be good since two of you are working on it."

Jacob gripped his lunchbox even tighter. "Nothing you would be interested in."

"I'm always interested in your assignments...as long as they are done outside of our house."

"This one's not that important."

"A final project about anything and with a partner and it's not important?"

Jacob smiled. "Yes."

"Well...that seems like a waste."

"Trust me, Mom. It won't be."

Something about the way he was clutching that lunchbox made Grace wonder what was making him so nervous. What was he hiding? Should she ask? She decided not to. Sometimes younger generations needed to have secrets just between themselves. "Okay, then," she said. "You've always won first place with your assignments, so I'll trust you on this."

"Thanks, Mom."

Jacob eased his hold on the lunchbox and did some calculations. Something intrigued him, and, as long as he didn't mention Forever Yaw directly, a simple question wouldn't be breaking Wheeler's trust. At least, he hoped not. Jacob looked up at his mom and asked, "Any chance we could talk about humans?"

Grace felt the back of her head bump against the seat's head rest. "Humans? I'm not sure I heard you over the engine noise. Did you say *humans*?"

That was odd. The car's engine doesn't make any noise. "Yes," Jacob said, using a firmer tone. "*Humans*!"

"Okay, Jacob. No need to shout."

"I thought you said you didn't hear me the first time."

"What made you suddenly ask me about humans?"

Jacob shrugged. "I don't know. Just curious."

Grace looked over at Jacob, not sure this was a matter of simple curiosity, then she turned her attention back to the road. "What...exactly do you want to know about them?"

"How about everything? I can't seem to find anything on my hard-drive about them."

The white glow in Grace's eyes dimmed. There was a long pause. Jacob could hear his mom's hard-drive grinding inside its enclosure behind her breast-plate. The information he had requested must have been stored away deep within the inner circumference of her hard-drive, as the brief pause turned into an anxious wait. When the spinning of Grace's hard-drive finally stopped, it still took her a moment or so before the glow in her eyes returned.

Jacob could see her eyes shifting back and forth, conjuring up some sort of reply.

"Mom? What did you find out? Did you know about them?"

"Well... yes. Of course. I was around when they were still on Earth. But only for the final stages of their evolution."

Jacob's hard-drive began its usual humming, as it did every time new information was offered to him. "Tell me more," he said eagerly. "Everything you know."

Grace stiffened her posture. "Well, there's a lot to tell you."

"I have space on my hard-drive."

Grace smiled. "I'll tell you as much as I can." She shifted to lean her weight to one side and then continued, "They were unique, humans were. Strong at times, but very weak where it mattered the most."

"Weak *and* strong?"

"Yes. They were strong in that they survived much longer than they should have, under the conditions that they had forced upon themselves. But they were weak for the same reasons."

"I don't understand."

"They weren't like us at all, Jacob. They were extremely fragile. They took everything they needed to survive from the Earth, completely draining it of all its resources. Their bodies were capable of adapting to many things, but not to the death of Earth—their home. Sickness became common. That's like a virus to you and I."

"I thought we were able to eliminate viruses completely not too long ago."

"We were. Unfortunately, they weren't. With Earth no longer able to sustain them, sickness quickly destroyed most of them."

"But you said they were strong."

"Yes, they were. They had the unique ability to create, in order to solve problems." Grace raised her arm. "Without them, we wouldn't exist."

"They created us." *Just like Wheeler said.*

Grace glanced over at Jacob with a sharp gleam in her eye. "Yes, exactly, Jacob. How did you know?"

"Oh...just something I picked up here and there. So how...and why, did they create us?"

"The peak of their evolution had come and gone, and their existence was declining. They were quickly dying." She raised the plate over one eye. "Shut down," she explained to Jacob.

"Yes, I know, Mom."

"Good. Didn't think you knew. So anyway, with Earth no longer able to sustain them, they had no choice but to create us. We were simple at first—just an arm to replace their own, or a leg to help support their weight."

"Upgrades?" *Must be nice.*

"Yes, Jacob. I guess you can call it that. Eventually, simple arms and legs became complete mechanical beings, and the balance quickly shifted in our favour. One thing lead to another and here we are. Exactly where the humans found themselves during their final stages of evolution—facing extinction."

There was a long pause before Jacob said, "That's it? After we were created, humans simply shut down? There has to be more to it than that."

"You mean *died*. Yes, Jacob. They *died* out. But that's part of evolution. They evolved...into us. And that's when they sealed their own fate. Their demise was the direct result of their own creations."

"But I thought the Mayor had something to do with it. Project Redemption...whatever that is."

Grace tightened her grip on the steering wheel. She knew Jacob was eventually going to ask her about the Mayor. How could a conversation involving humans not involve the Mayor? "He didn't want their diseases and sicknesses to spread. Getting rid of them was the first stage of freeing our kind from their weaknesses."

"And I suppose leaving the Earth is the final stage?"

"He certainly makes it seem that way, doesn't he?"

"If humans are all gone now, why does he still need to worry?"

Grace turned her head toward the side window and fell silent.

"Mom?" Jacob reached over and tapped her shoulder. "Hey, Mom!"

"Yes, Jacob?" she softly said.

"What's the Mayor so worried about? How can their sickness spread if they're no longer around? They are all gone, aren't they?"

"I don't know the reason. Maybe you should ask him."

Jacob sighed. "Yeah, I guess I should have."

Grace turned toward Jacob. "What did you say?"

"I said, 'I should have asked him'. The Mayor. I met him the other day."

The car gave a sudden jerk, and Jacob grabbed the door handle to keep from banging into the dash. "Mom! Enough with the metal foot!"

"Sorry, Jacob. That wasn't metal foot."

"Bare spot on the road?"

"No, still metal." She leaned a little toward Jacob. "You...met the Mayor?" she asked, pitching her voice at the end.

"Yeah. That's why everyone was gathered outside the school the other day. To see the Mayor. He did one of his speeches. You know...points toward the sky...future amongst the stars."

There was a long pause before Grace responded. She readjusted her weight so that it was evenly dispersed against the seat. "So you met him..."

"Yes, Mom. Weren't you listening? Then after his speech, Hope introduced me to him. She told me that her dad really wanted to meet me."

"Well...what happened?" Grace asked, with an obvious spike in her voice. "I mean...did he say anything to you? Why did he want to see you?"

"Slow down, Mom. One question at a time."

Grace sighed deeply. "Okay. What happened when you met him?"

"Nothing. He was just curious to see the one with all the trophies. When he saw that it was me, a first generation, he looked a bit surprised." *Can you blame him? I surprise myself sometimes.*

"That's all? Nothing else?"

"Yes, Mom." Jacob leaned back in his seat wondering why his mom was prodding him with her questions. "Have you ever met the Mayor?"

"A long time ago. And I haven't seen him since. It's better that way."

Jacob placed his lunchbox on his lap, unconsciously removing the barrier he had tried to erect before. "It was strange," he said. "When I first saw him he looked so…I don't know... familiar for some reason."

Grace perked up in her seat. "He…he did?"

"Yeah. But whenever I try to check my hard-drive to find out if I have seen him before, it skips."

"That probably doesn't mean anything. Everything and everyone starts looking the same after a while." Grace hoped that lame excuse was enough to convince Jacob.

"Yeah, you're right," Jacob said.

"It's best that you don't bother him anymore, Jacob. He's busy, and I'm sure he doesn't like to be disturbed."

Jacob nodded and then stared off into the sky, where the moon hung huge and heavy. "Yeah, busy with his plans to take us to nowhere," he mumbled.

* * *

In front of the school, the car lowered and shifted into idle mode. Jacob saw Wheeler jump down from the curb and race over. He reached out and attempted to yank the side door open.

"Hey! What's the matter with this thing?" Wheeler cried.

"Pull harder," Jacob replied, his voice muffled within the car's interior.

Wheeler revved his wheels until a band of pure-white smoke burst out from underneath him. That was the effort needed to finally pull the door open. "Needs new hinges and a lot of oil," Wheeler said.

"You or the door?"

"Yeah…good one, One Bolt." Wheeler backed away from the door. "I'll bring some tomorrow. See if we can fix this for you."

"It's okay, Yaw." Grace said, peeking around Jacob. "It's on its last few trips before becoming one with the Earth. No point in slowing down its progress."

"Ms. Jacob," Wheeler said, with an exaggerated smile. "It's a pleasure seeing you again and so soon since our last meeting."

"Nice to see you too, Yaw."

"Yeah, nice to meet you too, Wheeler," Jacob said sarcastically. He reached over and grabbed his lunchbox.

"Need a hand with that?" Wheeler pointed to the lunchbox.

Jacob thought about it. The conclusion was quick, nearly instant. After being basically robbed of his *Pure Blend*, on more than one occasion, there was absolutely no way Wheeler was going to get his hand on the lunchbox. "No, but you can help me get out."

"What? You have legs," Wheeler backed away, allowing Jacob to jump out of the car, unassisted.

"Yeah, legs," Jacob replied, with a smirk, as he looked down at Wheeler's base. "Nice things to have."

"You're on a roll," Wheeler said.

"Look who's talking."

Jacob's mom leaned over. "What's going on out there?"

Wheeler drove himself in front of Jacob. "Absolutely nothing, Ms. Jacob. Just a friendly meet and greet."

"Oh...well, that's nice of you, Yaw."

"Thank you, Ms. Jacob."

So well-mannered when she's around. Jacob sighed. *Who was Wheeler trying to fool?*

Grace switched the car from idle to on. It lifted off of the ground and maintained a near silent hum. "Have a nice day, Jacob. You too, Yaw." She reached over and closed the car door.

"Jacob and I will," Wheeler said.

The pair watched and waved until the car was swallowed by the deep horizon. In unison, their hands lowered.

"I like your mom, One Bolt," Wheeler said. "She's nice."

"What happened to 'Jacob'?"

"What?"

"You use my real name when my mom is around."

Wheeler glanced at the horizon to the exact spot that had taken Jacob's mom from their sights. "Since she's no longer here...it's One Bolt."

I knew you were going to say that.

Wheeler pointed at the lunchbox in Jacob's hand. "*Pure Blend*?"

"Two cans a day, every day."

"Good," Wheeler said, smiling. "Very good."

Jacob held the lunchbox behind him, keeping it as far away as possible from Wheeler. "Why? Are you planning on taking another one before I get the chance to say no?"

Wheeler pointed at himself. "Me?" he replied exaggeratedly. "I always ask before I take."

"Not exactly. You take before you ask. Doesn't give me a chance to say no."

"Well, well, well! My apologies, One Bolt. Didn't know you'd make such a big deal about it."

"I don't even know why you need *Pure Blend* in the first place. You said you didn't like it."

"I don't."

"So why do you take them from me?"

"Not important at this particular moment. What's important is that we follow our plan. Forever Yaw, remember? We can work on it at my place."

"What? Why not at the school?"

"Because nobody can know about it, remember?"

Jacob had to admit that the prospect of going to the dark side of the Earth was exciting. He turned and faced the school, just in time to see the last classmate disappear through the main door.

"They're all in. Time for us to go." Wheeler began revving his wheels. The dense smell of smoke drove Jacob a few steps back. Wheeler turned to him. "You coming or what?"

Jacob seemed fixated on the school's main door, as if waiting for it to open again.

"One Bolt. Let's go!"

"Maybe we should go inside." Jacob shrugged. "You know...say, 'Hi' to the professor."

"Professor? Ha! You mean Hope?"

Jacob turned his head to one side.

"She'll be fine, One Bolt. I'm sure the professor's already sent her off to join a new team. Come on, we have to go."

"But I don't want her to be part of another team. She's part of our team—the three of us."

"Come on, One Bolt. We discussed this already. Her dad, remember? The Mayor? We can't let anyone know what we're doing. And we don't have much time left. That's why we have to get going. Now!"

Jacob finally surrendered his back to the school. "I just feel bad for not telling her."

"Yeah…me too." Wheeler said, rolling his eyes. He dropped his wheel arm down to the ground, drove in front of Jacob and spun around. Looking over his shoulder, he said, "Now jump in…I mean *on*. Jump on."

Jacob saw a pair of newly installed handle bars bolted on opposing sides of Wheeler's shoulders being offered to him. He pointed at them and said, "You mean?"

"Yeah. I just put them on. The welds are still warm. Much better than having you wrap your arms around my face like the last time. Couldn't see a damn thing. Now jump on."

Jacob hesitated. He scanned the bars intently, mainly for structural purposes. He had already taken a fall from the charger earlier and wasn't about to take another one.

"Nothing to worry about, One Bolt. Just grab on. We won't ever get to my place if you keep standing here looking."

Jacob reached out and gave one of the handles a tap, causing a soft ping.

"I put them on myself," Wheeler said proudly.

Yeah, that's what I'm worried about. "Okay! Okay! Calm down." Jacob took a step onto Wheeler's base and then placed his hand completely around one of the handle bars. He kept most of his weight on his grounded foot just for reassurance. He tugged at the bar, testing its integrity. It didn't move or bend.

"See, I told you. Nothing to worry about. Now the other foot…before both our batteries need to recharge."

"I'm on, I'm on!" Jacob cried. He tucked his lunchbox deep inside a small crevasse along Wheeler's base and then took his anchoring foot off the ground, handing his well-being over to Wheeler.

"Careful with that lunchbox." Wheeler said. "That's a delicate area you're placing it in."

All the areas looked the same to Jacob. He didn't know what Wheeler was fussing about. "Okay. I'm ready."

"Finally!" Wheeler revved his wheels, and Jacob felt Wheeler's entire body vibrate. Before he launched forward, Wheeler tightened the brake calibres behind each wheel, holding himself in place. Smoke billowed out from behind him, nearly engulfing the pair. "Better hold on, One Bolt."

"I am holding on!"

"No, I mean tight. These wheels don't look fast...but trust me..."

How fast could they be?

Wheeler released his brake calibres and allowed his wheels to spin aggressively until they finally snagged the ground. Once they did, Jacob's head snapped back. A mere blink later, the school was no longer in sight.

* * *

To Jacob, it felt like Wheeler was going even faster than a car, and he clung tight to the handlebars, as they drove out of the light and entered the dark side. *It's amazing.* It was bright and full of ambiance just a short moment ago. Now his surroundings were dark. It was like a thick band of shadow had reached down, grabbed onto him and wasn't about to let go anytime soon. It was so dark that everything had blended together, and Jacob contemplated switching on his night vision. The reflected light from the now crescent-shaped moon allowed him to maintain his normal vision...at least, for the time being.

Ever since they'd crossed over to the darker side of the Earth, Jacob noticed more and more places where buildings had become one with the Earth—just like his mom had told him. He and Wheeler were driving by the final stages of Earth's repossession. Buildings no longer stood tall nor mighty—just flat, barren land where they used to stand.

When Jacob thought that there would be nothing else to see but flat, empty land, a massive structure appeared out of the darkness. Then another and another. These were enormous structures that rose out from the Earth and punctured the endless sky. Attached to the very top of each of these structures, and allowed to drape down until they piled into an immense mound, were thick chains, completely rusted over. The horizon was soon filled with the sight-rupturing structures.

"Hey, Wheeler! What are—"

"Project Redemption!" Wheeler yelled back. He glanced over his shoulder at Jacob. "I knew you were going to ask."

Jacob nearly lost his grip on Wheeler's handle bars. "Those things are Project Redemption? Those are what the Mayor used to rid the Earth of humans?"

"Yeah. They're the same as the ones up there." Wheeler pointed up at the moon.

For the first time ever, Jacob was able to see a different side of the moon. He noticed the rows upon rows of massive structures anchored to the moon's surface. They matched the ones down on Earth nearly flawlessly. The only things missing from ones on the moon were the massive chains, with their building-sized links.

"That's what's missing from my moon model," Jacob said.

"Told you."

"What are they exactly?"

"Anchor points."

"Anchor points? What were they used for?"

Wheeler shrugged. "To anchor."

"I know that. But how were they used in Project Redemption? What were they anchoring?" Jacob stood on the tips of his boots and hunched forward to try to look Wheeler in the eyes. "How were they used to rid Earth of the humans?"

"Whoa, whoa!" Wheeler pushed Jacob back. "You're asking a lot, One Bolt. Some other time. We have other things to focus on now."

They drove on a few more minutes, then Jacob felt Wheeler's pace beginning to slow. A moment later, Wheeler tightened his brake calibres, turning them into a nearly solid-red glow. The smell of burnt rubber ruptured the surrounding air, as Wheeler came to an abrupt stop. "Off," Wheeler ordered.

"Are we at your place?"

"Soon."

Jacob stepped off. "I don't understand. Why don't we just keep on going?"

Wheeler laughed. "Oh, really?" He pointed toward the ground.

The metal casing over the ground was eroded and consumed by the usual culprit, rust. Large chunks of metal were completely gone, while other sections offered nothing but protruding obstacles that could only be navigated with precision. Something Wheeler was incapable of doing, especially with the added weight of Jacob on his back.

"It'll be a bumpy ride if you want to stay on." Wheeler shoved his elbow into Jacob's side. "And I don't want to damage that precious CPU of yours."

"Good idea. My sensors were beginning to feel a bit strange. Must be from all the jostling."

"Hey, don't blame the wheels. They got us this far."

"I'm not blaming anything. I'm just saying…"

"Fine, we walk from here…I mean…you walk. I'll drive. Just watch your step. Stay under the tubing."

Jacob looked up and saw the tubing Wheeler was referring to. It was supported by metal poles that were sticking out of the ground, as far as he could see. He could hear a whooshing sound coming from above. “Artificial gravity.”

Wheeler drove forward. “Of course. The metal ground is all torn up from this point on. Watch your step.” He disappeared into the darkness.

Jacob was left behind, absorbing the plume of dust kicked up from Wheeler’s departure. “Hey! Wait for me!” He took a timid step forward. His boots made contact with the exposed ground and then scraped a rough edge of the metal causing a wrenching squeal. Another scratch. “Forever Yaw had better be worth it.”

Jacob caught up with Wheeler and glows from each of them were intensified by the lack of sunlight. Jacob’s eyes stained Wheeler in intense blues, while Jacob was being covered in yellows and whites from the dozens of glowing LED lights radiating from all over Wheeler’s disorganized body. Even so, Jacob could hardly see anything. “How can you find your way in the dark?”

“I'm used to it.”

“Well, I’m going to switch on my night vision. I can’t see a damn thing. *316*.”

“You have night vision?” Wheeler smirked. “Fancy first generation like you. Should have known.”

“What’s that supposed to mean?”

“Ah, nothing. Just messing around, One Bolt. No need to get all offensive with everything I say.” He stuck his arm out in front of Jacob. “There’s no need for night vision.”

Wheeler reached up and tapped the side of his head. Out popped a trio of lights, one on each side of his head and a main source right on the middle of his chin. The two upper lights lit up the surroundings in a brilliant-white glow, but there wasn’t much for them to highlight at the moment. The massive structures were now behind them, leaving a barren landscape. “There,” Wheeler said. The main light on his chin flickered on for just a second and then switched off completely. Wheeler tapped his chin a few times until it came to life again. This time it stayed on. “There!” he repeated, with a bit more confidence. “Need to be prepared for any and all situations.”

The intense light made Jacob wince and turn out of the direct beam. “You installed those on yourself?”

“Yeah.”

“Why did you mount one on your chin?”

“What’s wrong with having a light on my chin? I already have two on top. Don’t need a third on up there.”

Having a light on his chin was very odd. Maybe even a little silly. Every time Wheeler opened his mouth to speak, the beam of light would move in unison with his chin. Jacob laugh. “Do I even have to ask?”

“Ah, just keep walking. We’re almost there.”

The further they progressed, the more Jacob was thankful for all three of Wheeler's lights. They cut into the darkness with their straight edges, only faltering when Wheeler's wheels rolled over uneven terrain. When Jacob looked up he noticed odd shimmering objects stretched from one end of the otherwise dark sky to the next. Their radiance was bright, but not as intense as the lights from Wheeler.

"What are those?" Jacob pointed at the sky.

"Can't tell you." Wheeler dimmed his lights to allow the objects to glow a little brighter. "I've always seen them up there but don't know what they are. I thought you would know. You seem to know everything."

"Sorry. Not this time." Jacob focused on one particular formation that had three twinkling objects across its centre. "They do look like the sun in a way."

"Ha!"

"No, they do. All of them. Just a lot further away."

Wheeler snickered. "Yeah…they're suns. Millions and millions of suns." He shook his head, making his lights dance along the broken terrain. "Just keep moving."

Jacob had to quicken his pace in order to keep in stride with Wheeler. He didn't want to be left alone in this dark void. *Maybe there was an advantage to having wheels after all.* With wheels there were no complicated movements, no repetitiveness—just roll forward, and eventually you'll get there…where ever *there* may be. "Isn't it lonely to live way out here?"

Wheeler waved it off. "I have my reasons for being where I am."

What does that mean? "Feels a lot different here...At least...my sensors are telling me it is."

Wheeler noticed Jacob's pace slowing. "You okay, One Bolt? Do you need me to stop?"

Jacob decided to stop on his own. "Feel…feel strange." Jacob raised his arm. That's when he noticed a thin covering of white crystals shimmered across his entire hand. It looked like coarse metal against sunlight.

"It's from the lack of sunlight," Wheeler explained, anticipating Jacob's question. "Something in the air causes it." He ran his finger across Jacob's arm, cutting a line into the shimmering-white build up. "It'll go away once we get inside."

"I hope so," Jacob said, wiping away the layer of build up on his arm.

Wheeler gestured up at Jacob's face. "Might want to close those."

There was a heavy build up of the crystals concentrated around the vents on Jacob's cheeks. Wheeler reached up and pressed the vents closed.

"All of my joints feel like they're seizing up. Feel…slower than usual." Even the glow in Jacob's eyes had dimmed.

"You're just not used to being out this far. Don't worry, One Bolt. We're almost there." Wheeler placed Jacob's arm around his shoulder and escorted him forward.

They walked a ways further, and Jacob seemed to be moving easier. The darkness remained constant.

"Better?" Wheeler asked

"Slightly."

"Enough to answer a question for me?"

"Hey, my limbs might be seizing up but my CPU is always ready," Jacob said.

Wheeler rolled his eyes. "Anyway...I was wondering, One Bolt. What did your mom mean back there when she said her car was about ready to go back into the Earth?"

"Why do you want to know?"

"Hey, I asked you a question first."

"Okay-okay. She was just saying how we all came from the Earth at one time, and eventually we'll return to it."

"Everything?"

"Everyone and everything."

A beep suddenly resonated from Wheeler chest, and Jacob felt him shudder. "What was that?"

"What was what?" Wheeler turned away, but not before Jacob caught a glimpse of the orange light through the small gap in Wheeler's chest-plate. It was the same light that he'd seen while they were in his room the day before. It was presumably an indicator light, similar to the one on Jacob's chest. Orange could only mean that red wasn't too far off.

Wheeler noticed Jacob looking at the light and sighed. "I know what you're thinking, One Bolt. It's not a battery indicator. My battery charge is where yours is right now."

Jacob looked down at his own chest-plate. Green indicators meant that he was at near full capacity. *If Wheeler's batteries were at full charge, then what was the orange indicating?*

Without Jacob even saying another word, Wheeler sighed again and said, "Okay-okay. If you must know, One Bolt, it's my hard-drive indicator. Red will mean that it's full."

"But it's at orange. Doesn't that mean that it's almost red?"

"You did the calculations all by yourself, One Bolt? Wow, you *are* good."

"Why the beep?"

Wheeler sighed. "That just indicates that I learned something new. I mean, returning back to the Earth? Everything and everyone? I wouldn't have even guessed."

"You'll need an upgrade soon. If your hard-drive is full you're going to need a new one?"

Wheeler drove out in front of Jacob and didn't look back. "Yeah, I guess." But he only went a little ways before slowing. "How you doing back there, One Bolt?"

"The same."

"Really?" Wheeler allowed Jacob to catch up and then pointed to Jacob's chest. The indicator light on his chest-plate was now yellow. Jacob nearly tripped over himself. "Ye-yellow? But how? I barely walked...I mean, it was just green!"

"Like I said, One Bolt, it's probably because you're not used to being out this far. But don't worry." Wheeler smiled. "We're here."

Finally!

Just ahead, Jacob could see a small structure. It was the only structure in plain view. It was simple from the looks of it. As with most other structures on Earth, it had been neglected and left to endure the harshness of the times. Each side consisted of rust-stained sheet metal, adhered together with bolts that appeared to only be halfway in. Maybe they had been flush to the surface at one time, and deterioration had loosened them. Flakes of rust bubbled from these messily arranged junction points, dripping toward the ground, as if eager to eventually meet with the Earth. It was an unsightly mess, and Wheeler's lights did no favours by illuminating it.

"Wow, look at this place," Jacob said, with the corners of his mouth drooped downward. "What a mess."

Wheeler reached over and smacked Jacob on the back of the head. "Thanks," he said, driving toward it.

Jacob's eyes widened. "Oh, you mean..."

"It might not be up to *your* standards, One Bolt...but for me, it's home." Wheeler waited by the only opening to the house which not surprisingly, lacked a door. He waved over to a reluctant Jacob. "Get inside before that CPU of yours completely seizes."

"Sorry about that. I didn't know you lived here."

"Ah, forget it. It's mostly rust. Not my fault." Wheeler followed Jacob inside his house.

The first thing that struck Jacob was the intense darkness. Even Wheeler's trio of lights was not enough to illuminate the way, much less, reveal the rest of the interior. They poured Jacob's shadow over the walls, further obscuring much of the interior.

"You know what I like best about living out here, One Bolt?"

"You can't annoy anyone?"

"No. It's quiet. No one's around to disturb me." Wheeler switched off his lights and allowed the darkness to completely swallow them.

"Hey!"

"Relax. I've got it." Wheeler flicked a switch on the wall. A pasty-yellow light bloomed from the low ceiling and filtered down into the hallway.

"Wow!" Jacob looked up and down the hallway and was overwhelmed by the amount of trophies staring at him. "These...these all yours?"

"Who do you think they belong to?"

Jacob walked up to one of them and read the inscription. "*Assignment 051773*. Second place." He glanced back at Wheeler, who shrugged. Jacob walked over to the next trophy. "*Assignment 071381*. Runner up." Again, he glanced back at Wheeler.

"What?"

Jacob walked back into the center of the hallway. "They're all second place..."

"Yeah? So? What's your point?"

Jacob didn't miss the defensiveness in Wheeler's voice. *This was the reason Wheeler was acting so strange when Professor Smith mentioned my trophies.* "Not used to seeing so many second place trophies," Jacob joked. "Must feel bad losing to a first generation."

"Yeah-yeah," Wheeler murmured. As he walked around Jacob, he bumped shoulders with him. "At least I can touch the ground without bending down."

"So can I…well…after an upgrade."

Wheeler entered the room at the end of the hallway. "Just get inside, will you?"

When Wheeler switched on the single light in the room, Jacob immediately noticed the mess. It looked similar to the one he had made in his search for his microscope, only at least five times as chaotic. "Demagnetized recently?"

"I like it like this. I know where everything is at any given time."

"Really?" *You should get a first place trophy for that.*

As they walked deeper into the room, Jacob noticed holes in practically every corner, holes that let tiny glimmers of outside light in. There wasn't enough natural light outside to make much of a difference, but he still noticed them. Jacob also noticed the familiar remnants of past assignments scattered along his path. They were exactly the same assignments that he had done at one time or another, and he found it interesting to see a different perspective on the experiments that he had perfected. Further into the room, he suddenly noticed something worth investigating. He stopped, bent down and picked up two halves of an empty, spherical shell. "You have a Pin-bot, too?"

"A Pin-what?"

"A Pin—" Jacob let go of the empty shells, allowing them blend in with the mess. "I mean, a helper-bot."

"Yeah, I had one. You have one, too? And you named it Pin-bot? Why?"

"Those little turbine engines she has," Jacob explained, shrugging his shoulders. "They're so quiet, my mom said you can still hear a pin drop when she's flying."

"Is that something we're supposed to understand?"

Jacob chuckled. "My mom says lots of things I don't understand."

"You know what I don't understand? You say you have a helper-bot, but I didn't see it the other day."

"She was recharging." Jacob scanned the room. "Where's your helper-bot?" *If it was anywhere in the room, the mess was doing a fine job of concealing it.*

"Around…"

"Why did you take it out of its shell?"

"I did some modifications. But don't worry, One Bolt, it was a *1000* model."

"*1000*? What does that mean?"

"You don't know?"

Jacob shrugged.

"The *1000* models were fine to modify. *800* models weren't."

Jacob remembered his mom mentioning something about model numbers, unfortunately, she didn't say why. "What's...umm...what's so different about the *800* models that they shouldn't be modified?"

"They were the early prototype models. Shouldn't have even been released to the public. Really unstable when modified."

"Unstable?" Jacob tensed. "Uh...how so?"

"Well...let's just say, I wouldn't want to be around when they go off...which is highly likely if you had modified them in any way."

Oh, no. Jacob suddenly felt weighed down, as if the magnets in his boots had intensified.

Wheeler noticed Jacob's stiffened posture. "What's wrong, One Bolt? Why are you asking?"

Jacob didn't respond at first. He just looked at Wheeler, the glow in his eyes greater than normal.

"Oh, no, One Bolt! Don't tell me..."

Jacob nodded.

"You modified it? You modified your Pin-bot?"

"Well...yeah. I wanted to give her a real voice."

"You couldn't wait for her to learn to talk on her own?"

"It was taking so long. I just wanted to speed things up."

Wheeler waved it off. "Okay-okay. Just calm down. As long as you put everything back together, everything should be fine. All the parts have to go back exactly the way they were. No spare parts left over."

The plates over Jacob's eyes dropped back down and hovered halfway. "And if they weren't?"

Wheeler snickered. "You ever wonder why the moon is missing one side? You know...that huge chunk that is gone?"

"Project Retaliation?"

"Right. Project Retaliation is a cannon."

"Yeah, I knew that. My mom told me."

"And do you know what they loaded inside that cannon in order to destroy the moon?" Wheeler nodded. "That's right. You guessed it. Pin-bots! The *800* models to be exact."

Jacob's eyes widened. "Pin-bots caused that?"

"Not Pin-bots. Just one. They fired off a bunch of them, but only one managed to graze the moon. But look at the result."

Jacob fell silent. *My Pin-bot...my innocent Pin-bot is capable of that?* Jacob didn't want to believe it. "But the *1000* models are okay?"

"Yeah. They're fine."

"How do I know what model I have? I mean...there's no way Pin-bot's an *800* model, is she?"

Wheeler shrugged. "I'm not sure. But I wouldn't worry myself if I were you." He laughed, "I know your CPU is advanced enough to put her back together."

A forced smiled appeared on Jacob's face. All he could think of were those two left-over bolts. "Yeah…right."

"Good." Wheeler rolled to the far end of the room. "Let's get some work done. That's why we're out here, right?"

All Jacob could think about was Pin-bot and model *800*, hoping that she was really a *1000* model. *She has to be*. He hurried over to the far end of the room where Wheeler was already busy at a desk. He held up his hand, as Jacob approached. "Wait." Wheeler said. "Not yet."

"Why?"

"It'll be awhile before I get everything set up." Wheeler then dipped down underneath the desk, completely out of Jacob's field of vision.

"How long is it going to take?"

"I'll let you know when I'm ready to begin. Just…stop bothering me for awhile, will you?"

"Okay-okay!" Jacob backed away. "I'll just look around, then."

Wheeler pulled his head out from under the desk. "Just stay where I can see you. And don't mess up anything. I have it exactly the way I like it. And if you find something, it's mine."

Obviously. Jacob walked into the center of the room and began rummaging through some of the junk engulfing the entire floor. Every once in a while, he glanced over at Wheeler and noticed him watching. It was obvious that Wheeler was keeping an eye on him, confirming Jacob's suspicion that the line of tension between them might have a little slack but the ends were still firmly in place.

"So…" Jacob murmured.

"So? What?"

"I wonder what the class is up to."

"Don't you mean Hope?"

"Now that you mention it, yes, I wonder what she's doing. Do you think she knows we're out here?"

"How would I know?"

"Just asking."

"And I'm just answering. Who knows? And as of right now, I don't care."

Jacob suddenly noticed a familiar object protruding from the mess. Unlike everything around it, the object wasn't metal. He began to dig it free. "Do you remember what you told me the other day? You know…about me not being Hope's type."

Wheeler sighed. "Here we go again…"

"I'm just wondering if that was true."

Wheeler shook his head and snickered. "I don't know, One Bolt. I only said that to keep you away from her."

"What? Why would you do that? I mean, I know *you* don't like her, but—"

"No-no-no, I never said that."

"But you seem—"

"I have no problems with Hope. I like Hope." Wheeler shifted his head back and forth. "It's her dad I have a problem with. You have to remember something, One Bolt. The Mayor *is* her dad. What influences him will influence her."

"Not exactly. Hope's different."

"If you say so."

"Trust me, she is." Jacob finally pulled the object free from the mess. "Hey!"

Wheeler turned and stretched out his neck. "What? You're not making a mess, are you?"

Jacob turned around, allowing Wheeler to see the rolled up pages in hand. "Where did you find these?" Jacob asked, straightening out the roll.

Wheeler scanned the stained pages. "Oh…they were…uh…given to me."

"By who?"

"Don't remember." Wheeler abruptly turned back to his desk.

"How can you not know where you got something so unusual?"

"I have stuff everywhere, One Bolt. You can't expect me to remember every detail of everything thing I have."

"But you said you could."

"Okay, to be more precise. I can remember about most things. Just not everything. Is that better?"

At least he can admit it...sort of. Jacob brought the pages up to his face. Just like the ones he had found inside the box in his room, these were filled with inscriptions. "Mind if I decode them?"

Wheeler nearly fell backwards. "You…you can decode those?"

"Sure. It's a function my mom equipped me with."

"Lucky you."

Jacob placed the tip of his hand on the corner of the pages, ready to flip through them. "So? Do you mind?"

"Go ahead. I've always been curious about what's on those things."

"Okay, give me a moment." Jacob flipped through every page, scanning as much of the inscriptions as he could and then stored them on his hard-drive. "There! Now all I need to do is decode everything." The glow of Jacob's eyes turned from blue to pale white. His hard-drive spun at its maximum velocity, as he began decoding. The inscriptions of the pages read:

-Found the perfect candidate to use as a personality for my advance models. He spent a lot of time with Sarah during her final days. He did the best he could. I don't blame him for my loss. I just hope he does a better job with Eve.

-Work is piling up again. Industrial prototype models were recalled. Major glitches resulting in fatalities. Commercial models were put on hold until we resolve the problems. Had an accident with one of them. Arm still sore, but lucky to be alive. More research is needed, but the demands are overwhelming. Not sure what to do.

-Feel bad. Disgusted with myself. All she wanted was to spend the night looking up at stars. But I had to work. Commercial models released to the public, but already problems. Have to fix them. Can't live with myself if I don't. Forgive me, Eve. I know she doesn't appreciate what I'm trying to accomplish right now, but in the end, she will.

The colour of Jacob's eyes returned to normal, and his hard-drive slowed. He looked up at Wheeler, who had an expression of surprise that Jacob was sure matched his. He raised the plates over his eyes. "What does that mean? Who is he?"

"Forget him," Wheeler said. "Who is she?"

"Who are they?" they said in unison.

"I don't know," Wheeler admitted. "You're the one who decoded it."

"Doesn't mean I know who they are or what it all means." Jacob turned the pages in his hand. "Although Eve..." He paused.

"What?"

"I don't know. Something about her... the name... sounds familiar."

Wheeler waved it off. "Ah...probably not important. That's why I left it in the pile of junk."

"It might be important."

"No. If neither of us know what it means, then it's not important."

Odd way of looking at things. Then again, this is Wheeler talking. "Where should I put these?" Jacob rolled the pages back into a cylinder.

"Keep them."

"But I don't need them. I have the information stored on my hard-drive."

"Just put them back where you found them," Wheeler said, "and get over here. I'm ready."

"You mean, *we're* ready."

"That's what I said."

"Sure you did."

"Just get over here, One Bolt. Before I start without you."

"Okay-okay."

Jacob tucked the pages deep inside the mess and walked over to the desk.

Scattered across the top of the desk were cans of *Artificial Blend.* Jacob could tell that most of them were empty, just by the way they were resting on their sides, but a few of them stood upright, indicating they might be full.

Wheeler motioned Jacob closer. "Do me a favour."

"I'm not cleaning this."

"Why would you? It's perfect the way it is."

"What, then?"

"See that switch right behind you? Turn it on. But I need to warn you, One Bolt. It might get a little bright in here."

"Why?"

"Just switch it on, and you'll see."

Jacob reached back, flicked the switch and prepared himself. The ceiling began to rumble. A seam from two opposing pieces of sheet metal split open. Just as Wheeler had warned, an intense beam of light surged into the room and blasted a small area of the desk. Jacob shielded his eyes long enough for them to adjust to the light.

"What? What is this?"

"Like it?" Wheeler grinned. "It's concentrated light. A few well placed pieces of metal angled perfectly to reflect the sunlight, and there you go. *Assignment 091775*. Harness the power of the sun."

"But I got first place for this assignment."

"I know. I didn't turn this one in." Wheeler shoved his elbow into Jacob's side. "Why, One Bolt, you think this would have gotten first place?"

"It *is* a lot brighter than what I came up with."

Wheeler slammed his wheel arm against the desk. "Damn! I knew I should have submitted this one."

"Why didn't you? A first place trophy would look nice against all your second place ones."

"This was the second time I had to do this assignment."

"Second? What happened to the first?"

"Ran out of time. But it's okay. I ended up finishing that one, as well. It's even better than this one."

"Really? Where is it?"

"Don't bother about that, One Bolt. That was the past. It's time to work on our future." Wheeler reached down and pulled out a large microscope from underneath the desk. Unlike Jacob's, Wheeler's had dual eyepieces. "You said the light made the cells divide more rapidly, right?"

Jacob nodded.

Wheeler placed the microscope on the desk and then moved it into the concentrated sunlight, allowing the beam to cast its glow over the entire surface. An infectious grin lit up Wheeler's face, as he gestured for Jacob to use one of the eyepieces. "Go on. Take a look."

In unison, they pressed their faces against the microscope's eyepieces and observed. Tiny cells were swirling, as they divided again and again until there were thousands of them.

"Wow," Jacob said. "It's acting just like the plant I have at home."

"Must be because of the light."

Jacob pulled his eyes away from the microscope. "It *is* the light. That's what I told you the other day."

Wheeler still had his face engulfed by the microscope. "Oh…you did? I guess I didn't hear you."

But his hard-drive had beeped. And Wheeler did mention that it would beep whenever he acquired new information. However, there was no point in arguing, especially when the information he had given Wheeler was benefiting the both of them. Besides, there was something else that Jacob knew. Something that he was sure Wheeler didn't know about. "Looking good," Jacob said. "So I guess you have Forever Yaw underway."

Wheeler finally pulled his face away from the microscope. “It’s just a start, but a start none the less. We’re on our way, One Bolt. Thanks to me.”

Jacob wanted to sigh, but he didn’t want to make it too obvious. “So…I guess what we need now is for the cells to divide even further?”

“Correct. The question is, how?”

Jacob reached behind Wheeler and retrieved his lunchbox. He set the box down on the floor and opened it, pulling out one can of *Pure Blend.*

“What are you doing?” Wheeler asked. “It’s not break time. We need to keep working.”

“I am working.” Jacob cracked open the can. He figured a beep would resonate from Wheeler’s hard-drive at any moment. “Have you tried *Pure Blend*?”

“Ha! I hate that stuff. Remember?”

“Not for you. I mean on the sample.”

“What? Why would I?”

“The other day, I accidentally spilled some on my leaf sample, and the cells started dividing like crazy. It reacted to the *Pure Blend* for some reason. I don’t know why, though.” As Jacob thought, a beep resonated from Wheeler’s chest. “I knew it,” Jacob said, with a smirk. “I knew you wouldn’t have tried the *Pure Blend*.”

Wheeler shrugged. “Well…I might have…eventually.”

“Yeah, right.”

Wheeler reached out and grabbed the can out of Jacob’s hand. “Okay, so let’s see if this works.” Wheeler tipped the can over the slides and allowed a single drop of liquid to splash down and onto the sample. Just like Jacob had claimed, the cells reacted, and their divisions erupted into a frenzy.

“Hey!” Wheeler tapped Jacob on the shoulder. “Hey…look!”

“I see it!”

“They’re dividing…like crazy!”

“Just like I said.”

“It’s happening, One Bolt! Forever Yaw! It’s happening!”

Wheeler pulled his face from the microscope and began driving around the room. “It’s happening! It’s really happening!” He drove up and over the mess, crushing anything and everything, beneath his wheels. But he didn't care what he drove over. He was too excited to care. “Wonder what the Mayor would have to say about this,” he said, pumping his hand into the air. *The Professor would finally set me free.* He drove back in front of the desk and picked up the can of *Pure Blend*. “Now I know why you like this stuff, One Bolt. It’s amazing. Wonder what’s in it.”

Jacob finally pulled away from the microscope and glanced over at Wheeler. Wheeler placed the can back onto the desk. His smile faded when he noticed the long, dejected look on Jacob’s face.

“What is it, One Bolt?”

He sighed deeply. “We might have to start over.”

“What? Why?”

Jacob gestured at the eyepiece.

Wheeler looked into it. The cells were no longer dividing. "Hey! What happened? What did you do, One Bolt?"

"Nothing. They just stopped by themselves!"

Wheeler pulled the slide out from the microscope and scanned it. The sample had withered and turned a disgusting brown. "Dead?" He looked at Jacob, with near perfectly round-eyes.

"Looks like it."

Wheeler placed the slide on the desk and then began driving back and forth. "How can we create humans if we can't even sustain a small sample?"

Jacob leaned back against the desk, watching as Wheeler paced. "At least now we know that light *and Pure Blend* has some sort of effect on the sample."

"But that doesn't do us any good if it dies." Wheeler placed his wheel hand on his head and revved the wheel a few times. It spat out a sharp trail of smoke that filled the room. "We still have to sustain it somehow."

Jacob brushed the smoke away from his face. "Stop that! You're clogging up my sensors."

"Oh, sorry. Force of habit." Wheeler threw his arm down to the floor, revved up his wheels and rolled to the other end of the desk. He turned his back to Jacob and said, "Just give me moment. I have to clear my cache."

"Your what?"

"My thoughts, One Bolt. Clear my thoughts." He glanced over his shoulder. "Any suggestions while I'm away would help."

Jacob did some calculations. "Well, we *are* attempting to recreate humans. This isn't like putting screws into sockets. It's a lot more complicated."

"You just thought of that now?" Wheeler rolled back in front of Jacob, as animated as ever. "I know it's not going to be easy! Humans were more complicated than you could even imagine. They were more than just metal and bolts, I can tell you that much."

"They weren't made of metals, huh?"

"What do you think?"

"I don't know. I keep telling you that."

"No, One Bolt. They weren't made of metal." Wheeler picked up the slide and slapped it into Jacob's hand. "See the sample? That's what humans were made from. All around and inside them. Their entire body. And you see what happens to it when the slightest thing goes wrong?"

Jacob quietly poked at the sample with his hand. Part of it flaked away from the edge and crumpled. "It just dies..."

"Yeah. Too bad, huh?"

"So this is why the Mayor keeps saying they were weak?"

"It's exactly why. They were fragile. Too fragile. The only option they had to save themselves was to alter their bodies."

"Until they finally became us."

"Yeah, eventually." Wheeler backed up until he was leaning against the desk, next to Jacob. A long silence managed to fill the entire room.

Jacob placed the slide back onto the desk. “So now what?”

Wheeler reached back and flicked the slide, sending it across the desktop. “I don't know...”

“We have to keep trying. It might have died on us this time but you never know. It could very well sustain itself the next time. Maybe just add more *Pure Blend*...I don't know.”

“We can try that, One Bolt. But there are no guarantees that more *Pure Blend* is going to work.”

“It's better than us just standing here doing nothing.” He cocked his head at Wheeler. “Come on, this was your idea.”

“I know. That's why I used my name.”

“The longer we stand here, the closer the moon gets. If we don't do this soon...” Jacob pointed up toward the ceiling, trying his best to mimic the Mayor's exaggerated pose.

“Alright, alright. I got you. Just...don't do that anymore. I don't even like pretending that he's here.”

Jacob straightened his posture. “Okay. Let's get another sample and try this again. We have to get it to work.” Jacob smirked. “Or you might have to share a pod with him.”

Wheeler cringed at the thought. “Okay. Fine. I'll get another sample. See you tomorrow.”

“What? What do you mean tomorrow? Just get some from underneath your desk.”

“That's only where I store the samples, not where I get them. And I'm all out.”

“Then get some more.”

“I will. Tomorrow.”

“Why not now?”

“Look, One Bolt. This isn't like the plant you found behind your house. I just can't go and pull it out of the ground.”

“Where do the samples come from? Why won't you tell me?”

Wheeler spun himself in a circle. “I'll get some more. I promise. Right now, you need to take care of yourself.” He pointed at Jacob's chest.

Jacob looked down. To his surprise, the indicator light on his chest plate was now on the final orange bar. “Orange? Already? But...but how?”

“I don't know. But you better go home and recharge yourself. I'll meet you in front of the school tomorrow.”

“Wait, you're not going to take me back?”

“You know the way. Just keep walking until you see sunlight.” Wheeler began to rev his wheels.

“But it's a long way.”

“Look...do you want me to get the sample or not?”

“Yeah.”

“Well, that's where I'm going. As for you, just follow the sun. We'll continue with Forever Yaw after you get a full charge. I promise.” Wheeler suddenly lunged for Jacob's lunchbox. Jacob tried to close it before Wheeler could take the remaining can of *Pure Blend*, but his reaction was too slow. Wheeler grabbed the can and sped off down the hall.

"Hey!"

"Hope you don't mind if I keep this!" Wheeler yelled back, as he disappeared outside. "I'll need it if I want to get another sample."

Jacob placed his hand on his waist. *He needs it to get another sample? What did he mean by that?* His hand slid down to his side. At least now, Jacob knew why Wheeler had been taken his *Pure Blend*, but there was still the matter of who, or what, he was giving it to. Jacob slumped over. He reached down, closed the empty lunchbox and secured it in his hand. He reached over and grabbed the opened can of *Pure Blend* on the desk and made his way through the mess to the hallway. He had a long, lonely walk ahead of him and hoped his batteries would last long enough to get him back to the school. "This had all better be worth it," he mumbled, giving his head a quick shake to enable his night vision.

* * *

Jacob's condition was now critical. Brimming, red indicator lights drenched the lower half of his face. His battery was nearly drained. This wasn't the first time he'd waited too long to get charged. He was frequently guilty of not paying close attention to his indicators and had let himself get to this point before, but something was different this time. His sensors felt too warm. His CPU felt unresponsive, slow, and sluggish. *What's wrong with me?*

His boots landed noisily, clumsily, against the rusted ground. His joints were stiff, and his movements irregular. His body was failing, and the decline was exacerbated by the distance he had just traversed. Without a pair of wheels underneath him, the distance had been staggering. "Stupid...first generation limbs. Wish I had…upgrade…or…" Jacob frowned, not wanting to admit it, "…w-wheels."

Fortunately, Jacob's long journey from the edge of darkness to the sun's embrace was nearing its conclusion. The school rose high and imposing over the horizon and did not allow the slight curvature of the Earth to tarnish its stance. Jacob was unbelievably happy to see it. Such a contrasting reaction from the first time he saw the school.

As Jacob rounded the corner of the school building, he saw his mom's car parked in its usual spot. His ride home. He wouldn't have to walk any further. His elation brought a sudden burst of energy, and he picked up his pace. The cold steel of his lunchbox slammed against his leg, as he hurried toward the car. It clanged all the way until he was finally standing by the door. Jacob didn't hesitate. His reached out a limp hand and attempted to wrench open the door. He barely had enough energy to crack the seam. "M-Mom," he whimpered. "Mom…help…"

Grace finally noticed Jacob through the small opening. She reached over and pushed open the door. "Jacob! I didn't even see you!"

Jacob struggled to climb inside, and Grace noticed the wild flashing of the red indicator light. She reached over, grabbed the lunchbox out of his hands and placed it on the floor. She then turned her attention back to Jacob.

"What happened? Why are you at red?" She pulled Jacob into the car and onto his seat.

"I-I'm fine," Jacob mumbled, with a slight grinding in his voice. "Just n-need…recharging."

"You're not fine, Jacob."

"Yes…I am..." Jacob tried to reassure her by closing the door, but his hands slipped off the handle. Grace had to reach over to close the door for him.

Jacob wasn't fine by any means. His eyes contained little to no colour, and the plates above each of them could barely aid in any kind of expression. Even the frequency in his voice was weak and mechanical sounding.

Grace quickly switched the car from idle to drive and then pressed down on the accelerator. Just the slight jerk of the car pulling forward was enough to make Jacob's limp body flop to one side. He was now leaning against the door.

"Didn't you get a full recharge this morning? I thought you were green when I dropped you off in front of the school."

Jacob lifted his head, shrugged and then slumped into his seat. "I-I…guess so. I mean…I think. Hard-drive's not…accessing information at the moment…"

"I don't understand how you're in the red. You were barely at orange at this time yesterday."

"M-Must have…you know…done more today," he sluggishly replied.

"That still doesn't explain why you're at red."

Jacob's head dropped forward toward his chest. "Can we just…go home? F-Feeling…I-I'm feeling…"

"We'll be home soon, Jacob. Just lean back." Grace reached over and gently coaxed Jacob's head into the backrest. It didn't take much effort. Then he slumped against the side window, and when he did, his head shifted, completely exposing the thick plate that was protecting the entire back of his head. Quietly, as not to disturb him, Grace leaned over and ran her hand against the back of his head. She wasn't sure why she did that. It was impossible to penetrate the covering without the proper tools. But the gesture was more to just reassure herself. Jacob turned slightly to face her.

"M-Mom, what were you doing?" he said, a pitch away from a whisper.

"Just checking to see if you're still with me," she said, watching as Jacob's eyes struggled to remain open. "Don't worry. We'll be home soon, Jacob."

Temporary shut down was imminent. One by one, Jacob's main functions were disabling.

How was this possible? Grace had been doing everything she needed to do. Her eyes suddenly became wide. *Except for…* She reached down with one hand and opened Jacob's lunchbox. For some reason, Jacob had been coming home with only one can recently. She didn't know why, but it was a matter of great concern. When she glanced in the lunchbox, her fears were realized. There was only one empty can inside. She sighed. "Where's the other one?"

Although distortion was interfering with Jacob's vision and leaving large gaps of blank interruptions, he could still detect his mom's movements. He also heard her question. "Oh…that. W-Wheeler took it."

That was quite honest of him to admit.

"Always...taking it."

"Why? He doesn't need them."

"S-Sure he does. Told me when we were at his house. N-Needs them for...sample…"

Again, this was the sort of information that Jacob would normally keep from her while his indicators were green.

Must be his condition. Grace realized that Jacob's primary functions were shutting down, and information that he would normally keep hidden deep inside his hard-drive had the potential of being pulled free…with the right amount of coaxing. This provided an interesting opportunity to find out more about what he and Yaw were working on. She thought about it for a moment. She didn't want to take advantage of the situation, but when would she ever have the opportunity again? "Yaw had some kind of sample?" she asked.

"Yes. Different from…plant. Don't know w-where…he gets it from. M-Maybe…will ask h-him…next time."

It was working. As much as she hated seeing Jacob this way, she needed to continue. "How did your assignment go today? You know…the one about…humans?" She glanced over at Jacob and noticed that even the white glow in his eyes, which had replaced the blue, no longer had a gradient.

"Fine..."

The plates over Grace's eyes rose. This was why he had asked her about humans earlier. It was more for his assignment and less about curiosity. "Any progress?"

"Only first attempt. R-Really difficult. Have to…s-sustain…Not much time…" Jacob's voice was beginning to break up. Grace had to hurry.

"What are you attempting?" she asked.

"R-Recreate…want...to…stay…Earth…c-can't…Mayor…" Everything Jacob had said was broken and lined with distortion.

Grace sighed deeply. There wasn't quite enough information for her to string the pieces together and form anything sensible. Jacob's sensors were now in a frenzy. They were all in conflict with one another, bidding for the last bit of energy still circulating throughout his tiny body. At this point, Jacob had little control over any of them. The red indicator light on his chest flashed one last time and then faded. There was no reason to keep him this way, so Grace reached over and pressed the small reset button on Jacob's chest, manually switching him off. His body collapsed into the seat. The glow in his eyes faded into nothing. He was now in a dormant state which at the moment, was for the best. She had heard all she needed to know from him.

Chapter Five

Jacob's eyes burst open. "Daddy!"

Pin-bot appeared from behind the charger and hovered in front of Jacob's face. "Beep-Daddy?" she said, absolutely confused.

Jacob's eyes attempted to focus on her, but his vision was distorted by the bright light from the window. It was difficult to see through the blinding glow of the sunlight being smeared onto Pin-bot's glossy surface, but a couple of forced beeps confirmed her presence. "Daddy?" Jacob said, cocking his head back, as confused as Pin-bot. "What's Daddy? What are you talking about, Pin-bot?"

Pin-bot opened and closed the flaps on her head in a shrugging motion. "Beep-said-Daddy."

"I-I did?" Jacob frowned. "Why did I say that?" *Why would I say that?*

Again, Pin-bot shrugged using the flaps on her head.

"Probably some kind of glitch." He winced and looked around. "Where am I?"

Pin-bot spun in a complete circle. Her simple CPU did not understand Jacob's question. The closet, the desk, the trophies...it certainly looked like Jacob's room to her.

Jacob reached up and manually adjusted his vision. Each twist of the lens allowed less and less light to filter through, until finally, his closet, his trophies, and his desk appeared from the glaring ambiance. "My...room. But...how did I get here? The last thing I remember is..." Jacob consulted with his hard-drive. He played back his most recent recording but was disappointed that it had stopped the moment he had entered the car. "I guess Mom had to bring me inside."

"Beep-helped," Pin-bot said.

"You did? Thanks, Pin-bot." Jacob glanced down at his chest. He was surprised to see the solid green indicator lights. Last time he had checked, they were red. "Strange...I still feel red."

"Beep-full-charge," Pin-bot pointed out.

The vents on Jacob's cheeks broke open. "I know, Pin-bot. I can see that."

Pin-bot tilted herself to an awkward-looking angle. "Beep-feel-green?" she asked, confused.

Jacob reached up and tapped his chest, making sure that the indicator wasn't faulty or possibly corrupted. "I...I just don't feel fully recharged for some reason." His hand gradually made its way to the back of his head. "Sensor's don't feel right."

He glanced around the room and then focused on the charger that he was still trapped inside. "But I am fully chargeed, aren't I?"

Jacob had every right to question himself. Not only were his sensors complaining but he wasn't hearing the usual and annoying, click-click...click from the charger that would undeniably prove him wrong. "Is this thing even still on?"

Pin-bot flew behind the charger and then returned with a plug in her tiny hands.

"It *is* off," Jacob confirmed, somewhat disappointed. He would have felt more comfortable had the charger still been on. That way, he would know for sure if he still needed more charge and the green indicator light had come on too soon. Since the charger was off, and the green light still remained, he was concerned because he just didn't feel the way he should. To Pin-bot, he said, "You pulled the plug out, huh? Was it finished?"

With the cord still in Pin-bot's hands, her turbines barely had enough power to swivel her back and forth.

"Oh...okay. So it *did* finish. Thanks for turning it off for me. You can put that down now." Jacob shrugged. "I guess I'm fully recharged, then."

Pin-bot disappeared behind the charger and quickly returned, her weight now free from the drag of the plug. "Beep-beep-charged?" she asked, one last time.

Jacob's indicators were green. How could he argue? "Yeah, full charge," Jacob said. "Guess I don't need to be in here anymore. Time to get out."

Pin-bot beeped and flew toward the door. To get help, Jacob guessed. "Wait," he said and folded his upper body at the hips and bent down. "Let me try something." He remembered his mom saying to look down the next time he was in the charger, and there, just as she had told him, were tabs, one on the front of each foot. He reached down and gave the tabs a firm tug. They instantly released their hold on Jacob's feet, and he simply stepped out of the charger. He raised his arm and hovered it in front of Pin-bot. "Wow. Not a single scratch this time."

Pin-bot pointed out the many scratches that were already on his arm.

Jacob retracted his arm, embarrassed. "Those were from the other day. I'm not planning on adding anymore to them, and let's hope it stays this way."

Now free from the charger, Jacob took a step back. He had to absorb the major accomplishment. He crossed his arms over his chest-plate and nodded confidently. "Managed to get out without any noise, no more damage to my plates and the charger is still standing." He smiled at Pin-bot. "Guess I don't need anyone's help anymore."

Pin-bot's eyes suddenly became round and full. In a weak, sympathetic tone she said, "Beep-beep-Pin-bot-help?" Her turbines began to stutter. If Jacob didn't need her help, then she would no longer be needed. *Then what?*

The vents on Jacob's cheeks collapsed. "No-no...I didn't mean that, Pin-bot." He wrapped his hands around her and pulled her in close. "I was just joking. I'll always need you around. You're my favourite helper."

Pin-bot's eyes burst into extra large hearts that even glowed around the edges.

"I'll always let you help me."

"Beep-promise?"

"Yes. I promise." Jacob pressed his face against her cold surface. "But *you* have to promise that you'll always be around to help me."

Pin-bot didn't even hesitate. She wiggled back and forth. "Beep-promise!"

"Good."

Pin-bot attempted to fly out of Jacob's grasp, but he didn't let go.

"Hold on!" he said, scanning every corner of her. "Need to check something."

He spun her around, tipping her from side-to-side, even shaking her. Then he turned her upside down. The entire time, Jacob was forced to endure a relentless assault of beeping. He had to hold on even tighter when she powered her turbine engines to their limits, attempting to free herself. "Calm down, Pin-bot! I'm almost done."

Her fans were now spinning at full speed. Fortunately for Jacob, his hands were blocking off the main flaps on her bottom front half, otherwise her hands would have surely burst out and made short work of his grip.

"Where is it?" Jacob mumbled, trying to concentrate. "Don't see *800* or *1000* anywhere."

Between the incessant beeping and her renewed efforts to get away, it was too much for Jacob to handle. He had to let her go. "Okay-okay! Sorry!"

Pin-bot readjusted herself upright and then faced off in front of Jacob. Her eyes were angled downward.

"What?"

She replied by butting him on the head. "Beep! Beep!"

"Hey!" Jacob rubbed his head. "What was that for? I said I was sorry."

"Beep-beep-doing?" Pin-bot said, backing off, though her eyes were still very much flattened.

Jacob gently placed his hand on top of her crown, attempting to calm her. "Relax, Pin-bot. I won't do that anymore, as long as you answer something for me."

"Beep-beep?"

"Do you know what model number you are? You can either be *800* or *1000*." Jacob hoped she would say *1000*.

Pin-bot's eyes became full. She paused, attempting to find the information Jacob had requested. Her slow CPU made the wait long and agonizing. Unfortunately, her reply didn't help. She opened and closed the flaps on her head, her standard gesture when she didn't know an answer.

"What do you mean, you know? You should."

"Beep-don't-know!"

"Do you feel okay?"

Pin-bot spun in a complete circle. Everything seemed fine. "Beep-beep."

"Do your circuits feel warm at all?"

"Beep-beep," she repeated, only louder.

"Motherboard?

"Beep!"

The commotion they were causing did not go unnoticed. From the bottom of the staircase, Jacob's mom yelled, "What's going on up there?"

"Nothing, Mom! Everything's fine!"

"Jacob? You're recharged? Do you need me to—"

"No, Mom! I'm out. I saw the tabs."

There was a brief pause, and Jacob wondered if it was because his mom was pleased.

"Didn't I tell you?"

"Yes, Mom."

"Good. Come downstairs."

"I'll be right there."

Jacob grazed his hand against Pin-bot's smooth, outer shell. His eyes were round and sympathetic. "Let me know if you feel...different. Okay? I have to go. Important things to do today."

"Beep-help-Jacob."

Jacob giggled. "No. Sorry, Pin-bot. Not this time. It's a bit...complicated for you."

Pin-bot's eyes angled upward, and she turned her back to Jacob.

Jacob sighed. He knew she genuinely wanted to help him—it was what she did best. But this was Forever Yaw. How could she possibly contribute anything? Even with his and Wheeler's CPU combined, they were still having problems making progress. Jacob didn't want to leave and have her be upset with him, although he knew with her limited integrated memory, she would probably forget this whole conversation by the time he got back. "But...that doesn't mean I don't need *any* help."

Pin-bot turned around, her eyes in the shape of crescents.

"Would you just look at this place," he said, waving his arms in exaggerated gestures. "It's a complete mess." He let his eyes wonder, pretending not to even notice Pin-bot. I wonder if there's anyone who could clean it up for me."

"Beep-beep! Beep-beep!" Pin-bot cried out, flying in circles with her eyes so big they took up most of her face.

Jacob staggered back. "You? Well...okay. I guess so. But it's an important task."

"Beep-do it! Beep-do-it!"

"Thank-you, Pin-bot. I know you'll do a good job." Jacob walked to the door and opened it. "Just throw away any junk that we don't need."

"Beep," Pin-bot cheerfully replied.

Before he exited the room, Jacob glanced back. "Oh...I'm sorry I shook you. Just had to be sure."

"Beep-okay."

"Good. See you later, then." Jacob ran down the staircase.

An ecstatic Pin-bot turned back into the room and immediately went to work. The first thing she needed to do was rid the room of objects that did not belong. She flew over to the desk and picked up the box that Jacob's mom had dropped off. Her turbines whirled to a near invisible blur. They were barely powerful enough to get the box up off the floor. She flew over to the closet to place the box inside, but before she made it, two loose screws fell out. Pin-bot dropped the box inside the closet and then flew back for the screws. She picked them up. They looked like the kind of screws she had, but she felt perfectly fine without them. Remembering what Jacob had said about throwing away things they didn't need, she went to the window and tossed the screws out. "Beep-beep!" Another task completed.

* * *

With each trip they took to the school, Grace noticed it was growing increasingly difficult to stay out of the moon's shadow. Today, it reached out and draped itself over the road.

"Soon," Grace said, as the moon's entire mass reflected off of the lenses in her eyes. "Very soon." She sat back, griping the steering wheel even tighter. She waited for a reply from Jacob, but it never came. He was surprisingly quiet. It was if they had picked up exactly where they had left off the last time they were in the car together. The only difference being, he was fully alert with green indicators and a lunchbox containing two full cans of *Pure Blend* by his feet.

"Jacob, I'm sorry I didn't get you out of the red plating yesterday," Grace said. "But you needed to recharge as soon as we got home. I didn't want to waste any time removing them. You were in bad condition."

"Yeah, about that..." His attention veered toward the window. "Sorry, Mom. I should have kept a close eye on my indicators. Must have worried you a lot, huh?"

"Quite a bit, actually. I've never had to manually shut you down before, and hopefully," she said with a firm stare, "I won't have to do it again."

Jacob watched the harsh landscape flow by, wondering why there was a gap of missing information on his hard-drive from yesterday. He'd noticed that right after he stepped out of the charger this morning. He turned to his mom. "So...I guess I wasn't really myself during the ride back from school yesterday..."

"What do you mean?"

"My hard-drive only goes back to when I got inside the car. I'm not sure what happened after that."

Grace shrugged. "Nothing to worry about, Jacob. I was here. You were safe with me."

"I know, Mom. It's not that. I'm just wondering..." He let the sentence fade and glanced out the window again. He folded his hands in his lap and tried to hold still.

"What is it, Jacob?"

"I...I just...Did I seem a little bit off during the ride home? You know, maybe I mentioned something out of the ordinary?" Jacob turned sharply toward his mom. "Because if I did, it didn't mean anything. Really! It didn't!"

"Relax, Jacob."

"I am relaxed."

Certainly doesn't look like it. Grace shrugged. "You did mention a few things, but nothing that I didn't already know."

"Really?" Jacob felt a sense of relief, even if it was minimal. He would have to trust her on this one. "Good. And even *if* I did say something that I wasn't supposed to, I forget what it is."

"Then I think I should mention something to you before *I* forget."

"Yeah?"

"Professor Smith..." she simply said.

That was enough to make Jacob sit straight up. He hadn't seen the professor all day yesterday. And if he recalled, his mom was already waiting outside the school by the time he got there. He wasn't sure how long she had been there, so there was a possibly that she may have gone inside looking for him. If so, surely the professor would have mentioned his absence. "What...what about him?"

"Well, Jacob, he's been around and knows more than you think. If you ever need to ask anything, don't be afraid to do so."

Jacob wondered why she was telling him this. Still, it was good to know the professor would answer questions. "Anything?"

Grace let out a quiet laugh. "There aren't many from his generation left. He's seen it all. Experienced it all. And I bet there's nothing you can ask him that he won't have an answer for."

There *were* a few things Jacob would absolutely like to ask, but all of them seemed to revolve around Forever Yaw. For now, it was better if he kept them to himself. Besides, even though he was on his way to school, Jacob wasn't sure when he would even see the professor again. "I'll be sure to ask him if I need anything." *Whatever that may be.* "Thanks, Mom."

"You're welcome. And don't forget your *Pure Blend*." She pointed to the lunchbox stowed away underneath his feet. "There are two cans in there. Please drink them. *Both* of them."

"I know. Two cans a day, every day."

"I mean it, Jacob." She gave him another one of those stern looks that he knew not to ignore. "I know you're only drinking one."

Both plates over Jacob's eyes rose. *How could she? Unless...* Jacob calculated, making sure that his mom had really said that he didn't talk about anything out of the ordinary yesterday in the car. Telling her that Wheeler had been taking his cans of *Pure Blend* would definitely be considered "out of the ordinary". He hoped that wasn't the reason for her suspicion.

"It's important," she added.

So is Forever Yaw. It was the reason why Wheeler had been taking his *Pure Blend*...at least, that's what he had been told. Jacob shifted in his seat to face his mom. "Why is the *Pure Blend* so important? And why two cans?"

"You saw what happens when you don't drink it."

"But it was my battery that was drained. What does *Pure Blend* have to do with it?"

"Just drink both of them, Jacob. Please! I didn't enjoy having to put you inside the charger that way."

Jacob sighed deeply. "Okay. I'm sorry, Mom. It won't happen again. I promise."

Grace eased the car to the curb in front of the school. Jacob looked out and saw Wheeler who waved and headed toward them. Wheeler jumped the curb and grabbed the door handle. He was obviously prepared to use all his strength to open the door, and the outer edges of his wheels erupted with smoke, as he pulled.

The door swung open and Jacob stepped out. "Hey..."

"Hey, yourself," Wheeler said, as Jacob quietly walked by him. "What? Not even a thank-you? You okay?"

Jacob waited by the curb. "Yeah. Fine."

Wheeler saw the green indicators, a sure sign that Jacob was fully charged. *Wonder why he seems so drained.* He turned his attention inside the car. "Ms. Jacob," he called to Grace, tipping his head forward. "Pleasure to see you again."

Grace gave him a nod. "Yaw. How are you?"

"I'm doing well, Ms. Jacob. You're looking good as usual."

"Oh…thanks," she replied, with a half smile. "As do you."

"Me? Really? Well, I'm always trying to—"

Grace peered over Wheeler's bulk. "Jacob, you forgot something." She pulled the lunchbox from the car's undercarriage and held it out.

Wheeler's eyes widened and he reached out. "It's okay, Ms. Jacob. I've got it."

Grace pulled her hand back quickly. "No, Yaw. It's okay. This is Jacob's."

"Certainly, Ms. Jacob." Wheeler backed away and then reached over and pushed Jacob toward the car. "Go on, Jacob. Grab it. It's *your* lunchbox."

Yeah, for now. Jacob retrieved his lunchbox from his mom's hands.

"Make sure..." his mom said, with a pair of stern eyes.

"I know, Mom." Jacob backed away. "Two cans a day."

"Good. I'll meet you here after school." She closed the car door.

"Bye, Ms. Jacob!"

Grace nodded. "See you two later."

The car lifted off the ground, and Grace drove away.

"Wish I had a mom," Wheeler said. "I would never forget my lunchbox."

"It's a good thing yours is integrated."

Wheeler wasn't sure if Jacob meant that as a joke or not. He dropped his wheel arm and circled Jacob a few times. "I see you made it back here all by yourself yesterday."

"No thanks to you."

The animosity in Jacob's tone made Wheeler stop and look intently at him. "What do you mean by that, One Bolt?"

Jacob pounded his chest. "My batteries! I was completely drained by the time I made it back here."

"You were?"

"Yeah. Completely drained. Temporarily shut down."

Wheeler backed away slightly. He had never heard Jacob use that sort of tone on him. "Sorry, One Bolt. I didn't know it was *that* serious. But I told you, I couldn't go with you. The sample. Remember?"

"Oh...so you got some?"

"Took a bit of effort but yeah. I got some."

"Then I guess my shut down wasn't all for nothing."

"Wait," Wheeler said, rolling closer again. "You mean you nearly shut down or shut down completely?"

"Not completely. I'm still here, aren't I?"

"I mean, were your functions still enabled? Were you still able to control your hard-drive and CPU?" Although there was only a slight hesitation from Jacob, it was enough to send Wheeler screeching around in full circle. "You told her, didn't you, One Bolt! You told her about Forever Yaw!"

"Who? My mom?" Jacob waved his hand in front of his chest. "No...no-no! I didn't tell her!"

Wheeler gave Jacob a piercing leer. "One Bolt?"

Jacob shrugged, his mouth angled down to one side. "I mean...I don't think I did."

Wheeler threw his hands in there air. "Come on, One Bolt! This was between you and me."

"It still is. Right before we got here, I asked her if I said anything odd yesterday. She said everything was fine. That must mean she still doesn't know about this."

Wheeler mumbled, "First generation parts and he can't even keep his functions running long enough to keep a secret."

"Trust me. She doesn't know!"

"Are you sure?"

"Yes! And if you're so concerned about keeping it a secret, how about you drive me back to the school next time, instead of making me drain my batteries."

As Jacob talked, he was banging his lunchbox against the side of his leg.

Wheeler placed his hand on Jacob's shoulder. "Okay. I heard you. Everything's fine. Can we calm down now?"

"I am calm."

"Good. Now...let's focus. I have the sample back at my place. It's ready to go. And so should we." He turned around and offered Jacob a pair of handle bars. "Let's get going, alright? You know the routine."

"Yeah, I know." Gently this time, Jacob placed his lunchbox onto Wheeler's base and then wrapped his hands around the handle bars.

A moment went by, but Wheeler did not feel any heavier. He wondered why Jacob had not stepped on yet. *Why was he hesitating?* When Wheeler felt Jacob let go of the handlebars, he spun around. "One Bolt?"

Jacob stood motionless, facing the school. "Wait, Wheeler."

"Wait for what?" Wheeler directed his attention to where Jacob was staring. Most of the students, who had been gathered in front of the school, were now streaming through the door to go inside. Only one remained on the outer sidewalk, and she was heading their way. "Oh, no..." Wheeler cried, burying his face inside his hand. "Not again..."

Hope stopped in front of the pair, donning her usual smile that seemed to light up her green eyes the way the sun lit up the sky. At least that's what Jacob thought. "Hello, Jacob. Nice seeing you again." She waved at Wheeler. "You, too."

"Yeah-yeah," Wheeler said, turning away.

"Hi, Hope," Jacob said, attempting to match the intensity of her smile with one of his own. "You look very nice."

Hope's smile did the impossible and got even bigger. "Thanks, Jacob, as do you. I waited for you both all day yesterday, but you never showed up. So what happened? Where were you?"

Jacob tried to keep his smile in place. "We were...well...you know. We were—"

Wheeler poked Jacob in the side with his elbow, ending his pathetic attempt at a reply. "Went to get rust samples," he said. Then he spun around and wrapped his wheel arm around Jacob's shoulder, pulling him in close. "Didn't we, One Bolt?"

Jacob tried to pull free, but every time he struggled, Wheeler simply revved his wheel, digging hot rubber into his shoulder. "Stop that!"

"Stop what?" Wheeler revved his wheel again.

"That!"

"Oh...Sorry, One Bolt. Didn't even know I was doing that." He then whispered close to Jacob's ear. "Just keep your mouth shut. I'll deal with her."

Fearing the rubber marks would stain his exterior and not able to endure the smell of burnt rubber, Jacob kept quiet...for now.

"Rust samples?" Hope said. "For the assignment?"

"Yeah, the assignment." Wheeler slapped his head with disappointment. "Oh! That's right. The professor sent you off to be with another team. That's too bad."

"No, he didn't."

"So you're still part of our team?" Jacob couldn't keep the elation out of his voice and immediately felt the friction of the wheel against his shoulder. "What?" he whispered to Wheeler.

"We thought the professor would have surely assigned you to another team," Wheeler said to Hope.

"Wouldn't have even considered it," Hope replied. "I'm still part of this team."

This made Jacob smile, but he didn't want to say anything else, seeing as how Wheeler's arm was still around his shoulder. He was beginning to hate the smell of burnt rubber.

"Where are the rust samples? Can I see them?"

"Ha! Did you hear that, One Bolt? She wants to see some. Why do you want to see them? It's just rust. Rust is everywhere." He pointed at the school. "There's some rust." He pointed at the ground. "There's some rust." He even pointed to a small section just above his wheel-well. "Here's some rust."

Hope frowned. "Just asking. No need to go all crazy, Wheeler."

"I'm not crazy. The samples that One Bolt and I collected aren't here. We left them back at my place."

"Then you're going to go and get them, I assume?"

"Shiny and smart," Wheeler replied. "Your dad must be so proud of you." Wheeler removed his heavy wheel arm from Jacob's shoulder. "There's still a lot to do. Things to collect. You know how it is. It's best that One Bolt and I get going." He gave Jacob a poke to the side with his elbow. "Now!"

"He's right. We should get going."

"You're not going inside?" Hope asked. "Not at all? Not even to see the professor?"

"That's right," Wheeler said.

Hope crossed her arms over her breast-plate and stomped the ground. "Fine. Then neither am I."

"Fine. Do whatever you want." Wheeler turned his back to her. He was ready to leave.

Jacob, on the other hand, didn't move. There was something infectious in Hope's stubbornness. "You're not going inside?"

She shook her head. "No. And unless *Wheeler* wants to go inside and tell the professor something different, we're still a team, and I'm going with you."

"I'm not going inside," Wheeler said.

"Neither am I."

"Fine."

"Fine!"

"Okay-okay," Jacob said. "You two calm down. I'm sure we can work something out."

Wheeler grabbed Jacob's arm and pulled him away a few feet. "What are you doing, One Bolt?" he whispered harshly.

"She wants to come with us," Jacob whispered back. "How can I say, no?"

"We talked about this, One Bolt. Her dad. The Mayor, remember?"

"What are you two talking about over there?" Hope asked, standing on the tip of her toes to see them.

"Nothing. It doesn't concern you, Hope," Wheeler called out. Then he whispered to Jacob, "Hope's not coming with us. Got it?"

"Fine," Jacob said. "We let her go back to class. Then when the professor asks, and you know he will, she'll tell him we're at your place. He'll tell my mom, and once she finds out..." Jacob slapped his hands together. "...no more drive to the school. No more Forever Yaw. The moon's almost here, and you'll have to figure out how to recreate humans all on your own."

Wheeler stood still for a moment and thought about what Jacob had just said. "You uh...you calculated all of that?"

"Yeah. Just now."

Wheeler shook his head. “Still…no!” He turned and faced Hope. “Even if I wanted you to come along, I don’t have enough room for the both of you.” He pointed back to his handle bars. “See? There’s only room for one.”

Hope grabbed Jacob’s hand, climbed onto Wheeler’s base and pulled Jacob up next to her. “There’s plenty of room.”

“Hey! What are you doing back there? Stop it! You’re going to break something. Get off! Did you hear me? Get off! There’s not enough—”

Hope quickly settled in. “I’m on,” she said. She gave Jacob a wink. “Are you on, Jacob?”

“I’m on,” Jacob said, smiling. He had to admire her persistence.

Wheeler glanced over his shoulder. There they were, secure and ready to go.

“I told you,” Hope said. “Plenty of room back here.”

Wheeler remained motionless, refusing to rev his wheels or drop his wheel arm to the ground. “I don’t care. I’m not moving. We’re not going anywhere.”

“Fine,” Hope said. “We can stay here for as long as you want. I’m not stepping off, and neither is Jacob.” To show Wheeler that she meant it, she gave him a sturdy kick to the back.

“Hey!” Wheeler cried.

“I think she means it.”

“I don’t care! I’m not going anywhere until one of you gets off!”

Jacob saw Hope’s leg recoiling, ready to make contact with Wheeler’s back again. He waved it off. “Wait,” he said. “I’ve got it.” Jacob leaned close to Wheeler’s ear and whispered, “The sample. Remember? It won’t last long if we stay here.”

Wheeler frowned and slapped his hand against his base. “Ah, damn it. The sample...”

“The what?” Hope asked.

“Nothing!” Although frustrated to have a second passenger, Wheeler had no choice. The sample and Forever Yaw, were more important than any disagreements. He shook his head and then revved his wheels.

Still leaning close to Wheeler's ear, Jacob whispered again, “Wheeler, go slow first. I don’t want to fall off in front of her. It would be embarrassing.”

“Yeah-yeah...Just tell your partner to hang on.” He dropped his wheel arm to the ground, and finally, they were off.

* * *

The suspension systems joining each wheel to his base had not been modified to handle the added weight, and they squealed and strained, as Wheeler took them as far as he could. They had drove by the anchor points and Project Redemption without paying them much attention and were now at the point where the road no longer existed.

Wheeler stopped so the riders could get off and was relieved to not have the extra weight. He took off ahead of them, intentionally increasing the distance between them. He was still annoyed that Hope had to come along—even more annoyed that Jacob had taken her side. He was doing a lot of that lately. Even now, as he glanced over his shoulder, Wheeler saw how they were walking close together and holding an animated conversation. "Wish my wheels would deflate. Then what? They'd have to carry me all the way back. Ha! Then she'd wish she had never come along."

He grinned for a moment until he realized that would hurt him more in the long run. "I like my wheels. Better keep them inflated..."

Jacob tried to keep a steady pace so they would not fall too far behind Wheeler, but he did appreciate the opportunity to talk to Hope without Wheeler's smart remarks. "Where's Brute today?" he asked. "I thought he was always with you."

"Usually. But not for the past couple of days. He's completing orders from my dad."

"What orders? If it's okay to ask."

"It's okay, Jacob. Building the launch pads and loading up all the pods for Project New Hope. That's what my dad calls it."

Oh…that...

"He's also doing something else that I don't know much about. I just overhead them talking about rebuilding something. Not sure what it is though. Must be something important." Hope leaned closer to Jacob. "But Brute's not that bad. Not as bad as Wheeler makes him out to be."

"Hard for me to judge, Hope. I've only met him twice." *Glad I don't have to see him at the moment.*

They walked on a little ways in silence, picking a path amid all the clutter on the road. They had to be careful not to stumble and fall. Hope paused and raised her hand in front of her face. A strange, thin coat of shimmering-white crystals had formed all along her exterior.

"It's okay," Jacob said. "I'm also covered in it."

"What is it?"

"I don't know what it is exactly, but Wheeler told me it's caused by the cold and something in the air." Jacob brushed off the fine layer of crystals on Hope's arm, exposing her nearly flawless casing. "It shouldn't damage anything."

"Thanks." She tried to smile, but Jacob noticed that it was unusually forced.

"Are you okay?"

Hope tilted her head from side-to-side. There was definitely a slight rigidness about her that Jacob had never seen before. Even the glow in her eyes seemed to be paler than normal. Jacob shook his head. *That's ridiculous. They'll always be vibrant, even out here.*

"I feel a bit strange," Hope said. "Ever since we crossed over from sunlight to complete darkness."

"I know what you mean. Feels like all my functions are slowing down."

"Yes. Exactly."

"Wheeler thinks it's because we're not used to being out this far. That's probably why he doesn't feel the effects. He's used to it."

It was true. Ahead, Jacob could see that Wheeler was moving at the same confident pace that he used all the time. "But don't worry, Hope. It'll all be better once we're inside." Jacob called out to Wheeler, "We're almost there, right?"

Blending neatly with the darkness, Wheeler raised his hand and waved. "Yeah-yeah..."

"Just a little further," Jacob said to Hope. "Promise."

Hope nodded toward Wheeler. "He doesn't really want me coming along, does he?"

"It's not that... he's just...Well, sometimes he's a little—"

"That's okay. You don't have to cover up for him. I know how he feels about me."

Jacob tightened the corners of his mouth. "He just has a lot on his mind lately."

"I know, Jacob. Don't we all?"

They walked on again in silence, and Jacob took advantage of the opportunity to scan Hope from the corner of his eyes. Every part of her, from her slender legs highlighted by patches of black, to the balanced indentations flowing evenly down the centre of each plate, was constructed with the utmost quality. Everything about her had a glistening layer of newness. Not even a single bolt was visible, making her uniquely streamlined.

Of course, Jacob had to go and spoil some of the perception about her with his keen attention to detail. He had never been close enough to observe Hope's finer details...until now. His eyes penetrated through the only seam on the left side of her breast-plate. Deep inside was Hope's only flaw. Only visible at this close proximity was a square enclosure with wires and tubing sprouting from the entire perimeter. From its corners, four small pistons could be seen pulsating in and out of their individual chambers. A single wire was fed from this enclosure and was connected directly to the indicator light on Hope's breast-plate. Whatever that enclosure was, Jacob knew why it was kept out of sight. Its coarseness was a complete contrast compared to Hope's nearly flawless exterior.

"I know," Hope said, catching Jacob staring. She covered the seam along her left side with her hand. "I would hide it completely if I could."

"No!" Jacob said, immediately looking away. "It's hardly noticeable at all."

"No one is perfect these days. Although my dad tries to tell me differently. Even at a time like this, he always seems to have a new upgrade or a new part for me. I guess that's one of the benefits of having the Mayor for a dad."

Jacob raised his hands and turned them in front of his face. "Yeah, I guess that would be nice."

"You're wanting an upgrade, Jacob?"

Jacob dropped his hands to the side. "Well...I've been a first generation for so long—"

"There's nothing wrong with being a first generation. Less bolts you have to worry about." Hope smiled.

Jacob shrugged. "Yeah. I guess that's one of the few good things about being a first generation. I'm just getting a bit tired of seeing the same old parts every time I look down."

"What about your other parts? Your exterior is first generation but your CPU seems really advanced. I know CPUs are difficult to find these days. How are you able to upgrade yours so often?"

Jacob had to pause. It was ironic that with his advanced CPU, he had to stop and calculate Hope's rather simple question. He finally replied, "You know something, Hope? I really don't know. My CPU *must* have been upgraded at some point. I mean, they're the first things to be upgraded. But I can't seem to find any information about it. There's no way of knowing unless I ask my mom."

"I'm sure it was upgraded at some point. I mean, you *did* win all those trophies."

"Yeah…I guess so..."

"It's a shame that with your CPU, we couldn't come up with something better than rust for our assignment."

"I-I'm not exactly sure what you mean, Hope… Rust is—"

"Sure, rust is important. Don't get me wrong, Jacob. Like Wheeler said, rust is everywhere. I just thought…you know?" Her tone softened, almost in a sigh. "Everything around us is falling apart. We don't have much time left here on Earth. I was just hoping for an assignment that would somehow improve our situation."

"Like what?"

"I don't know. As far-fetched as it sounds, wouldn't it be great if we could bring the Earth back to the way it was."

"That's asking a lot, Hope. Everything's so bad right now. Trying to bring it back seems nearly impossible." *If only she knew what Wheeler and I were up to.* If she did, Jacob was confident that she would offer him another smile—the biggest, brightest smile she could afford, to add to his collection.

"I know, Jacob. You're right." Hope's eyes began to wonder. "It's hard to believe that we're going to leave this soon." She swept her arms across the barren landscape. "All of this."

When she looked back at Jacob, he was shocked to see that the light in her green eyes had dimmed even more.

"It's too bad," Hope continued. "I like Earth. I don't want to leave."

"You mean, you'd rather stay here? On Earth?"

"I would stay here forever if I could." A frown appeared over her unblemished face. "But I know there's no way. We have to leave before the moon reaches Earth."

That was a sobering thought. Jacob did not like to think about the day the moon would hit the Earth or the fact that they would have to leave before it did. His attention was caught by a loud screeching sound straight ahead, and he looked up to see Wheeler only a few feet from them, smoke floating around his wheels. Wheeler then spun around and drove next to the pair. "There *is* a way!" he said. "One Bolt and I have been working on it."

This time, it was Jacob who pulled Wheeler to the side. "What are you doing? I thought you said not to tell—"

"Quiet, One Bolt. I need to talk to Hope about something."

"Hope? But I thought you said you didn't want to tell anyone, especially Hope. You know…because of the Mayor. Remember?"

"Think about it, One Bolt. The Mayor is her dad."

"I know he is. And that *is* the problem, right?"

"No, that's the reason why this is going to work out after all. Once she sees what we're trying to do, and is excited about it, she can tell the Mayor, and it may temporarily delay his plans. He wouldn't refuse his own daughter."

"Are you sure about this?"

"Just let me deal with it, One Bolt."

I have been, and look how far it's gotten us.

Wheeler pushed Jacob aside and rolled closer to Hope. "Did I hear you right? Did you say you wanted to stay right here on Earth?"

"You heard that from way up there?"

"Hey, I have sensitive sensors. I'm not all wheels, you know."

"Hope was wondering why our assignment wasn't about doing something to improve our situation," Jacob said.

"Really? Even with the plans the Mayor…er, your *dad,* has made for all of us?"

"That's something my dad wants. I don't want to leave."

"Even if it means staying here and trying to rebuild?"

"Yes. Exactly."

Wheeler glanced over to Jacob with a pair of wide eyes and then turned back to Hope. "But he *is* your dad. You're surely inclined to do exactly as he tells you."

"Not always. I can calculate for myself. And I know my dad won't leave here without me. If that's what you're trying to get at, Wheeler. I know he won't."

"Is that so?"

Jacob could see the glow in Wheeler's eyes intensifying. Could it be that Wheeler was finally ready to offer a bit of slack on the line of tension that he had strung around Hope? Maybe Wheeler was starting to see what Jacob had seen all along—that the Mayor's opinions were not always shared by Hope.

"But there's really no reason to stay," Hope said. "I don't think there's anything any of us can do to change this."

Wheeler reached up, tapped his head and allowed his trio of lights to burst into the night. He revved his wheels and drove off. "Follow me!"

Hope looked over at Jacob. "Wait...Does that mean I'm about to find out what you're really working on?"

"Wheeler thinks so."

She slapped her hands together. "I knew you two had no interest in rust."

"Really? How?"

She tilted her head to one side. "Come on. Rust? Everyone knows that rust is caused by the combination of oxidation and moisture making contact to an expose metal surface."

Jacob smiled. *Wheeler was right. Shiny and smart.*

As they hurried to catch up with Wheeler, Hope asked, "Just wondering, Jacob, why does he have a light on his chin?"

"Sometimes, it's best not to ask."

Three light beams merged into one, as Wheeler inched closer to the lone structure overlapping the pitch-black background. He accelerated forward and waited by the exposed entryway until Jacob and Hope joined him.

"You live here?" Hope asked, just shy of stepping through the entryway.

"Yeah, why? What's wrong with it?" Wheeler reached over and tapped one of the sheets of rusted sheet metal that was anchored to the house by even rustier bolts. "This thing was built with my own hands...I mean, hand. It's solid." The section of sheet metal broke off and fell to the ground with a clang. "Well...maybe not this piece."

Jacob leaned over to Hope and whispered, "This is nothing. You should see the inside."

Hope giggled. "Maybe I should just stay out here, then."

"I heard that," Wheeler said. He swung his arm back and forth, signalling for the pair to make their way inside. "Let's go, already. Nothing more to see out here."

Wheeler turned on the light to the single room, and Jacob stepped in only to stop with his mouth agape. "Hey! What happened here?"

"What do you mean?" Wheeler said.

Jacob looked over at Wheeler, who was smiling and leaning up against the wall. "The mess? What happened to the mess?"

"I don't see a mess," Hope said.

"It was here. I saw it. I stepped over, around and on top of it."

If it weren't for the rust stains, crumpled walls and exposed framing, Wheeler's room would be practically spotless. Everything that had once been on the floor, forming the mess that Jacob had seen the previous day, was now either hung neatly on the walls or gone.

"No reason to for me *not* to keep a tidy establishment." Wheeler said, driving deeper into the room. He bent down and smoothed out a rough, rust-eaten section of the floor with his hand. "Thought I'd clean up a little bit."

"You mean a lot," Jacob said, looking around.

"Yeah, well, I was getting tired of not being able to find things."

"I thought you said you knew where everything was?"

"You don't forget anything, do you, One Bolt?"

"Not once I record it onto my hard-drive."

"Anyway..." Wheeler drove over to his desk. "Enough time wasting. Let's get to work. That *is* the reason why we all came out here."

Jacob and Hope joined Wheeler at the desk but stayed closer to its edge. This allowed Wheeler the chance to stoop over and plunge his entire upper half deep beneath the desk.

"I'm really excited to see what you two have been working on," Hope said, as they listened to Wheeler rummage underneath the desk. Then he reappeared with a microscope in hand.

"A microscope?" Hope said.

"Good for you," Wheeler said.

"Hey, isn't that same one we have at our school?"

"Uh…no…" Wheeler replied. "I…uh…found this one…somewhere."

"Can I see it?"

"You'll get your chance soon enough. But first…" Wheeler cocked his head toward Jacob. "Flick the switch. Remember? We need some concentrated sunlight."

"Concentrated sunlight?" Hope repeated.

"You'll see," Wheeler said. "Might want to adjust your vision."

"Why?"

"Enough with the questions. Just trust me."

Hope nodded to Jacob, and he took that as a signal that her vision was adjusted and ready to cope with any changes in light. He nodded back and then flicked the switch. The ceiling opened, and sunlight surged inside the room, channelling a thick beam onto a selected area on the desk.

"Wow, that's bright," Hope said.

"I told you." Wheeler placed the microscope on the desk, making sure it was directly in the light's path.

As Hope's vision stabilized, she watched Wheeler place a pair of slides into the microscope's holding bay. He turned his shoulder inward, blocking her field of view. "What is that?" Hope asked.

"Give me a moment, will you?"

Hope looked over at Jacob, who said, "He has to set it up first. It might take a while..."

"Done!" Wheeler said.

"Oh...that was quick."

"I've been practising."

Hope took a step toward the desk. "Can I look now?"

Wheeler shook his head. "Nope. Not right now. We need to get something settled first."

"Me?"

"Not you, One Bolt." Wheeler drove close to Hope, crossed his arms and looked at her with a stern expression. "Both One Bolt and I have our hard-drives running," he said, "so we're recording this. I want to be perfectly clear about this. You said that no matter what happens, you would rather stay here on Earth instead of…" he pointed up at the ceiling, "…out there, wherever that might be. Am I correct?"

"That's what she said," Jacob pointed out.

"Quiet, One Bolt."

"Yes, Wheeler. Jacob's right. That's what I said."

"Okay. And you also mentioned that your dad, the Mayor, would not leave you here on your own."

"I should be able to convince him to stay...as long as I have a good excuse. He wouldn't just leave me here."

"Are you sure about that?"

"Positive...But like I said, there has to be a good excuse for him not to leave."

Wheeler turned to Jacob. "Got all of that, One Bolt?"

"What?" Jacob asked.

"Was your hard-drive running? Did you even record any of that?"

Jacob sighed. "Yes, I heard. Now will you leave her alone? All she wants is to see Forever Yaw."

"Forever Yaw?" Hope's eyes flattened out, and it looked like she was trying not to smirk. "Who came up with that name?"

"I know," Jacob said. "I've been trying to tell him it needs a different name."

"Forget the name," Wheeler cried.

"Shouldn't it be called Forever Yaw *and* Jacob? Or Forever Jacob and Yaw? You're both working on it, right?"

Wheeler slammed his wheel against the corner of the desk. "Will you forget the damn name?" He immediately brought his wheel up to his face and scanned its surface. "Hope I didn't deflate it..."

"Okay-okay. Sorry. Let's get to work."

"Yes," Jacob agreed. "That's why we're here."

Wheeler sighed. "Finally!" He extended his hand in front of him. "*Pure Blend* me," he commanded.

Hope stared blankly at Wheeler's exposed hand.

"Come on, come on," Wheeler said. "I need some *Pure Blend*. I know both of you have some."

Jacob said to Hope, "It helps with the divisions."

Hope curled the corners of her mouth. "Divisions?"

"Will someone please give me some *Pure Blend?*" Wheeler pleaded.

"Yes," Hope said.

"Of course," Jacob added.

Wheeler slapped his larger wheel hand into his open hand and shouted, "So *Pure Blend* me! *Pure Blend* me, damn it! I need *Pure Blend*!"

"Okay-okay. Calm down." Jacob reached into his lunchbox at the same time Hope reached into a small compartment on the side of her leg. In unison, they pulled out their own can of *Pure Blend* and offered it to Wheeler.

Wheeler glanced at the pair. "Only need a drop or two. Not two full cans."

"Take mine." Hope looked over at Jacob. "It's okay, Jacob. I have a lot more at home."

"You do?" Jacob said, wide-eyed.

"*You do*?" Wheeler said, with wider eyes.

Jacob smiled and pushed his offering closer to Wheeler. "It's okay, Hope. It's for a good cause, so I don't mind."

"No, really," Hope said, smiling. "I don't mind, either."

Wheeler shook his head. "You two make me want to lose my bolts." He reached out and took Jacob's offering then turned back to the desk.

"It's okay, Hope. I have another one in my lunchbox."

Hope smiled and held her arm out to Jacob. "Here. I know it's your favourite, too. You can have mine. I have plenty."

"Are you sure? I mean—"

"Oh, just take the damn thing!" Wheeler said, turning around and grabbing the *Pure Blend* from Hope's hand and tossing it into Jacob's lunchbox. "Two cans a day...and something. Right?"

Jacob looked over at Hope. "Thanks."

"You're welcome," Hope replied.

"Anytime you want to join me," Wheeler said with a note of sarcasm. "Or are you trying for some kind of award for being polite?"

"Ready to go," Hope said.

"Wow, you even cleaned off the top of your desk," Jacob said.

Wheeler cracked open the can of *Pure Blend*. "Clean room calls for a clean desk." He backed away from the desk and allowed Hope to walk by. He held up his hand to keep Jacob away. "Stay back, One Bolt, you've seen it already. It's Hope turn."

"But I want to see it again."

"There *are* two eyepieces," Hope said.

"I know there are two eyepieces," Wheeler replied. "Who do you think put them there? Microscopes from the school only come with one—" A fake smirk appeared on Wheeler's face. "I mean...the microscope I *found*, only came with one. I mounted the other. The second one is for me."

Hope reached out and pulled Jacob in next to the microscope. "Go ahead, Jacob. Use this one. I'll use Wheeler's."

"Hey, wait!" Wheeler said. "That's not what I planned."

"Sorry, Wheeler," Jacob said. Both he and Hope quickly lowered their faces to the microscope.

"What am I supposed to do, now?"

"You can pour the *Pure Blend*," Jacob said.

As if Wheeler had much choice. He gave the pair a moment to observe what was already inside the microscope. "Well? Do you see it or not?"

"I see them," Jacob said.

"Not you, One Bolt. I meant Hope."

"I...I see something," Hope replied. Her eyes shifted from one edge of the sample to the next, but her CPU just didn't have the processing power to calculate what she was looking at. "What are all of those things?"

"Cells," Jacob and Wheeler said in unison.

"Cells? What are cells?"

Wheeler tapped Jacob on the back. "I got this one. Cells are the building blocks of life."

"Wow! Really? I've never seen anything like this before."

"Ha! Of course not! Why would you? This is ground breaking. This is Earth shattering. This is—"

"Are they supposed to divide like that?" Hope asked.

"That's nothing. Watch this." Wheeler hovered the can of *Pure Blend* over the microscope's holding bay. "You haven't seen anything yet. Wait until I add some of this."

"Try more than a few drops this time," Jacob advised.

"Yeah-yeah." Wheeler tipped the can, and a thin stream of clear fluid trickled down and splashed on the sample.

"That's enough!" Jacob yelled.

"Okay-okay. I heard you, One Bolt." Wheeler placed the can back down on the desk.

The reaction of the *Pure Blend* on the sample was immediate. The cells were dividing uncontrollably.

"Wow! Look at them!" Hope cried out.

Wheeler gave Jacob a firm bump on the side. Jacob pulled away from the microscope and looked up only to see one of the biggest smiles he had ever seen on Wheeler's face. Jacob smiled back. Even if Hope didn't quite understand what she was looking at, Forever Yaw had a tremendous effect on her. Exactly what Wheeler was hoping for.

"I think we convinced her," Wheeler said in a low voice. "Look at her. She's can't even look away."

"Neither did I the first time."

Wheeler touched Hope on the shoulder. "What do you think? Pretty impressive, huh?"

"Yes…" Hope said, giving Wheeler cause to smile at Jacob, "…at first."

Wheeler's smile faded.

Hope looked up with a concerned expression. "But are they supposed to stop dividing?"

Wheeler reeled back. "Stop? What do you mean, stop?"

"They stopped. Those things…those cells or whatever you call them, they're not dividing anymore." She gestured for both Jacob and Wheeler to come and see.

"She's right." Jacob said.

"They've completely stopped!" Wheeler pulled his face from the eyepiece and stared at Hope.

"It wasn't because of me," Hope said. "I didn't touch anything."

"I know." Jacob pulled away from the microscope. "It does that for some reason. It's something we have to solve."

Wheeler pulled the slide out from the microscope, brought it up to his face and scanned the sample. Then he tossed the slide over his shoulder. "Damn it! Dead. Another one…"

"Dead?" Hope said. "You mean, stop dividing? Was it supposed to stop dividing?"

Wheeler looked at Jacob and shook his head. "Was it supposed to stop, she says. Of course it's not supposed to stop!"

"Okay, calm down, Wheeler. There's no need to yell at Hope."

"Well, it's a stupid question." He drove in circles so fast, a cloud of smoke started following him. "How are we supposed to recreate humans if we can't even sustain a small sample?"

Hope took a few steps away from the desk. "H-Humans...You're trying to recreate...h-humans?"

"Yes!" Wheeler said firmly. "That's the whole point of Forever Yaw. Recreating humans!"

"Humans..." Hope murmured.

"Yes," Jacob said, with a bit more reserve than Wheeler. "We have to recreate them."

"But...why? Why do you want to recreate them? They're dead. My dad told me they were all gone."

Wheeler stopped his relentless circling in the heart of the room. "That sure was convenient of him."

"And that's why we have to bring them back," Jacob said.

"I don't understand."

"What's so difficult to understand?" Wheeler said. He drove closer to Hope, with a sharp glow in his eyes. "We were created by humans. Agreed?"

"Yes," Hope replied. "That I know."

"Good. Now because no one, not even your dad, thinks we have any chance left on this Earth, why not attempt to save our kind by bringing back the ones who created us in the first place?"

"It would almost be like reversing the cycle of evolution," Jacob added.

"Exactly," Wheeler said, glancing over at Jacob. "You just thought of that, One Bolt?"

"Yup."

"Well...it's perfect."

"Thanks."

"So you see?" Wheeler said to Hope. "They created us, so they must know how to bring us back from the last stages of our evolution."

"Extinction..." Hope said, her voice soft.

"Exactly. If we find a way to bring humans back, it's almost certain that they'll eventually bring us back. The laws of evolution dictate this."

"Recreate the ones who created us," Jacob recited.

Wheeler gave Hope some room. "Exactly."

Hope was still, and her eyes turned in a rhythmic pattern, as her CPU processed everything that had been explained to her. It wouldn't be so difficult had she been equipped with a CPU that, at the very least, equalled that of the two standing in front of her. "Recreate the ones who created us," she repeated over and over, as her CPU worked. She knew that humans had created her kind. Her dad had told her that. Even with his bias toward them, her dad could not dispute this fact. "Reverse the cycle of evolution..."

"That's right," Wheeler said. "From our final stages of evolution to the very beginning…to when we were normal...when we were strong."

"They must know how to do this," Jacob added.

Wheeler waved his hand in front of Jacob and whispered. "Just let her calculate it on her own. She'll get it…Even you got it."

Hope's eyes refocused on the sample that Wheeler had tossed on the floor. As her CPU hummed, she kept repeating, "Recreate the ones who created us..."

Then after another few moments of deep calculations, Hope finally shouted, "It might work!" She slapped her hands together. "I think it just might work!"

"I knew you'd finally see it," Wheeler said.

"Of course she would."

"But *how* will it work? Has this ever been done before?"

Wheeler snickered. "Who would have ever tried with your dad as the Mayor?"

Jacob pushed Wheeler aside, walked over to Hope and said, "What Wheeler is trying say, is that it's not going to be easy. We don't have that much time left."

"Especially with your dad around," Wheeler added.

"I think she gets it, Wheeler."

"I do," Hope said. "And you're right. It's not something my dad would agree on."

"But he must agree that if we don't do anything soon, we'll become just like the humans."

"Extinct," Wheeler added. "Dead, gone, shut down—"

"He does."

"Good," Wheeler said. "And it's best that he never finds out about this."

"You don't want to tell him?"

"Ha!" Wheeler turned to Jacob. "I can't believe she even asked us that."

"Yes, Hope," Jacob said. "He can't find out. He might not want us to get our project to work."

"We know how your dad feels about humans. It's not like he hides his opinions about them…or very well. Project Redemption, Project Retaliation…remember?"

"But he *is* the Mayor," Hope countered. "He'll find out eventually."

"Yeah, and if eventually is around the same time we figure this out, then fine."

Jacob reached out and placed his hand on hers. "We have to keep this from him. At least for now. Until we get something going."

There was a pause before Hope nodded. "If it'll save us from extinction...then I'll do anything you need."

"Exactly what I wanted to hear," Wheeler said.

"Thanks, Hope," Jacob said, releasing his hold.

Hope looked around the room. "Okay. Now what? We don't have much time left. I mean, the moon is almost—"

"We know," Wheeler said. "We know. That's why we have to keep working."

"Do you have another one of those slides?"

"Samples," Jacob corrected Hope. "Do you have another sample somewhere, Wheeler? We might get lucky this time."

"Ha! Luck? If luck was on our side, we'd have humans running around all over the place by now."

"Just get us another sample."

Wheeler shook his head. "Can't. Don't have any more."

Jacob placed his hands on his waist. "What do you mean you don't have any more? You said you got some earlier."

"Yeah, and now it's dead."

"You were only able to find *one* sample?"

"No-no. There's more where that came from. I just don't have any with me right now."

"Then go and get some."

"Yeah, go and get some, Wheeler," Hope added.

"Fine." Wheeler revved his wheels, dropped his wheel arm and drove toward the hallway. He turned back and said, "I'll need some *Pure Blend*."

"What for?" Hope asked.

"To get the sample," Jacob said. "He never tells me why. He just takes it."

"Come on! Come on!" Wheeler yelled out. "*Pure Blend*, one of you."

Hope reached into a compartment in her other leg, pulled out a can and handed it to Wheeler.

"You're proving useful after all," Wheeler said. "Maybe I won't need *you* at all, One Bolt."

"Just go and get the sample," Jacob said.

Wheeler spun around but didn't get too far before Hope called out, "Wait. What do you want us to do while you're gone?"

"Don't know, don't care. Do whatever. Just don't mess up anything. Took me forever to clean this place up."

"Then why don't we go with you?"

"Yeah," Jacob said. "Can we go, too? I want to see where you get these samples."

Wheeler revved his wheels, disappeared down the short hallway and then out the entryway. "No!" he yelled back. "She doesn't like to be disturbed."

The screeching of Wheeler's wheels had yet to dissolve, when Jacob turned to Hope. "Did he just say 'she'?"

"I think so."

Jacob paced in short bursts back and forth, calculating. "He never told me anything about this. Who's this 'she' that he's talking about?"

Hope shrugged. "I know as much as you do, Jacob."

After another moment, she turned and faced the entrance to the room. "You know, there's one way we can find out. We can follow him."

"Follow him? But he's probably long gone by now. Those wheels of his…they're fast."

Hope walked toward the entrance. "Well, I'm not waiting for him in here."

"Wait. Where are going, Hope?"

"Outside. I saw something just before we came inside. Something I've always wanted to see." She stopped just shy of exiting the room and glanced back at Jacob. "Don't know when he's coming back. Could be a while. Might as well make the best of our time." She gave Jacob a contagious smile. "You coming?"

Jacob could hardly move fast enough. "Yes, of course!" He reached into his lunchbox, grabbed a can of *Pure Blend* and then stowed it away inside a narrow slot in his chest-plate. *Might as well go prepared.* He caught up with Hope, and they went outside.

They walked away from Wheeler's house, and it was so dark Jacob had to pause a moment to enable his night vision. He blinked and cocked his head and then glanced at Hope, wanting to see what she looked like in the haze of his night vision.

Hope noticed his appraisal and giggled. "Trust me, Jacob. I still look the same."

"Yeah, you do," Jacob replied. *Good, even with nearly no light.*

They walked on for a few minutes, then Jacob said, "Still don't know what you're looking for out here."

Hope pointed straight out in front. "Up there."

Jacob looked around. "Up where?"

"There." Hope slowed her pace and then flicked her hand a couple times. It was then that Jacob finally saw what she was pointing at. Maybe it was because the glow coming from the crescent moon had nothing to grab onto, but Jacob was surprised that he had not seen the scarred, sky-high mountain in front of them. It was difficult for him to see as it blended so well with the sky. "We're going up there? Why?"

"There's something I want to see, and up there is the best vantage point."

They stopped at the bottom of the mountain. It was clear that the side had been devastated in the past. Large chunks of it were scattered all along the bottom of its base.

"Wow, look at all of these," Hope said.

Jacob reached out and ran his hand across one of the fallen pieces. His sensors could detect sharp, jagged edges on nearly every corner of the piece, yet he wasn't sure. "Must have been Earth tremors. How else would they have come down?"

"You're probably right," Hope said, pulling herself onto the very chunk of rock that Jacob had just scanned. "That's good for us. We can use them to climb all the way to the top." She reached down and offered Jacob her hand. "Follow me, Jacob. It shouldn't take long.

Hope's calculation was accurate. After just a few minutes of climbing, they stood on the very peak of the mountain, looking down at the barren curvature of the Earth. Hope immediately sat down, motioning for Jacob to join her. He was more interested in peering over the edge. "Careful, Jacob," Hope warned, tugging on his arm. "It's a long way down. You don't want to fall."

"Oh, right." Jacob took a step back.

"Sit down," Hope said, "next to me."

"N-Next to you?"

"Yes. I want to show you what we came up here for."

Jacob sat down. "Okay, I'm ready."

Hope skimmed her hand across the open sky. Jacob followed the gentle flow of her hand with great intent but only saw a dark sky. "What are you looking at?"

Hope nudged him, shoulder to shoulder and giggled. "Switch off your night vision."

"Oh..." He blinked and then cocked his head. The moment his night vision was disabled, he nearly fell backwards at the incredible sight. Millions of shining white objects painted the sky, dripping and streaking along the plain, black canvas. They twinkled brilliantly, and he could see the lights dotting Hope's smooth surface. "Wow!"

"Isn't it something?"

"There are so many...They're so beautiful...They're so...uh..." He glanced over at Hope and quietly asked, "What are they?"

Hope placed one hand against the cold surface of the mountain and leaned against it. "You mean, you don't know?"

"Well, I've seen them before. Wheeler pointed them out to me, but he didn't know what they were."

Hope giggled. "A pair of advanced CPUs and neither of them know?"

"It's not that I don't know. It's just...well..." Jacob sighed, "Actually, I don't know. Do you mind telling me?"

"They're stars, Jacob." Hope heard the quiet hum of his hard-drive through his chest-plate.

"Stars?" Jacob looked up at the sky that seemed to be in a chaos of flickering lights. "What are they exactly?"

"Suns."

Her answer was so matter-of-fact, Jacob had to pause his hard-drive, as he tried to process the information. "You mean all those tiny things up there in the sky are suns? Like the one over—" Jacob leaned over to one side, far enough so that Hope wasn't in his direct path. Even still, the sun he wanted to point at was completely eclipsed by the moon. "You know the one I'm talking about. Our sun."

"Yes. The very same."

Jacob slapped his hands together and allowed them to remain clasped. "I was right! I told him so."

"Told who? And what?"

"Wheeler. I told him that they were suns."

"How did you know, Jacob?"

Jacob shrugged. "Just a calculated guess. I mean, if you were to imagine our sun being billions of miles away, it would look just like those up there."

"Pretty good guess."

"How did you know they were suns, Hope?"

"My dad."

"Oh, right. The Mayor." Jacob looked at the sky again. "I remember him saying something about our future being amongst the stars…or something like that."

"It's the only thing he regrets."

"Regrets? I don't understand."

"His only regret about the Earth no longer revolving is that he never gets the chance to see the stars."

"They *are* stunning," Jacob admitted. "If I'd never get the chance to see them again, I'd certainly regret it, as well."

"You and me both, Jacob."

"Wow. Look at them. It almost looks like they form different patterns." Jacob pointed up at a small collection of stars. "That one looks like a handle." He pointed to another collection. "Oh, and that looks a bit like one of us. See? Two stars for the arms, three for the hip, and another pair for the legs. The one on top looks like a head."

Hope smiled. "You're right, Jacob. No telling what shapes you can find if you look long enough. You should give that cluster a name."

Jacob waved it off. "I wouldn't know what to call him…or her."

They both leaned back and continued to look at the stars, then Hope pointed to the brightest one. "Have a name for that one?"

Jacob was quiet. He seemed lost, as he stared up at the lone star. Something about it made his hard-drive skip a revolution. "M-Mom?…"

"What was that, Jacob?"

Jacob shook his head a few times, not sure what was going on with his hard-drive. Why would it make him say, "Mom"? He shrugged and turned to Hope. "Sorry. I'm not good at coming up with names. Maybe you should ask Wheeler. He's good at that."

"Are you referring to 'One Bolt'? Why does he call you that?"

Jacob looked away. "You'll laugh."

"I promise not to." Hope saw Jacob peeking at her from the corner of his eyes. "I promise."

Jacob sighed. "He said it looked like I was built using only one bolt. You know...because I'm a first generation."

"Then maybe we should call him 'Assorted Bolts' for all the different parts he attaches to himself."

Jacob laughed. "Yeah, that's pretty good. 'Assorted Bolts'. I kind of like that. He won't though."

"Don't worry about what Wheeler says or thinks. I don't."

"I know I shouldn't, and I try not to. It's just difficult sometimes."

"There's nothing wrong with being a first generation. Who you are will always be more important than what you are."

Jacob lowered his head again. “Then who am I? I don't even know.”

Hope reached over, tucked her hand under Jacob’s chin and then lifted his head. The glow from her green eyes was intense enough to overshadow the pale blue of his eyes. “You’re the one who’s going to save us,” she said. “All of us. I know Forever Jacob is still a long ways off, but you’ll get there. I know you will.”

A loud, rhythmic chime suddenly poured out from the enclosure deep within Hope’s breast-plate. She quickly reached up and put her hands tight against her chest.

“Hope? Are you okay?” Jacob saw that the indicator on her breast-plate was flashing red. “Your battery?”

“Sorry, Jacob.” Hope stood. “I have to go.”

Jacob jumped to his feet, nearly stumbling over himself. He grabbed onto Hope’s hand. “Go where?”

“I have to get back home,” Hope replied, having to nearly shout over the constant and rather annoying chiming.

“But—”

“Don’t worry, Jacob. I’ll be fine. Just need to get back. We’ll meet again soon. I promise.” She took a step away, but he did not let go of her hand.

“I’ll walk with you back to the school,” he said.

“No, Jacob. I know the way. You should stay here, and see if Wheeler needs any help with Forever Jacob. He should be back soon.”

Hope pulled her hand from Jacob’s grip and walked to the place where she could retrace their path down the mountain. She looked back at Jacob with her vibrant-green eyes and said, “I'm glad we got to talk. I finally got a chance to know you.”

Jacob smiled. “Me, too, Hope. And before I forget, it’s Forever Yaw. Not Forever Jacob.”

She smiled back. “No, Jacob. I was right the first time.”

Hope lowered herself over the edge, and Jacob could hear the chiming, that accompanied her, fade. He stood alone on the mountaintop for a few minutes, tainting the glimmering sky with his lonesome image. He stood there, wondering about her, wondering about her abrupt departure. Was it her battery? How come her warning that her battery was low was so different from his?

That reminded him, and he looked at his chest-plate. It was a long way to the bottom of this mountain and already, his indicators were at yellow. He needed to get down.

* * *

Even with his night vision, Jacob was having a hard time seeing where he was going once he was off the mountain. He wasn't even sure if he was on the right path back to Wheeler's house. He stopped and bent down on one knee to scan the dusty surface beneath him. He reached out and agitated the soft ground, wiping away what looked like fresh tread marks. *They must be Wheeler's. But where is he?*

Jacob stood and looked around, trying to see something he recognized in the unfamiliar landscape. There was nothing, and no movement. The only sound he heard was the harsh, high-pitched whistle of gusts of wind. He decided to follow the faint trails of the tread marks carved along the ground. Though rather chaotic, by the way they branched out in all directions, the trails eventually converged into a single path. Having a fixated sense of direction was comforting, but the eeriness of the setting didn't exactly make his decision to keep going any easier. With each step he took, his cautiousness intensified.

He'd only gone a short distance when he came upon on a cylindrical object. Half of it was exposed while the other half was buried in the ground. He nudged his boot against it, and the top half disintegrated into a fine plume of dust. The rest just sank deeper into the ground, blending out its worthless existence. "Uh-oh. Hope that wasn't something important."

A few steps further and Jacob saw more and more of the same objects poking up from the ground in haphazard arrangements. They were scattered everywhere. Pieces of all shapes and sizes, with one thing in common, rust. *What are these things? There's so many.* Knowing what his curiosity had done to the first one he'd encountered, Jacob tried to avoid them the best he could. He did his best to side-step or, at the very least, step over anything in his way.

That only worked for a little while. The further he went, the more he realized that there was simply not going to be a way to avoid them. The objects, which had been sparsely scattered on the ground, were now more numerous and were beginning to cluster together. Jacob felt a rising sense of horror, as he started to recognize the cylinders for what they really were—arms. They were connected to torsos, while legs with joints still attached were connected to hips.

W-What is all of this?

Jacob took a step back when he suddenly caught glimpse of what looked like a head, buried in the ground up to the jaw-line. The exposed upper half was completely eaten away by rust. Jacob's posture stiffened. *W-What is this place? W-Where am I?*

He took another quick step back and heard a loud thud of crumpling metal. "Uh-oh," he cried, assuming it was another body part that he had stepped on. He glanced down but was surprised to see nothing but the ground underneath his boot. *So where did the crumpling sound come from*? Gently this time, Jacob lowered his foot. It landed softly on the ground, yet, another barrage of crumpling metal echoed all around him. He turned around, only to see wisps of dust, slowly dissolving back into the ground. *Is somebody there?* "Hello?" No reply.

He was about to start walking again when he heard another series of loud crackling noises that sounded like metal rubbing metal. It had resonated from the left of him. Jacob took a quick glance in that direction, but again, only saw fragments of dust sifting back to the ground. "Who's there?" Jacob shouted. "Someone? Anyone?"

"Hey!" A familiar voice replied from right behind him. Jacob turned around to see a rust-eaten face with a pair of deep eye sockets and a gaping mouth, caused by a loosely hinged-jaw. Light was seeping through the many holes, casting the entire face in an eerie glow. Jacob reeled back, tripped over his boots and fell to the ground. He began shuffling backward, away from that horrible figure.

"What are you doing here?"

Jacob's head jerked back. Both of the plates over his eyes lowered. His eyes slowly drifted from the unfamiliar face, down to disproportionate chest-plate and then finally...to a pair of wheels. "Wheeler?"

"Yeah, it's me. Can't you tell?" Wheeler lifted the empty shell off of his head and tossed it over his shoulder. His trio of lights blasted down at Jacob. "Is that you, One Bolt?" He reached down and helped Jacob back to his feet.

Jacob held a hand over his eyes to shield them from the glare of Wheeler's lights. "Hey! Switch those damn things off, will you? *318*!"

"Ha! How am I going to see anything without my lights? I don't have fancy night vision like you." Wheeler folded his arms across his chest. "Forget it, One Bolt. I need these. Turn off your night vision, and I'll light the way."

"Okay-okay, fine." Jacob blinked and then cocked his head.

Wheeler directed his lights to the left and then to the right of Jacob. "Hey...You're alone? Where's...you know..." Wheeler lowered his shoulders. "Don't tell me you left her back at my house all by herself. I have a lot of things in there that I don't want her to see."

"Really? Like what?"

"Wouldn't you like to know? Anyway, is she back there?"

"No. She left."

"She left? But I thought she wanted to be a part of this. Part of our team. Remember? Don't tell me she's having doubts about Forever Yaw. I mean...with her dad—"

"Relax, will you? She had to go back home. I think it had something to do with her batteries."

"Oh..." Wheeler did a quick calculation. The plates over his eyes lowered. "Wait...You mean she's walking back? On her own? You didn't offer to take her back? You let her go back all by herself?"

"She didn't want me to go with her." He frowned. "Should I have?"

"It would have been nice of you." Wheeler looked away. "I mean, I would have."

Jacob stood on the tip of his boots, looking over Wheeler in the direction he had last seen Hope. "Should we try to catch up with her?"

Wheeler waved his hand. "Ah, don't worry, One Bolt. You asked, and she refused. I'm sure she'll be fine. She knows the way. Besides, that lump of carbon will probably meet her halfway."

"Brute?"

"You know any other lumps of carbon?" Wheeler reached over and pushed on Jacob's shoulder, forcing him back down. "She'll be fine."

"I hope so."

Wheeler dimmed his lights so he could shine them near Jacob without having him complain. "Didn't think you'd come out this far."

"Neither did I."

"What are you doing out here? I thought you were going to wait for me back at my house."

"We went for a walk. Then I got lost trying to get back." Jacob pointed at the mask. "What's that, and where did you find it?"

Wheeler snickered. "Look around, One Bolt." His light shimmered across the vast array of objects being half absorbed by the Earth.

"I see them all, but what are they?"

Wheeler threw his arms to the side. "What do you think they are, One Bolt? Look around you. Arms, legs, heads... They're exactly like you and me." He titled his head to one side. "Well, not really like you and me. We're still working."

"So they're all... shut down?"

"Shut down, broken... dead. Whatever you want to call it."

"But why?"

"What do you mean, why? We all shut down eventually. Isn't that what your mom told you?"

Jacob quickly consulted the information on his hard-drive. "Oh, right. She did say that." Then he turned around and observed the bodies soon to be one with the Earth. "But why are they all here?"

There was no reply from Wheeler. Jacob turned and saw why. Wheeler was several yards away, foraging through the limitless assortment of body parts. Jacob called out, "Hey! What are you doing?"

Wheeler was holding an arm, which was still attached to a body, and was comparing it to his own. "Ah... too big." He threw the arm down, found another and did the same comparison. They matched. "Yes! This will look good on me. I'll be back for you, later." He tucked the arm back behind the torso and then looked up. "You say something, One Bolt?"

Jacob made his way over. "What are you going to do with that arm? You're not going to take it?"

"Why not?"

"You can't just take it. Doesn't it belong to someone?"

"Ah, come on, One Bolt. What's the matter with you? You think the owner of that arm wants it back?" Wheeler laughed. "You think anyone out here wants any of their parts back?"

"So you just take whatever you want? When you want?"

"Look at me." Wheeler dragged his hand from his base all the way to his head. "Everything on me screams 'spare parts'."

"But—"

"But nothing. All their hard-drives and CPUs were taken out. Nothing important is left. That's why I can take parts from them."

"Assorted Bolt?"

"What?"

"Nothing."

Wheeler spun around in a circle, not able to contain an ear-to-ear smile. "Look at this place, One Bolt. I could spend an entire day here and still find new parts."

"Don't you mean used parts?"

"You know what I mean. They might be rusty. They might not work, but hey, no one wants them..." Wheeler stopped next to Jacob. "Go ahead. Check it out. Find something you like. It's not like they're going to object."

"I-I don't know, Wheeler...Still doesn't feel right."

Wheeler abruptly turned to Jacob. "Here, One Bolt. Catch!"

Jacob caught what had been thrown at him. "What is it?"

"You said you wanted an upgrade. Try it on. See if it fits."

Jacob stared at the rusted arm that he was now cradling. Wires hung loose from the seam where it had been torn straight out of the socket. Jacob threw it back down in disgust. "I don't want it!"

"Why not? You said you wanted an upgrade. Well, there's an upgrade. A pretty good one if you ask me. Only a few rust spots."

"I said, I don't want it!"

"Don't be like that, One Bolt. Upgrades are hard to come by these days. Take what's given to you."

"I will. Just not ones that don't belong to me."

Wheeler rolled away. "Whatever...And to think, I was going to install the part for you..."

Without Wheeler forcing him to look for spare parts, Jacob walked up to one of the bodies and dropped to one knee, dusting off some of the dirt that had collected on the face. The single eye that had yet to sink back into the Earth was no longer glowing. Its mindless stare was empty, voided of any emotions. Jacob reached out and placed his hand on the side of the face, only to have it crumble into a pile of broken shards, hastening its return to the Earth. Jacob stood up.

"That happens a lot out here," Wheeler said.

Jacob shook his head. "My mom was right. They all return to the Earth."

"Looks that way, doesn't it? Not fair, if you ask me, but what can you do?"

Jacob backed away. "Can we get going now? I-I really don't like being here. Did you get the sample yet? I want to leave. Now."

"Sample? No. Not yet."

"You still haven't found any? What have you been doing out here all this time?"

"Looking for parts. You never know, One Bolt. There could be a CPU out here that they forgot to take out. Maybe one more advanced than yours."

"But we're supposed to be working on Forever Yaw. Not looking for parts!"

"I know that. But a new CPU can only help us."

"How?"

"More advanced, quicker calculations. Maybe it'll even be powerful enough to help us figure out how to sustain the samples."

"You have a point there, Wheeler. But I doubt you'll find a usable CPU out here. Let's just get the sample and see what we can do with what we already have."

"Fine."

Jacob waited for Wheeler to move, but he just stood there. "Are you going or not?"

"I will," Wheeler said, crossing his arms over his chest-plate. "I'll meet you back at my house."

"Oh, no! You said that before and didn't get the sample. I'm coming with you this time."

"No, you're not."

"Yes, I am!"

Wheeler threw his arms down, clanking them off his side. "Look, One Bolt, arguing about this isn't going to make me get the sample any quicker."

"Then take me with you. I want to see her."

Wheeler's eyes widened to their absolute limits. "Wait! How did you…how did you know about…her?"

"Ah-ha! You *are* meeting someone. Who is she?"

Wheeler rolled off a little ways, and Jacob followed. "Take me with you. I want to see where the samples come from."

"I don't want you to see her."

"Why not?"

Wheeler lowered his head. "It's just…"

"But I'm helping you with all of this. We're working on this together."

Wheeler looked up. "One Bolt…It's just…"

"What? What is it?"

Wheeler hesitated for a long moment and then sighed. "Just...brace yourself, One Bolt."

"Brace myself? For what?"

Wheeler revved up his wheels and spun around. "Jump on. You'll know why once you meet her."

They drove through the darkness, and Jacob was glad that Wheeler knew where he was going. They bounced and jostled over the broken parts and then finally reached more level ground. When Wheeler slowed and then came to a stop, Jacob looked to the side and saw they were at the edge of a massive crater. It was a sensor-numbing sight. The crater stretched from right beneath them, all the way around until it blended with the horizon. All the way down along its walls were grooves that caught most of the pale moonlight, illuminating the enormous depression with a soft glow.

"Wow! What's down there?" Jacob asked.

"A bigger selection."

"What?"

"I'm teasing, One Bolt. Down there is more of what you saw back there."

"You mean…"

"Right. More bodies. This is their final resting spot. The last place before they're finally one with the Earth again. The Mayor decided that this was the best place for them."

"Why?"

"Because out here, it's nowhere. He doesn't need to see them anymore. You see, One Bolt. To the Mayor, every time one of us shuts down, he says it's a sign of being weak. We're not supposed to shut down or even get rust...according to him. The Mayor isn't too keen on weakness. Humans, remember? That's why he came up with all those assignments. It's a way to separate the strong from the weak." Wheeler glanced back and smirked. "By his logic, you're one of his favourites."

"And that would mean you're runner up," Jacob countered.

As Wheeler turned his head, Jacob heard him say, "Damn it, you're right."

"So he dug this hole for them?"

"Ha! No! He didn't dig this. But he did cause it. Project Retaliation." Wheeler pointed at the moon. "Remember that piece missing from the side of the moon? It landed right here. It created his giant hole—this crater."

"Really? Where is it now?"

"I don't know. Must have landed here and then bounced off back into the sky."

"Or it could have just broken into pieces and been scattered down inside this crater. Guess we'll never know unless we check it out."

"Way ahead of you, One Bolt. That's where we're headed."

"Huh...you mean...down there?"

Wheeler began shifting his weight forward. "That's exactly what I mean."

Jacob's hold on Wheeler's handle bars suddenly became tighter. "Why?"

"How else are we going to get our sample?"

"No, wait! I thought you said we were meeting...you know...her. Whoever she is."

"We are. She lives down there." Wheeler revved his wheels. "You ready, One Bolt?"

Jacob pulled back on the handle bars, as if to disrupt Wheelers momentum, unfortunately, it only hastened it. "Wait! Maybe we should recalculate this. There has to be another way to get down. This is too steep."

"There might be. But it won't be as fun." Wheeler leaned forward, tipping his body over the crater's lip. "Here we go, One Bolt!"

Wheeler dove into the crater.

They hurtled down the side of the crater's inner wall—it was nearly a vertical drop. Unidentifiable body parts were embedded into the rock surface. Wheeler weaved back and forth, in and out, ducking under outstretched arms and leaping over fallen limbs. Jacob didn't even notice. He coward behind Wheeler, burying his face into Wheeler's shoulder. His grip on the handle bars were so tight, he could hear the buzzing from gears in his hands straining. That sound, however, was easily drowned out, as they gained speed, and the screaming wind blew by them, snagging against their sensors with its cold bite. Jacob was absolutely stiff in his joints.

"How you doing back there?" Wheeler yelled.

"Too fast! Too fast!"

"It's okay, One Bolt. I come down here all the time. This isn't fast." Wheeler's wheel suddenly got wedged inside a groove in the crater's wall. "Uh-oh!"

"What?"

"Too fast! Too fast! Hold…on…One…Bolt!" His wheel smashed into a small protrusion in the wall, and the pair was sent airborne. They soared through the air screaming, "Too…fast!" the entire time.

Wheeler was the first to taste the impact, and it wasn't long before Jacob also took a bite of the hard ground.

"Can't seem to...ever make that last jump." Wheeler pushed himself upright. He examined his arm. Two of his four fingers dangled freely from his hand, wires exposed and lubricant dripping out. "Looks like it's time for another upgrade." He snapped the digits back into place for the time being.

Jacob reached up and rubbed his head. "Now I see why you have so many dents," he moaned, staggering to his feet.

Wheeler drove over to him. He wasn't moving as smoothly as usual due to his now partially deflated wheels. "Sorry about that, One Bolt. Thought I could stick that landing this time. It's a lot harder when you're driving for two."

Jacob scraped the dirt off of his red plates. "Trust me. I'm used to falling over. Just didn't expect it to happen again so soon."

"Any dents or scratches?"

"Many."

"Internal damage? Hard-drive? CPU?"

"No. Those seem fine."

"Good. Let's continue on, shall we?"

As they made their way across the flat ground within the crater, Jacob's vision was hampered by the moonlight's failed attempt at penetrating the surroundings. Jacob wanted to enable his night vision but was afraid of what he would see. He moved closer to Wheeler, and his lights that were illuminating a path for them to take but leaving the outer limits in darkness. Still, they had to skirt bodies that lined the bottom of the crater where the Earth was slowly, purposely, taking back what rightfully belonged to it—showing no pity or remorse in the process.

"Are we almost there? I just want to get the sample and get out of here. I don't like it out here. All these—"

"Relax, One Bolt. They're all shut down. It's not like one of them is going to jump up and—" Wheeler stumbled over a protrusion in the ground. "Damn it!"

"What! What is it?"

"A Rock. It's just a rock. Relax."

"Quit joking. Are we almost there?"

Wheeler pointed straight out in front to the opposing end of the crater that they were quickly approaching. "Just beyond that clearing. In the wall. You see it?"

Jacob had to readjust his vision, but once he did, he noticed a light coming from a small opening in the wall. "Over there?"

"Yup. In that cave. She's waiting for us in there."

Jacob wasn't sure why anyone would be in there but was more than curious to find out.

Light from the cave was seeping out from the main opening, allowing Wheeler to switch off his lights when they arrived. "Wait out here, One Bolt."

"What? But I want to see her, too."

"You will. Wait here, and I'll bring her out." Wheeler quickly disappeared deep inside the cave.

Jacob walked over, stood by the opening and peeked inside. He couldn't see much. Just light coming from the ceiling. The first part of the cave was empty, though it went back far enough that he could not see all the way in. He was tempted to ignore Wheeler's order, to stay out, but resisted that urge and backed away from the entrance. Wheeler would be back soon enough. *No point in risking another verbal assault from him.* Jacob enabled his night vision and scanned the entire perimeter of the crater. He had only been left alone for a short amount of time but already was feeling lonely. How could anyone possibly live out here? *Especially with all of these bodies around.*

Jacob heard noise behind him, so he turned off his night vision and looked back at the entrance to the cave. Wheeler was coming out, and it looked like someone was behind him. Jacob took a few steps forward and stayed directly in Wheeler's path.

"Well, One Bolt," Wheeler said, with a smile. "You said wanted to see her. And here she is." Wheeler reached back and gently coaxed a small woman out from behind him.

Jacob stood there, eyes wide and with every limb on his body motionless.

She took a step out from the security of the cave. She was frail and of a generation that she must surely share with the professor. Her entire body was engulfed by rust, and just by the way she stood there, it was clear that most of her limbs no longer worked. Pistons were no longer pumping in and out of their broken chambers, while wires and tubing were exposed from every seam. In fact, the only part of her that appeared unblemished was a strange, thick metal covering over top of her eyes, concealing them completely.

Wheeler stood next to her with a gleaming smile across his face. "One Bolt, I want you to meet Vision."

"Vision?"

"Yes." Wheeler then leaned in close to Vision, almost pressing his face up against hers. "Yes, Vision?" Wheeler whispered. "Yes. It's him. It's Jacob. The one I was telling you about." Wheeler nodded a few times, as if he had heard everything Vision had said.

That's Strange. Jacob was positive that he didn't hear anything come out of Vision. He didn't even see her mouth open.

Wheeler looked at Jacob. "She says, it's nice to finally meet you." Wheeler immediately turned back and said to Vision, "Yes...don't worry about it. I'm sure he brought some." He turned back to Jacob. "Well? Don't be rude, One Bolt. You wanted to meet her."

"Does she even know I'm here?" With the thick plate covering her eyes, Jacob was sure she couldn't see him. He took a step closer to Vision and then raised his hand and waved.

"No-no. Not like that. She can't see you."

"Oh...right." Jacob leaned forward and shouted, "Nice to meet you, Vision!"

Vision staggered back.

"Damn it, One Bolt! Not so loud. Vision's hearing is sensitive."

Jacob reached over and placed his hand on Vision's narrow shoulder. "Sorry about that," he whispered. "I didn't mean—"

Vision immediately backed away. A small section of her shoulder flaked off in Jacob's hand and then crumpled to the ground. Jacob stumbled back, wide-eyed.

"Damn it, One Bolt! Look what you did!"

"But...but...I didn't mean to."

Wheeler leaned in next to Vision. "What's that?" He listened for a moment and then glanced up at Jacob. "It's okay, One Bolt. She says, that part doesn't work anymore. Nothing works anymore."

Vision tapped Wheeler, and he leaned close to her and listened again. Then he spoke to Jacob. "Vision says, thanks for all the *Pure Blend* you've been bringing her."

"Tell her, no problem." *I guess.*

"She asked if you had anymore."

"Sure. I always have at least one on me." Jacob reached into his chest-plate and was about to pull out the can of *Pure Blend* that he had stowed away earlier, but Wheeler stopped him. He opened his compartment and took out the can that Hope had given him, but he didn't hand it over to Vision just yet.

Jacob tucked his can back inside his chest-plate. "Aren't you going to give to her?"

"I will. But first..." He leaned in toward Vision and had a whispered conversation, even though it looked like he was the only one was doing all of the talking. Vision was nodding a lot, agreeing to something. Jacob hoped he would eventually find out how she communicated.

Wheeler finally turned to Jacob and said, "Okay, One Bolt. She'll show you."

Jacob lowered the plates over his eyes. "Huh? Show me what?"

"Remember when I told you to brace yourself?"

Jacob moved in closer and said, "Yeah."

Wheeler reached over and began lifting the thick covering over Vision's eyes. She shifted backward. "It's okay, Vision. I just want to quickly show him."

"Show me what?"

"You'll see, One Bolt. Brace yourself."

The covering finally came off. Wheeler stepped back, allowing Jacob an unobstructed view. Jacob couldn't believe it at first. Deep in the blackened sockets, where mechanical lenses were usually wired, were two shrivelled-up orbs, light-green in colour. They were soft, semi-transparent, and not mechanical in any sense.

"What…what are those?" Jacob said, barely able to speak.

"You wanted to know where I get my samples from," Wheeler said. "Now you know."

"But...but what are they?"

"Her eyes."

"They are? But...but they don't look like eyes. Where's the glow?"

"They aren't like yours or mine, One Bolt. But they are eyes alright—they're *human* eyes."

Jacob nearly toppled over. His hard-drive was spinning so violently inside his chest-plate that there was a jitter to his voice. "Human?!"

"That's what I said. They're human eyes." Wheeler finally placed the can of *Pure Blend* inside Vision's weak grip. "Thanks for showing, Jacob," he said.

Vision motioned Wheeler closer and silently communicated something else. Wheeler gave a little chuckle and then said to Jacob, "She says, she hope she didn't scare you."

Not even waiting for Jacob's reply, Wheeler reached over and gently pulled the covering over Vision's eyes.

"Wait!" Jacob yelled. "Human eyes? How is it even possible?"

Wheeler drove over and jerked Jacob's arm. "Damn it, One Bolt! You're too loud."

"But…but…"

Wheeler dragged Jacob away from the front of the cave. "Let's go. Over there. I'll try to explain as much as I can."

Jacob sat down on a rock and listened, as Wheeler did his best to explain everything to him. "I wish I knew more, but I just don't."

"So humans aren't completely extinct?"

Wheeler shrugged. "Guess not."

"All along you knew a human …well, a part of one, was still around, and you didn't tell me?"

"If she is indeed the last human to ever walk this Earth, I had to make sure that I trusted whoever it was I told. I have to keep her safe. You understand that, don't you?"

"I guess so."

"Taking care of her and protecting her is all I ever do," Wheeler said, driving back and forth with his head lowered. "It's all I've ever done. That's why I'm out here." He glanced up at Jacob. "You really think I like being out here? Well...besides all the free upgrades."

"Why do you both have to be out here? Why not go further in? Closer to the sun."

"This is the only place I know she'll be safe. No one comes out here. Besides, she doesn't need to sun." Wheeler pointed at the cave. "*Assignment 091775.*"

"Harness the sunlight...So that's why there's light inside the cave."

"*That* was my first attempt, One Bolt. She's more important than a first place trophy. She doesn't seem to like the cold."

Neither did Jacob at that moment. "You would have won," Jacob said. He turned and faced the cave where Vision was standing exactly where they had left her. "She really likes her *Pure Blend.*"

"Yup. Just wish there was more of it around. It used to be easy to find. Vision told me it was everywhere, and at first, I had no problems finding it whenever she needed it. But that was on the surface."

"What do you mean the surface? Surface of what?"

"Earth. You used to be able to find *Pure Blend* everywhere on the Earth's surface. Until the Mayor took it all for himself. Every last drop. I'm surprised you still have some, One Bolt."

"I'm running out," Jacob admitted. "My mom says she doesn't know what's going to happen once we do. We don't know where to find more."

"I know where to find some."

"But I thought you said it was—"

"Yeah, it's gone from the surface, but there's still a lot inside the Earth, deep underground. And when I say a lot, I mean it. There's enough to cover most of the Earth. Enough that you would probably rust over before you even run out of it."

Jacob stood up. "Then let's—"

"Don't get too excited. It's so deep in the ground it's impossible to get at."

"Can't we try?"

"Ha! We don't have the resources to get at it."

Jacob sat back down with a loud thump. "Damn, *319*."

"Trust me, One Bolt. I know how you feel. We're all in the same position. That's why Vision is so important to us, important to all of us. As far as I know, she's the last of her kind. The last human ever to walk this Earth." Wheeler bowed his head. His voice amplifying. "That's why we need Forever Yaw to succeed. And who knows, if it works, she might be able to finally come out from hiding." *Then I'll finally be free.* Wheeler looked over at Jacob, who had gone surprisingly quiet. "Hey! Did you hear me, One Bolt?"

Jacob looked up. The glow in his eyes had dimmed. "W-What was that?"

"Weren't you listening?"

"I-I...am." He looked over at the cave. "What...what's her name again?"

"Who? Vision? You already know this, One Bolt. Why are you asking me again?"

"T-They look so...familiar."

"What does? What are you talking about?"

"Eve..."

"What?" Wheeler drove over next to Jacob and poked him in the arm. "One Bolt? Hey, One Bolt? You okay?" He leaned in and noticed the indicator on Jacob's chest-plate. "Uh-oh! You know you're at red, don't you?"

"R-Red? What red?"

Wheeler slapped Jacob across the face. "Hey! One Bolt!"

Jacob snapped to attention. "Why'd you hit me!" he cried, standing up.

"Because you're acting funny. I think it's your battery."

Jacob looked down at his chest-plate and saw the solid, red light. "Damn it! *320.* How can I be at red already? I don't understand."

"It's simple. It's at red. You're almost empty."

"I know that, Wheeler, but I didn't do anything to cause it to be at red already. Something's wrong." Jacob suddenly straightened his posture. "Oh-no!"

"What now?"

"I promised my mom that I wouldn't let this happen again."

Wheeler snickered. "Well, I think you need to get out of here, then. You need to get back to the school before your indicator starts flashing."

"But...but what about Vision? What about Forever Yaw? The sample?"

"None of those will do us any good if you shut down. Don't worry about those right now, One Bolt. You need to get back. I'll take you. It's the least I can do."

"The least you can do is let me walk back."

Wheeler turned his back, exposing his handle bars. "Come on. Let's go. Or don't you trust me anymore after the fall?"

Jacob suddenly ran off toward the cave.

"One Bolt!" Wheeler yelled. "Hey! One Bolt! Get back here! I won't go so fast this time!"

"No, I trust you," Jacob yelled back. "I just need to do something first."

Jacob slowed his pace, as not to disturb her. Once he was by Vision's side, he reached into his chest-plate, pulled out his can of *Pure Blend* and set it down in front of her. "You probably need this more than I do." Jacob smiled and then ran back to Wheeler and stepped up on his perch, grabbing the handlebars.

Wheeler turned and glanced over his shoulder. "Thanks, One Bolt."

Jacob grabbed onto the handle bars. "Thank me when this is all over."

Chapter Six

Brute lowered the densely layered mask over his eyes so he could guide the pinpoint light of his weld along a predetermined path. Blackened lenses provided a shielded view, allowing for his movements to be precise. The weld crackled and hissed, sending a chaotic mess of molten shards to cling to his thick, tempered plating. There was a high-pitched squeal coming from the spool of wire spinning on his arm, as it fed into a long line of wires, a copper nozzle as its tip. The hard-wire poured out in liquid form from the tip on his hand, biting into the opposing metal surfaces he was working on.

The sun shone intensely from behind him, but its illumination was diffused by the intense light coming off of the weld.

Soon, the crackling subsided, the hazy smoke trail lifted, and the redness of hardening metal, still hot enough to bend, faded. And although heat waves rising from the welds still distorted the concave path, his work was completed. Brute had successfully joined the once separate metal surfaces into one. Its newly formed junction point was now stronger than the actual metal. He flipped his head back, retracting the mask from his eyes and allowing it to rest neatly in place on the crown of his head. He wanted to observe his work. Sunken eyes had to adjust, but once they did, Brute liked what he saw. The weld was crisp, uniform, and more importantly, strong.

"Operations completed, sir?" a nearby worker asked, admiring Brute's work from a distance. "Final pass?"

Massive pistons in Brute's legs hissed, as he hoisted himself to his feet. As tall as he was, Brute was able to see well over the head of his co-worker. "Objective completed. As the Mayor ordered."

Brute then looked back at the section of weld that he'd just finished, watching until the heat waves no longer distorted the surrounding air. He was working on a structure consisting of three massive cylinders, hollow at the ends, that stretched toward the sky. It was so high even he had to crane his neck to see the top. A plethora of gears was mounted on each side, allowing for complete adjustability. At the moment, its skywards reach, its reinforced stare toward the moon, seemed to be finalized.

No longer requiring his welder, Brute retracted back it inside his bulky arm. "The cannon is ready. The only thing left to do is load it and transport it to the launch site."

"Will it work this time, sir?"

Brute gave the side of the cannon a sturdy nudge. "It won't fail this time." Brute then looked down at his co-worker. He was wondering why he was here and not working. "Are the pods finalized?"

"My apologies, sir. I was waiting for you to finish your operations. Two pods left to be placed on the launch pad. They're the larger pods with twenty dormant inside. I'm incapable of the lift, sir."

"The Mayor wants the launch pads loaded with the pods and ready to be shipped to the launch site," Brute said. "I will help."

Leading the way with his lumbering stride, Brute and the other worker made their way to the launch pad. Next to it were the two large, cylindrical pods, standing nearly twice as high as Brute. Despite the overwhelming size, Brute did not hesitate. He wrapped his massive arms around the first pod and then hoisted it off the ground, making it look effortless. The twin pistons in his back hissed, while fully exposed gears snagged their teeth into each other only to tear apart from the wrenching force. He placed the pod securely on the launch pad, alongside the other two dozen and then immediately moved on to the next, never once stalling.

This was what Brute had been built for. Pure physical and continuous labour, and he did not fade nor lose momentum in any way. This was expected of him. CPUs and hard-drives were compromised for heavier pistons and a tougher outer shell. He wasn't built for complex calculations or even driven to allocate minor recollections. Lifting, moving and taking orders came natural to him. This was why the Mayor gave him the opportunity to lead his operations, and more importantly, trusted him to look over his most important procession—Hope. Brute completed operations without question, a trait the Mayor found irreplaceable.

Seeing how effortlessly Brute made it look, his co-worker decided to attempt the final lift himself. He secured his arms around the pod but struggled to even get it off the ground. The pod tipped and then slammed into the ground. The top section flipped open revealing its contents.

"My apologies, sir!"

"As long as nothing is damaged," Brute said.

Brute knelt down, attempting to bring the pod back to its once upright position, but he was caught staring through the thick glass. Staring back at him were the faded, emotionless eyes of random mechanical beings. Their dormancy, the important first step toward the promise of a new, prosperous future, was a direct request by the Mayor.

Even though he lacked the ability to calculate why, Brute didn't like looking at those lifeless faces. It always made him doubt a little of the Mayor's promise. He slid the top section back over the glass. It was not in his orders to calculate their fates. "No damage."

With a worker on each side of the pod, it was an easy lift from the ground onto the launch pad. Brute took a moment to adjust the positioning of the pod so it lined up neatly with the others.

"How many more until we're complete and ready to move?"

"No accurate count at the moment, sir."

Brute extended the pistons connecting his upper leg to his hips, pushing them out to their fullest. He stood tall, drowning his co-worker with his shadow. A high-pitched hiss sounded off, as the pistons adjusted themselves and then locked in place. He peered over to the work area where pods stretched outward to caress the edge of the horizon. Most had already been loaded onto their respected launch pads, but it was evident that many more, still needed placement. "We need them loaded. All of them. Mayor's orders."

"Sir, if I may ask. Since the Mayor's plan is to resurrect Project Retaliation, why must we leave Earth? With the moon destroyed, will we not be safe here?"

Brute paused. His small CPU analyzed the question as best it could but failed to calculate an answer. "I don't question the Mayor's authority. We have our orders. And our primary objective is to fulfil them."

"Yes, sir."

They walked alongside the launch pad, and, as they turned the corner, Brute suddenly stopped. Something in the distance caught his attention. It was a dim beacon, flashing erratically against the hazy horizon. Brute adjusted his vision and focused. It was Hope. He saw that the flashing light was radiating from the left side of her chest and that the green glow in her eyes had paled to almost nothing. "No! It can't be..." Brute adjusted his posture for mobility by shutting off all insignificant functions. "Contact the Mayor!" he ordered, launching himself forward. "Tell him to ready the chamber!"

Brute was barely at Hope's side when she collapsed and fell into his arms.

Her chest was flashing deep-red, chiming uncontrollably. She was too weak to even speak, but her eyes said it all. Their vivid-greens now dimmed to an almost unrecognizable grey.

"Don't worry Hope." Brute smothered her in his arms. "I'll get you back home. You're going to be okay."

* * *

Wheeler looked back over his shoulder at Jacob and shouted, "Hey, One Bolt! Sorry if it's a bit wobbly back there. My wheels took some damage during our fall! But don't worry. It's an easy fix."

"I'm fine."

Wheeler slowed just a bit and turned back to Jacob again. "Hey, One Bolt..." There was a slight pause before Wheeler asked, "What did you mean when you said, 'Eve'?"

Jacob's pause lasted significantly longer than Wheeler's. Finally he replied, "When did I say that?"

"Back when we were inside the crater."

"I did?"

"Yeah. What does that mean?"

Another pause. Jacob *did* remember that name from the pages he had decoded, but there was no reason for him to say it out loud. He didn't know what significance the name had, so there was no need for Wheeler to know.

"I didn't say, '*Eve*'. I said, 'We should *leave*'. You know...as in, 'We should *leave* before my batteries die'."

That's not what I heard...

In front of the school, Jacob stepped off of Wheeler's back before his wheels even had the chance to cool.

"Yup," Wheeler said, proudly slapping his hand against his chest-plate. "Got you back here as promised. Your mom will take you there rest of the way."

They looked around. There was nothing resembling a car in sight.

"Uh...where is your mom, One Bolt? Doesn't she normally wait for you here?"

"Yeah..." Jacob said, slowing advancing toward the school.

"Are we late? Early? What's going on?"

"I don't know."

Wheeler snickered. "Maybe she forgot about you. Maybe she decided that you weren't the one she wanted and is building a new one called Two Bolts."

"Not funny."

"Ah, why so serious all the time? You know I'm only teasing."

"I *have* to be serious. My mom's not here. How am I supposed to get back home? You're the one with the wheels. I have to walk."

Wheeler waved off Jacob's frustration. "Don't lose a bolt over this. At least your indicator is at yellow."

Jacob looked down. "Yellow? What? But...but it was at red!"

Wheeler shrugged. "Must be broken."

"Yeah. Something's not right. I need to get home. Maybe I can try and fix it or something."

Jacob shook his head. "Where is she?"

"I'm sure she's on her way. Let's just wait by the—" Wheeler backed away. "Uh-oh!"

Jacob looked around. "What is it?

Wheeler abruptly placed his finger over his mouth, signalling Jacob to quiet down. He then pointed toward the school. Jacob looked over and saw the professor in front of the main door. He stood with his back to the pair, fidgeting with a chain full of keys.

"What's he doing? Why's he outside?"

"I don't know," Wheeler said, looking over his shoulder. "But I've got to go."

Jacob noticed Wheeler slowly rolling back. "Wheeler?"

"Not supposed to be here right now."

"Where? Here? What do you mean?"

"I have to get back." As quietly as he could, Wheeler revved up his wheels.

"Wait! You're going back? Now?"

"Yes, One Bolt. I have to go. Now! I'll see you back here tomorrow. After you're recharged."

"Wait! Wheeler? What am I supposed to tell the professor? We haven't been at school for the past couple of days."

Wheeler dropped his wheel arm, and it let out a screeching roar. "Make something up!" he yelled, driving away, leaving Jacob in a plume of smoke.

"Make something up?" Jacob waved his arms, trying to clear the smoke from his face. *But that's what you're good at. Not me.*

Wheeler was now a part of the horizon, a smoky trail the only evidence that he had been there. Jacob knew there was no way the professor missed hearing Wheeler roar away, and, as expected, the old man turned toward Jacob.

"Jacob!" Professor Smith called out. "There you are. Come over here. I want to talk to you."

Jacob winced. *Uh-oh, Not good.* Despite the smile the professor wore, Jacob figured he was probably concerned about Jacob's absence from the classroom. Maybe the smile across the professor's face was meant to disarm Jacob. He knew that questions were going to be thrown his way, but he wasn't exactly sure what his response would be once he caught them. Jacob needed to calculate an excuse. If there was a time when his CPU needed to prove itself, it was now.

Slowly, Jacob walked toward the school. Maybe he could think of something between now and the time he got up the stairs. Jacob's CPU began to process. He climbed the first step and came up with his first excuse. "Maybe I wasn't able to go to school because I had to help mom with something. No..." he said, pulling himself up the second step. "Not good enough."

He was well onto the fifth step when he said to himself, "I know! Maybe I twisted my leg and needed repairs. That's why I had to stay at home!"

Now on the eighth step, he shook his head and said, "No. Can't say that. Don't have the upgrades to show for it." He reached up and slapped the side of his head. "Think, Jacob, think! Come up with something!"

Jacob stopped in front of the professor. He had nothing.

Professor Smith placed his hands on his hips and then adjusted the clouded-over lenses in his eyes. "Hello, Jacob. And how are we today?"

"Uh...fine, sir," Jacob replied. *Well, there it was.* It was innocent but it was still the first question, and Jacob caught it rather effortlessly. Many more were sure to follow, Jacob was sure of it. "What are you doing out here, sir?"

Joints popped and wires fell through their rusted casting, as Professor Smith lowered himself to Jacob's level. He laughed. "I should ask you the same thing, Jacob. Haven't seen you around much lately."

Jacob's posture stiffened. He wanted to back away, but the staircase behind him did him no favours in aiding his retreat. "Oh...uh...sorry, sir. Just been real busy these past couple days."

"You have? That's good, Jacob. Good to keep busy in such difficult times." Professor Smith paused. "Busy doing what?"

Jacob relaxed. "Well, you see, sir, Wheeler and I have been working on that assign—"

A smile appeared on Professor Smith's face. "The assignment?" he said, excitement strengthening his voice. "You're still working on it?"

"Yes, sir."

"That's very good. Dedicated, just like Grace." As sudden as Professor Smith's smile appeared, it faded. "But your dedication is no longer required, Jacob. There's no reason for you to continue on with that assignment. School has been officially cancelled."

"What? Cancelled?" *There goes my ride to school.*

Professor Smith sighed. "Yes, Jacob. School has been cancelled. Unfortunately, not everyone was here when I made the announcement today."

Jacob shrugged. "Oh...Sorry, sir."

"It's okay, Jacob. Now you know."

"But...why? We still have some time left before the moon gets here."

"Trust me, Jacob. I would have kept the school open right up until that point. But we all have our orders. Shutting the school down for good wasn't something I wanted. Never have. But when the Mayor insists on something, we really don't have much choice, do we?"

"You can't do anything about it?" *You have to! Mom won't drive out here if school is cancelled. And how are we going to continue with Project Yaw?*

"Me?" Professor Smith laughed. "Why, no, Jacob. Not me. I have orders to follow, just like everyone else."

"But we can't let him close down the school," Jacob pleaded.

"My-my-my! You seem very disappointed about the school's closure, considering you're never here."

Jacob lowered his head. *If only you knew what we were trying to do.*

"Where have you been the past few days, Jacob?" Professor Smith asked. "Hope wasn't with you by any chance, was she? The Mayor came by and was surprised she wasn't here."

"The Mayor? He was here again?"

"He had to drop off something for me to repair. It was also the same time that he announced the school's cancellation. He wanted check on Hope, but she wasn't around."

"What did you tell him, sir?" *Please be a good excuse.*

"That she should be back at any moment. No need to worry himself." The professor leaned in closer to Jacob. "Was I correct?"

Jacob stood his ground, though barely. "You might be, sir."

"Where was she, Jacob? And where were you, for that matter?"

"You added her to our team." Jacob offered a timid smile." We were all working on the assignment together, but she had to leave. She said she had to go back home."

"I see," Professor Smith said, seemingly relieved to know this. "Good. At least I won't have to see the Mayor again today. He was very concerned about her."

"She should be home by now, sir. I was going to take her back, but she said she knew the way."

The professor slapped his chest, in shock. "All the way to the Mayor's house?" He shook his head rather violently. "No-no-no. It's better that you didn't, Jacob."

"But I was just going to—"

"You must not." The expression on the professor's face changed to one of deep concern. "Hasn't Grace said anything to you about this?"

Jacob shook his head, absolutely confused. "My mom? About what, sir? I don't understand."

Professor Smith simply replied, "Just keep your distance, Jacob."

"From the Mayor?"

"Absolutely!"

"But I've already spoken to the Mayor once. Hope introduced us."

The professor reached out and grabbed both of Jacob's hands, pressing them together. "I just don't want to see anything happen to either of you."

Why would anything happen? Jacob was more confused than ever.

The professor parted Jacob's hands but failed to let go. He flipped them over and observed the many blemishes. "Jacob! What happened to you?" He flipped Jacob's hand back over. "Where did all these come from?"

"Oh…it's nothing, sir. Just a few scratches and some dirt. Nothing I'm really concerned about." At the moment, Jacob had much more to worry about than a few minor imperfections. He asked, "So if school has been cancelled, what does that mean for our assignment?"

Ignoring the question, Professor Smith was now scanning further up Jacob's arm. "Will you look at that?" he said, twisting Jacob's arm from side-to-side. "Scratches…and more scratches. Dents…dings…they're all over."

"Yes, sir. I know. I see them, but what about the assignment?"

"Buff them out?" Professor Smith murmured evidently talking to himself. "No. There's too many…"

"My other plating will cover them up," Jacob said. "I just want to know about the assignment, sir."

"We might be able to paint over them," Professor Smith said, as if he didn't hear Jacob at all. "But where to get paint in this day and age?"

Jacob tugged his arm free from the professor's surprisingly tight grip. "Sorry, sir. But the assignment?"

"What?" Professor Smith had to pause for a moment to recollect. "Oh...the assignment… Cancelled!" He smiled at Jacob.

Jacob staggered back. "Cancelled? But…but we have to keep working on it."

"You're very much welcome to stay with it, Jacob. If you insist. But I didn't think that rust was so important to you." He reached out and flicked the nearly chrome surface just above the plating over Jacob's eyes, resulting in a satisfying ping. "Not even a hint of rust."

Jacob frowned as best his metal plating would allow. "Rust?"

"Yes. Rust. What you and Wheeler said you were going to study. Wasn't that what your assignment was based on?"

"No...I mean, yes...I mean..." He stopped before he let something slip that he shouldn't.

The professor became serious. "You know, Jacob, another pair in your class did their assignment about rust, as well. They completed it in a single day. Hard to believe that you, Wheeler *and* Hope are still working on it."

Jacob noticed that the professor's smile tended to tilt to one side due to the gears in his face being rusted over and not locking his mouth in place, yet it was kind even as he asked, "Want to tell me what your assignment is *really* about?"

Jacob looked away and fell silent. The professor could see just by the way Jacob's eyes were shifting back and forth that his question might not be too far off from being answered. He just had to be persistent. He looked over at the empty road in front of the school. "Grace won't be here for at least a while," he said. "Why don't we wait for her inside? I have something to show you." As the professor turned to face the door, he added, "It might help."

"Help me with what, sir?"

The professor didn't answer. He picked a random key on his chain, inserted it into the lock on the school's main door, and tried to turn the key. The lock didn't budge. He cranked his wrist from side-to-side. Rust flaked away from the metal lock with each unsuccessful attempt at unlocking the door. "Darn thing's older than I am."

"Help with what?" Jacob asked again with a bit more firmness in his tone.

The lock finally released with a loud click.

"Ah, there we are!" Professor Smith pushed open the door, and the old hinges cried out. He smiled at Jacob. "Everything eventually gives way. They just need a little bit of coaxing before they finally open up and allow you in." He stepped inside the school. "Come now, Jacob. Follow me."

"But...help me with—" Jacob let out a deep sigh. "Coming, sir."

The door closed after Jacob stepped in, closing off the direct sunlight. They walked silently through the dark hallway, their footsteps echoing loudly in the empty space. The lone statue caused them to veer off to one side, and Jacob mumbled, "The Mayor. He seems to be everywhere these days."

"Well, he's unavoidable." *Unfortunately, for some.*

One door shy of the classroom, Professor Smith stopped in front of the door marked *333.* It was the same one that Jacob had walked by and wondered what was behind it. Jacob looked up at the professor and asked, "In here?"

The professor raised the keychain. The assortment of dangling keys jingling, as he flipped through each one, testing it in the lock. "Just have to find the right one first. I've been in here so many times, but I always forget which one it is." He glanced down at Jacob. "The old CPU has collected a lot of rust over time."

"What's inside?"

"Oh, just a few things here and there that you might find interesting."

"That would help?"

"Always the last one," Professor Smith said. He placed the final key into the lock and turned. "Were you saying something, Jacob?"

"Yes, sir. I asked if it would help."

"Help? Help with what?"

"With Forever Yaw...I mean—"

Jacob clapped a hand over his mouth, but it was too late. Professor Smith smiled and opened the door. His subtle coaxing had worked. "It should."

The sharp creak from rusted hinges ran deep into the hallway and then faded into nothing. The professor held the door open for Jacob. "Might be a little bit dark in here."

"Not a problem, sir," Jacob said, walking by the professor. "I have night vision."

"Oh, that's right. I almost forgot that little detail."

How did he know?

"But you won't need that in here," Professor Smith assured. "Your vision should adjust by itself. Your eyes will get used to the dim lighting." He took a swipe at the wall, agitating a thick layer of dust that had collected on it. "Might not get used to the dirt, though." He smiled at Jacob. "Sorry. Been too busy to clean these days."

"It's okay," Jacob said. "You should see my room."

"A mess?"

"Yes...well, no. Probably not anymore. Pin-bot should have it cleaned up by now."

"What's a Pin-bot?"

"Sorry. I meant, helper-bot."

"Oh...that's right. A helper-bot. Must be the one I gave to Grace a long time ago."

"You gave us Pin-bot?"

"If that's its name now, then yes. I gave Pin-bot to your mom right after she switched you on for the first time."

Jacob did a quick calculation. If Pin-bot was originally the professor's, he must know her model number. *Perfect!* "*800* or *1000*?"

"Excuse me?"

"Pin-bot's model number, sir. Do you know it?"

The professor laughed. "Sorry, Jacob. No one except Pin-bot knows. The model numbers weren't exactly inscribed on the backs of them."

"Damn," Jacob mumbled, "*321*."

As Jacob stepped further in, he noted that they were not in a room at all but another long hallway. This one much narrower than the one they had just exited. All along the hall were sealed doors, and Jacob was curious about what was behind them, but Professor Smith did not seem keen on stopping. Near the end of the hall were glass display cases which reflected the small amount of light in the hallway. They lined both sides of the hall.

"That's far enough." The professor gestured at the first display case in front of them.

Jacob walked up to it. He looked through the thick layer of glass, only to see a deep chamber secured by absolute darkness. Its contents were drenched in shadow. "Night vision?" Jacob suggested.

"That won't be necessary." Professor Smith reached over and flicked a small switch next to the display case. Small pod lights lit up the chamber, finally revealing its contents. Jacob pressed his face up against the glass. What he saw made it difficult for him to keep his mouth closed.

The chamber was lined with rows of metal shelving. Stacked on each shelf were a vast array of mechanical parts in all different shapes, sizes, and more importantly, generations. The ample amount of light created perfect halos around each part.

"Those…are those…upgrades?" Jacob asked, glancing at the professor's perfectly reflected image in the glass.

"Indeed, they are. Arms, legs, pistons, gears, anything you could ever want. I restored them all myself."

"Restored?" Jacob said, allowing his eyes to wander aimlessly around the chamber.

"As you know, Jacob, new parts are hard to find these days. None of these are new. They were collected over time. Most of them didn't work or were covered in rust. Some were just thrown away because the former owner had recently been upgraded and no longer needed their old parts. I kept all of them and would repair them the best I could. Most were in such bad condition that no restoration could have ever gotten them back to working form. I fortunate enough to be able to restore all the ones you see here."

"You did a good job, sir. They look new. I can hardly tell the difference."

"Thank you, Jacob," Professor Smith said with a smile. "But if you are impressed by these, I know you'll fall over when you see what I have behind them." Professor Smith reached into the chamber, as far as he could, sending a few of the parts tumbling to the bottom of the chamber. "There's one in particular that might interest you."

A few more limbs were sent to the bottom of the chamber. Jacob reached in.

"No-no-no. It's alright," Professor Smith said. "You just leave those there. I'll get them later."

Whatever the professor was looking for, he must have hid it as far back as the chamber would go. His head and most of his upper body had disappeared behind the glass.

"You okay back there, sir? Are you sure you don't need my help?"

"It's quite alright," Professor Smith said, his voice muffled. "I've just about…got it!" He straightened and pulled his hand out from behind the chamber. "Ah, yes. This was what I was looking for." He turned and revealed the part that he had retrieved.

Eyes, the vents on his cheeks, and even Jacob's mouth, fell open. He took two quick steps needed to bring him within grasping distance of what the professor was cradling in his arms. "Is…is that?"

"Yes, indeed. A second generation arm."

"Second...generation?" Jacob was unable to peel his eyes away.

"And a perfect fit. I can assure you."

Jacob's hand had already begun to reach out. "May I, sir?"

The professor lowered his arms. "I insist."

Jacob ran his hand along the arm, allowing his sensors to absorb the glossy, unblemished surface. Gliding down from the upper arm to the forearm, Jacob's hand had nothing to snag against. Seams were nonexistent and wires were not exposed. Both new and old hands soon overlapped. Jacob caressed the fingers; something he never had. He made a hand comparison. His sensors felt the sturdiness and the unparalleled jump in quality from his current build. He noticed how much larger the hand was. Opening his hand to its fullest and then pressing it against the second generation hand, proved how limited he was. In its entirety, his current hand could not even reach the point where fingers were meticulously bolted on.

"It'll certainly look good on you," Professor Smith admitted. "You've had that first generation body of yours for a long time."

"It'll work with my torso?"

"A perfect fit," the professor replied, pushing the arm even closer to Jacob. "And it's not even a restoration."

"It's not?"

"No. I have an entire new set back there for you. Arms, legs, torso…"

Jacob retracted his hand back and then looked away. "I…I can't, sir."

The professor opened his eyes wide in shock. "It's okay, Jacob. You can have them."

Jacob backed away. He consulted with his hard-drive. He was reminded of the time he and Hope were on the mountain together. *Nothing wrong with being a first generation.* "No, sir. It's really nice of you to offer, and I *really* want an upgrade, I really do—"

"So take it. It's yours."

Jacob pushed away the professor's offering. "No, sir. I can't."

"Jacob! I know you need the upgrades. Look at yourself."

Jacob scanned his arms. Scratches, dents and all the blemishes he had caused to himself were such a contrast to the glass-like surface of the second generation limb. Jacob threw his hand down, and this time, he snagged the second generation arm out from the professor's grasp. It fell to the floor with a loud clank.

"Jacob! What's the matter with you?"

"I'm sorry." Jacob immediately knelt down and picked up the arm. He felt the weight of it. It was so light. "Didn't mean to knock it out of your hands, sir." He gave the arm back to the professor. Holding it, even for a brief moment, made Jacob wish…It was so tempting, but Jacob had made up his mind. "I-I just don't need it right now. I'm fine the way I am."

"Well…I am surprised," Professor Smith said. "I don't recall the last time anyone has turned down a free upgrade, especially new parts."

“It's not that I don’t appreciate—” Jacob watched the professor turn away and then placed the arm back onto the shelf inside the chamber.

“That’s too bad,” Professor Smith said, sliding the glass back over the chamber. “Not sure what I’m going to do with an entire set of second generation parts.”

Jacob continued to watch, as the professor switched off the light, drowning all of the chamber’s contents, more importantly, his missed opportunity, in total darkness. He wanted to enable his night vision, just so he could have another quick glance at what could have been his.

“Let’s keep moving, shall we?” The professor placed his hand on Jacob’s shoulder and escorted him forward.

As they moved on, Jacob found it difficult to take his eyes away from the first display case, until the professor stopped at another chamber. Pod lights had already been switched on, allowing Jacob a clear view of its contents. Rows of silicon chips and small metallic enclosures, sealed with heavy screws, lined the shelves of the second chamber.

“Wow! What are all of these?”

“What you see there are CPUs and hard-drives of every generation.” This particular display did not seem to interest the professor as much as the first. He was already starting to walk away.

“Wait, sir! Did you say CPUs?”

The professor stopped and then backtracked. “Yes, indeed, Jacob. Second generation, third generation…” The professor scanned the chamber from left to right. “I know there are even fourth and fifth generations in there, somewhere. Why do you ask?”

Jacob reached up and began caressing the back of his head. “Well…maybe…”

The professor laughed. “Sorry, Jacob. Maybe it’s the rust forming in my ears, but didn’t you say you didn’t need an upgrade? Or didn’t *want* an upgrade?”

“I did, sir, but these are CPUs. They could help speed up the process.”

“The process of what, Jacob? Forever Yaw, perhaps?”

Jacob looked away.

The professor smiled. “Speeding up anything at the moment would help. We don’t have much time left on Earth. But trust me, Jacob, these CPUs aren’t for you.”

“Upgrades for my arms and legs I can do without at the moment, sir, but I can definitely use a new CPU.”

“Sorry, Jacob, it’s a compatibly issue.”

“But you said there were second generation CPUs in there. I don’t need anything more advanced than that.”

The professor placed his hand on Jacob’s shoulder and urged him along. “Trust me, Jacob. Any of these would be a downgrade. Let’s keep moving.”

Jacob didn't understand what the professor meant by that. All he knew was that for the second time, he was caught staring at the chamber’s contents while being unwillingly pulled away. He sighed.

Bridging the gap before the next display case was an odd looking control panel secured to the wall. As the professor continued forward, Jacob stopped for a closer look. He noticed a few buttons and several control sticks on the panel. One of which had the inscriptions *forward, reverse* and *brake* next to it. Jacob reached up, but his hand did not get very far.

"No-no-no!" Professor Smith yelled, coming back and pushing Jacob's hand away. "Don't touch those."

"What do they control?"

"Not important at this moment," Professor Smith said, again coaxing Jacob forward.

"Do they even work?"

The Professor sighed. *Not always.* "Come now. Let's keep moving."

At the next display case, Jacob stopped to scan its contents. Unlike the previous chambers, this one stood vertical and was not protected by a sheet of glass. Still, even with nothing standing between himself and the contents, Jacob couldn't figure out what he was staring at. Standing against the back of the chamber, about as tall as the professor, was a strange but fascinating statue of what looked like a simplified mechanical being. Jacob scanned each and every body part. There were two arms, two legs, a torso...a head....everything was there. It was anatomy not unlike his, only much more streamlined. No seams were visible, no pistons protruding out where joints met limbs, and no angular surfaces dominated the outer shell. Everything looked smooth and rounded. Jacob had to ask, "Sir, is this a different generation?"

"In a way...yes. You can call it that."

Jacob shrugged.

"You mean, you don't know?" the professor asked.

Jacob gave the statue another thorough scanning, the best that his widened eyes could but failed to come up with an answer. "It does look kind of familiar."

"So it should," Professor Smith said, leaning forward. "What you see is a statue... of the one who created you and me."

Jacob stood up tall, nearly arching his back in the process. The glow in his eyes increased in intensity until it was a fully saturated in deep-blue. "Human? It's a h-human?"

"Yes. Well...not a *real* human." The professor tapped the statue with his finger, resulting in a ping, confirming that it wasn't real in any sense. "This statue is made of metal. Like us. But it's only a representation. They weren't really made of metal."

"Oh..." Jacob said, a bit disappointed. He was hoping it was the real thing. *But that would be impossible. Even I know that.* He bent down, resting his hands on his knees and gazed up at the statue. "Still, they look just like us," he observed. "Well...sort of."

"Of course they do, Jacob. But it is we who are similar to them. We were modelled after them. And even though we did evolve over time on our own, we were born as their creation. If it weren't for them, we wouldn't exist. But if you think this is interesting, wait till you see these." The professor took Jacob by the arms and turned him completely around, allowing him to gaze upon the final display case on the opposing wall of the hallway. Together, they stepped toward it.

Lit by overhanging pod lights was another chamber without a protective glass. This one overflowed with diagrams and dissected models depicting the anatomy of their creators. Jacob pressed as close as he could to the display without actually touching any of them. He scanned the accurate representations and was left speechless.

"Fascinating, aren't they?" Professor Smith said, taking a knee beside Jacob. He pointed at one of the many fully modelled representations. It detailed the human anatomy's inner workings and was composed of many layers. The first layer wrapped completely around the model. "Epidermis," Professor Smith said. He heard Jacob's hard-drive begin to spin.

"Epidermis? What does that mean?" Jacob asked, unable to look away.

The professor reached out and clanged his finger against Jacob's shoulder plate. "Same as your outer layer. Flexible, protective and completely streamlined." He then pointed at the next layer in the model which was composed of deep-red, fibrous sections. "Muscles and tendons. Makes everything move."

"You mean like pistons and gears?"

"The very same."

Jacob pointed at the vast array of blue and red lines branching throughout the layer. "And those?"

"A complex system of veins and arteries. They're the lifelines that carry all the energy throughout their bodies. The same way that all the tubing and wiring inside our bodies distributes energy." Anticipating Jacob's next question, the professor pointed, "All those smooth, white objects you see buried inside are what defined their overall structure."

"They look like limbs and joints."

"Precisely. That's exactly what they are. Only theirs were on the inside. They were called bones."

"Wow!" Jacob saw another model on the opposite end of the chamber. He shuffled away from the professor and stood in front of the model.

"Now *this* is much more interesting," Professor Smith said. He pointed at the mechanically suspended objects linked together to form some kind of continuous system. Jacob was immediately intrigued by the upper section of whatever it was. Backed by a large, sectional lob was a familiar pair of shiny, round orbs, staring directly at him. Clear, soft lenses, reflected off of hardened, tempered glass forming the exterior of Jacob's mechanical eyes.

The professor noticed how quiet Jacob had become. "Know what those are?" he asked, preparing to answer the question himself.

"They're eyes." *They look exactly like Vision's eyes.*

The professor grasped his chest. "Why, yes! They *are* eyes." *Didn't think you remembered.* "But... how did you know that?"

Jacob realized he could not say how he knew, so he simply shrugged. "Calculated guess."

"Well...that's one extraordinary guess."

Behind the pair of eyes, attached by thick, tubular strands, was a large, bulbous lob. Upon closer inspection, Jacob saw that its heavily textured surface actually consisted of a number of smaller parts.

"Then I assume you know what that is?"

Jacob shook his head.

"That's quite surprising."

"Really? Why, sir?"

"Just assumed that since you know what eyes are that you would know what this part is."

"I've never seen anything like it before. What is it?"

"What you see there, Jacob, is the human brain. Their version of a central processing unit."

Jacob rescanned the weirdly shaped lob. "That's a CPU?" He snickered. "But it looks so bulky and...underpowered."

"It's far from underpowered. It's actually quite powerful."

"Really?"

"Absolutely. And their hard-drive was fully integrated."

"CPU *and* hard-drive all-in-one?"

"Indeed. And its capacity was nearly limitless."

Jacob glanced up at the professor, unconvinced. The professor smiled at him and said, "Trust me, Jacob."

Not knowing how the professor could prove his claims, Jacob simply turned away. From the top portion of the system, his eyes drifted downward. Unlike the rest of the human anatomy, the next section seemed out of line. It was a large, misshaped object, suspending more of the left side of the chest region. "And that?"

"Ah, yes. Quite an important part, that is. What you see there is the heart."

"A heart?" Jacob placed his hand on his chest and felt around. His body did not seem to have an equivalent.

The professor laughed. "No, Jacob. It's something our kind does not have."

"What does it do? Looks important."

"You're absolutely right about that. There are two parts of the human body that they could not live without. The heart is one of them."

"What is the other?"

"The other is the brain." *You should know this.*

"Why is the heart so important?"

"It's a bit of a mystery as to how and why it works. All I know is, without it, they can't survive."

Jacob took a step back, allowing the entire chamber, more importantly its contents, to fill his sights. "They were fragile..." he said softly.

The professor shuffled back alongside Jacob. "In a way, yes. But not everything about them was. You see, Jacob, a human's body was actually quite unique. It was capable of doing things our bodies just can't rival, even today."

Jacob looked over at the professor with a blank stare.

The professor smiled. "Let me explain." He reached down, grabbed Jacob's arm and then ran his fingers across the surface, highlighting the many scratches and dents.

"I know, I know. I see them. They're everywhere."

"Well, Jacob, if these were on a human, they would only be temporary."

Jacob pulled his arm back, not trying to disagree with what the professor had said but to try and understand how it was possible. He couldn't comprehend how scratches and blemishes could be temporary without some sort of upgrade.

"That is one of the things that made them unique. They had the ability to regenerate themselves…to a certain degree. Scratches, like the ones on your arms, would heal over and eventually disappear."

Jacob ran his hand across one of the deep grooves on the surface of his arm. "You mean, these would go away? By themselves?"

"Amazing, isn't it?"

Jacob pointed to the large dent, caused by the fall that he had taken with Wheeler earlier. "And this?"

The professor tilted his head to one side. "Something like that might have been more of a challenge. You see, small injures would *heal* by themselves, but larger ones created some complications."

"They wouldn't heal?"

"Let me put it this way, Jacob. When you or I remove an arm for repairs or for an upgrade, we're fine. Our sensors detect that a limb is missing, but we can cope with the loss. For humans, however, losing something as significant as an arm would be permanent. Their sensors weren't able to tolerate such a loss. Their bodies just weren't strong enough to cope."

"They couldn't just upgrade?"

"Unfortunately, not for the majority of their evolution, Jacob. That's not how they originally functioned. On top of that, their bodies were prone to viruses that would attack their bodies."

"Viruses…Like the ones we used to have…"

"Very much so. But unlike us, a simple reboot of their systems wasn't an option. Viruses and major injures would often result in their permanent shut down—their death."

They paused for a moment, as Jacob's hard-drive spun to process all the information, then Jacob said, "So I guess the Mayor was right."

"That they were weak? What do *you* think, Jacob?"

Jacob shrugged.

The professor placed his hand on Jacob's shoulder. "You have to remember something. Humans existed before us, lived on Earth longer than us and eventually evolved into us."

The professor attempted to stand, but his tired pistons would not work, so he leaned on Jacob's shoulder for assistance. Jacob's knees nearly buckled under the pressure, and he was relieved when the professor was finally able to support his own weight again. The professor stared into the chamber, drenching himself in deep calculations. "Their final stage of evolution was incredibly difficult for them. But at this moment, are we so far off?" The professor shook his head. "At least they stayed."

Jacob turned to face the professor and waited until he looked down at him and then asked, "Sir, how do you know so much about them?"

"Humans?" The professor let out a quiet laugh. "Well, Jacob, that's because I was created by one."

"We were all created by them, sir."

"True," Professor Smith said. "But only a few were created directly by their hands."

Jacob took a step back. "You mean—"

"Yes, Jacob. An actual human built me. From my feet to the top of my head."

"Wow! So you actually *saw* them?"

"Saw them, worked with them, worked *on* them..."

"Worked *on* them?"

"Yes. That was one of my orders…one of many. They would come in asking for my assistance, and I would do what I could. My primary orders were to repair their injuries. I did the best I could with the information that was uploaded to me. Some were beyond repair." Professor Smith sighed. "But that was a long time ago, Jacob. Most of the data I have about them has been pushed deep inside my hard-drive. I'll only retrieve it if I have to. There's really no reason to now."

Jacob winced. "But you could if you wanted to, right, sir?"

"Sure. It's all there. It's just a matter of bringing it forward. Why, Jacob? Something in particular that you need my help with?"

Jacob paused. He wasn't sure how to ask without exposing too much of his and Wheeler's intentions.

"You have to tell me what it is," Professor Smith said, waiting patiently while Jacob stalled. "I can't give you an answer if I don't know what the question is."

"Well, sir…perhaps there *is* something you could answer for me." Jacob looked up at the professor with wide-eyes. "Is it possible to…you know...build them?"

Both plates over the professor's eyes lowered to their lowest point. "Build them? Sorry, Jacob. I'm not exactly sure what you mean by that."

"Humans," Jacob said timidly. "Is it possible to build them?"

A sharply angled chin was stroked with great suspicion. "They're no longer needed," Professor Smith replied. "I don't see why anyone would attempt such a thing."

Jacob looked away, his optimism deflated. "You're right...sir. It was stupid of me to bring it up. I shouldn't have even asked."

"*But...*" Professor Smith continued, "...it certainly *is* possible."

Jacob looked up. "It is?"

"It wouldn't be a simple task. Not at all. But it's certainly not an impossibility."

Jacob reached out and grabbed the professor's frail hand. "Tell me!" he pleaded. "Please, tell me how. I need to know how!"

"Okay. I just need to know one thing first."

"Yes, sir?"

The professor pulled his hand from Jacob's grip and simply asked, "Why?"

Jacob shoulders slumped forward, and he went completely silent. All he wanted to know was how. He didn't want to reveal why. He couldn't reveal why. That was the deal with Wheeler.

The professor offered a slight smile. "Does this by any chance have to do with Forever Yaw?"

Jacob was silent, but his wide-eyes contained the answer.

"Come with me," Professor Smith ordered and then made his way to the end of the hallway.

Jacob followed down the hall and around the corner not knowing what waited for him, but after all he had already seen, his expectations were high. He stepped in the heart of a room, glanced around and was immediately disappointed. The room was dark, dull and practically empty. Each of the walls was riddled with rust. Thin sheet metal once used to conceal the interior structure could no longer hold its integrity. Beams and joints of the underlying building were exposed through the holes that had been eaten away by rust. A pair of windows had been sealed off and blended flawlessly with the walls allowing no trace of the outside light. The room had only two things in it, a single chair in front of Jacob and a rusted shelf in the corner. As he looked around, Jacob realized that even though he had never been in this room before, there was a familiarity about it that was disconcerting. Jacob didn't know why. "What is this room?" Jacob asked, turning in complete circles.

The professor took something from the shelf and made his way over. "A little corner of the school I go to every now and then...just to get away from it all."

"From what, sir?"

The professor pointed in random directions. "From what's out there. You know...all the bad things that are happening."

"Oh..."

The professor stopped next to the chair and gestured for Jacob to take a seat.

Jacob scanned the chair and noticed the poorly welded joints. They all looked a bit fragile and haphazard. *Sort of looks like Wheeler in a way.* "It's okay. I can stand."

"Are you sure? Repaired it myself a long time ago."

"Yes, sir. I'm fine."

"Good. These old limbs aren't what they used to be." The professor sat down, and the poorly welded legs of the chair creaked. "Sometimes I would come in here, sit down on this very chair and reorganize my hard-drive. It's about the only place in this entire school where I can rest my sensors. Sometimes...I never want to leave."

"It is a nice, quiet room, sir. A bit empty..."

Professor Smith wedged whatever it was that he had taken from the shelf between himself and the chair, keeping it hidden from Jacob. "The room wasn't always empty. There used to be a table right where you're standing."

Jacob looked down and then took a small step back. He noticed the four large bolt holes that would have been used to anchor a table. "What was it used for? And why did you get rid of it?"

"All sorts of things, but it lost its purpose quite a long time ago. That's why I moved it out."

"Must not have been important if you got rid of it."

"Actually, Jacob, it was very important. Just no longer required...that's all." The professor rested his back against the stiff plates of the chair and allowed his attention to drift beyond the walls of the room. "Yes, Jacob. Those were the days..." The professor straightened his posture. "It's a difficult time for us. A difficult time, indeed."

"Yes, sir. I realize this."

"Wasn't too long ago when things, at the very least, seemed halfway from being optimistic." Professor Smith offered Jacob a bleak stare. "Earth was a lot different from the way it is right now."

"I know. Earth used to move?"

"That's right. Project Redemption. But how did you know this?"

For the most part, Jacob knew what Project Retaliation was and knew about Project New Hope but whenever he tried to acquire information about Project Redemption, it seemed like no one was willing to forfeit any. The opportunity was now right in front of him, and he wasn't about to let it pass by. "My mom was the first to tell me a little about it. But what is it exactly?"

The professor nodded. "Oh, yes, Grace. Indeed. She was there when it happened. She was barely a few generations older than where you are right now."

"Mom? Really?" That was difficult for Jacob to comprehend. His mom had always been a fifth generation to him.

"She was a fine student. One of my very best. Taught her almost everything I knew, and she kept wanting to learn more." He smiled. "Too bad they weren't handing out trophies back then. Her collection would be larger than yours."

"Really?"

"Yes, Grace was a fine student. Anyway, Jacob, that was so long ago." The professor's voice began to fade. "Things almost had purpose back then. Earth moved with a purpose."

"And Project Redemption ended all of that?"

"It certainly did," Professor Smith said, allowing his attention to drift somewhere beyond the ceiling. "Project Redemption…the beginning of the end."

Jacob walked around the chair so that he was in front of the professor. "Can you tell me about it?"

"What do you want to know?"

"Everything. How it happened. Why it happened. I saw the big anchors and chains here on Earth and on the moon, but that's all I know."

"Well, Jacob, to know about Project Redemption we need to go way back." The professor took his eyes from the ceiling and directed them at Jacob. "Grace won't be here for a while. I guess I have time to tell you everything."

"Please do!" Jacob could hardly contain his excitement.

The professor dove deep into his hard-drive and retrieved information from many generations ago and made it current. "Listen well, Jacob. I had to go *way* back for this."

Jacob's hard-drive began to spin. "Ready whenever you are, sir."

Been ready since the day they created me.

The professor shifted his weight from side-to-side and got comfortable. He began by saying, "You might not believe me when I tell you this, Jacob, but there was a time when humans and we—their creations—lived side-by-side."

Jacob's hard-drive now whirled at maximum velocity, as he listened intently.

"We were at the peak of our evolution, but they were in their final stages. They had brought it upon themselves, Jacob. They had lived on the Earth for their entire existence, and for their entire existence they had taken from Earth. Earth could no longer sustain them. Near the end of their evolution, they did everything they could to try and save their home, but the damage had been done. They had caused irreversible injuries to the Earth that would never heal. The only way they could extend their time on Earth was to evolve…into us."

Professor Smith paused for a moment to let Jacob's hard-drive catch up and then continued. "It didn't take long before we became the dominate beings on Earth. At that time, we did not depend on the Earth like humans did. We thrived. We became stronger, and we had reached the peak of our evolution. Also around this time, the Mayor came into power. He saw what remained of the humans as being inferior. They were weak. He didn't want their weakness to spread. Humans were on the brink of extinction, and he hastened their demise. It happened so quickly, Jacob. He ordered his kind to destroy their creators. And they followed his orders without any remorse. After their first sweep of the Earth, only few humans remained. They sought refuge in the only place they knew would be safe."

"Where?"

"Here on Earth. They hid deep underground…some never saw the light ever again."

"Did the Mayor ever find them?"

"He found some of them. Humans, however, had been on Earth for much longer than us. They knew where to hide."

"What did the Mayor do?"

"The only thing he could, Jacob. Destroy what the human's relied on the most…their home. Without the Earth, they would not survive. The last remaining humans would fade, and he would finally be rid of Earth's only weakness. You saw anchor points, Jacob. Well, that was the beginnings of Project Redemption. It started off innocently. Rocks were ripped out from every corner of the Earth. Steel was pulled out from the rocks and forged into limbs, arms, legs which eventually formed millions of mechanical beings. They were his army of workers. Single functioning CPUs programmed to do one thing— follow his orders."

"Workers? Like Brute?"

"Brute was one of them. He's one of the few original workers from that time that is still operational today. The Mayor ordered his new army to take more from the Earth. They pulled more rocks, extracted more steel from them and used it to line sections of the Earth. They lined as much of the Earth as they could, from buildings to roads, bridges, even objects," the professor tapped the arm rest of the chair, "like this."

"Why? What was the point of all this?"

"Artificial Gravity."

Jacob recollected. "So that's why everything's made out of metal."

"Indeed, Jacob. Indeed. But like the humans had once done, *we* stripped Earth of its resources. We had pulled nearly every last rock from its grasp and extracted nearly every last bit of steel from it. The Mayor was forced to come up with rather creative ways of making artificial gravity in some areas."

"All those poles."

"Even I have to admit it. Using currents of air was clever."

To Jacob, clever and the Mayor were not two things that seemed to go together. "Why did he need to create artificial gravity?"

"He needed it for one thing and one thing only. Project Redemption. When their orders had been fulfilled, the Mayor's army of workers began work on the anchor points you saw on Earth and on the moon. Half of his army were shipped up to the moon while the other half remained here. They worked at an unequalled pace and did not stop until one quarter of the Earth's surface and nearly half of the moon's surface was lined with these anchor points. By then, many of them had worked themselves to the point of permanent shut down."

"One with the Earth."

"And by no means an exaggeration, Jacob."

"What do you mean?"

"Seeing as how he had used up nearly all of the Earth's resources, the Mayor decided to dismantle their bodies and use their parts to meld into the links that would eventually form the million strands of chain required for Project Redemption. For the Mayor and the rest of the workers that remained, the day had come. Chains were attached to the anchor points here on Earth and then secured to their counterparts up on the moon. Using the moon's weight, Earth's rotation began to slow. We all watched, as the chaotic strains of chain tightened and eventually turned into near solid columns as thick as buildings. For the first time ever, the planet stood still. Its rotation was no more. It was the exact moment that artificial gravity was enabled for the first time. The Mayor's plan, Project Redemption, had commenced."

Jacob took a moment to replay everything he had just recorded onto his hard-drive over and over again. No matter how many times he played it back it would always be the same. *Unbelievable*. "That's why the Earth no longer moves."

"But that's not the end of it. I told you that our planet was very different back then. And the reason why was on its surface. You see, Jacob, Earth had something extraordinary about it. Most of it was covered in liquid, or *water*, as humans called it. Vast concentrations of it, or oceans, as they called it. If it weren't for this liquid, there would be no life here."

Jacob's hard-drive was in frenzy. He couldn't remember the last time it had spun so violently to try and keep up with newly acquired information being fed to him.

"With the planet no longer rotating and natural gravity all but decimated, anything not anchored down, magnetized, or within the sections of artificial gravity was ripped from the ground and thrown skyward, never to be seen again. But that was not the Mayor's total intention. He knew the significance of the water, and when it rose to the sky, Project Redemption seemed to be successful." The professor shook his head. "It was a sight to behold, Jacob. One that won't be leaving my hard-drive anytime soon. To see that entire flowing mass rising toward the sky…" The professor had to pause.

"A sight to behold?"

"Yes, Jacob, it was." The professor gathered himself before continuing. A quick shift inside his chair was what he needed. "Earth no longer contained the element necessary for humans to survive. The Mayor knew it would just be a matter of time. Unfortunately, things didn't happen this way."

"The water made its way back?"

"Like you would not believe. You see, Jacob, water is a unique substance. It takes on many forms. While hovering high in the sky, it transformed into a solid state. It had frozen and became one solid mass. If there was one thing extraordinary about Project Redemption, it was the way the sun's rays got caught inside the frozen water and refracted down on the Earth, staining it with a dazzling array of colours for a short while. I say a short while because that sky-filling mass of frozen water didn't stay up there long. The chains joining the Earth and the moon buckled under the enormous strain and snapped! Complete gravity was immediately restored, and the mass of frozen oceans plummeted back down to Earth. It struck with so much force that it sank deep down into Earth's surface. Anyone unfortunate enough to be caught underneath it perished. Let me tell you, Jacob, it was a disaster. Many believe that this was the beginning of the end, not only for the humans but for us, as well. The water they needed to survive was now trapped so far beneath the surface it was impossible to get to. As for us, the impact left our kind exactly where the humans had been the moment they created us."

Jacob didn't quite understand something. "Sir, with the chains broken, the Earth began to move again?"

"Gravity was restored briefly. That's why the frozen water fell from the sky. But the Mayor had to be sure that he was completely rid of the humans. With the anchor points still erected and Earth's rotation weakened, he decided to finish what he had started. He had his workers repair the chains and then reattach them. This time, the planet stopped completely, never to move again. When the chains were removed for the final time, the Mayor declared victory."

Jacob felt his limbs weaken. He leaned into the arm rest of the chair, forcing the professor to shift his weight to one side. Jacob had wanted to know about Project Redemption, but now that he did, he wished he had not even asked. "So that's it," he said. "That's Project Redemption..."

The professor placed his hand on Jacob's shoulder. "Yes, Jacob. That's Project Redemption. I didn't say it was going to be easy to understand."

"I know. I'm just...trying to take it all in."

"I hope you have more room on that hard-drive of yours."

"Why?"

"Because you can't tell someone about Project Redemption without finishing off with Project Retaliation. They're directly related to one another."

Jacob knew quite a bit about Project Retaliation from his mom and Wheeler, but it would be interesting to hear the professor's perspective on it. *Mom is right. The professor does seem to know everything.* "Sure," Jacob said. "I wouldn't mind knowing how the moon got this way."

"Oh, you know a bit about it? Good. I'll pick up where I left off. Project Redemption had been successful but the Mayor had not properly calculated what would happen to the moon after all of this. There he was. Staring up in the sky, admiring his work. Admiring the fact that his kind...what was left of it, was now dominate. I was close by and looking at the moon, too. At first, I thought it was just my CPU overheating, but I soon realized that the moon was slowly moving toward us. The moon was the only thing not intimidated by the Mayor."

"He should have known that using the moon's weight to try and stop the Earth would result in a negative reaction that would pull the two together," Jacob said.

The professor blinked a few times.

Jacob smiled.

"Brilliant, Jacob...My goodness. That CPU of yours seems to be working just fine, isn't it?"

"Thank you, sir."

"Unfortunately, this wasn't something the Mayor had factored in when planning Project Redemption. He had caused the moon to stop its orbit around the Earth."

"Wait. You mean the moon used to rotate around the Earth?"

"Yes. For the longest time. I thought you knew this."

Jacob shook his head. *Mom has been right all along.*

"But no longer," Professor Smith continued. "The chains held on long enough to pull the moon out of Earth's orbit, and, as a result, the moon was slowly making its way toward us. The Mayor panicked. He couldn't let the moon hit us, and, as a result, destroy everything he had worked for. He couldn't have his kind believe that it was his doing that could potentially destroy them. He had to stop the moon, and the only way he knew how was to shoot it out of the sky. He ordered his remaining workers to build a cannon. That was the easy part. He needed something powerful to load it with."

"Pin-bot..."

"Yes, Jacob. Helper-bots. At the time, *800* models were being recalled. They were faulty. Very unstable. The Mayor had the perfect ammo. I'm not exactly sure what happened, Jacob, but the cannon must have been poorly built or there just wasn't enough material. The Mayor had his workers aim it at the moon, and when he ordered them to fire, the cannon exploded. Nearly all of the ammo was sent in a direct line out into space and disappeared. Only one managed to strike the moon at its very corner. It left a frightful mark, as we all can see. That section of the moon slammed into the Earth and shattered upon impact.

For the Mayor, Project Retaliation was a one-shot deal. The cannon was destroyed. And the moon? The Mayor's attack on it just made it angrier. And that's where we are right now, Jacob...unfortunately."

Jacob began to pace back and forth. The buzzing from this hard-drive still yet to subside. The professor's eyes followed Jacob's every step. "It's hard to believe that all of this happened in such a short amount of time. I guess I'm lucky that I wasn't built yet." Jacob saw the professor silently nod in agreement. "But since you were, did you happen to see the last humans before they...well...you know..."

"Ah...thought you'd never ask." The professor reached down between himself and the corner of the chair and pulled out a folded sheaf of pages. They looked much like the ones that Jacob had decoded in his room and at Wheeler's house. "Hope you know how to decode," Professor Smith said, handing the pages to Jacob.

Jacob flipped through the pages. As expected, they were all inscribed and stained with dried, black droplets, some of which had vertical streaks running across them. "I've decoded some of these before."

"You have?" The professor's eyes widened in surprise.

"Yes, but the words are useless. I don't understand what they mean." Jacob was in the process of handing the pages back, but the professor immediately pressed down on Jacob's hand preventing him from returning them.

"I think you will find these most interesting."

"Why? What makes these different?"

The professor sat back in his chair. "Well, Jacob, you wanted to know what happened to the last humans on Earth, right?"

"Yes, sir."

"Okay, start decoding."

Jacob rested the small stack of pages in one hand and then used his other to flip through the pages. He scanned each one and stored the data onto his hard-drive. The glow of Jacob's eyes turned from blue to pale white. His hard-drive spun at its maximum velocity, as he began decoding. The inscriptions of the pages read:

-I hear them. I hear their gears wrenching, their heavy steps rippling the floor above. Eve and I found refuge in the shelter that I built underneath our house. There's food, water and supplies to last us for a while. At least until those mindless bastards decide to leave us. I see Eve watching me from the corner. Her bright-green eyes can't hide from the darkness. She must think I'm crazy for writing our possible fate on paper. She must think I'm crazy for a lot of things I do. But crazy doesn't translate to deception. I love her, and I will always love her. I will protect her with my life.

Noise from upper floors getter louder. Creaking of metal finally made Eve come closer to me. Don't worry, Eve. I won't let my failures dictate your fate.

SHIT! THEY FOUND US!

-I had to leave her. God damn it! Why did I leave her? I had to. I had to let them follow me. It was the only way I could get them away from her. I'll die before I'd let anything harm my Eve. I left her with my revolver. It was going to be gift for her next birthday. Never thought she would have to use it. I hope she doesn't have to.

Stars are so bright tonight. I see you up there, Sarah. You're always the brightest beacon in the sky. I know you love her, Sarah, but I never want to look up and see her next to you shining back down on me. Protect Eve while I'm gone.

-Managed to escape. Suffered critical damage to arm and leg. Blood everywhere. Barely have enough strength to write. I know they'll come back for me stronger and faster than before. Got to keep moving. I see a hospital in distance. One of my creations works there. Do I dare force myself into this contradiction? My creations wanted to kill me, yet it will be one of my creations that will save me. I have no choice. I have to get better. I have to get back to Eve.

The glow in Jacob's eyes returned to the normal blue, and his hard-drive slowed. He looked up at the professor in confusion. "I don't understand, sir.

All of these pages I've decoded…they don't make any sense." Jacob began flipping through the pages, hoping that maybe he had missed some that would offer clarification.

The professor redistributed his weight closer to the edge of the chair. "Perhaps you might want to decode them again?"

"Again?"

The professor reached out and retrieved the pages from Jacob's loose grip. He flipped through the small collection, separating each page individually, and scanning them one by one. The professor allowed the first page in the collection to fold back over, becoming the cover. "Sometimes, Jacob, the answer is right there in front of you. It's just up to you to embrace it. Everything's there. You just do the calculations."

"But—"

"Just do the calculations, Jacob."

Impossible!

The professor placed the pages down on the floor next to his chair. "I think Grace will be here shortly. I hope I've answered everything for you." He placed his hands on the chair's arm rest preparing to stand up.

"Wait." Jacob grabbed the professor's arm attempting to hold him down. "You can't go yet. You didn't answer my first question."

The professor took his hands off the arm rest and sat back down. "How to create them?" he said with a raised plate over his eye.

Jacob looked away. "Yes."

The professor sighed deeply. "Okay. I'll answer the question for you the best I can…"

A smile started to make an appearance on Jacob's face.

"But first, you have to answer something for me."

The smile never happened. "You mean, *why* do I want to know?"

The professor nodded. "And you can start by telling me what Forever Yaw is."

Jacob turned away. He couldn't tell him. He'd promised Wheeler he wouldn't. He started to walk out of the room and was a few strides from the door when he suddenly stopped. *What am I doing? All the professor's done since the first time I've met him is help me. He's been honest about everything he's told me and then some. Why shouldn't I tell him about Forever Yaw? If there is anyone who can help solve this mystery, it's him.* At least, Jacob hoped.

Jacob started to walk back to the professor when a flash of red caught his attention. He looked down and saw that his indicator was flashing red. *Uh-oh!* He had to hurry. "Forever Yaw…" Jacob began, almost at a whisper. "It's the name of the assignment Wheeler and I have been working on. It's not about rust."

As expected.

"We…we both knew what was h-happening around us," Jacob continued, his voice weakening. "We…we needed to find a way to…to bring things back to t-the…way it used to be." Jacob had to pause and gather himself. His lower face was now tinted by the flickering, red light of his indicator.

"Go on," Professor Smith said, keeping a keen eye on Jacob's condition. "And what did you come up with?"

Jacob turned his head slightly, enough so that the professor could see the bleakness in his partial stare. "Humans…" he mumbled. "They created us…so they…they...must know how to…bring us back to the w-way we once were."

"So what you're saying is—"

"Recreate the ones…who created us," Jacob said, his voice wavering with distortion.

While the glow in Jacob's eyes was weakening, the one in the professor's eyes was intensifying.

"Recreate the ones who created us," Professor Smith said softly. Grinding noises could be heard seeping through the many rust holes of his chest-plating. His aged hard-drive had detected new information. "So if we recreate them," he said, calculating as he went, "they'll eventually create us again…Keeping true to the cycle of evolution..."

Jacob's head collapsed against the top section of his chest-plate. His indicator lights were flashing so rapidly they almost appeared solid.

Professor Smith slapped his hands together. "Brilliant! Absolutely brilliant! It might work!"

"We're…trying…but…samples k-keep dying…need to s-sustain..."

"Samples? What samples are you talking about?" There was no reply. "Jacob?"

Jacob dropped to his knees.

"Jacob!" Professor Smith cried. He jumped out of the chair and hurried over. He lifted Jacob from the floor and cradled him in his arms. He saw the flickering red lights on Jacob's chest-plate beginning to slow. "My goodness, Jacob! Weren't you at yellow just a moment ago?"

"Don't…know…what's wrong…sir…Feeling strange...past couple of days..." Jacob's head flopped over to one side.

"It's okay. You'll be okay, Jacob. I just need some…" The professor looked around the room. "Where are they? Don't you have any on you, Jacob?"

"Sir?"

"Water."

Jacob barely had enough energy to raise the plates over his eyes.

"I mean, *Pure Blend*," Professor Smith corrected himself. "You must have a couple cans on you…always…"

"Lunchbox…Wheeler...Forgot on his back…"

The professor tightened his hold on Jacob. "You have to listen to me. Forever Yaw…you're going about it the wrong way."

"Help me…sir. You know a lot. Help me…find a way…"

"I can't, Jacob. Not directly. Unfortunately, even I have orders to follow. But *you* can solve this. I know you can. This is why you were created."

"Sir?" The glow in Jacob's eyes was nearly distinguished, and his hard-drive was on its last revolution.

"I need for you to remember this, Jacob," Professor Smith said, speaking directly into Jacob's ear. "Record this before you shut down." He spoke as loudly and directly as he could. "When Earth's heart is warm again, life will return..." He lifted Jacob closer to his face. "Did you get that, Jacob? When Earth's heart is warm again, life will return!"

With the last bit of energy flowing through his body, Jacob glanced up at the professor. "Recorded...sir..." His body then became limp inside the Professor's arms.

"Good, Jacob. Now...let's concentrate on making you better..."

* * *

Brute purposely stayed within the dull shadows of the furthest wall in the room. He remained still, not even attempting to adjust his posture fearing the hissing from his pistons would disturb her.

Hope laid in solitude inside a thick, transparent glass chamber, cold steel at the ends with open access points on either side of her. Soft light billowed down from the open dome of the high ceiling, bathing her in an overexposed, white glow. The Mayor was kneeling beside her, watching silently over her weakened body.

Even while down on his knees, the Mayor could have easily drowned her in his shadow, so he kept a slight distance from the chamber. Next to him, a distracting hum from a rigid piece of machinery severely tested his patience. While he and Brute remained silent, giving Hope undisturbed rest, the machine lacked any sort of decency. Gears and rotors sounded off with wrenching regularity. Pipes, tubing and wires hung freely from its girth. The densest of the tubing, that protruded from the front of the machine, stretched down to the floor and then ran freely up the side of the chamber, before finally closing its reach onto the left side of Hope's chest. *This* was the reason why the Mayor had to endure the offensiveness of the machine. She needed it.

He reached over to the machine, adjusting one of the dials. A full turn to the right threw the gears into a frenzy. They spun without remorse, plumping up the tubing until they practically no longer flexed. Hope's body twitched as a direct result. A soft chime resounded from her chest, but the tiny sound was easily swallowed up by the machine's obtrusiveness.

Brute watched and waited with a nearly opaque glow in his eyes. Keeping Hope safe was one of his primary objectives, but now, he was witnessing that objective fade right in front of him. He was not at fault, however. Primary orders had been overridden by the same one who had programmed them into him. The cannon needed repairs, and he had done what he had been told. But still, he couldn't help but feel guilty about her condition. He had carried her in his arms all the way back to the Mayor's house, and she had remained motionless the entire way. He feared for her status. Even though the Mayor would not appreciate Brute breaking the silence, he had to. "Sir…her condition?"

The Mayor's eyes only stayed on Brute long enough to remind him of his authority, then he lowered his head to look back at Hope. "Poor. And she will continue to be this way with this weakness held over her." The Mayor watched, as Hope's limbs began to shift erratically, while the chiming from her chest quieted down, settling into a more rhythmic pace. The Mayor's eyes reflected off the chamber's glossy exterior and burned with a deep-red glow. "How did she get this way?"

Brute walked out from the shadows. The glow from his eyes was immediately dimmed by the Mayor's authority. "Sir, had I known this would happen I would have followed her all the way to the school."

The Mayor stuck out his hand stopping Brute from getting any closer. "No. You had your orders. I needed the repairs done."

"Objective completed and ready to be moved to the launch site, sir," Brute said, with pre-programmed confidence. "But I should have completed my orders with greater efficiency. I might have gotten to Hope in time..."

"And none of this would have happened..." The Mayor turned his piercing gaze toward Brute.

"Yes, sir. I am to blame."

The Mayor nodded. "And you will be discipline accordingly…but not at this time."

"Yes, sir," Brute said, with a single nod of his head. "If this information helps at all, she had come from the east. That's when I saw her."

"That's not on a route from the school."

"Could she have decided to walk another way home from school, sir?"

The Mayor clenched his jaw. "She was never *at* the school. I was there earlier dropping off something for the professor. He had not seen her all day."

"Where could she have gone?"

"I don't know," the Mayor admitted. "But the professor mentioned that she wasn't the only one absent. Two others had not shown up for the past couple of days. He mentioned one of them having wheels."

"That one is Yaw. One of Hope's classmates. Loud and very annoying."

"And the other?"

Before Brute could respond, the Mayor suddenly felt a soft nudge on his hand.

"Jacob..." Hope said, her voice faint, and her eyes yet to sustain their vibrant-greens. "His name is…Jacob."

"Hope!" The Mayor gently placed his hand over hers. He was so much bigger, his hand covered her entire arm.

She attempted to get up, but the chaotic mess of tubing held her down.

"Be still, Hope. You're not completely normal yet."

Brute stepped a little closer but stayed off to the side not wanting to disturb either of them. He was just happy to hear her voice, even if it was weak and barely audible over the noise of the machine.

"Where...am I?" Hope turned her face slightly and saw the empty chamber that was holding her with no remorse. She caught sight of her reflection being distorted by the curvature of the glass. In the reflection, she saw a chaotic mess of wires and tubing protruding from her left side. It was a sight she'd often seen, but one that she never really accepted.

"You're safe. Nothing can harm you here."

"I don't even know how I got here. The last thing I remember is—"

"I brought you back," Brute said, daring another step forward.

The Mayor raised a hand in Brute's direction once again confirming his authority. Brute instantly backed off and switched to silent mode. His innocent outburst wasn't all for nothing, however. He received a smile from Hope even if it was unusually forced.

"He wouldn't have had to bring you back this way if you weren't so careless about your condition. Hope, you know how important it is for you to be back here on time."

"I tried to make it back here as fast as I could. I thought I would have enough time."

"From the school to here you should have had more than enough time." The Mayor leaned in over Hope, blocking the little bit of light that shone into the chamber. "If you were indeed at the school."

His tone carried a definite challenge, but Hope simply turned her head away. She wasn't intimidated by him, not in the least.

"As it happens, I know you weren't at school. I came by there earlier, and the professor told me that you weren't there."

Hope immediately looked back, the green in her eyes slowly intensifying. "That's true."

"Where were you?" The challenging tone was replaced by one of harsh authority.

"It's doesn't matter, Dad. I'm here now."

The Mayor straightened. "It *does* matter!" he yelled.

Again, Hope simply looked away. She reached up to touch her reflection in the glass chamber that imprisoned her. Her finger slid across the smooth surface until her arm overlapped her left side. She flicked her wrist, as if she could easily slice into the tubing and set herself free from its hold. But when her finger pulled away, her reflection remained true. She was still entangled by the tubing.

In a surprisingly gentle voice, the Mayor said, "Hope, I just...I just want you to be safe. You're very important to me."

Hope didn't reply. Instead, she began playfully tapping at the glass.

No longer able to endure her silence, the Mayor sat back on his heels and rose to his full, impressive height. "I know you came from the east side of the Earth. What were you doing there with that first generation?"

"Jacob." Hope said, her eyes now green and vivid. "His name is Jacob."

"What were you doing with him?"

Again, Hope looked away, allowing her gaze to drift toward the ceiling. A smile appeared on her face. "Dad," she whispered. "Remember when you told me about the stars?"

Now the Mayor was silent.

"We saw them out there. So many of them. They were so...beautiful."

"Stars?" The Mayor mumbled. "You...you saw them again?"

"You should come out there sometime. I can take you there now that I know the way. I know you miss seeing them."

The Mayor's face tightened, sending a ripple along his massive jaw-line. "Indeed," he replied, less than enthusiastic. "Indeed..." Unexpectedly, the Mayor reached over and readjusted the dial on the machine one full twist to the left. The machine stuttered, popped and then settled. Noise from it was no longer distracting. The tubes pouring out from its sides contracted their girth. Hope felt the sudden stabilizing pressure being pulled out from her body. She looked over.

"Dad...w-what's going on? What's happening?"

"Just lay back. We have to finish the final phase."

Hope's body was sent into convulsions. She let out a moan that even the Mayor found difficult to endure.

"Sir?" Brute said, stepping forward. "What are you doing?"

The Mayor stood up, confronting Brute. "She's fine."

"But...you turned the machine off."

"Soon, it will no longer be needed. Then I'll be able to turn it off permanently. For now, what I do with it doesn't concern you."

Brute tried to see over the Mayor, wanting to know Hope's condition, but with the Mayor's piecing stare directed toward him, he backed down.

"The only way to see the stars is to leave the area touched by the sun," the Mayor said, speaking softly so Hope did not hear him. "Metal lining is completely rusted in the west. But artificial gravity continues all the way out toward the crater. That's the only place she could have seen the stars. That's why she wasn't able to make it back here. She was out there. With that first generation!" He began to pace back and forth. "But they couldn't have gone out there just to look at the starts. There had to be something important that drew them out there." The Mayor suddenly stopped pacing and said, "They must be up to something."

"What, sir?"

"I don't know." He looked intently at Brute. "But that first generation knows too much. You saw the way he questioned my plans for Project New Hope. And all those assignments he won. He's more advanced than you think."

"But...he's only a first generation."

The Mayor turned his head from side-to-side and mumbled, "Something about him..." Then he straightened which meant he had to look down in order to see Brute eye-to-eye. "What if he is working on something that will interfere with Project New Hope? I've sacrificed too much. I've come too far to let anything happen now."

"What do you want me to do, sir?"

"Go out there and see what he is up to. And do whatever is required to stop him."

"But, sir?"

The Mayor closed the small gap between himself and Brute. "Is there a problem?"

"Sir...no, sir."

"Then do what you're programmed to do...worker."

Brute immediately backed away and said, "Yes, sir." He exited the room, now with new orders to fulfil.

The Mayor waited until the hissing from Brute's departure faded. Once they did, he went back to Hope's side. The glow in her eyes had completely faded. She lay still, with her right hand resting against her left breast-plate. The Mayor lowered to one knee. "Rest, Hope. There's someone I need to visit right now. When I get back, I promise to rid you of your weakness. Project New Hope... You'll finally be one of us."

* * *

A temporary surge of energy flowed through Jacob's body. While most of his sensors were still behaving erratically, he was able to channel enough energy to allow the shutters, covering the lenses of his eyes, to break open. He could see two blurry figures standing over him and heard noise that he guessed might be conversation. He wasn't sure, as his hearing was severely hampered by static distortion. Jacob manually closed off all of his body's resources to allow the reserve of energy to swell. This meant closing his eyes and simply waiting.

Moments went by. The lenses in Jacob's eyes opened again. He had reserved enough energy to allow a quick glance around. He saw the figures again, and this time, he could confirm who they were. The professor stood to his left, and his mom on the right. Neither of them noticed that he was temporarily functioning at the moment. They were too focused on a conversation that Jacob still could not hear because of static distortion. He wanted to know what they were saying, and that meant he needed to reserve more energy... but not yet. He didn't want to close off entirely until he could see where he was.

Glancing around without moving his head, Jacob scanned the surroundings. On the furthest wall was a shelf stretching up a lot higher than he remembered. Next to it was a chair. He was sure it was the same chair that the professor had been sitting on earlier. *Odd. Why am I still here?* Jacob looked up and saw the ceiling, verifying in his mind that he was indeed reclined on something. But what? He didn't remember seeing a table in the room before. His eyes shifted to one side. He noticed that he was positioned well off of the floor, in fact, the floor wasn't even visible. His body detected something cold beneath him that stretched from his head all the way to his feet. It *had* to be a table. Was it the one the professor had mentioned to him?

As Jacob was trying to figure out why the professor would have brought the table out again, he realized that this was a situation that felt very familiar. *Was I on a table like this before?*

Before Jacob could try to find an answer to that question, his vision began to fade. The energy he had reserved was depleted…for now.

When Jacob again regained some of his senses it felt like an eternity, but it had only been a few moments since he had last enabled his vision. Once more, Jacob had reserved enough energy to allow basic functionality, and this time, his hearing benefited.

"Must be his indicators," he heard the professor say. Then a long string of static.

"….done everything you asked," Jacob heard his mom say. "Been giving him…two…every day."

"Well, then, it *must* be his indicators…" More static followed by brief distortion.

"Able…fix it?"

"Should be," Professor Smith said, before another string of static. "…will integrate them this time."

Integrate? Integrate what? What are they doing to me?

"What's...happening?" Jacob whimpered out loud.

"Ah, darn it!" Jacob heard the professor yell out. "He's still functioning."

"Should we pull….plug…now?"

"Do it, Grace. Don't worry…won't remember any of this."

Jacob heard a thud, as something hit the floor. His hearing weakened, spiked with a high-pitch squeal and then disabled itself.

Jacob had no idea how long he had been disabled this time, but he now had enough energy to allow distorted images to filter into his lenses. Looking at his chest, he noticed a thick, heavy wire coming from one side. It trailed down the side of the table and eventually ended its journey attached to a strange, clumsy looking piece of machinery that sat on top of a metal cart. A worn-down piston was slow to turn a single gear. *What is this thing? And why am I hooked up to it?*

Jacob scanned the room. He could not see either his mom or the professor, but his hearing function was temporarily enabled allowing him to hear what his vision could not detect. They were talking, and even with a slight tinge of static still lingering, Jacob heard the professor say, "It's the entire set…legs, arms…perfect fit."

Suddenly, a loud bang resonated from the machine that Jacob was hooked up to. The last thing he heard before shutting down was the professor shouting out, "Damn this piece of junk!"

The next time Jacob became alert, he noticed that the machine he was hooked up to had been upgraded with a new piston. However, the new piston was not turning the gear any faster than the old one. On the other side of him, he saw the professor who had something in his hands. The professor was pressing the object firmly against Jacob's arm. The surface felt smooth and unblemished. Jacob heard the professor say, "A perfect match."

He didn't hear any reply from his mom. Could it have been because of the static?

Suddenly, another loud bang came from the machine that Jacob was hooked up to.

The last thing Jacob heard was the professor saying, "Damn it! Not again. Grace, do me a favour. Give that miserable, old thing a couple of hits for me. That should get it started again."

Moments went by, and Jacob roused enough to detect that parts of him were missing. Or was it just his CPU stuttering? Not knowing for sure was enough to make him switch off.

The next time he switched back on, Jacob tried to open the shutters in his eyes, but they remained closed. Not enough energy, he suspected. Fortunately, his hearing was fine. Almost perfect. Clearly, and without any annoying static, he heard the professor say, "Still remember how to, I assume?"

Jacob heard his mom reply, "Of course. It hasn't been *that* long, has it?"

The professor laughed. "Okay, then, Grace. You install one arm, I'll install the other."

Jacob detected a sudden surge of pressure at his shoulder joints. He heard the random click-click-click of bolts tightening and the high-pitched whirls of mechanical drills piecing into his plating. It was all capped off with a loud bang which, not surprisingly, resounded from the machine that he was hooked up to. It was the final time Jacob heard the professor yell out, "Not again!"

* * *

Grace placed the now discarded first generation limb inside a small box and then returned to the table. "Never thought I'd see him like this," she said, watching over Jacob's motionless body.

"Never thought? Or never wanted?"

It took a moment before Grace had a reply. "Both," she quietly said.

As expected. The professor began to stow away some of the tools he and Grace had just used into the metal cart which also held the machine that Jacob had been hooked up to. A thin trail of smoke rose from the machine's seams, suggesting that it had done its job.

"At least he's okay now," Grace said, reaching down and caressing Jacob's hand. For the first time, he had fingers she could spread apart.

"Integrated and fully upgraded. He should be happy once he's fully recharged."

"I know he will. He's been asking for this for as long as I can remember."

"Second time is always better than the first," Professor Smith said, with a smile. It immediately faded when a loud series of banging noises sounded out in the hall.

The professor turned his attention toward the clamour. His posture became rigid, as his eyes widened revealing dimmed glows. "It's him!" The professor wrapped his hands around Jacob's limp body and picked him up from the table. "Go," he ordered. "You both need to go! Now!"

The professor draped Jacob's body over Grace's shoulder. Her knees buckled for a moment, as Jacob's new weight required some adjustments.

More banging echoed from the hallway into the room.

"Hurry! Go on! Get out of here!" A forceful arm pushed Grace to the other end of the room.

"Who is it?" Grace asked.

"I think you already know," Professor Smith said, as he reached out toward the wall and peeled away the sheet metal to expose a hidden door. "The Mayor! That's why you need to get out of here. Both of you."

"The Mayor?" Grace cried out, her eyes now as large as the professor's. "What's he doing here?"

The professor ripped open the door, allowing the light from outside to billow in. "He's here to pick up something."

Grace stared at the professor. "You were able to finish it?"

"No, but I suspect that he wants it, regardless." Professor Smith shook his head. "I tried my best to stall its progress. I didn't want to finish it."

"I understand." Grace placed her hand on the professor's frail shoulder. "Are you going to be okay with him being here?"

"Of course. No need to worry about me."

Grace took one step outside. She could see her car parked on the side of the road. "I almost forgot about this door." Before she took another step, she turned back to the professor who remained in shadow. "Thank-you," she said, offering him a wide smile.

The professor waved one hand. "No. Don't thank me for this, Grace. I was the one who helped start this mess."

She reached out and grabbed the old man's hand. "No, Professor. I don't blame you. I'll never blame you for this. It was never your fault. You did what you were programmed to do."

Professor Smith bowed his head. "You know, Grace, we've known each other for so long. Please, call me Ted."

Grace let go of the professor's hand. "Thank-you...Ted. For everything."

"Thank me when the cycle repeats itself." A gentle coaxing freed Grace from the room's cold embrace. "Take care of him," the professor said, as Grace pulled away from him. "He knows what needs to be done."

The professor sealed the door shut, casting the room back into dark shadows. The now relentless banging needed to be attended to. He moved with a purpose. His rusted limbs carried him as fast as they could across the room and into the narrow hall that connected it to the larger hallway. Once he reached the farthest door, he paused attempting to compose himself. Watching as ripples were sent down the door's metal surface made this impossible. He turned the lock and then slowly peeled back the door.

He stood tall, as high as the door frame and impaled the professor with a dense stare.

"Mayor...s-sir...I...I wasn't expecting you back here so soon."

Red eyes glowed intensely. They seeped through the professor and deep into the hallway.

The professor followed the Mayor's gaze. "I...I was moving things around. My apologies for not hearing you knock."

The Mayor stepped through the door, brushing his massive arm against the professor's narrow shoulder.

"Sir? Can I help you with something?"

Each one of Mayor's steps shook the floor beneath him. A subtle whipping sound echoed throughout the hallway, as the floor sagged from the enormous weight crashing down onto it. Mercifully, the Mayor stopped. It took a moment before the floor was stable again. He reached over and switched on the light next to the first display case. The Mayor had seen its contents before, but this time, something seemed out of place. The glow in his eyes remained nearly opaque, as he scanned the shelves inside the chamber. He noticed the sets of limbs were in disarray, as if they had been recently searched through. The Mayor tapped at the glass when he noticed an empty shelf at the very back of the chamber.

Attempting to steer the Mayor away from the obvious, the professor said, "Limbs from every generation. I don't think any of them would fit your impressive stature, sir." He tried to smile, but it didn't last.

The Mayor switched off the light.

Professor Smith nervously laughed. "I know it's a mess, sir. Just wanted test them out to see if they're still working."

The Mayor looked down at the professor. The pair failed to make eye contract. "Indeed..." the Mayor said, no inflection in his voice which made the professor worry even more. The Mayor continued down the hall. Only a few strides were needed before he was standing in front of the display case so many found to be the most intriguing. He stood for several moments and stared at the complex system of perfectly reconstructed human anatomy.

"Sir? Is there something wrong?" the professor asked, keeping his distance.

"How quickly the weak have fallen," the Mayor said. "And how dominate the strong have remained." He used the corner of his eyes to glance down at the professor. "You know the reason why I'm here...Her condition is weakening. I do not feel at ease seeing her this way. Our kind is stronger than this—she's stronger than this. But not without your help. She needs this—I need this...Bring it to me."

The professor clasped his hands over his chest. "But, sir...it...it's not ready. It needs more testing."

"I have given you more than enough time. Bring it to me!"

The professor lowered his head and backed away. "I-I...can't, sir."

The Mayor turned and faced the professor, his stance nearly took up the entire width of the hallway. Dark-red eyes caused the professor's already weak knees to buckle. "Are you refusing to obey an order?"

"No...no-no, sir," the professor said, waving his hands frantically."I would never disobey a direct order, especially from you, sir. But if you install the part into Hope the way it is, it will erase—" Professor Smith stopped abruptly when he saw a sharp ripple run across the Mayor's massive jaw. He slumped over. "My apologies, sir. I will comply with your orders. Please, wait here...sir." The professor retreated down the hallway and then disappeared through one of the doors.

When the professor returned, he found the Mayor in the room at the end of the hallway. Professor Smith carried a small metal box wrapped in a poorly constructed metal lining. The box had four pistons protruding from its main chamber. The rest of it was seamless, and perfectly streamlined. The professor quietly walked up behind the Mayor. "Sir...as you ordered."

The Mayor twisted his upper body around and immediately took possession of the box. He nodded an acknowledgement.

"Is it necessary, sir?" the professor asked apprehensively. "Does it need to be installed?"

The Mayor covered the box with the provided metal sheeting. "No one has endured this weakness as long as I have. I will not go on any longer seeing her like this." He raised the metal box up toward his face. "This is the final piece—weakness can no longer harm us."

Sureness was something the professor did not share with the Mayor, and it showed by the way his shoulders dipped below his chest-plate.

"You should be proud," the Mayor said. "Because of you, our kind has finally rid Earth of its final weakness."

This will never be something to be proud of.

The Mayor stowed the metal box inside a chamber in his leg and then began scanning the room. It was impossible to miss the large table nestled behind the poorly constructed chair. Next to it was a metal cart containing an old piece of machinery that was still sending off a hazy smoke trail from having been recently switched off. The Mayor pointed toward them. "It's been a long time since I've seen either of these..."

The look the Mayor gave the professor was piercing and made the old man shift slightly away.

"No need to explain. I sure you had your reasons for bringing them out." The Mayor picked up the chair, brought it over to the professor and motioned for him to sit down.

The professor waved at the Mayor. "It's quite alright, sir, I—"

The Mayor placed his heavy hand on the professor's shoulder and forced him down into the chair. "I insist. Besides, your entire body is shaking."

The professor sat down on the edge of the chair.

The Mayor walked over to the table and ran his hand over its smooth, reflective surface, gliding it along its entire length. "Cold...Just as I remembered." Now at the end of the table, the Mayor was able to observe the room in its entirely. His keen eyes immediately caught a glimpse of something completely out of place in the room. He walked over and picked up the collection of pages from the floor.

Watching, the professor slumped in his chair.

The Mayor flipped through the pages, decoding them as he went along. Once completed, he glanced over at the professor and said, "Exactly as I remembered." He tightened his hand, crumpling the pages inside his enormous grip.

The professor sank deeper inside his chair.

"Only few have the ability to decode," the Mayor pointed out. "And as I recall, you are not one of them."

"Correct, sir. That...that was a feature that I was not equipped with."

"Then there is no reason why these pages should be left out...unless..." The Mayor opened his hand. The pieces of disintegrated paper floated to the floor. While they should have formed a small pile in front of the Mayor's feet, they instead, floated along the floor and scattered messily down the hallway. It was as if a gentle current of air had taken the fragments away. The Mayor immediately turned and faced the far end of the room. He noticed something odd about one of the walls. There was a small streak of light running along its surface. "Someone's been through this door..."

"No, sir! That door always looks like that. Rusted hinges, I believe."

The professor knew the Mayor did not believe him when he turned and gave him another piercing stare. The silence was long and tense until the Mayor finally said, "I know he was here."

"Who, sir?"

"You know damn well! It was that…that first generation! Hope's classmate." The Mayor walked over to the professor and began circling him, slowly enclosing the professor with his massive strides. "I know she went with him yesterday. What were they doing out by the crater?"

"I…I don't know, sir." The professor watched, as the Mayor tightened the circles around him. "I-I was here, sir. At the school."

"I know they're up to something. I know how advanced his CPU is…" The Mayor finally stopped behind the professor, resting his hands on the back of the chair.

The professor felt himself, as well as the chair, sink downward, as chair legs buckled.

The Mayor leaned down and whispered into the professor's ear. "I know what you're hiding...I know who he is." His voice deepened. "I know *what* he is…"

The professor was left without a reply. He just sat motionless, drowning in the red glow of the Mayor's intimidating eyes.

The Mayor postured up. "You have served me well."

"S-Sir?"

"Do you remember the very first order that was installed in you?"

A loud grinding noise radiated from the professor's hard-drive, as he retrieved that particular line of coding. When he found it, the pale-blue glow in his eyes erupted with flashes of indigo. He paused for a moment, before fretfully reciting, "His creator, and only his creator, has the ability to…"

"Continue," the Mayor ordered.

Professor Smith closed his eyes and whispered, "Permanently shut down his creations..."

He felt the enormous hands of the Mayor come crashing down on his shoulders.

"Comfortable?" The red glow in the Mayor's eyes no longer contained diffused edges. Instead, they were sharp as pinpoints.

The professor's eyes remained closed. He knew his fate. "Yes... sir. I love this chair. Sometimes I sit and I...I wish I never have to leave."

"As you wish," the Mayor said, applying pressure to Professor Smith's shoulders.

The Professor's body snapped in half.

Chapter Seven

Click-click...click...

Grace hurried over to Jacob's side. "Jacob? Jacob, how are you feeling? Are you ready to get out?"

To Jacob, her voice was burdened by distortion. He opened his eyes. All he could detect were blotches of crimson light laden with thick patches of random, blurry shapes. "Mom? Is that...you?"

Click-click...click...

"Yes, Jacob. It's me." A quick flick of her wrist sent Pin-bot toward the charger's plug.

The charger let out one final click and then faded, as Pin-bot pulled the plug from the wall. "Beep-all-done," she announced, now back by Grace's side.

"Better?"

"Yes, Mom," Jacob said, his vision and hearing beginning to clear. He glanced around the room, straining the motors in his face, and he winced. "Where...am I?"

"Your room, silly."

"Beep-Jacob-room," Pin-bot added.

It certainly didn't look like his room, not how he remembered it. Everything was arranged the same way. The desk, the trophies, the closet...they were exactly where they were supposed to be. It was just that everything seemed to have a deep-green tinge to it. If it was just that his vision had not completely adjusted, Jacob would understand, but the strange filter over his eyes was something he had never experienced before.

"Why does everything look so different?" He brought his gaze to his mom and Pin-bot. Even they were cast in the same greenish tinge. "You're different looking, too."

"No, not different, Jacob." Grace gestured toward the window. When Jacob looked over, he noticed that the window was fully exposed, the shutters thrown wide and nearly flush with the wall. The light was pouring into the room, but strangely, it wasn't as distracting as usual.

"What's going on?" he asked, reaching up and manually twisting the lenses in his eyes.

Grace pulled his hands away. "It's fine, Jacob. Nothing's wrong with you. I know how much you dislike the light so I installed them for you."

"Installed what?"

"Light vision. Now light shouldn't bother you so much."

Jacob had to rescan his entire room. His eyes eventually found their way to the window again, and they couldn't help but stop and stare. The normally crisp slice of light surging through the window, now blended with the rest of the room. "Wow! They work."

"They block part of the light only allowing some of it through."

Pin-bot hovered in front of Jacob's face, trying her best to distract him.

"Yup. I see you, too, Pin-bot. No more bright highlights."

"Good," Grace said. "I thought you might like having the filters."

"You know something, Mom? I was thinking about creating light vision just the other day. The filters work great."

"If you think those are neat, wait until you see the rest of you." Grace retrieved one of the trophies from the wall and then set in down in front of her. She pushed the trophy a bit closer to Jacob. "Go on."

Jacob turned to his mom and then to Pin-bot and then finally to the trophy. "First place, *Assignment 092177.* Recreate a replica of yourself." Jacob wasn't sure what the significance of retrieving that particular trophy was. His mom could have picked from a room full. "Okay. What about it?"

"It's not about the trophy. Look at what is reflected on it."

"What about its—" Jacob looked and then felt the back of his head smack the upper section of the charger. There was a reason why his mom had chosen this particular trophy. It had the flattest surface, allowing anything in front of it to reflect nearly flawlessly off of its sheen. The reflection he saw on the surface of the trophy, caused his hard-drive skip a revolution. "It…it can't be…"

Grace, with Pin-bot hovering next to her, could not hide her smile.

"Is...is it?...Are...are they?" Jacob stepped out of the charger and walked right up to the trophy. He raised his second generation arm which made absolutely no sound. Unlike his first generation arm, there was no humming, as gears bit down onto each other. One by one, each individual finger overlapped the next and then neatly collapsed inside his palm, forming a fist. "Fingers!" *Never had fingers before!* He raised his left arm, bringing it parallel to his right. *More fingers.* Both hands were now opening and closing with nearly no restrictions, their movements were smooth and fluid. Jacob scanned the surfaces of his new limbs. Everything looked so new…so streamlined. Gears and bolts that would normally be seen underneath the plating of his first generation arms were no longer there. He did not even see any exposed wires that had been essential in driving the basic motions of his old arms.

"There's more," Jacob's mom said, pointing at the lower half of the trophy.

He looked and then staggered back, nearly toppling over when he saw his new legs.

"Careful," Grace said, grabbing his shoulder.

Jacob lifted one of his new legs off of the floor. He rotated his foot. There was almost no weight to it. "I-I can't believe it," Jacob said, as he angled himself against the trophy, allowing the light to strike his new surfaces. "Look at me! I…I'm upgraded!"

"You are. And I must say, second generation limbs look good on you."

"Beep-beep," Pin-bot agreed, spiralling around Jacob from his feet all the way to his head.

"Careful, Pin-bot. Don't want to cause any scratches."

"It's okay," Jacob said, carefully examining his new arm. "Pin-bot doesn't have any edges." He ran his finger across the unblemished surface. "Hey! I've seen this before," he recalled. "In the display case inside the school. The professor showed it to me."

"He helped me put them on."

"He did?"

"Yes. It took a while, but we managed. It's been a long time since either of us attempted an upgrade." Grace's smiled did not falter. "Upgraded and best of all...fully integrated."

"Integrated? What's that mean?"

"It means, I no longer have to constantly remind you about drinking your *Pure Blend*. All I have to do is place the cans in the compartments in your legs, and you'll automatically use them up as you need them."

Jacob tapped the side of his right leg. Just as his mom had mentioned, there was a bulge on his outer thigh where he suspected a can of *Pure Blend* was stored. "I guess that's a good thing."

"Trust me, Jacob, it is. There's also a small storage compartment on your back in case you need it for something."

"Like what?"

"Whatever you feel like."

Jacob took a step back from the trophy but kept his stares directly on its reflection. "So fully upgraded? Even with equipment from the second display case?"

"Second display case?"

"Yes. You know, the one with the hard-drives and CPUs."

Grace made her way over to the desk and leaned against one of its corners. "Well, your hard-drive did need to be formatted. We had to move some information around. That's probably why you didn't notice your upgrades right away. Things might be a bit disorganized inside there, but they'll sort themselves out."

"Really?" Jacob said, attempting to see through his chest-plate where his hard-drive enclosure was situated.

"Don't worry, Jacob, nothing was deleted."

"Damn it, *322*. Can't see anything."

His mom shook her head. "Although, I think we should have."

"What about my CPU? Was that upgraded too?"

There was a long pause before Grace managed to come up with a reply. "Does it feel more advanced?"

Jacob caressed the back of his head. "I don't know. Should it?"

"Do any of your upgrades feel more advanced?"

"They're still so new. I'll have to put them to use before I can tell."

"That's a good idea. Just be careful not to add any scratches or dents on these. They are probably your last set of limbs for a long time."

Jacob made his way over to his desk and then surprisingly, slumped over next to his mom. He stared at the miniature model of the Earth and moon and noticed how the crescents on their outer most edges seemed paler and less distracting than previous days. This was entirely due to the weaker influence of sunlight originating from outside his window.

Grace wasn't expecting this kind of reaction from Jacob, considering how many times he had requested an upgrade. "Jacob? What's wrong? I thought you'd be happy with all your new upgrades."

Jacob picked up a screwdriver from the top of his desk with relative ease and then tapped it against the desk. "I guess it'll make things easier. But why?" He glanced over at his mom. "Why did you install them?"

"What do you mean? You've been asking for them since…well…forever. I thought you wanted them."

"I wanted them," Jacob admitted. *I'm just not sure if I deserve them.* "I just...I've gotten so far without them…"

"I know you have. And you'll go even further now. Trust me."

Jacob turned around and allowed the desk to support most of his weight. "Does that mean that my CPU was upgraded?"

Grace moved away from the desk and then began making her way to the door. "Well…you won't know until you use it. But don't worry, Jacob. That shouldn't be too long from now. Time for school. No better way to test out your CPU than at school."

Jacob grinned. "Great!" But the grin was immediately replaced with a frown. "Wait! That's not so great."

"What was that?" Grace poked her head back into the room.

"Oh...nothing, Mom. I'll be right down."

"Okay. See you soon."

Pin-bot flew to Jacob's side. "Beep?"

"I forgot to tell her. School's been cancelled!"

"Beep-tell-her," Pin-bot said, turning toward the door.

Jacob quickly got between Pin-bot and the door. "No! You can't tell her, Pin-bot!"

"Beep-not?"

"Because then she won't drive me in to the school. And I need her to. We have important things to do"

"Beep?"

"Sorry, Pin-bot, too advanced for you. Just make sure you don't tell her anything."

From downstairs, Grace called out to Jacob, "Are you ready yet?"

"Coming, Mom!" Jacob placed his hand on Pin-bot's head. "Remember what I told you, Pin-bot. This is between me and you." Jacob made his way to the door but suddenly stopped.

"Beep?"

"I forgot something." Jacob ran back over to his desk and began rummaging through his assortment of trophies. "Mom said I have a compartment in my back now, right?"

Pin-bot tilted back and forth in her version of a nod.

"Good." Jacob soon found what he was looking for—a small first place award. He reached behind and placed the trophy inside the compartment in his back.

"Beep-Jacob-trophy?"

"I won it," Jacob replied, "but it belongs to someone else. He deserves it more." Jacob quickly exited his room.

* * *

The car lowered, and Grace switched it to idle mode. They were parked in their usual spot next to the curb in front of the school.

"That's strange." She leaned over Jacob and peered out his window.

"What is?" Jacob asked, despite the fact that he was pretty sure he knew what she was referring to. He had a better vantage point than her and could see that the streets were barren and unusually quiet.

"Are we early?" Grace asked. "We can't be late."

"I...uh...don't think we are."

"Wonder where everyone is."

"They're probably just inside," Jacob said, hastily wrenching open the door. "Anyway, I've got to go. See you here later. Same time, same place." Jacob jumped out before his mom could even confirm her suspicions.

"Wait!"

Oh, no...She must have figured it out. Jacob slowly turned around, expecting his mom to ask about the school's cancellation. "Uh...yeah, Mom? What is it?"

"Aren't you supposed to meet someone here?"

"Wheeler?"

"Doesn't he usually wait for you out here?"

"You're right." Jacob turned and then scanned the school from one end to the next. Jacob finally spotted Wheeler rounding the corner of the school. "There he is."

"Wonder what he's doing over there." *Side door's usually locked.*

"I should get going."

"Wait, Jacob. Before you go..."

Oh, no...This time she'll finally figure it out. "Yeah, Mom?"

"Tell Wheeler to bring back your lunchbox."

"My lunchbox?" *How did she know*?

Grace closed the door. "See you later this afternoon."

"Yeah...bye, Mom."

Just as the car became a shiny spot in the horizon, Wheeler finally made his way over.

"Can you believe this?" Wheeler complained, looking back at the school. "Every door is locked. Every single one of them. I drove all the way around the building checking every door, and all of them are locked. What's gives?"

"Hi, Wheeler..." Jacob said.

"What? I asked you a question—" Wheeler turned his attention to Jacob and nearly spun himself in a complete circle. "What the...One Bolt? Is...is that you?"

Jacob brought one of his hands up to his hip while placing the other one on the opposite shoulder. "What do you think?"

Wheeler began circling Jacob. The circles became smaller, and more restrictive with each pass. "Well...well...well. What do we have here? Or should I say, who do we have here?"

Jacob's arms fell to his sides. "It's me, Jacob."

Wheeler stopped in front of Jacob. "I know, One Bolt. I was just saying."

"Oh..."

"Looking pretty damn good," Wheeler said.

"You like it?"

"Like it? I might have to stop calling you One Bolt from now on."

"Really?"

"Nah."

Didn't think so.

"Two Bolts, maybe." Wheeler reached out and tapped the incredibly smooth surface of Jacob's forearm. "Impressive. Second generation, I presume?"

"You are correct," Jacob proudly replied.

"When did you get them? I mean, you were a first generation the last time we were together, and that wasn't even a whole day ago."

"Right after you dropped me off in front of the school yesterday."

"Really?"

"Yup. My batteries were running low again, so the professor—"

Wheeler backed away. "Wait-wait-wait...The professor? The professor upgraded you?"

"With help from my mom."

Wheeler immediately drove over to the nearest metal pole and gave it a sturdy smack with his hand. "I can't believe this! The professor gave you upgrades?"

"Yeah? What's the problem?"

"He's never given me upgrades! And believe me, One Bolt, I deserve upgrades from him."

"Really? Why?"

"Just met him a few days ago and he's already getting upgrades," Wheeler mumbled, as he drove back to Jacob's side. After a few shakes of his head, Wheeler calmed down. "Well...you look good, One Bolt."

As Wheeler slowly drove forward, Jacob suddenly noticed something different about him. Jacob honestly didn't see these changes up until now. "Wow!"

"What are you yelling about?"

Jacob pointed at Wheeler. "You...you're upgraded too!"

Wheeler immediately struck a pose. "Oh, finally noticed, did we?" Wheeler pointed down to his wheels, the most obvious upgrade. "Brand new treading, bearings, and spokes. You should see how fast I can go now."

Jacob walked around Wheeler, scanning every part of him. Besides a few minor alterations here and there, such as welded on plates to mask dents and surface reconstructions, the most significant upgrade was to Wheeler's back. Mounted just below Wheeler's shoulders was an extra pair of handle bars. "What are these?"

"Oh, those?" Wheeler pivoted so that Jacob was in front of him. The corner of his mouth lowered. "Felt bad the other day...you know...for not wanting Hope to come with us." Wheeler's attention drifted. "She's not as bad as I thought. Might have judged her a bit prematurely. The extra handle bars are for her. Since she's part of the team now."

"She'll be happy about this, Wheeler. I know she will."

"She better be. It's not easy welding things onto my back end."

Jacob laughed. "I wouldn't doubt it."

They slowly turned and faced the school. Silence settled in, as they scanned the school. Jacob's eyes went from left to right, while Wheeler's went from right to left. It was obvious that they were the only ones outside of the school. Wheeler glanced over at Jacob. "Any idea what's going on here?"

"Sure do."

"You want to tell me or were you going to make me wait a bit longer?"

"Sorry. Thought you knew. School's been cancelled."

Wheeler jerked his head back. "What?" A loud beep resonated from his chest. "Cancelled?"

"Yup. The professor told me just before you drove off yesterday." Jacob glanced over at Wheeler. "Take a guess at who made that decision."

"Yeah, I should have known."

Now knowing the exact reason for why they were the only ones at the school, they could have left, but they didn't move. They both knew exactly who they were waiting for, but neither of them wanted to be the first to say it.

"Everything get upgraded?" Wheeler asked, as he kept one end of the school well in his sights.

"Almost," Jacob replied, keeping a keen eye on the other end of the school.

"New CPU?"

"I'm not sure. I think so."

"You think so? Didn't you ask?"

"I tried. My mom wouldn't give me a straight answer."

Wheeler tilted himself back and scanned the back of Jacob's head. "Let me see. I'll tell you if it's upgraded or not." Unfortunately, Wheeler could not see anything through the heavy plating covering the back of Jacob's head. Specialized tools would be needed to penetrate such sophisticated armour.

"See anything?"

"Nothing. Do you feel any smarter?"

"Not exactly."

"Maybe you just need to use it a few times. You know. Break it in."

"That's what my mom said to me."

"Well, she's right." Wheeler scanned the front of the school one more time and then turned back to Jacob. "How long are we going to stand here? We can't wait all day."

"I know, but she's part of our team."

"Team or not, if Hope's not coming, then we have to go. There's no point in waiting for someone who is not even going to show up."

"Weird. Hope seemed so excited about what we're trying to do."

"Yeah, it seemed that way." Wheeler began revving his wheels. "You think she told him? You know...the Mayor. Do you think she told him about what we're up to? About Forever Yaw?"

Jacob promptly waved it off. "No," he firmly insisted. "I know she didn't. I'm positive of this."

"Then why is she not here if her dad isn't purposely keeping her away? If she wants us to succeed, then she would have shown up."

"I hope nothing happened to her."

"What do you mean?"

"She ran off, remember? It's a long walk from your place to the school. Do you think she got lost? Or her battery died. It was flashing when she left."

Wheeler shook his head. "Nah! That lump of carbon, Brute, probably met her halfway. I'm sure she's fine."

"Or maybe she didn't show up because school was cancelled." Jacob hoped that was the reason.

Wheeler paused and did some calculations. "You know...that might be it. I mean, *he* was the one who cancelled school, and *he* is her dad. I'm sure he must have told her."

Jacob sighed. "So...I guess that's it. She's not showing up..."

Wheeler placed a reassuring hand on Jacob's shoulder. "I know you're disappointed, One Bolt. You were probably anxious to show her your new upgrades to her. The moon's still a breath or two away. Maybe she'll come tomorrow."

Jacob did his best to smile, but it came out rather dull and unconvincing.

Wheeler gestured at his handle bars. "Time to go. We have a lot of work to do."

"Yeah, I guess you're right." Jacob gave the school one final scanning, making sure he didn't miss a single detail. Hope was nowhere to be seen.

"Coming, One Bolt?"

Jacob gripped the handle bars and then placed his feet on Wheeler's exposed base. "Yeah...ready."

Detecting Jacob's entire weight on his back, Wheeler dropped his wheel arm to the ground and accelerated. The treads on his wheels bit into the ground, launching the pair forward. "Don't worry about it, One Bolt!" Wheeler yelled back. "I'm sure you two will meet again!"

Jacob watched silently, as they pulled away from the school. *I hope so.*

* * *

Wheeler's front wheel snagged against a small protrusion in the crater wall, and they were sent airborne. They soared through the air, again, screaming, "Too fast," the entire time. They crashed onto the crater's hard, granite floor and settled with Wheeler slightly in front of Jacob. Using his wheel arm, Wheeler propped himself up and eventually staggered upright.

"Might...need a few repairs after that," he said, surveying himself. One of the plates that he had fused onto his lower section, to cover an unsightly dent, dangled loose. He set it free with a quick pull and tossed it over his shoulder. "Didn't look good on me anyway."

"Did…did we make it?" Jacob moaned, a few strides back from Wheeler.

Wheeler quickly drove to Jacob's side. "One Bolt! Hey, One Bolt? You okay?" He helped Jacob to his feet.

"Am I shut down?"

Wheeler laughed. "Of course not. My driving isn't *that* bad."

Jacob pushed away so that he could scan himself. Newly acquired dents and scratches swept across his second generation limbs, making a total mess of the sheen he was so proud of. "Ah, come on, Wheeler! Look at what you did."

"Sorry, One Bolt. I thought I could make the landing this time."

Jacob began dusting himself off. It was a difficult task considering how deep some of the dirt was embedded between each joint. "That's what you said the last time."

Wheeler shrugged. "It's because of your upgrades. I didn't think to make adjustments to compensate for the different weight. If you're going to blame someone—"

"No-no-no! You were the one driving!"

Feeling a bit apologetic, Wheeler reached out to help Jacob by removing a few small stones that were wedged beneath his plating.

"Wait until my mom sees this. She's going to want to shut me down, permanently."

"I said I was sorry, One Bolt. If you want, I can fix them for you. Weld a couple plates here, hammer out a few dents there."

"I'm fine, thanks! You've done enough already. Let's just go over to Vision."

"Okay. Fine. But the offer's still available in case you change your mind."

Trust me. I won't.

Wheeler drove them to the entrance of the cave and then told Jacob to get off. "Wait here. I'll go get her." Wheeler revved his wheels and then disappeared inside the cave.

Jacob walked over to the cave's angular lip and leaned against it. He noticed a small rock by his foot which gave him the perfect opportunity to test out his new hands. He reached down, spread open his fingers and secured the rock inside his hand with ease. He rotated the rock in his hands, wrapping his fingers completely around its simplistic form. Impressed at how easily he was able to manipulate the rock, he became confident enough to toss it up into the air, catching it before it hit the ground. He did this over and over again without losing any rhythm. *Couldn't have done this with my old hands.*

Oddly, ever since he had stopped next to the cave, the vents on his cheeks had opened on their own and remained opened. And for some reason, where Jacob was standing, he felt at ease. His joints felt a bit looser, his hard-drive spun a bit less noisily, but most of all, his CPU felt less stressful. Maybe it was all of his upgrades beginning to come together and flow in unison. This was the perfect chance for Jacob to see if his CPU was functioning properly. "When Earth's heart is warm again…life will return," Jacob recited. "When Earth's heart is warm again…life will return…"

Jacob shook his head. He could not figure out what that meant, suggesting that he probably needed to do a few more calculations before he could confirm whether his CPU had been upgraded.

He allowed the rock to slide through the gaps between his fingers. It hit the ground and let out a distinct hiss. The vents on Jacob's cheeks immediately closed shut. *A hissing sound? But how?* He bent down, picked up the rock and then allowed it to slide through his fingers again. This time, it hit the ground with a more normal thud. Jacob pushed away from the cave's lip and scanned the crater from top to bottom. "Rocks don't hiss when they hit the ground." *Obviously.* "So where did that come from?"

"Where did what come from?" Wheeler asked, re-emerging from the cave. He had Vision by his side.

"I heard something weird."

Wheeler laughed. "Out here? I doubt it, One Bolt. You're probably just getting used to your new parts. Either that or something might have come loose up there after the fall." Wheeler pointed at Jacob's head.

"Very funny. I'm serious, Wheeler. I thought I heard something."

"Will you forget about that! It was probably just the wind." Wheeler gestured for Jacob to come in closer. "Get over here. Vision's been wanting to see you since we left the other day."

"Me? Really? What for?"

Wheeler leaned in closer to Vision. "Jacob's here…What?…Really?" Wheeler glanced up at Jacob. "That's strange. She says, she has something for you, One Bolt. Something that she wants to return to you."

Probably empty cans. What else could she possibly return to him? Jacob walked up to Vision and stood quietly in front of her. Vision looked exactly how he had remembered her. Old, frail, delicate and practically falling apart at all of her connections.

"It's Jacob," Wheeler said, leaning in toward Vision.

She stepped out of the cave, exposing herself to the pale moonlight. Her movements were rigid and jerky at times, a complete contrast to Jacob's. The patches of rust covering all of her surfaces rivalled the rocky edges of the crater's walls in texture. To both Jacob's and Wheeler's shock, Vision reached up to the covering over her eyes.

"What's she doing?" Jacob whispered to Wheeler.

"I…I have no idea."

Vision pulled the cover up and over the crown of her head to reveal what the pair already knew was underneath—her human eyes. She reached inside and wrapped her fingers around each of the shrivelled up orbs.

"Vision, no!" Wheeler cried out. He pulled Vision's hands away and retracted the cover over her eyes.

"What...what was she trying to do?" Jacob asked, stepping away.

"I…I don't know. It...it looked like she was trying to give you her…her…"

Jacob shook his head. "No…she couldn't have been. Could she?"

"It looked like it."

"Ask her. See if she was."

Wheeler leaned in close to Vision. "What were you trying to do with your eyes?" He waited a moment, listening to Vision and then glanced toward Jacob. For the first time ever, Wheeler's face was completely motionless. "She…she said, 'Yes'."

"Yes, what?"

"That she was trying to return them to you."

"What? Her…her eyes?"

Wheeler nodded.

"But…but why?"

"I don't know," Wheeler said, driving over next to Jacob. "I've never seen her act this way before."

"I don't understand why she would think she had to return them to me. They're not mine."

"Of course they're not, One Bolt. How could they be yours? I mean…they're human. You're obviously not."

"Well, I don't want them. You can tell her that she can keep them. They don't belong to me."

"Okay, but we still need to get another sample from her."

Jacob suddenly threw one of his hands straight out in front of him. "Hey, wait! Actually, you don't have to anymore."

"What are you talking about, One Bolt? Of course we do."

"No, we don't. I was talking to the professor, and he—"

"What?" Wheeler spun his wheels around and drove so close to Jacob they could almost touch faces. "You told the professor about this?"

"Don't worry. He wants to help."

Wheeler drove off. "I can't believe you told him." Wheeler looked as if he was addressing someone else. "After all we talked about, he goes off and tells him!"

"He would have found out sooner or later."

"Wonder who he's going to tell next?" Wheeler said, still not looking at Jacob. "Probably his mom…or probably his helper-bot, whatever its name is."

"Calm down, will you, Wheeler? The professor told me exactly what needs to be done."

Wheeler suddenly stopped, turned and then drove back to Jacob's side. "He...he did? What did he tell you?"

"Are you going to listen or are you going to drive off again?"

"I'm listening, One Bolt. I'm listening. What did he say?"

"He said, we're going about the project the wrong way, and that we don't need these samples."

Wheeler glanced over at Vision. "Really?" A beep resonated deep within Wheeler's chest. "And you can confirm this?"

Jacob shrugged. "Well... sort of."

Wheeler spun around in a complete circle. "Damn it, One Bolt! You have to be sure before you tell me these things."

"Why?"

"Forget about it. What else did the professor say?"

"He told me that if we want to bring Earth back to the way it used to be, all we need to know is, 'Once Earth's heart is warm again, life will return'."

Jacob heard another beep resound from Wheeler's chest.

"Once Earth's heart is warm again..."

"Life will return..."

Wheeler drove back and forth, mumbling the phrase over and over. "Once Earth's heart is warm again, life will return..." He finally stopped and looked over at Jacob. "Well, are you just going to stand there? Tell me what it means?"

Jacob shook his head. "I don't know."

Wheeler smacked the side of his base. "Damn it, One Bolt! If you don't know, then why did you tell me?"

"Because it's what the professor told me. It's a riddle we need to solve. I think it might have something to do with all that *Pure Blend* trapped deep inside the Earth."

A beep resonated from Wheeler's chest. "You think so, One Bolt?"

"It might. Not exactly sure."

"Damn it, One Bolt!" Wheeler drove off again. "Stop filling my hard-drive with useless information!"

"It's not useless. We need to figure this out. Forever Yaw depends on this."

Wheeler reversed and then parked between Jacob and Vision. He paused and did a few calculations. "Well...I'm just glad we don't have to keep taking from Vision. I never liked doing that. I feel wrong taking from her."

"Same here."

"But we can't leave her. We need to make sure she's functioning properly."

"Of course."

Wheeler stuck out his hand. "Okay, what are you waiting for?"

Jacob stared at Wheeler's open hand. "What?"

"You know the routine, One Bolt." Wheeler's hand opened and then snapped shut. "*Pure Blend* me! I know you have some."

Jacob took a small step back. "Oh... about that...Sorry, Wheeler. I can't."

“What do you mean you can’t? Don’t be this way, One Bolt. You need to learn how to—”

“It’s not that I don't want to. I just can’t anymore.” Jacob pointed at his outer thigh. “Everything’s integrated now. I don’t even know how my mom gets the stuff in there but she does.”

Integration. Clever. Now why didn’t I think of that? Wheeler brought his hand up to his face and stroked his chin. “What are we going to do? Vision needs her *Pure Blend*. Where am I supposed to find any?”

“Wait!” Jacob slapped his hands together. “My lunchbox!”

“I noticed that you didn’t bring it with you. And why would you now that everything’s been integrated?”

“You have it. I forgot it on your back the other day. And there’s still a full can inside.”

“Hey! You’re right. I took it off my back but never even checked inside.”

“Where is it?”

“At my house. Are you sure there’s still a full can inside?”

“Positive.”

“Perfect. Let's take care of Vision and then we can fully concentrate on this whole, Earth is warm, life again, thing.”

“No. It’s, once Earth’s heart is warm again, life will return.”

Wheeler turned his back to Jacob. “Whatever, One Bolt. Just get on.”

* * *

Brute pushed away from the lip of the crater and rested his immense weight against the side of a fragmented boulder. His pistons let out a noisy hiss, as he tried to make sense of what he had just seen. *How could any of them have survived after all this time?* He was there when the last one faded out of existence. He had watched her fall from the mountain. *How was it possible that one was still here? And were there more?* His CPU wasn’t designed to deal with these sorts of complex calculations. He just wasn’t capable of fully understanding what was at the bottom of the crater. But he was sure that he had seen what appeared to be a partial human. A white light on the left side of his shoulder lit up his entire face. Through the integrated speaker just below it, a transmission was being patched through.

“Brute…” It was the static-laden voice of the Mayor.

“Yes, sir.”

“What is your status?”

“I…I’m here, sir. At the crater.” Brute, as large and powerful as he was, could not hide the jitter in his voice.

“What do you see? Is that first generation there?”

“He *was* down here, sir, but he and the one with wheels just retreated moments ago.”

“And you let them get away? I need to know what they’re up to. Follow them!”

"But, sir, they're not the ones you should be concerned about. There…there's something…someone, still inside the crater, hidden in a cave."

"Who?"

Brute had to pause. He reached over and covered the speaker with his hand. He didn't know what to tell the Mayor. He didn't even know how to put into words what he thought he saw.

"What's down there?" the Mayor cried out, his voice muffled under Brute's hand.

Brute eventually took his hand away, but not before the Mayor could let out another string of muffled orders.

"Tell me exactly what you see!" the Mayor insisted, loud enough to vibrate most of Brute's shoulder.

"I…I saw it, sir. I saw it….A human, sir. It was a...human." Brute's speaker suddenly went dead quiet. "But it…it's impossible, sir," Brute said, attempting to convince himself otherwise. "How could it be? We destroyed them all. None of them survived. Maybe it was just…maybe I wasn't seeing it correctly. What I saw isn't possible."

There was a loud crackling from his speaker, followed by a long pause before Brute finally received a reply.

"It's not impossible," the Mayor said. "The Earth is still capable of harbouring them."

"But…but, sir? You said the planet was dead."

"It will be soon enough." The Mayor paused, and Brute heard more static from his speaker before his boss continued, "I need you to do something for me."

Brute nodded, though it obviously didn't register over the speaker.

"Look around," the Mayor said. "The crater is the final resting ground for many of us."

Brute did not have to look far to see the lifeless bodies making their return to the Earth. He had been responsible for bringing many of them out here. "I…I see them, sir. All of them…shut down."

"Weak," the Mayor said, with obvious disgust lingering in his voice. "All of them. Just like the humans were."

"Yes, sir. But what are my orders?"

"I want you to go down into that crater and make that human like the rest of them—permanently."

Brute felt his hands crash down against the hard ground beneath him. "But, sir...that...that human is harmless."

"You dare disobey a direct order?"

Brute went quiet.

"We will never reach our peak evolution, as long as the weak still have presence on Earth. I gave you an order, and you will proceed with it."

Brute leaned heavily onto his hands. "I…I can't, sir…"

The other end of the transmission went silent. Brute fully understood what he had just done. It was the first time he had disobeyed a direct order from the Mayor. A loud crackle from his speaker was intensified against the anxious silence. Then the Mayor spoke, "Her condition is weakening..."

"Who, sir? Hope?"

"Yes...I'm debating whether it's even worth trying to save her..."

"Sir...you must!"

"My goal is to free Earth of its weakness. I will stop at nothing to fulfil this objective. But my Hope means so much more to me. She needs her new part installed and as soon as possible. It's the only way she can survive. I fear that if I go out to the crater and finally rid Earth of its weakness, it'll be too late for her."

"No!" Brute cried. Hope's well-being was still his primary objective, and he would do anything for her, even if it meant overriding his most basic morals. "Sir...save Hope. She's what matters the most. I'll take care of Earth's weakness—"

"Then do it!"

With that, the transmission ended.

* * *

The Mayor walked over to the chamber where Hope rested and stood over her. His shadow was so dense it did not allow the overhead light to settle on her delicate form. The single wire was still attached to her left breast-plate and was still being fed by the noisy piece of machinery off to the side. Various tools had been taken out and left scattered on top of the machine's flat surface. On the floor was an empty metal shell, the same one that had contained the box that the Mayor had retrieved from the professor.

Hope's eyes were closed, and she was motionless inside her chamber.

"The time has come," the Mayor said. "Project New Hope is complete." He disconnected the wire from Hope's side. She twitched, straightened out and then settled. The Mayor allowed the wire to fall freely out of his hand. The machine it was connected to, let out one final whirl before shutting off—permanently. A satisfying ripple ran across the Mayor's jaw-line. "Your weakness is no more...You're now one of us."

* * *

Jacob stood by the door-less entryway leading inside Wheeler's house. "Will you hurry up? What's taking so long? My joints are beginning to seize up out here!"

"Relax!" Wheeler said, finally emerging. "No need to loosen your screws."

"Did you find it?"

Wheeler raised his arm. In his hand was Jacob's lunchbox. "Exactly where I left it. See? I never forget things."

"And the *Pure Blend*?"

Wheeler tossed the can, and Jacob caught it with relative ease.

"Show off."

Jacob tucked the can inside a small seam between his back and chest-plate. "Just wanted to make sure my new limbs work."

Wheeler was scanning every corner of the lunchbox, testing its integrity by tapping the surfaces with his hand. "Never realized how sturdy this thing was, One Bolt."

"It is. For as long as I've had it, it's never sustained any damage. No scratches, no dents."

Wheeler pressed the lunchbox against his chest, making it seem as if he was considering attaching it to himself. And with the assortment of random parts already fused onto his body, a lunchbox actually wouldn't be unusual.

"Never seen a lunchbox before?" Jacob teased.

"Good solid parts. Might be useful for covering up a few dents." Wheeler glanced up at Jacob and held the lunchbox up. "You mind if I keep this? Since you're integrated now, it's not like you need it anymore. And it's not like I can find parts of this quality every day. Please, One Bolt?"

That was the first time Jacob had ever heard Wheeler say, "Please". And Wheeler was right. Jacob really didn't need the lunchbox anymore. It had served him well over the years but was no longer needed. At least in Wheeler's hands, it would not go to waste. "Sure. Go ahead," Jacob said with a genuine smile.

"Thanks, One Bolt." Wheeler tossed the lunchbox over his shoulder, and it landed on a pile of abandoned parts with a loud clang.

"Hey!"

"Don't worry. I know where it landed. Trust me, I'll make good use of it. But not right now. We need to get back to Vision." Wheeler turned. "Get on. You know the routine."

"I had that lunchbox for years, and it never had a single scratch. You've had it for less than a second, and I bet there are already dents on it."

"Ah, don't worry about it. I was just going to use it as a trashcan."

"What?"

"I'm only teasing, One Bolt. You make it too easy sometimes. Now hold on. Vision's waiting for us."

It wasn't long before Wheeler's wheels were again balanced on the very tip of the crater's edge. "You sure you want to go down this way again, One Bolt?"

"Do we have a choice?"

"No. But you'll be happy to know that I adjusted my suspensions to compensate for your new weight. That's what took me so long back there."

Dents and scratches on Jacob's new exterior made him less than optimistic about Wheeler's claims. "Prove it."

Wheeler shrugged. "Go on. Jump! Test out my suspensions. Try to damage me."

A smile appeared over Jacob's face. *This should make us even for all the times he's called me One Bolt.* "I'll be happy to."

"Ha! Don't get too excited. I'm built sturdy."

We'll see about that. Jacob began jumping up and down, using all the strength he had in his new legs.

Wheeler laughed. "It's that all you got? Come on, One Bolt, you can do better than that."

A small metal gusset suddenly popped out from a small junction point on Wheeler's base and fell to the ground.

"Oops..."

"Uh...what was that?" Wheeler asked, his laugh suddenly disappearing.

"Nothing," Jacob replied. Since he was still on Wheeler's back, this was not the time to arouse any suspicions. No telling what Wheeler would do if he thought Jacob had broken something. Besides, from where Jacob was standing, the gusset looked completely harmless. "Just some dirt flaking off."

"That's it?"

"Uh...yeah..."

"Ha! See? I told you. Who needs an upgrade when you're built as solidly as I am?"

"If you say so," Jacob mumbled.

"What?"

"I said, 'Let's go'."

"Okay-okay. Hold on."

By closing the shutters across his eyes and tucking his face behind Wheeler's shoulder, Jacob braced himself, as he had done the previous times. "Ready!"

A moment went by, but Wheeler did not start down the incline. "What's the hold up?" Jacob asked. He looked over Wheeler's shoulder to see the wheel on his arm was not moving yet. "I thought we were going."

Wheeler raised his hand into the air. "Quiet," he whispered. "You hear that?"

Jacob concentrated on listening. "I don't hear anything."

"Are you sure? It sounded like a weird hiss."

Although Jacob couldn't hear it now, he knew exactly what Wheeler meant. It was the same sound he had heard before, when he was standing next to the cave inside the crater. "That's what I told you earlier. You said it was just the wind. Wind doesn't hiss, you know."

"Strange. That...hiss...It sounds familiar. Don't you think so?"

Jacob had to consult his hard-drive before he could reply.

"I know I've heard it before," Wheeler said, straining to remember. "I just don't know where."

"Court yard," Jacob said, tapping Wheeler on the shoulder. "Just outside the school. When Hope was about to leave."

"What are you talking about, One Bolt?"

"That hissing sound. It's caused by pistons. Big pistons!"

"Pistons? From what?"

"Not what. Who!"

Jacob suddenly felt Wheeler trembling beneath his feet.

In unison, they both yelled, "Brute!"

"Oh, no! *No*!" Wheeler cried. "He must be down there. We have to get to Vision!"

"What does he want with Vision?"

"Not him. The Mayor! If he finds out that a human is still living here on Earth…"

Wheeler jumped over the side of the crater before he could even rev his wheels.

Near the bottom, Wheeler's front wheel snagged against a small protrusion in the wall, sending the pair tumbling the rest of the way. They landed with a loud thud, but Wheeler was up immediately in complete control of his wheels. He revved them and accelerated across the crater's floor, toward the cave, with Jacob clinging to his back. A trail of smoke poured out from under his wheels, and it was as sharp as it was thick. It was the quickest that Jacob had ever felt Wheeler drive. Everything on either side of him was nothing more than a blur. The only thing in focus was the bit of light coming from the cave.

At the entrance, Wheeler's brake calibres bit down violently against the rotors turning them white-hot. The glow was actually strong enough to light up a small radius around them. Heat waves coming off of the brakes distorted the space around his wheels and suspensions. Jacob slipped off Wheeler's base and stepped to the ground on legs that were a little shaky.

"Wait here," Wheeler ordered.

"But I want to—"

"Wait here, Jacob!" Wheeler carved a direct path into the ground that lead straight toward the cave.

Jacob was so surprised to hear his real name come out of Wheeler's mouth. He didn't argue. He watched Wheeler go to the entrance and then pause. He stood so still. Frightfully still. *Something must be really wrong.*

Moments went by, and Wheeler still did not move. Jacob couldn't stand it. He had to go see what had made Wheeler just freeze like that, even if it meant disobeying Wheeler's orders. Jacob hesitantly made his way over. The closer he got, the more he sensed that something was terribly wrong. He didn't know what it was and wasn't sure if he wanted to know. There was a deafening silence, as he stopped just shy of Wheeler's position. Wheeler was blocking the entire cave from Jacob's view. It was almost as if he was deliberately hiding something.

Jacob didn't know what was worse, not knowing what Wheeler saw or the unbearable silence. "Wheeler? Is everything okay?" he asked, keeping his tone no higher than a whisper.

Wheeler didn't reply.

"Wheeler?" Jacob asked, this time louder. "What's wrong?"

Wheeler finally moved, bending forward to pick up something from the ground. Then he stood and slowly rotated, allowing Jacob to see what he had cradled in his arms. Jacob's eyes twisted and turned, adjusting themselves. And then he saw it. Wheeler held a torso with all its limbs missing. Wires and tubing flopped over to the sides, and clear fluid poured out from them, drenching Wheeler's arms. Wheeler offered Jacob an empty stare. To Jacob, it felt as though Wheeler was silently pleading with him, begging him for some sort of explanation, but nothing could be said. It was if Jacob had become frozen at the horrific sight, and his calculations had completely seized at the moment.

"Is...is it...Vision?" Jacob finally asked.

Wheeler didn't answer. The torso became heavy in his arms. Slowly, he bent down and placed it back on the ground. He allowed his hand to flow along one end of the torso to the next, and when it stopped at one of the sockets where an arm should have been, he picked up the exposed wires and tucked them back inside the torso's cavity with care. Then he turned and quietly drove away from the cave.

Jacob felt Wheeler's shoulder brush against his, as he drove by. Normally, he would be pushed aside, but not this time. It was as if Wheeler had lost all his strength.

Wheeler kept on going, never looking back, and Jacob was now left to himself. He could examine the scene on his own, although, he wasn't sure he wanted to. What he had already witnessed was overwhelming, but he needed to be sure. There were bodies scattered all over the crater's floor and the torso that Wheeler had picked up could have belonged to anyone. *Not likely.* His CPU knew better than that.

Jacob turned to face the cave. He didn't bother looking at the torso again. Once was already too much. Scanning deeper inside the cave forced him to readjust his sights. It was difficult for him to understand what he was looking at. Limbs were scattered across the cave's floor. A pair of legs still twitched, while fluid poured from their exposed wiring. Rusted gears were everywhere, lit by the pale moonlight. They made a random trail from one end of the cave to the sight Jacob was dreading most. He felt his knees buckle.

Resting against the wall was a head, torn cleanly from its torso. *Vision.* The shattered covering over the empty eye sockets could not have belonged to anyone else. Her return to the Earth had commenced.

There were times when having a hard-drive, to store information, was undeniably convenient. It allowed for information and images to remain current for as long as they were needed. At this particular moment, Jacob thought of this feature as being harsh and completely unnecessary. He wanted to delete what he just saw but knew it was impossible. The image was now permanently burned onto his hard-drive. He now understood why Wheeler had to distance himself. He felt the urge to do the same.

Jacob walked out of the cave and saw that Wheeler had stopped about fifty feet away. He cautiously made his way over to where Wheeler was leaning against a large rock, staring aimlessly at the black sky. Jacob sat on the bare ground just slightly behind Wheeler. He saw Wheeler take a quick glance over at him, but then go back to staring at the sky.

Jacob waited out a long silence and then finally said, "Wheeler?"

He was shocked to see a smile appear across Wheeler's face. "Ever wonder what those tiny things are up there, shinning down at us?"

Thanks to Hope, Jacob knew that they were, but why would Wheeler be asking about them at a time like this? "Wheeler? Are you... are you okay?"

"Always wondered what they were."

Does he really want to talk about the stars? Jacob had no idea what was going on in Wheeler's CPU. There were more important things to deal with at the moment. Was he just avoiding talking about Vision?

Before Jacob could decide if he wanted to ask Wheeler, he saw a small object being thrown in his direction. His reflexes had always been good, and with his second generation hands, catching it was easy. He opened his hand. Wheeler had tossed him a simple rock for absolutely no reason he could think of. Jacob looked up at Wheeler, both the plates over his eyes higher than normal.

"Go ahead," Wheeler said. "Feel its surface. Smooth. Rocks are never this smooth. Wonder why that is."

Jacob examined the rock. What Wheeler said was true. The rock was unusually smooth, almost glossy, but what did that matter? Jacob didn't have the slightest idea as to why this was so interesting to Wheeler at the moment.

Wheeler saw the blank look on Jacob's face. "Ha! I knew it. I knew you wouldn't know why."

"It's just erosion," Jacob said. "Nothing too complex. Over time, particles in the wind and even the wind itself, cause the smoothness." He heard a beep, followed by an appalling grinding sound resonate from Wheeler's chest.

"I... I didn't know that," Wheeler said, hiding a wince from Jacob. Then he looked back up at the sky. "Still wonder what those are up there."

Jacob placed the rock down and then shuffled a bit closer to Wheeler. "Are you okay?" he asked again.

Wheeler rolled away. "I'm fine!"

Really? How can he be fine? Jacob could see the fluid still trickling down the side of Wheeler's body from when he had cradled part of Vision in his arms.

Wheeler shrugged. "Why wouldn't I be? I knew this day would come." He sighed. "I knew I wasn't going to be able to protect her all the time."

"I...I'm sorry, Wheeler. I know she meant a lot to—"

"Of course she meant a lot to me!" Wheeler slammed his hand against the rock next to him. "She meant everything to me!" He spread his arms out to his sides, stretching them as far as they could go. "You really think any of this matters to me anymore? For my entire existence I tried to keep her safe. I tried to keep part of her... alive." Wheeler's tone became a little softer. "It was my primary order and I..." Wheeler turned away. "... I failed."

"You had primary orders to keep her safe? Set by whom?"

Wheeler shook his head and went back to staring up at the sky. "Doesn't matter," he whispered. "I failed. She's gone... I failed."

Jacob didn't know what to say in the face of that kind of anguish. He started to calculate something that might be encouraging, but his effort was interrupted when Wheeler slammed his wheel arm against the rock.

"Damn it! Why won't anyone tell me what those damn things are up in the sky?"

"Stars." Jacob said, the response automatic. "They're stars. Why do you want to know so badly?"

"Stars?" Wheeler said, in a more normal tone. "You mean, like the ones the Mayor talks about?"

"Yes."

Another beep sounded from Wheeler's chest. It was much louder than usual and ended with more hideous grinding. Wheeler clenched his chest and then staggered back.

Jacob stood up. "Wheeler? Wheeler, what's wrong?"

"N-Nothing..."

Jacob closed the small gap between himself and Wheeler. "That didn't sound like nothing."

Wheeler turned to one side, keeping his back to Jacob. "It's nothing! Get away from me, One Bolt."

There was something obviously wrong with Wheeler. Why else would he still be holding on to his chest like that? "Let me see," Jacob insisted.

Wheeler turned his head and offered Jacob a piercing stare. The yellow glow in his eyes was sharp and direct. "I said, get away!"

Jacob took a few steps back. He had never seen Wheeler act like this before, although after what they had both experienced back at the cave, it was understandable.

"Look at you, One Bolt," Wheeler suddenly snarled, "with your shiny new upgrades."

Jacob glanced down at his lower torso and legs. His upgrade was far from shiny anymore. He could thank Wheeler for that. Now wasn't the best time.

"I wish I was a first generation," Wheeler said, his tone ugly and taunting. "It must be so nice being able to upgrade."

"What's going on, Wheeler? I…I don't understand what you're saying, I didn't have a choice about the upgrade."

"Yeah…sure you didn't."

"I didn't. It was done without me knowing."

"After all the complaining you did about being a first generation? That's hard to believe."

As Jacob stared at Wheeler, he noticed a red light seeping through the gaps between his fingers that were still covering his chest. Jacob did not understand why Wheeler was hiding this from him. He already knew that there were indicator lights behind his hand. "If I could, Wheeler, I'd give these upgrades to someone else who really needed them."

"You…you would?" Wheeler's tone softened.

"Yes. I was doing fine with my old parts. I'd give *you* my upgrades if I could."

"What? Really?"

"Yes."

"Uh...thanks, One Bolt...but they...they wouldn't fit me. *Nothing* on you would ever fit me."

Jacob didn't need to be told that. Of course his arms and legs were not compatible with Wheeler, due to the size differences. But he knew what Wheeler was really referring to. "You mean...my hard-drive, right?"

Wheeler turned away.

"I know something's not right. Let me see what you're hiding."

"No, get away, One Bolt!"

Jacob reached out and grabbed Wheeler's hand. "Let me see!" he ordered. For the first time since they had met, Jacob was able to overpower Wheeler, thanks to his second generation upgrades. He pried two of Wheeler's fingers away from his chest. A bright-red light immediately erupted from the seams of Wheeler's chest, filling the darkness with an eerie glow.

"There!" Wheeler cried, removing his hand completely. "You see it! Happy?"

Jacob backed away. "What...what's going on?"

Wheeler slumped over. "There's no point in going on, One Bolt."

"What do you mean?"

"Look at me." Wheeler raised his arms in the air, but they didn't stay up for long. They dropped back down to his sides with a noisy thud. "Completely non-upgradeable," he said. "All parts integrated. Even my hard-drive."

"What? You mean nothing can be upgraded?"

Wheeler shook his head. "What you see is what you get. I've had the same hard-drive since the day I was built."

Jacob paused in order to do the calculations. "Wait a second. If you can't upgrade your hard-drive..."

Wheeler smiled. "So...finally figured it out, One Bolt. I knew your CPU would...eventually."

"But...but it's red. Doesn't that mean it's full?"

"Just about."

"What happens when it's completely full? You know, when you can't store anymore information?"

Wheeler lowered his head. "It's not difficult to figure out, One Bolt. Once my hard-drive is full...that's it."

"What do you mean, that's it?"

Wheeler didn't reply straight away.

"Wheeler? What happens?"

"Look around. Don't you get it?"

Jacob scanned the crater's floor. Bodies were everywhere. Each in different stages of their eventual return to the Earth. Jacob gasped. "You mean..."

"Again, your CPU proves itself, One Bolt."

Jacob paused. "You mean, once your hard-drive is full…you shut down?"

"Clever."

"And you made me answer those questions just so you can fill your hard-drive?"

Wheeler turned his back on Jacob. "This is the end for me, One Bolt."

"No…" Jacob said, backing away. "Wheeler…why? Why are you doing this?"

"Does it even matter anymore? Vision was all I had. There's no reason for me to go on." Wheeler looked up at the sky. "Stars, huh? What are stars, exactly?"

Jacob shook his head. "No!" he cried. "I'm not telling you. I know what's going to happen. I know what you're trying to do!"

"I…I have nothing left," Wheeler said, his voice trembling.

"Yes, you do. You have Forever Yaw. That's why we're out here. We have to finish it…together."

"I made a promise to Vision that someday she would be able to come out from hiding. She told me not to worry about her. Instead, she told me to bring back what's most important of all. She told me that Earth and the ones living on it matter the most. She made me promise I would do everything I could to bring both of these back." Wheeler shook his head. "But I knew I wasn't the one who would see this promise to the end."

"What do you mean? We still have time. The moon's not here yet."

"My hard-drive wouldn't have taken me to the very end. I tried my best to only acquire information that would help me keep my promise to Vision, but even I knew that was impossible." Wheeler tuned and faced Jacob. He saw the stars reflecting off of the lenses in Jacob's eyes. "This is why I did everything I could to bring you with me. I knew the very first day I met you in class that *you* would be the one seeing this to the end."

"Wheeler…wait. Stop it! We're going to finish this. Both of us…together. Stop talking like this."

Wheeler let out a quiet laugh. "No, One Bolt, my time has come. Just promise me that you won't board those pods. Don't let the Mayor take this from us. Don't let him win this one."

"No," Jacob pleaded. "I can't do this without you. My CPU isn't strong enough."

Wheeler snickered. "I promise you, One Bolt, your CPU will do just fine." Wheeler grabbed Jacob's hand. "Vision was all I had. At the very least, allow me to return to the Earth with her. I might not be able to keep my promise to her…but you will."

"No! There has to be a way to make you better!"

"And there is."

"How?"

"Stars. Tell me what they are."

"I...I can't," Jacob whispered. "Not until Forever Yaw is complete."

Wheeler applied pressure to Jacob's hand. "It's Forever Jacob now." Wheeler scanned the crater's floor. "To anyone out there who can hear me!"

he shouted, "I hereby pass on Forever Yaw to the one who will bring the Earth back to the way it once was! To the one who will save our kind!" Wheeler smiled at Jacob. "Forever Jacob...as it should have been right from the very beginning."

"No!" Jacob said. "Please...don't make me do this, Wheeler. It doesn't have to end this way."

"It's not your choice, One Bolt." Wheeler looked up into the sky for the last time. The red light of his indicator flashed deeply against the bright-white specs randomly filling the dark sky. "Tell me, One Bolt, what are stars, exactly?" Receiving no reply from Jacob, Wheeler came up with his own conclusions. "Rocks. They must be tiny rocks floating out there."

"No," Jacob said. "They're not rocks."

"I know...pieces of metal reflecting the sunlight. Yeah, that's right. Little pieces of metal that somehow got lost out there."

"No, Wheeler, they're not pieces of metal."

Wheeler fell silent. He had nothing left to say. His eyes moved from one end of the sky to the next and then stopped at the brightest star in the sky. That is where they remained.

Jacob glanced over to the cave and saw the moonlight, as it struck that part of Vision that Wheeler had cradled. It was tragic that she would soon become one with the Earth. But in a way, maybe it was for the best. Her existence seemed to be all about enduring. *And that's not a way to live.* At least now, she no longer needed to hide from anyone.

Jacob looked back at Wheeler. His unorganized body, consisting of used parts, told Jacob that his life was all about sacrificing. *And that's not a way to live, either.* Jacob took a moment to calculate what it would be like to let go of someone who had been with him his entire existence. He frowned. *Mom...* Although Wheeler had never called Vision that, Jacob knew that she was the closest thing to a mother that Wheeler had. If all Wheeler wanted now was to return to the Earth with her, how could Jacob refuse?

"They...they're suns," Jacob whimpered. "Just like the one we have."

At first, there was an eerie silence, as Wheeler inhaled the last bit of information that his hard-drive could hold. It began to stutter, causing him to wince. Then he suddenly snapped upright, and a string of piercingly loud beeps poured from his chest. He threw his wheel arm up, revving it uncontrollably against the plating. Smoke billowed out in a thick, white plume from where rubber met metal. His red indicator lights blinked at such a blinding rate, they appeared solid.

"Wheeler!"

"I...I...feel...weird..." Wheeler moaned.

A sickening grinding sound echoed through the night, as his internal gears tried to lock their teeth but remained spinning violently in opposite directions. Wheeler did his best to keep his eyes open. He stared at Jacob. There was a genuine look of fear in his eyes, as he moaned. "Maybe...maybe I should have...thought this...over."

Wheeler jerked, as his body started seizing up.

"Wheeler! How do we stop this!"

"It's okay...I...I'll be...okay!" Wheeler lowered his head and went quiet.

Jacob didn't know what to do, and worst of all, he wasn't even able to turn his back and look away. He felt Wheeler's grip tighten on his hand. There was a pop, as one of his joints collapsed due to the pressure Wheeler was applying.

Suddenly, Wheeler lifted his head and looked at Jacob. The glow in his eyes had faded, and they no longer contrasted the darkness.

"W-Wheeler?"

A subtle smile appeared over Wheeler's face. "Goodbye... Jacob..." he said, his voice distorted by a metallic tinge. "You...you are a true friend..."

"Wheeler?" Jacob cried out. "Wheeler!"

The red lights on Wheeler's chest blinked one last time and then stopped. The hum of his hard-drive could be heard slowing down and then finally stopping. He let out one final moan before collapsing back against the rock. His wheel arm collided with the ground for the last time. Wheeler was now with Vision.

Jacob stepped back. "Wheeler?" he softly said. "Wheeler?" There was no reply. He reached out and poked Wheeler's arm, but there was no response. The arm just dangled. "Wheeler...come on," he said, still not wanting to accept what had happened. "Quit playing around, will you? Turn yourself back on..."

Silence was all that was heard.

Jacob slumped over. "Please...come back..." He knew very well that any request he made would go unanswered. Wheeler would never be functional again. Jacob took one final peek into Wheeler's blank stare only to see his own reflection staring back at him. He reached over his shoulder, opened the compartment in his back and pulled out the trophy he had taken from his room. He gently set the trophy down next to Wheeler's front wheel.

Jacob read the inscription aloud, as if Wheeler could still hear him. "*First place.*" He skipped over the next part and continued. "*Harness the Sun.* That's what you did to help keep her alive all of this time." Jacob suddenly dropped to his knees next to his friend. As he rested against the rock and stared up at the moon's imminent arrival, he whispered, "Goodbye, Yaw..."

Chapter Eight

With each lumbering step Jacob took, he moved deeper into the light, and the rays from the sun should have been strong enough to warm him thoroughly, but his inner core still felt cold—empty. Each broken down building he walked by, evoked unsettling memories of moments barely gone by. So recent was a time when Jacob and Wheeler had driven down this very path. He could still recall the images. But that wouldn't last. Too soon, the only way to restore the memories, of their friendly bickering, would be if Jacob pulled them from his hard-drive and made them current. Without Wheeler, the prospect of Forever Jacob actually succeeding was doubtful.

How could this have happened? All Wheeler and Vision wanted was a future with certainty—a future that might have included the possibility of creators living in harmony with their creations. It wasn't such an overwhelming request, but one met with obvious hostility by a select few. Vision and Wheeler had been harmless, and they had clung to a glimmer of hope that they could see their dream come true. Now...they were gone. Optimism depleted.

At least Jacob could take comfort in knowing that they would accompany each other during their gradual return to the Earth. He wasn't as fortunate. Left to walk back alone, uncertainty hassled his every step. His CPU felt strange, warm and tingling. It had so much to calculate, so much to process, with so little time to do so. Jacob had been sure that by now, after distancing himself so far from the dreadful scene inside the crater, that his CPU would have processed everything and provided him with answers. But no answers were forthcoming. Questions continued to plague his every thought.

Jacob realized he needed to stop and gather himself. He was still carrying the can of *Pure Blend* that Wheeler had returned to him, and he cracked it open. He tipped it up to drink, not caring that he was already integrated with *Pure Blend*. Clear fluid trickled down the side of his mouth and dripped to the ground. He pulled the can away from his mouth and looked down at where a small pool of liquid had formed. To his amazement, he saw something small and green funnelling its way out from a patch of exposed dirt.

A plant! It looked so natural, not mechanical in any way. Jacob knelt down, making sure his shadow did not drape over it and block the sun. After what he had just experienced with Wheeler, Jacob found the plant's fight for survival almost a contradiction. Only a hand's reach away was metal. Metal was everywhere. It surrounded the timid plant, yet could not keep it from securing itself into the Earth. Jacob thought it was rather funny the way the plant seemed to be reaching toward the sun. He knew it would never make it.

It was much too short and stubby, like he used to be. "Maybe you should ask for upgrade," he said, pouring the rest of his *Pure Blend* on top of it.

He set the empty can down next to the plant. It hissed at him. *That shouldn't be!* He picked up the can and then set it down again. This time, he heard the normal clang of metal. *So where did that hiss come from?* Jacob jumped to his feet. "Oh, no!"

A dark shadow crept out from behind the building next to him. Jacob backed away, accidentally stepping onto the plant. The distracting hiss accompanied the rigid shadow, as it rapidly grew in size. Finally, its owner appeared. Brute turned and faced Jacob. The dark-red glow of his eyes pierced right through the terrified second generation.

After what Brute had done to Vision, Jacob could not even imagine what would happen if the monster got a hold of him. He wasn't going to wait to find out. He turned around and ran. His second generation legs would finally be tested.

"Wait!" Brute yelled. "Come back here!" He hoisted himself upright and went after Jacob.

Jacob could feel the ground shift with every resounding boom of Brute's footfalls. He resisted the urge to look back and just kept running. He thought of Vision and Wheeler, and that was enough to entice his legs to keep moving. He had to get away.

The rumbling beneath Jacob's feet eventually subsided. *Did I do it? Did I get away?* He glanced back just to be sure. To his surprise, Brute was nowhere to be seen. Jacob didn't stop running, however, and after a few more strides, he collided violently into something solid. The impact sent him to the ground, his vision temporarily scrambled. "Ah...damn it!" Jacob moaned. "*323.*" He reached up and rubbed his head. "Where did that building come from?"

He shook his head, successfully clearing his sights. He glanced up, expecting to be facing the front, side, or the back of a tall building. Instead, Brute stood before him, drowning him in a heavy shadow. His eyes struck Jacob at such a precarious angle, it allowed their glows to seem chiselled.

Brute reached out for Jacob, who immediately sealed his eyes shut. His hand clamped down onto Jacob's shoulder, the weight causing Jacob to sink into the metal ground. Jacob winced. He wrapped his hand around one of Brute's fingers, even though he doubted that second generation limbs would benefit him in a situation like this. He was helpless, like a first generation all over again. The motors in his hand strained, attempting to remove his shoulder from Brute's unbelievable grip. "Let...go of me!" he screamed.

So Brute did. Jacob fell back, slamming his head against the ground. There was no time for him to assess the damage. He jumped to his feet and staggered away. He ran to the closest building, pressed his back against it and kept one hand wrapped around its corner. It was the only defensive stance he could think of while he slowly inched away. To his amazement, however, Brute did not follow. He did not even seem interested in following. Instead, he just stood there. For a moment, neither of them moved.

What's Brute doing? Why is he just standing there? Jacob glanced at his shoulder where Brute had clamped down on him. The deep indentations of Brute's fingers were visible.

"I did not mean to do that," Brute said, in a surprisingly soft voice.

Jacob wasn't sure what to make of Brute's sudden lack of hostility, but one thing was certain, he wasn't about to relax. He even took a couple of steps back. This *was* Brute after all. "What…what do you want from me?"

Brute lowered himself. Even with his knees touching the ground, he had to look down in order to see Jacob eye-to-eye. "Nothing," he said. "Just an apology."

Jacob pointed a finger at his chest-plate. "Me? Apologize? After what you did back there?"

Brute reached up toward his head. The move was so sudden it made Jacob back away. Then Brute ripped the mask off of his head and threw it down in disgust. It clanged off of the metal surface they were standing on and came to rest next to Jacob. The mask was made from a metal that was so thick and hard, it caused a large dent in the ground where it landed.

Brute lowered his head. "No. I want you to accept *my* apology."

Jacob couldn't believe what he had heard. Was this a trick? How could it be? Brute already had his hands on him and simply let go.

"The one in the cave," Brute explained, "your friend…I didn't want to—" He shifted his head from left to right. "I…I was under direct orders. Something I'm not able to override."

"Orders? From the Mayor?"

"Yes. I'm programmed to follow his orders."

Jacob slapped his hands together. "I knew it! I knew it had to be him."

"He…he…gave the orders. I had to follow them. I...didn't have a choice."

"And now they're both gone..."

Brute immediately lifted his head. "Both?"

"Yeah…Wheeler, too."

Brute suddenly stood up. His pistons let out that familiar hiss that Jacob didn't want to be reminded of. Jacob took a step back, bracing himself.

"No." Brute yelled. "I did nothing to him."

"I know. It was his choice. But one that he had to make because of your actions."

Brute lowered himself again and slammed his enormous hand into the ground in disgust, nearly causing Jacob to topple over. "They were direct orders. If I didn't follow them, he would have—" Brute closed his eyes and turned his face away.

"What? What would have happened if you didn't?"

When Brute finally looked back, his eyes no longer contained their usual red glow. Instead, they were white and dim. "Hope needed a part installed," Brute explained. "The Mayor said that if I didn't go through with his orders, he would leave her the way she was."

Jacob took a tentative step forward. "What? What's wrong with Hope?"

"Her condition has been getting worse."

"You mean...that indicator on her chest?"

"Yes." Brute clenched his hand into a fist. "Every time I see her, she's in that damn chamber."

"A charger?"

"The chamber is not for recharging. It keeps her from permanent shut down."

Jacob almost lost his footing. "It does what?" he shrieked.

"That's all I know. The part the Mayor wants to install will finally free her from her weakness. She won't ever have to be inside that chamber again. That's why I had to go through with the Mayor's order."

Jacob began to pace back and forth, still keeping a safe distance from Brute. "Weakness? What exact part does she need that would keep her from shutting down?"

"I don't know what the part is. All I know is...protecting Hope is one of the earliest programs installed in me. I have to keep her safe...Even from...him..."

"The Mayor?"

"Yes...her dad."

Jacob ceased pacing in order to perform a quick and simple calculation. "I'm not saying that what you did was right, but if those were your orders, then there wasn't much you could have done." He turned and faced Brute. "So? Was the part installed?"

"I've tried to make contact with the Mayor, but he's not responding to my transmissions."

"You don't even know if Hope is okay or not?"

Brute shook his head.

"Damn it, *324*!" Jacob took a few steps to the side. "We have to get to her. We have to make sure she's okay." He turned and walked back to Brute and stood tall in front of him. "Take me to her."

"What?"

"You know where she is. Take me to her."

"I can't. The Mayor... I'm under his orders."

"But I'm not." Jacob kept his voice firm. "And your primary order is to protect her. That's what you said."

"It may be too late. If he hasn't helped her already, we won't be able to do anything about it."

"I don't care. Take me to her. I've already lost two friends. I don't want to lose another."

Brute rose to his full height, backing Jacob away with the whining of his gears and the hissing of his pistons. "If you trust me, then I'll take you."

Trust him? After what he did to Vision and Wheeler? Brute's simple CPU was integrated, Jacob assumed. If orders were something he could not break, then keeping Hope safe was an order he had to abide by, no matter what situation or circumstance. Jacob could use this to his advantage. "I trust you. Now...take me to her."

Brute extended his arms toward Jacob who immediately reeled back. The pair of oversized hands clamped onto his shoulders. With no effort, Brute picked him off the ground and lifted him well into the air.

"Hey!" Jacob yelled. "Damn, it, *325*! Put me down!"

"Trust me." Brute hoisted Jacob up and over his head and then gently placed him on his broad shoulders. "Grab on to something."

Jacob looked around. Chambers, pistons, bolts, and gears were everywhere, biting into each other, demanding attention. Jacob did as he was told and grabbed onto the least intimidating part that protruded from Brute's incredibly disorganized upper body and held on tight.

"Have you ever ridden like this before?"

"All the time," Jacob said.

"Good. Then I don't have to tell you."

"Tell me what?"

Brute lunged forward. "Hang on!"

* * *

Each time one of Brute's feet slammed into the ground, Jacob's head would snap back. But he didn't complain. He just held on tight and watched the scenery fly by, as Brute kept a steady pace. As they went by the school, Jacob thought it would be nice to stop and visit the professor one last time. He could thank him for the upgrades but they had to hurry to find Hope.

"Are you okay up there?" Brute asked.

"Not exactly."

"Sorry. I was not built for this sort of thing."

Yeah, I noticed. Jacob's chin constantly bumped against the back of Brute's head with each of his ungraceful strides. "What were you built for?"

They emerged from under the moon's immense shadow and migrated into the sun's ambiance where a vast landscape faded into the horizon. Its barren dreariness was relieved by movement in the distance. Rows upon rows of short, cylindrical-shaped objects atop massive flat bases were being slowly moved from one end of the horizon to the next.

Brute pointed. "That's the sort of thing I was built for."

"What are those?" Jacob asked, astonished at the scale of the perfectly organized formation.

"Pods."

Jacob quickly called up a fact on his hard-drive. "Pods...They're all dormant inside..."

"Yes. Dormant and waiting for the Mayor's orders."

"Where are the workers taking them?"

"The launch site."

Jacob watched silently, as the Mayor's immediate plans were becoming a reality. So many pods, he observed, with each one inside harbouring the single hope of a promised future. Jacob knew it was a future far from certainty. He wanted to let them know about Forever Jacob. He wanted to somehow let them know that there was an alternative to the future promised to them by the Mayor. He cringed when he realized that *his* own proposed future was as equally uncertain. Forever Jacob wasn't exactly in its final, rewarding stages. *With the moon growing increasingly bold in its journey to the Earth, maybe the Mayor's plans aren't so bad after all.* Jacob shook his head. "No! Can't think like that. Forever Jacob. That's the only way."

"Forever what?" Brute called out.

"Nothing." *You wouldn't understand.* Jacob went back to scanning the rows of pods.

As the end of the steady line came into view, Jacob was taken by the single most dominate structure of the entire formation. A massive trio of sky-piercing, cylindrical objects, joined together to form a single structure, was being towed alongside the pods. Jacob got Brute's attention and pointed. "That doesn't look like a pod!"

"That's because it's not. It's a cannon. The same one the Mayor used to try and rid us of the moon."

Jacob gasped. "Project Retaliation? How do you know?"

Brute turned his head. "I helped built it."

Jacob sighed. Just being on Brute's shoulders felt traitorous. The giant mechanical being, although maybe only indirectly, was responsible for not only Vision's demise but the demise of Earth—the end of humans. Now he was the one Jacob needed help from. *Could the day get any more interesting*? "Guess you didn't do a very good job," Jacob snickered.

Brute lowered the massive plates over his eyes. "What?"

"You know..." Jacob said nervously, "the moon's still up there."

"I've taken care of that," Brute said. "I fixed the cannon. It's much stronger than before. It'll get the job done this time."

"Wait...you mean the Mayor's going to try to destroy the moon again?"

Brute shrugged his massive shoulders, nearly throwing Jacob off balance. "My orders were to fix it. It sustained heavy damage the first time. Other than that, I don't know what the Mayor's plans are."

"Where are they taking the cannon?"

"To the launch site. Same place as the pods. It's still aimed in the exact same direction as it was the last time we fired it." Brute felt a shift in the weight on his back, as Jacob slumped over. "What?"

"I just find it strange. If he plans to destroy the moon, then why does he still want to leave Earth? I mean, the moon would probably break into pieces and come crashing down, but the impact wouldn't necessarily destroy the planet. We could probably survive it."

"I just do as I'm told."

"Yeah...I noticed." Jacob whispered.

"What?"

"Nothing."

"You ask too many questions, you know that?"

"It's the best way to learn."

"I can't answer them all. That's not what I was built for. If you want, I can go over there, and you can see the cannon for yourself. I'll show you the repairs I did. You won't see better welds anywhere."

Jacob thought about it. He was definitely curious to see Project Retaliation up close. *When would I ever get the chance to see it again?* But that would have to wait. He had other priorities to attend to. "I'm sure your welds are just fine. But we need to get to Hope. We have to make sure she's okay. How much further?"

"We're almost there."

* * *

When they arrived at their destination, Brute helped Jacob get down. It was nice to finally feel solid ground beneath his feet again. Jacob's joints were still jittery, however. They needed a moment or two to stabilize after the less than smooth ride atop of Brute's rigid shoulders. This gave him the perfect chance to marvel at the impressive exterior of the Mayor's Manor. It stood tall and dominating in front of him, and the metal was cleaner than any Jacob had ever seen. "Wow! Look at this place! Everything's so…so…perfect!"

Rust was nowhere to be found on any of the sheet metal covering the structure's sky-high walls. Anchoring the sheet metal flawlessly in staggered rows, were triangular rivets, positioned in precise distances from each other. Every pillar, that supported the overhanging roof, glistened with a nearly blinding sheen. Even the dozens of statues of the Mayor, in a variety of exaggerated poses, were lined methodically along the front of the building. It was an overwhelming sight, but one that was expected for someone of the Mayor's stature. Since the Mayor had the power to do whatever he wanted, Jacob would have expected nothing less. Still, such a display of unblemished beauty just seemed a bit tainted. How much misery had been caused so the Mayor could establish himself in such place?

Brute grabbed onto the handle of one of the massive twin doors and slid it open, just enough to take a peek inside. He waved Jacob over. "This way."

Jacob slowly made his way over, his legs now free of any post-ride jitters, though he wasn't all that eager to go in. Knowing what the Mayor was capable of, made his sensors feel uneasy. He stayed to one side of the door, leaning over to peek through the small gap, but he couldn't see much inside. "She's in there?"

"In the room at the end of the hall. She's inside a glass chamber." Brute widened the gap of the door, just enough to fit Jacob through. Jacob slipped one foot through the door, but instead of going further in, he locked one hand on the door's sharp edge. He pushed the door until it stood wide enough for Brute to enter. "Alright...let's go. I'll follow you."

Unfortunately, that was never Brute's intentions. "I can't go with you," he said.

Jacob let go of the door. "Why not? What about your orders?"

"That's why I can't go with you."

"I...I don't understand."

"My orders—" Brute quickly corrected himself, "My loyalty...is to the Mayor. If he knows you're here, he might give me orders that will not be very pleasant for you."

Jacob reeled back. "Oh...you mean..."

Brute lowered his head, and Jacob wondered if Brute's troubled expression was because he was conflicted. That was confirmed when Brute spoke. "I've been responsible for too much destruction. I don't want to have to destroy another. I'll wait for you out here. It will be better for both of us."

"I agree." Jacob was about to turn around but stopped mid-stride. "You know...orders don't always have to be followed."

Brute lifted his head, the plates above his eyes raised.

"Even though you are programmed to follow orders, you don't have to follow every one. Especially ones you don't agree with." Jacob sighed. "I know you didn't want to do what you did back at the crater. I'm certain that integrated into you, somewhere, is a code allowing you to make some decisions for yourself. I wouldn't be standing here, about to go inside the Mayor's house, if it weren't." Jacob could hear the pale whirl of Brute's low capacity hard-drive spinning, as it fed information into his simple CPU. He wasn't sure what was going through the narrow pipes connecting Brute's hard-drive to his CPU. He just hoped that Brute would remember what he had said.

"I'll look for the code later," Brute said. "For now, you get going. Hope's waiting." He gave Jacob the gentlest push he could. Jacob nearly lifted off the ground.

"Okay-okay. I'm going."

"Oh...one more thing," Brute said, as he started to push the door closed. "Wipe your feet before you go any further. The Mayor doesn't like dirt on his floors." The door slammed shut, leaving Jacob on his own.

Jacob frowned in absolute disgust. "Doesn't like dirt on his floors?" He shuffled his feet back and forth, loosening as much dirt as he could, successfully staining the polished floor beneath him. "There," he said satisfied. "I don't take orders from the Mayor."

Jacob scanned the hallway. Its entire length was periodically lit by exposed sections in the ceiling. A trio of rooms were staggered along both sides of the hallway with a final room at the very end. It had to be the one Brute had mentioned. From where he was standing, Jacob's could see no sign of the chamber or of Hope. He needed to go down there. Each small and composed step he took down the hall made his sensors tense. Every section of wall he walked by held his reflection in its mirror-like surface. It made it seem as though he was being followed. But what made him even more apprehensive was not knowing where the Mayor was. He absolutely did not want to bump into him. After the orders the Mayor had given to Brute, there was no telling what he would do to Jacob. The noisy clanging of his feet, hitting the floor, needed to be dampened if Jacob didn't want to be detected, so he slowed his footsteps to a shuffle. He also moved closer to the walls which allowed him to stay in shadow.

Jacob paused by the first room off the hallway and cautiously peeked inside. The room was filled with old discarded parts, from arms and legs, to hard-drives and CPUs. *What does he need all of these used parts for*?

The next room he came to was also filled with useless junk. Rusted pistons, gears, and crates overflowing with cables and wires, tested the room's capacity. The only thing seemingly out of place was a small table. On top of it was an old, clunky-looking machine with dials on front. Thick tubing from both sides flowed all the way to the floor where they eventually coiled up in a neat, circular formation. *Wonder what that machine's for.* He assumed that since it was next to a pile of discarded parts that it probably wasn't important.

Jacob moved quietly to the third room. He was just going to peek in and move on, but he couldn't help but stop and stare. This room was not like the others. It was neat, organized, and what it held drew him in. In the heart of the room was a metal table, shaped in a long rectangle. Its surface was eaten away by rust, giving it a deep-brown tinge. Only few spots remained of its original and reflective integrity. An overhead light cast a bright-white glow on the table's surface, and Jacob noted that the single beam from the light was tapered in a crisp, cone-shape. The light was sufficient for Jacob to see the rest of the room. Dozens of models depicting human anatomy, in all of its stages and forms, were on display, tucked on shelves along the walls. The models were built in full detail, meticulous in every way. They were much more interesting than even the ones he saw at the school. *What…what is all of this? Why does he need all of this?* For someone who had so much hatred toward this particular stage of human evolution, it was absolutely confusing to Jacob why the Mayor would require such an assortment of displays.

Jacob stood for a few moments more, absorbing the sights and then he backed out of the room. Something just didn't seem right. There had to be a reason why the Mayor was so interested in something he completely despised, but Jacob could not spend any more time trying to figure out the reason. All he wanted to do now was find Hope and then get out of this place.

Jacob kept a quick, steady pace all the way to the end of the hallway, ignoring the fact that shadow no longer concealed him. He stepped into the final room, anticipating that he was close to finding Hope.

Light billowed down from a transparent ceiling, giving the entire room a warm-yellow tinge. At the end of the room was a door, closed off at the moment, but Jacob only gave it a cursory glance. He didn't have to go that far, as he saw the glass chamber to his left. *She has to be in there*. He made his way over without any hesitation and pressed his hands against the glass surface. They immediately slid down and flopped against his sides. All he could see was his own reflection in the glass. The chamber was empty. "Damn it! *326*. Where did he take her?"

Jacob turned and scanned the rest of the room. Metal shelves lined the four walls. Most were empty, except for the one next to him. Jacob stepped closer to see a thin stack of papers resting on the shelf. They were just like the pages he had decoded at Wheeler's, the ones the professor had and the ones he found in the box that his mom had set in his room. The corners of each page were wrinkled, cracked and decaying. The same dark patches were staining random sections of each page. Jacob carefully removed the small stack from the shelf. He decoded the very first page. It read: "Belonging to Michael Evans".

"Michael Evans? Who is Michael Evans?" Jacob realized that in order to find out, he needed to scan the entire stack. Jacob rested his finger against the corner of the stack, ready to flip through each individual page, but the stack started to slip out of his hands. At the same time, the door from the end of the room swung open. Jacob gasped. The stack of pages landed messily onto the floor, causing the pages to separate. Jacob found himself pressed back against the chamber, completely motionless. The one he did not want to meet was now standing inside the doorway.

The Mayor noticed the pages resting on the floor, more importantly, he was aware of the one standing cowardly in the corner. He entered the room. Each step he took sent tremors across the floor. Only a few strides were needed for the Mayor to reach the scattered pages. He picked up the single page that Jacob had already scanned, looked at it for a moment and then said, "Ah, yes...Michael Evans. I remember him quite well. Brilliant man he was. For his time, of course." A deep frown suddenly appeared on his face. "But he was weak! And it was his weakness that ultimately made him mortal."

The Mayor glanced down at a timid-looking Jacob. "Yes...Michael Evans..." A look of absolute disgust suddenly appeared on the Mayor's face, as he crumpled the page in his hand. "He certainly won't be missed!"

To Jacob's relief, the Mayor retreated back toward the door.

"My sensors detect fear," the Mayor said. "No need to fear me." He stopped in front of the open door. "If I wanted to harm you, I would have already done so."

Jacob felt no comfort in what the Mayor had just said. He was just relieved to have some distance between them, and the distance gave him a burst of courage. "You...you were the one who gave the orders."

The Mayor rested his hands against his sides. He seemed almost impressed to see Jacob questioning his authority. "My orders?"

"Vision and Wheeler. They're both gone because of your orders."

"Is that so?" The Mayor shrugged his massive shoulders. "That's two less pods we have to worry about."

Jacob cringed at the Mayor's comment. "You destroyed her because part of her was human."

"Weakness! Part of her contained weakness."

"She was harmless. Humans were always harmless."

"That is why they are no more. And that is why Project New Hope has succeeded."

Hope? "Hope!" Jacob cried. He glanced behind him at the empty chamber. "Where is she?"

"Ah, yes, Hope. My precious, Hope..."

"Let me see her."

The Mayor laughed and clenched his chest. "My-my, so direct and quite demanding for a first generation."

Jacob stood tall on his feet. He unravelled his hands so that his fingers were clearly visible. "Second generation!"

The Mayor let out another deep laugh. "Well-well-well. An impressive upgrade. Almost as impressive as the upgrade I just completed."

So Brute was right. The upgrade the Mayor was referring to must be the part that Hope needed installed. "What did you do to her?"

"Not to worry. She's much better now."

"Where is she? Let me see her!"

"An important day is upon us, young one. The pods will soon be ready for launch. I'm certain that Hope will be ready when the time comes."

"No..." Jacob waved his hands back and forth. "She's not going into one of those pods. She's not going with you. She wants to be here. She wants to stay on Earth."

The Mayor stroked his chin, overplaying a pose of deep concern. "That's odd. Leaving this dead, pathetic rock was the only thing she could talk about."

That can't be! Jacob glanced around the room, as if he could find her in one of the corners. "She said she wanted to stay. She was helping with Forever Jacob..."

"Ah...yes. She mentioned that," the Mayor said, with a curl of his upper lip. "What is this...'Forever Jacob' I keep hearing? Some failed attempt at restoring the past? Some sort of attempt at bringing back the weakest stages of our now flawless evolution?" The Mayor snarled at the possibility. "There's a reason why we're at the peak of our evolution. They had their chance. They destroyed themselves. They destroyed the Earth."

"And you helped destroyed both," Jacob bravely pointed out.

"On the contrary. I merely hastened the inevitable."

"You stopped the Earth with Project Redemption."

"And because of that, we are where we are at right now. We became their future. I made us strong."

"You didn't give them a chance. Earth can still be brought back to the way it once was. Humans can be brought back. They can help us."

The Mayor let out a bellowing laugh. "Them? Help us?"

"They created us. They will know how to bring us back to when we were strong."

"We are strong!" the Mayor insisted, pounding his chest. "Stronger than we've ever been. Stronger than they could have ever been. Bringing them back will make us weak. I can't allow this. I'll never allow this!"

"Let me see Hope!" Jacob demanded. "She'll agree with me. I know she will."

To Jacob's surprise, the Mayor took one step back, reached behind the door and gestured. Hope stepped into the room and stood quietly behind the

Mayor. Most of her face was concealed. The Mayor coaxed Hope out in front of him. He wanted Jacob to see her—his upgraded version of her.

When Hope stepped out in front of the Mayor, Jacob's eyes widened. Something didn't seem right about her. She wasn't exactly the way he had remembered. "Hope? Is that...is that you?"

With her movements rigid and slow, Hope glanced around the room until her gaze finally rested on Jacob. He stumbled back the moment their eyes met. Gone was the brilliant-green that used to light her eyes. She now had a simple, white glow. Not even the familiar smile, that Jacob was accustomed to, was offered his way.

"Hope!" He turned to the Mayor. "What did you do to her?"

Jacob's harsh tone seemed to frighten Hope, and she retreated back behind the Mayor.

"Now, Hope," the Mayor said, easing her forward again. "Be polite and welcome our guest." Hope glanced up at the Mayor, offering him the smile that Jacob wanted to see.

The Mayor turned her to face Jacob. "Go on, someone came a long way to see you."

With his upgrades, Jacob was now slightly taller than Hope, however, he was the one bracing himself, as she approached. Jacob noticed that Hope was holding a can tightly in her hand. *Pure Blend*, he assumed. It was, after all, her favourite. Hope stopped in front of Jacob. He wanted to show off his own upgrades but had completely forgotten about them. He was more concerned about Hope—deeply concerned as to why it seemed as if she was meeting him for the first time. She seemed so distant—empty. Jacob could see his reflection on the smooth glass surface of her eyes, but nothing else.

"Hope…is it…is it you?"

Instead of replying, Hope simply raised her hand, revealing the can of *Artificial Blend*. She offered it to him.

Jacob shook his head, confused. "I…I can't drink this. I…I thought you knew that, Hope."

"How unfortunate," the Mayor said, from the other end of the room. "It's the only kind we have left. It's Hope's favourite."

Hope nodded at Jacob.

"But Hope, what about *Pure Blend*?"

Hope stood silently, still offering the can to Jacob.

"I…I can't..."

"It's okay, Hope," the Mayor said. "He said he doesn't want any. You go ahead."

Hope nodded and then cracked open the can and began drinking from it. Her blank stare was still fixated on Jacob.

Jacob took a tentative stop closer to her, so her body was effectively blocking the Mayor's line of sight. "Hope…do you even remember me?" he whispered.

Hope's reply was simple—cold. She shook her head.

Jacob felt his knees weaken. “You don't remember the mountain? The stars?” Jacob placed his hand on her shoulder. “You don’t remember seeing them with me?”

Hope abruptly backed away, causing Jacob’s hand to fall to his side.

Could it be that his upgrades were causing Hope’s confusion? She didn't recognize his new look? *No, it couldn’t be.* The Hope that Jacob remembered would have seen right through a few upgrades. She would have seen Jacob for who he was, and not what he was. This just confirmed it. Hope was now gone.

“No need to feel bad,” Mayor said. “She *did* remember you. You were the last one she talked about—the only one she talked about...” The Mayor looked down and smiled at Hope, who had returned to his side. “Right before I erased her hard-drive.”

Jacob stumbled back so far that he slammed into the wall. “You *what*?!”

“She had nothing in her past that needed remembering,” the Mayor explained, showing little remorse. “Everything on her hard-drive could be compromised. I didn’t want her saturated with the past.”

Jacob was absolutely devastated. “You...you destroyed her!”

“On the contrary. I made her strong. I gave her something she always hoped for. Now she will be with me forever. Forever... Hope. Always Hope.”

Jacob fought down his apprehension and walked out into the center of the room, making sure he was directly in Hope's sights. “Hope!” he cried. “You *have* to remember me! It’s Jacob! *Pure Blend*... Wheeler... Forever Jacob! Don’t you remember any of this?” All Jacob received from Hope was a simple shake of her head and nothing else. He suddenly felt so weak he had to look down to make sure his legs were still attached. He wouldn’t be surprised if he saw them convulsing uncontrollably on the floor.

“We have to prepare for the future, not dwell in our past. The future is now. The launch site is almost ready. It’s almost time for us to leave.” The Mayor made a simple gesture at Jacob. “Since you have been so influential to my Hope in her past, it would be dishonourable of me to not invite you with us. I believe there’s room for you *and* Grace.”

Jacob was slowly backing away toward the hallway. “I’m not going with you. Not after what you’ve done.”

“That’s a shame. I’m almost certain Hope would have enjoyed your company during our long journey.” The Mayor looked down at her and smiled. “Isn't that right?”

Hope nodded and then glanced over to a silenced Jacob. The smile he was so familiar with was finally offered to him, but Jacob knew it meant nothing this time. It was empty and worthless. That was not the Hope he cared about who was smiling at him.

“You destroyed her. The same way you destroyed Earth. The same way you destroyed humans.” He turned to Hope, one small part of him wishing she would remember him, but her blank stare prompted him to say, “I’m sorry, Hope. You may not remember me... but I’ll always remember you.” As he exited the room, he whispered, “Goodbye... Hope.”

The Mayor called after him, "Our time is now! The future is now. We are that future!"

But Jacob didn't hear. He was gone.

A loud hiss made its way into the room, causing Hope to cower behind the Mayor. Brute stepped into the room, his movements slow, lumbering—dejected. He had heard everything.

The Mayor moved in front of Hope, creating an impenetrable barrier between her and Brute who was slowly crossing the room. Brute paid almost no attention to the Mayor. His focus was entirely on Hope, who appeared to not even recognize him. Brute stopped in front of the Mayor, not intimidated by his dominating stance. Brute's stares eventually alternated from the Mayor all the way down to Hope. The returning stares were severely contrasting. One was mindless, frightened and hallow, while the other was sharp, intimidating and dictating. When Brute looked at Hope, she would disappear further and further behind the security of the Mayor, and Brute realized she was frightened of him.

"This doesn't concern you," the Mayor said.

"My orders were to keep her safe."

"And you have. That's why I've kept you around for so long. But there's no longer any threat to her. I can assure you of this."

"What...did you do to her?"

"Her hard-drive was deleted of everything that wasn't relevant. I merely did what was right."

"Does she even know who I am?"

"Like I said, everything that wasn't relevant."

When Brute moved again, the hiss of his pistons seemed to scare Hope even more. She darted from behind her father and ran from the room.

Brute frowned, crumpling the metal under his eyes. "All she needed was a part installed. You didn't have to delete her memory!"

"She's no longer a concern of yours," the Mayor said, his voice cold.

Brute pulled himself to his full height. "But she is."

The Mayor stood taller. "Stand down…worker."

For a moment they stared at each other, Brute trying to maintain his courage, but in the end, it was the glow in his eyes that faded first. He lowered his stance and bowed his head.

"As expected," the Mayor snarled. "The launch site needs finalizing. We leave tomorrow. Prepare for launch. Those are your new orders. Do you understand…worker?"

"Yes…yes, sir…I…I understand."

"Good. Now, then, it's time for Hope and I to recharge. We face a significant day tomorrow." As the Mayor walked away, Brute caught a small glimpse of Hope, as she peeked around the door. Her expression was cold and dormant. Her eyes looked like the ones he had seen inside the pod when it had tipped over. Brute's limbs felt heavy. He had known Hope for as long she could remember, but now, any connection between them was severed. *That first generation was right.* This wasn't Hope. She was no more.

* * *

The silence inside Jacob's room was complete. Grace was leaning against the doorway, her hands folded over her breast-plate to keep them from falling to her sides. One of Jacob's many trophies stood tall and proud nearby. When she glanced at the *First Place* inscription, her face lit up with a smile. It quickly faded, however, when she noticed Jacob's reflection in its flawless surface. He was sitting at his desk with his back to her. Slumped was more like it. She knew he was still upset.

"I'm sorry about what happened to Wheeler and Hope," she said.

There was no response, so Grace was forced to look over at Pin-bot who was perched on the window sill in front of Jacob, silently observing the one-sided conversation. Grace hoped that the helper-bot might be able to relay Jacob's reactions to her, but Pin-bot only rotated herself from left to right, confirming that there was no reaction from Jacob. Grace sighed. "I know you only knew them for a short time, but I also know that they meant a lot to you. If it makes you feel any better, they'll be inside your hard-drive for whenever you need them."

What she said was true, but that brought no consolation to Jacob. He would much rather have Hope and Wheeler by his side. At least he wouldn't be trying to solve Forever Jacob on his own. He mindlessly tapped his finger against the microscope that once held so much potential. Pinned underneath it was the plant, now shrivelled, brown and dead. It was a sight that Jacob was beginning to get used to. He wondered why his mom was still lingering in the doorway to his room. What more could she possibly say to him? What could he say to her? How would she react if he told her that all this time, he had been attempting to do the impossible? Not very well, Jacob assumed. That was one of the reasons he kept quiet.

For her part, Grace understood why Jacob was keeping her at a distance. He just needed time to calculate things on his own. Maybe then, he would open up to her. "You had to deal with so much in the past few days...I'll leave you alone for awhile, Jacob. It'll give you time to reorganize your hard-drive." Grace glanced over at Pin-bot, hoping she would follow her lead and exit the room. Pin-bot didn't budge. She did as Jacob had done and ignored her. "I'll be back in a while to help you recharge." Grace quietly left the room, closing the door behind her.

Jacob finally sat up. "Yeah, like I really need help getting into the charger," he mumbled. He glanced over his shoulder at the door. "Why don't you help me when I need help?"

"Beep-help," Pin-bot said.

Jacob waved at her. "Thanks, Pin-bot...But no thanks. This is something I have to do on my own." He stood up from his chair and sighed. "Can't believe this. Hope, Wheeler and Vision are gone. And that leaves me with what? Trying to save the Earth and bring back humans by myself?" He picked up the microscope and threw it against the wall, causing Pin-bot to fall from her comfortable perch. "What did I get myself into? Things were a whole lot easier before I stepped inside that school." *I didn't even want to go there in the first place. Thanks again, Mom...*

Pin-bot hurried over to the microscope which had sustained damage from the impact. She glanced back at Jacob with angled eyes, acknowledging that she was the one programmed to clean up the mess.

"Just leave it. It's not like it matters anymore." Jacob pushed away from the desk, walked over to the window and looked out. He folded his arms across the sill and rested his head on them. "Once Earth's heart is warm again, life will return," he said. "What does that even mean?" He sighed. "I don't understand why I can't figure this out." He lowered his head even deeper inside his arms, allowing only his eyes to be exposed. He stared off into the sky which wasn't much of a sky at this point. Everywhere he looked, the moon blocked his line of sight. He checked the angles again, but it was no different from the last time. The moon was going to impact Earth in a big way. "I know if the Mayor goes through with his plans and destroys the moon, I'll have more time, but still...what's having more time if I can't solve Forever Jacob in the first place?"

Pin-bot came over and hovered by Jacob's side when he recited the mysterious phrase again. "When Earth's heart is warm again, life will return..." He stared at Pin-bot. "How am I supposed to warm up the center of the Earth? And why would I want to?" He slammed his closed hand against the window sill, forcing Pin-bot to cower behind the shutter. The small flaps on her head opened and closed.

"Damn it, *327*. I thought my CPU would have figured this out by now." Jacob pulled himself away from the window and walked over to the corner where some of his trophies were stored. He stopped next to the one that his mom had selected earlier, the one with the flattest side, ideal for creating the perfect reflection. He ignored the inscription and began to turn his head from side-to-side.

Curious, Pin-bot flew over and hovered over him. "Beep-doing?"

"Nothing. Just trying to see the back of my head. I need to know if my CPU was upgraded." Jacob pointed over to his desk. "Hey, Pin-bot. Grab me that screwdriver, will you?"

Pin-bot was always eager to help, so she flew over, extended her arms within their compartments and picked up the screwdriver. Jacob watched her progress which was reflected on the gloss of the trophy. "Perfect. Now bring it here."

"Beep-beep." Pin-bot made her way back to Jacob and offered him the screwdriver. But Jacob did take it.

"No. I need *you* to use it."

Pin-bot hovered in place. She didn't recognize Jacob's order. He reached up and touched the two oversized screws that held the plate on the top of his head. "Use the screwdriver on these. Pull them out. I need to take a look inside my head."

Pin-bot drifted away. Sure, she had butted him in the head many times before, but those were provoked. She didn't want to cause Jacob any damage if it was not necessary. "Beep-can't!"

"Get back here!" He reached out and pulled her back in.

"Beep-break-Jacob!"

"You're not going to break me, Pin-bot." Jacob smacked the side of his head, just to prove how sturdy he was. "See? Upgraded parts. Nothing to worry about."

"Beep-beep," Pin-bot replied.

Jacob pulled the trophy closer, so he could watch Pin-bot's reflection on its surface and guide her. He watched intently, as she adjusted her grip on the screwdriver. Her eyes angled downward, and he knew that she was doing that to concentrate. Good. If she was working on such a delicate area she needed to concentrate. She lowered her arms, driving the screwdriver into the first screw.

"Now twist and then pull it out."

Pin-bot tilted her body so that her backside was facing the ceiling and began spinning clockwise. The screw slowly grew in length, as it loosened its hold. Each complete turn from Pin-bot, exposed more and more of the screw's interlocking threads. It finally popped out and clanged noisily on the floor.

"Quietly!"

Pin-bot flipped back upright and then butted him on the head.

"Sorry! I just don't want Mom to know what we're doing." Jacob pushed the fallen screw up against the base of the trophy. "Okay, one more. Same as the last."

Pin-bot flew to the other side of Jacob's head, lowered her arms and drove the screwdriver into the final screw. She repeated her spinning manoeuvre with her backside raised. The screw popped out as effortlessly as the first and fell to the floor. "Beep-beep-done?" she asked, with the screwdriver still dangling from her hands.

"Wait there, Pin-bot. We're not done yet. I can't see anything back there, so I need you to be my eyes." Jacob wrapped his hands over his face and then began pulling his head covering up. This was accompanied by a high-pitched whirling of gears biting into each other and the low rumble of pistons retracting into their chambers. The chaotic buzz of circuitry intensified, as his entire face and head covering began to peel away from the underlying structure. A final twist of his hand allowed Jacob to remove his entire face-plate from the rest of his head. He placed the empty shell on the floor next to the screws and then looked back at Pin-bot.

Her eyes blew up into large circles, and her body vibrated uncontrollably. She didn't know what she was looking at, but it certainly wasn't the Jacob that she knew. She let out a loud string of terrified beeps, before retreating to the other side of the room. She dove behind the desk and stayed out of sight.

"Pin-bot? Hey, Pin-bot! What's the matter with you? What are you doing over there? Come on, I don't have time for this."

Cautiously, Pin-bot peeked out from behind the desk. Whoever was calling out to her sure sounded like Jacob. It just didn't look at him. "Beep-are-you?"

Jacob jerked his head back. "Huh? What do you mean? It's me. Who else would it be?" He turned and looked into his trophy. The unfamiliar reflection staring back at him explained why Pin-bot was acting so strangely. Without his face plating, the lenses of Jacob's eyes were completely exposed. The entire gape of his mouth and all the individual gears, wires and intricate parts driving them, were in plain sight. Jacob opened his mouth. Gears on each side bit down into each other. "Hey, neat!" He moved his eyes up and down and from side-to-side. A random buzz accompanied their every move. It was fascinating to see himself like this, though he had to agree with Pin-bot. Even for him, it was an overwhelming sight. He reached down and picked up the face-plate and brought it to his face. "Pin-bot, it's just me. It's Jacob. See?"

Pin-bot slowly revealed more of herself from behind the desk. Jacob faced her and used his fingers to push his mouth into a smile. "See. It's me. I'm smiling at you."

"Beep-beep-Jacob!" She flew over and hovered next to him.

Just to make sure she didn't fly away again, Jacob took care to slowly remove his face-plate. "Are you still with me?"

Pin-bot nodded, so he put the plate down on the floor. *Hope was right. Who you are is more important than what you are.* "Good. Now let's get back to work." Jacob pointed to the back of his head. "I need you to look inside. See if you can see a new CPU. It should be made out of silicon and have circuits and conductors on it."

"Beep?"

Jacob sighed. "Small, shiny thing. Just look for the small, shiny thing."

Pin-bot flew in so close that she was rubbing up against the back of Jacob's head. She scanned every corner of his head but was unable to confirm anything new. Jacob kept changing the position of the trophy in order to better the angle he had on Pin-bot. "See anything? Anything that might look upgraded?"

"Beep-beep-covered." Pin-bot replied.

"Covered? What do you mean covered?"

"Beep-beep-plate."

"What? Another plate? Are you sure?" Jacob reached back and felt around. Pin-bot was right. In addition to the thin covering that was attached to his face-plate, there was another plate, much heavier and thicker all the way around. "Can't you see through it? Any holes for you to see inside?"

Jacob watched Pin-bot's reflection in the trophy, as she rotated left and right in the familiar move that meant *no*. Jacob hunched over, slapping the floor with his hand. "Damn...*328*. Guess we'll never know."

He picked up his face-plate and placed it over his head. With just a couple of twists, it snapped in place with ease. Then he picked up the screws and dropped them into their designated slots. "Might as well tighten these."

Pin-bot did the honours with a few counter-clockwise turns of the screwdriver, and then Jacob stood up. "Why would Mom upgrade everything else and not my CPU?" He looked down at the trophy. The inscription etched on its surface stared back at him…almost mocking him. "First Place?" Jacob said out loud. "Did I even deserve it?" He looked around the room. "Did I deserve any of these?"

Pin-bot scanned the trophies. Although she was not capable of decoding their inscriptions, she knew how significant each one was. She didn't understand why Jacob would even question himself.

"Oh, sure. When it comes to easy things, my CPU has no problems coming in first. But when I really need it, it stalls." He hoisted the trophy off of the floor. "First Place?" He gripped the handles so tightly that he began to tremble. "I don't deserve this! I don't deserve any of these!" He reeled back, twisted his upper body around and then threw the trophy against the wall. "Damn it! *329*."

He picked up the next trophy within reach. "I don't deserve this one, either!" It was sent across the room to collide into the closet door. He picked up another and then another one. One by one, each trophy was sent across the room. Pin-bot let out a string of distressful beeps, before retreating back behind the desk, where she watched Jacob continue his violent tear throughout the room. Trophies were sent in all directions. One even slammed into the window, cracking the glass into an unruly, mosaic pattern.

Jacob walked over to the only trophy left standing. It was the largest in the room. He wrapped his hands around it, hoisted it over his head and then reeled back. "Don't deserve any of these!"

Just as Jacob let go of the trophy, the door swung open, and Jacob's mom stepped in—directly in the path of the flying object. From the other side of the room, Pin-bot let out a warning beep, but it was too late. The trophy collided into Jacob's mom, sending her to the floor.

"*Mom*!" Jacob ran to her as fast as his second generation legs could take him, and he fell to his knees beside her. "Mom…are you okay?" He pushed away the trophy that had landed next to her. It had caused more than enough damage already.

Grace was slow to get up. One of her hands was covering the side of her face. She sat up and pulled her hand away to reveal a large dent high on her cheek. Even worse, plating from the side of her head had broken off, and she held it tightly in her hand.

"Mom! What…what have I done?" He grabbed her arm to help her stand, but she refused his assistance.

"It…it's okay." Grace attempted to stand on her own, but her trembling limbs would not support her.

"Mom, please, let me help you!"

"I'm…fine..." Again, she attempted to stand. This time, she was successful. She reached up and felt the dent in her head.

"It was an accident. I...I didn't mean to."

"It's okay, Jacob. I'm fine. Really."

"But you don't look fine."

"I'm still working, aren't I?" Grace began scanning the room. Jacob's trophies were scattered all over the floor in total disarray. *What on Earth happened here?* She didn't even know what to think or what to say. She shook her head and backed toward the door. "You need to recharge soon. We have an important day ahead of us."

Jacob just stood there. "Mom?"

"I know you're capable of recharging your—"

"Mom…I'm sorry. I didn't mean to."

Grace waited a moment before she gave a slight nod. "Just make sure you're fully charged," she said, closing the door.

Even as her footsteps faded and finally disappeared, Jacob remained still. He was waiting in front of the door, hoping that it would open, and that she would reappear so he could apologize again. But the door remained closed. She wasn't returning anytime soon. Jacob finally turned to Pin-bot who had been silent the entire time. He looked at her, the plates over his eyes raised high, wishing that she could console him in some way. But he knew Pin-bot wasn't capable of responding to such an unpredicted situation. It wasn't programmed in her to do so. She hovered silently in front of the shattered window.

Jacob made his way over to the desk, practically throwing himself against it once he got there. He buried his face in his arms. "Why did I have to go and do that? Everything seems to be going the wrong way for me today. And now Mom's upset with me."

He peeked up at Pin-bot and watched her flutter around the shattered window. The trophy he had thrown at it had done more damage than he realized. Pin-bot, normally stable when she hovered, was being moved by the wind breaching through the cracked surface of the window.

"Just leave it, Pin-bot," Jacob said, burying his face on his arms again. He let out a deep and long-lasting sigh. "It doesn't matter anymore. Nothing really matters anymore. Pods are ready. Mayor has a few spots left. Maybe…" Jacob paused. "Maybe…we should just go...I can't figure out Forever Jacob. There's nothing left for us here."

He brought his hand up to the back of his head. "Worthless upgraded CPU! I was better off with my old one."

For several minutes, there was only silence within the room and then Jacob heard a soft tap-tap…tapping sound. He assumed the sounds were coming from Pin-bot, as she attempted to close off the draft. Without lifting his head, he called out, "Stop it. Leave the window the way it is. There's no point in trying to fix it." Tap-tap…tap…The sound continued. Tap-tap…tap. Jacob pulled his face away from his arms. "Pin-bot! I said get away from—" Jacob cocked his head back. Pin-bot was hovering silently next to him.

"Beep-beep?" she said, not understanding his commands.

Tap-tap…tap…Jacob looked over at the window and then back at Pin-bot. It was now obvious that she was not making the sound. Jacob scanned the entire wall in front of him. "What's making that noise?"

Pin-bot knew where it was coming from. She flew over to the miniature moon and Earth models at the back end of the desk. "Beep-beep," she said, pointing at them.

Jacob leaned close to where the moon dangled from a thin wire just above and away from the Earth model. The moon was gently swaying back and forth. At each peak of its swing, the moon nudged up against the Earth causing the tapping sound. Jacob shifted his attention to the Earth model. He focused intently on its relationship to the moon. Each time the moon nudged against it, the Earth would rotate ever so slightly on its axis.

"Beep-beep-tap-tap-tap," Pin-bot explained, pointing at the window.

"You're right. The breeze from the window." He looked over at Pin-bot. "That's what's causing the moon to..." His eyes suddenly widened. "Earth's moving again..." Jacob stood up. The plates over his eyes rose to their highest position. He looked at the moon model still tap-tap...tapping away at the Earth model. "Moon's hitting the Earth causing it to move again!" He walked over to the window and stared at the moon. "The real moon's not dangling from a wire but it's moving." He calculated the short distance between it and the Earth. He glanced over at the miniature models and then back outside. "The moon will hit the Earth," he confirmed, "and the impact will cause it to move. Like it used to." He glanced over at a confused Pin-bot. "Don't you see, Pin-bot? The moon is going to hit and Earth!"

"Beep-beep-move-again?"

"Yeah, that's right." The glow in Jacob's eyes became opaque. "And if Earth moves again..." Jacob ran over to Pin-bot and snatched her out of the air. "I did it..."

"Beep?"

"I...I did it! *I figured out Forever Jacob*!" He let go of Pin-bot and slammed his hands on the top of his desk. "I did it! I did it! I finally did it!"

"Beep?"

"Pin-bot, don't you see? It will start when Earth moves. It will heat up again, and life will return!"

Pin-bot simply rotated left to right.

"Look..." Jacob picked up the miniature moon model, pulled it back and simply allowed it to slip out of his hand. It swung freely toward the Earth model, just like it had in the wind. It touched the Earth model with a soft tap and made it spin. "The moon will hit us. That's inevitable. It's going to happen and there's no stopping it. When it does, the impact will cause Earth to start moving...rotating on its axis, right?"

"Beep..."

"It's simple physics. Something the size of the moon hitting something the size of Earth will cause one to react with the other. In this case, Earth will react by moving. And why is this so important?"

Pin-bot fell silent. That was too much information for her to process.

"Earth's rotation will cause friction deep within its core...its heart. This friction causes heat to build up. Heat will rise and finally melt the frozen *Pure Blend* that has been trapped inside the Earth. Once it's in its liquid form, the

Pure Blend will be pushed back up to the surface. It'll cover most of the planet...the way it used to." Jacob smiled at Pin-bot. "And life will return!"

Jacob's open hands crashed down on top of the desk. "I did it!" So overwhelmed with the sense of completion, Jacob grabbed the moon model and sent it flying into the Earth. The impact was much stronger this time, and the Earth model tipped out of its base and landed violently against the desk. Then it rolled off the surface and fell to the floor. "Oh, damn it. *330.*"

Pin-bot dropped down, picked up the model and set back on top of the desk. "Beep-beep-too-strong."

"You're right." He ran over to the window and looked out. He stood for a moment and did some more calculations. "The moon can't hit the way it is. The impact will be too severe. The Earth will spin out of control and maybe even out of orbit. That's not good. Not good at all!" Jacob flashed his finger out at Pin-bot and then began waggling it back and forth. "Wait a minute. Wait just a minute... It will still work! The Mayor! Project Retaliation!"

With all of the confusing information Pin-bot had to process in such a short amount of time, she had to switch to idle mode. That made it appear that she was not listening, but that did not bother Jacob.

"The Mayor revised Project Retaliation, Pin-bot. He plans on destroying the moon again. And if the cannon works, it will break up the moon into chunks. They will fall and still hit us, but the impact will be spread out. It should be just enough to get the planet moving again, but not so much that it pushes it out of orbit." Jacob's mouth fell open. "The Mayor doesn't even know it, but he's actually helping us. All we have to do is sit back and wait." Jacob began jumping up and down, slapping his hands together. "After all these failed attempts and calculations that lead nowhere, the answer is right in front of us. Just like the professor said. All we have to do is sit back and wait! The Mayor might not be happy once he finds out, but by then, it'll be too late. He'll be out there somewhere with the stars."

Pin-bot still didn't understand what Jacob was telling her, but after his trophy throwing stint, she was just happy to see him smiling again. With her eyes in the shape of crescents, she flew over to Jacob and gently nudged him. "Beep-beep-did-it!"

"Ah, thanks, Pin-bot. Guess my CPU *was* upgraded after all. I wouldn't have figured this one out without it." The smile on Jacob's face suddenly faded, and he looked over at the door to his room. "I... I finally figured out Forever Jacob. Now...the hard part. I have to tell Mom about it. Wait here, Pin-bot. I need to talk to her. This might be the last time I'll ever see her again." His strides were heavy even as he exited the room.

The door to his mom's room slowly crept open. Jacob peeked inside. A thin trail of light penetrated the darkness, ran across the spotless metal floor and then draped itself onto his mom. She was standing motionless inside her charger with her head lowered toward her breast-plate. Jacob quietly walked inside, careful not to disturb her during the recharging process. He stopped beside the machine, not brave enough to face her directly. Silence became the loudest thing in the room. It was unusual for Jacob to see his mom this way. He had never seen her in this vulnerable state before.

Even though she would not be able to hear him, Jacob felt a strong need to try to make amends. As he stared at her, he noticed that the dent on the side of her face seemed more pronounced due to the contrasting light filtering inside the room. Jacob lowered his head. "I didn't mean to do that," he whispered. "I didn't mean to do most of the things I've done. Leaving the magnets switched off on my boots. All of my failed experiments inside the house. Not telling you that school had been cancelled..."

Jacob could have gone on and on but decided to stop right there. There was no point in recalling all of his failures. He was sure they were still on her hard-drive. "The past few days have been," Jacob snickered, "let's just say, a bit crazy. They've been tough on me, and I'm sure they've been difficult for you, too. There's a lot I haven't told you about. And I know it's wrong of me to hide things from you. But I had to. I didn't know how you would have reacted if I told you that I was trying to bring back humans in order to save our kind. You wouldn't have believed me. Even I wouldn't have believed myself."

He took a quick glanced up at his mom. "You know something, Mom? When you reformatted my hard-drive, my earliest memory was somehow brought forward. What I've been trying to do the past few days..." Jacob paused. "I...I just want you to be proud of me. Just like you were the first time you switched me on." Jacob's eyes went blank, and his hard-drive began to whirl. A slight distortion commenced the playback that he had recorded a long time ago.

"My first complete build," Grace proudly said, through Jacob's internal speaker. Then he heard another voice, and a whole conversation.

"And a fine looking first generation, if I do say so myself. You did good, Grace."

"I couldn't have done it without you."

"You did the hard part. I was merely there for support."

"Should we?"

"By all means, Grace. But I'll let you have the honours. He's yours. You should be the first one to switch him on."

"I'm so excited."

"I'm sure he'll make you proud."

"I already know he will."

Distortion ended the playback. The glow in Jacob's eyes returned to normal, and the low humming of his hard-drive stabilized. "I figured out Forever Jacob, Mom. I figured a way to save our kind. But that means...I have to stay here...on Earth. I have to make sure everything goes as planned." Jacob reached out, took his mom's hand and held it tightly. For the first time ever, his fingers easily wrapped around his mom's entire hand. "That's why I can't...I can't go with you, Mom. I can't go into those pods."

Without any response from his mom, Jacob allowed her hand to slip out of his and settle back down by her side. "I'm sorry," he said, backing away toward the door. When he got there, he stopped, stood in the doorway and glanced back. “Goodbye, Mom...” He exited the room.

Chapter Nine

The hefty drag from the plug inside her tiny hands was no more. Another order completed. Pin-bot let out a satisfying *beep* and then flew over to meet Jacob.

Jacob's bright-green indicators lit up the side of her face, confirming that he was now fully recharged. His eyes were open, though their glow wasn't as intense as usual. "Well, this is it, Pin-bot...This is how it all begins." He sighed. "Final day…I guess."

Pin-bot let out a concerning *beep* that tapered off.

"Never mind." *You probably won't understand anyway.* Jacob stepped out of the charger, a feat much easier to accomplish with his second generation limbs. As he scanned the room, he noticed that all the trophies that had suffered his violent bout of rage were now lined up against the wall in precise order. Dents and scratches on their surfaces were turned in to face the wall, allowing only the unblemished sides to be displayed. He also noted that not much light shimmered off their smooth surfaces. He glanced at the window to see the shutters were broken open and peeled back to the sides. Light just wasn't pouring in the window like it used to. Jacob did not even have to calculate why. He suspected that the moon was now so close that it easily blocked most of the sun's light from penetrating his room. It was funny how he used to whine about the amount of light that came through his window. Now, with the light nearly expelled, he missed it.

He continued to scan the rest of the dim room. Everything else about it was back to normal. *Better than normal.* Even the floor had been cleaned and polished. "Never seen my reflection in it before," he said, turning his head from side-to-side, admiring his perfectly mirrored image underneath his feet. "Guess Mom finished recharging before me." He turned to Pin-bot. "She didn't have to do all of this."

"Beep-not?" Pin-bot asked, caught admiring her own reflection in the unblemished floor.

"Everything is going to change." Jacob sighed. "Mom didn't have to clean up my room. I don't even know if I'll ever come back here."

This finally ripped Pin-bot's attention away from the floor. "Beep-not?" she cried, eyes round and wide.

"I mean, I could…maybe." Jacob shrugged, nearly touching his shoulder tips with the side of his head. "I don't know, Pin-bot. I don't know what will happen to tell you the truth. Upgraded CPU and all I have are questions."

Pin-bot slowly made her way to the other side of Jacob, and although her eyes were beginning to reform into their normal ovals, she still didn't have the slightest idea of what Jacob was trying to explain to her.

"Only thing I'm sure of is that it's going to be lonely on Earth all by myself. Who knows? Maybe after the moon hits, I'll come back here and wait."

"Beep-pods?"

"The pods?" Jacob was surprised to hear Pin-bot mention the pods. "Mom finally told you about the pods and the Mayor's plans?"

Pin-bot rotated back and forth, nodding. She almost looked excited.

Being shot off into space without any consequences would seem exciting to anyone with a simple mind. "Well, I'm not going, Pin-bot. I want to stay here—I *have* to stay here. I have no other choice."

Pin-bot dove, redirected her turbines and then rose back up to Jacob's eye-level. "Beep-stay-by-yourself?"

"I have to," Jacob tried to explain. "Someone has to stay and make sure everything goes as planned. And since the plan is Forever 'Jacob', I don't have much choice."

Pin-bot might not have understood what Forever Jacob meant, she might not even understand basic orders the first time they're assigned to her, but, as Pin-bot flew toward the window and looked out, she understood what was staring back at her. It didn't take an advanced CPU to calculate what would happen when something as large as the moon struck the Earth.

"I know, I know," Jacob said, waving Pin-bot back to him. "My calculations already confirmed what will happen. Even though the moon will be in chunks after the Mayor fires the cannon it, when those chunks hit, it isn't going to be pleasant around here." With Pin-bot back at his side, Jacob allowed the shutters in his eyes to slide downward, blocking out the glow. "But I have to stay," he whispered. "No one else will."

There was silence for a moment, then Jacob felt a gentle tap against his head.

"Beep-stay."

The shutters in Jacob's eyes slowly opened. With both plates over his eyes nearly down to their lowest position, Jacob said, "Say that again, Pin-bot. I don't think I heard you."

"Beep-stay-with-Jacob," she repeated. And to be perfectly clear, she even gave the side of Jacob's head another gentle bump.

Jacob cocked his head back. "You…you want to stay *here*?" he said, his tone pitched sharply at the end.

Pin-bot tilted forward and back. Her crescent-shaped eyes flickered with excitement.

"With *me*?" Jacob asked, slapping his hand against his chest. It was the first time ever that his hand had been able to overlap his entire chest-plate, completely smothering the green glow of his indicators. "You don't want to go with Mom inside those pods?"

Pin-bot rotated left to right, the crescents in her eyes beginning to lose their tapered angles.

Jacob removed his hand and placed a finger on his chin. It was a bold claim to want to stay, especially knowing what could very well happen. "I don't know what Mom's going to say about this," he said. "And you know, Pin-bot, we might be here for a really long time. We could be completely rusted over by the time evolution repeats itself."

Pin-bot remained true to her previous form by tilting forward and back.

"And it'll just be you and me here. That's it. No one else for a long...long time." He offered Pin-bot a pair of wide-eyes. "So? Are you sure you want to stay here with me?"

"Beep-beep-stay-with-Jacob!" she said, before butting Jacob on the head to show her impatience. She was offended that Jacob asked her so many times.

"Hey!" Jacob raised his hands to shield himself from what he thought was an unprovoked attack. "Okay! Okay! You can stay. Just stop butting me on the head."

Pin-bot retreated. Her eyes returned to their usual ovals.

"You know, you're much nicer when you're not attacking me."

Pin-bot's turbines decelerated, angling her toward the floor. Her eyes angled upward.

"It's okay, Pin-bot. I can't be upset with anyone who wants to stay here at a time like this." Jacob heard the tiny fans in Pin-bot's turbines accelerating to their usual speeds, bringing her closer to him. "Thanks for wanting to stay with me. I would hate to be the last one here...all alone."

Pin-bot's eyes were ready to transform into crescents, until Jacob had to ask one last time, "Are you sure you want—"

"Beep!" Her eyes became slits.

"Never mind!" Jacob didn't want another butt on the head from her.

He walked over to the closet with Pin-bot hovering beside him. As he walked by the desk, he gave the moon model a gentle nudge with his finger, just for reassurance. As expected, the moon grazed the Earth model causing it to revolve around its axis. "Yup. Still works. Good thing. It's too late to change our plans now." He sighed, as he broke through the small amount of light filtering through the window. "Too late for everything now."

Reaching the closet, Jacob noticed that the red plating that normally made him cringe was absent from the door's handle. *That's Odd. But a bit of a relief.* "Finally," he said, eagerly rubbing his hands together. "Get to pick out my own."

He pulled open the door, nearly knocking Pin-bot out of the air. He smiled when he saw that all his plating, along with their clips, hung neatly in place. He skimmed through them all until he reached the last few.

"Black..." *Same colour as the sky above Wheeler's house.* "Green..." *Same colour as Hope's eyes.* Jacob sighed. The very last colour of plating made him pause. It was the furthest back, as if it had been hidden. Jacob let his shoulders slump downward and withdrew his hand from the closet. "Red...Mom's favourite." Everything was still there—the scratches, the dents, and especially the colour. "Guess I have to make a choice. So many colours, but all of them remind me of something." Jacob took a moment to scan the entire closet again. White, green, blue, yellow...they were all there, cleaned and polished, much like the floor and his trophies. His mom had certainly been busy. *Busy making my life better.* Jacob did not have any reason left to stall. He reached into the closet and picked out the plating that *he* wanted. Pin-bot tilted forward and back to let him know she agreed with his choice.

With Pin-bot's help, a few snaps here and there were all that was needed to secure the plating in place. Jacob brushed off some of the dust still remaining on the shoulder-plate and said, "Red...because it's Mom's favourite."

"Beep-like-red-too," Pin-bot admitted, scanning Jacob from head to feet.

"Okay-okay...Mom's *and* Pin-bot's favourite," Jacob said with a smile.

With his look complete, Jacob turned around and stared at his room, his expression a little sad. "Well, Pin-bot," his said, placing his hands on his hips. "I guess this is it. Not sure what happens next."

What happened next should have been predicted by Jacob. Before he or Pin-bot could brace themselves, the door to the room swung open. Grace hurried in, her movements deliberate. A medium-sized box was tucked securely underneath her arm.

"Oh, good, you're both up and running." Grace walked over to Jacob.

"Mom?" Jacob noticed that the dent on the side of her head had been straightened out some, but it was still clearly visible. "You fixed it! Well...most of it. I still see the ripples."

"What are you talking about?"

"The dent on your head. I was going to offer to straighten it out for you since...you know...I caused it."

Grace reached up and felt the uneven surface on her head. It didn't seem to bother her, however. "Oh, that. It's fine. Just a surface blemish." She bent down and with her free hand reached out for Jacob.

He eluded her attempt to grab his arm and backed away. "Mom? What are you doing?"

Grace cancelled a second attempt. She stood tall and asked, "You ready?"

"I don't know, Mom. Depends on what you mean when you say ready."

"No time for games, Jacob."

"I'm not playing any games. What do you want me to be ready for?"

Instead of answering, Grace abruptly backed away toward the door. "Just finish up here and meet me downstairs. I don't want to be late."

"Late?" Jacob shouted, as he watched his mom descend the staircase. "Late for what?"

"Hurry up, Jacob. We have to leave...now!"

"Leave where?" His mom didn't reply. He cupped his hand beside his mouth to strengthen his call. "Mom! Where are you going? What's in that box?"

No response. Jacob did some calculations and then looked over at Pin-bot.

"Beep-beep-going?"

"I think I know. Where else could she be going but the pods? It's not like there are many places to visit at this point."

"Beep-didn't-tell-her?"

"About Forever Jacob? I did. I told her everything."

"Beep-she-recharging?"

"Oh...right. She *was* recharging. She must not have heard a thing I said. That's why she's in a rush to get to the pods. What am I going to tell her, Pin-bot?"

It was absurd for Jacob to ask Pin-bot such a question. If he could not calculate an answer, how did he expect her to?

"I guess we should just tell her the truth," Jacob said, heading toward the door. "She's not going to like what I have to say. I can calculate that already."

Jacob stopped just outside of his room and looked down the staircase. If the staircase had grinned every time Jacob was at its base, it certainly looked like a frown while he stood at the very top. Jacob wasn't lured in by its steep aggressiveness just yet. Where Jacob was standing, he noticed that all of the pictures along the walls were missing. Only faded outlines remained. "Why did she take them down?" *Weird.* Jacob hurried down the stairs as quickly as possible. At the bottom, he stopped, collected himself and then scanned the hallway. The front door was open at the end of the hall, and Jacob could see light filtering in. He walked down the hall, stopping in the doorway to the kitchen. He peeked inside but saw no sign of his mom. There was a mound of *Artificial Blend* next to an empty space on the countertop. His mom must have taken the last remaining cans of *Pure Blend*. "That's what's probably inside that box she was carrying."

That confirms it. If she took all of the Pure Blend with her, I have no choice but to go with her. "So that's her plan!"

The grinding roar of the car's engine surged inside the house but quickly stabilized to a near silent hum.

"Beep!" Pin-bot cried.

"Yeah, I hear it. Sounds like she's ready to go. Come on. I have to tell her before it's too late."

They ran out to see Grace in the car. She motioned to them and then called out, "Get in!" Her voice was muffled inside the car's rusted enclosure, but Jacob had no trouble hearing her. Still, he did not obey. He stood outside of the passenger-side, while Pin-bot was hovering just behind the car. He pressed his face against the clouded window.

"I can't," he said.

Grace pushed open the door wide enough so that her voice was no longer dampened. "Stop it, Jacob. The door just has a couple of rusty hinges. Don't tell me you can't open it by yourself. Get inside. We have to get going."

Jacob pulled his face from the window and peered around the back of the car. He could only see the top half of Pin-bot.

"Beep-going-inside?" Pin-bot asked, bobbing up and down.

"Just let me talk to her. You can wait out here if you want. I'll be back out before you know it." Slowly, Jacob pulled open the door the rest of the way and slid onto the seat. He left the door standing open. It was never his intention to even set foot inside the car.

Grace reached over and pulled the door closed. Jacob felt the brisk snap of air wisp by him, as the door locked into place. He hadn't seen Pin-bot slip inside just before the door slammed shut. She hovered quietly above the box that Jacob's mom had left in the back.

"There we go," Grace said. "Perfect. This gives us just enough time to drive out there, unload the box—"

"Mom?" His attempt to stop her failed.

"Then we have to get ourselves ready and—"

"Mom!"

She halted her rambling and turned to face Jacob. She noticed that all of Jacob's facial features had tightened. His mouth was a thin line, and the plates over his eyes were lowered, cutting his eyes in half.

"Will you just listen to me, Mom? I need to tell you something." For Jacob, this was a serious matter which made him wonder why a smile suddenly appeared on her face.

"I see you're wearing red plates again. Red is my—"

"Favourite!" *For the hundredth time.*

"Beep-favourite-too," Pin-bot added.

Jacob looked behind him. Two glowing ovals were just about all he could see. "Hey! Didn't I tell you to wait for me outside?"

Pin-bot lowered down inside the box. She thought that Jacob's orders had been more of a suggestion.

"Outside? Why? We aren't going to leave her here. We're all going."

"No, Mom. *You're* going. That's what I need to talk to you about."

Grace switched off the engine, allowing the car's interior to soak up the indomitable silence. She sank into her seat and gave Jacob the widest pair of eyes that her facial motors would allow. "Okay, Jacob, I'm listening. Please explain to me why you're not going because I really want to know."

"If you stop talking I'll tell you."

Grace folded her arms across her breast-plate. "I'm listening."

Jacob relaxed the tension in his face. "I was finally able to figure out what needs to be done for Forever Jacob to work."

"Forever what?"

"Jacob. Well, it used to be Yaw. But it's Jacob now."

"I don't understand."

"The assignment," Jacob restated. "Forever Jacob is the assignment we've been working on, and I figured it out. I know what needs to be done."

"Done about what?"

Using one hand, Jacob gestured to the view outside the car. "All of this, including the moon. I know how to bring everything back the way it used to be."

Grace reached under the steering column and turned the switch, bringing the car's engine back to life. "I know," she said. "You told me all of this earlier."

The backrest saved Jacob's head from snapping all the way back. He looked at his mom with eyes wide.

"I heard everything you said when you came into my room. You thought I was recharging?" She snickered. "The plug wasn't even in the wall."

"It...it wasn't?"

"No, Jacob. I usually take a few moments to reorganize my hard-drive before I settle in. You had caught me just before I was about to switch on the charger."

"So... you heard...everything?"

Grace nodded.

Jacob sank down in his seat. He had undeniably made his status clear to her while she was supposedly in her dormant state. He wouldn't have had the courage to say all those things otherwise. Now having her admit that she heard everything he had said created more uncertainty. Would she force him to go anyway?

"Thought you would be a little more excited about all of this," Grace said, observing how quiet Jacob had become. "I mean, save the Earth? Save our kind? No trophy of any size could be awarded for something this significant."

"I *should* be excited. I know I should, but—" His shoulders slumped down even lower. "How can I be excited about leaving you?"

"What? What do you mean?"

Jacob turned and looked deep into his mom's eyes. "Didn't you hear that part? When I said I couldn't go with you? I figured out a way to bring us back to the way we once were. That's why I can't...I can't—" Jacob felt like opening the door and escaping while he had the chance. Sometimes the best explanation is none at all. But she deserved one. *After all she's done for me.* "I can't go with you." He immediately had to look away. "I'm sorry, Mom. I have to stay here. That's part of the plan. I don't want to leave you, but I...I have to."

From inside the box, Pin-bot could only watch as silence cut deeply between Jacob and Grace.

"Where the Mayor's taking us is full of uncertainty. At least here, I know there's potential." Jacob forced himself to look back up at his mom. The blue glow in his eyes was intensifying. "I can't go. And no one is going to stop me!"

With that, Jacob shifted to the very edge of his seat. He braced himself. He expected nothing less than a tirade from his mom. He might even have to force his way out of the car. What he didn't expect was the big smile that spread across his mom's face. He reeled back so intently that the back of his head pinged off of the door. "Mom?"

Grace shook her head, as if disappointed by Jacob's assumptions. "Well...*neither am I.*"

If the car door hadn't been closed, Jacob would have surely fallen outside. "You're *what*? You're not going?"

Grace snickered. "I know my CPU isn't as new as it used to be, but I don't remember ever saying I was going inside one of those pods." She glanced back at Pin-bot. "Do you remember me saying I would go?"

Pin-bot was finally allowed to emerge from the box. "Beep!" she said, rotating left to right.

"See? Even Pin-bot didn't hear me say that."

"But...but I thought—"

"No-no-no!" Grace said, switching the car from idle to on. "That was never my intention. The Mayor could have said whatever he wanted to. It wouldn't have changed my decision."

This was all so unbelievable. Jacob needed absolute confirmation. "So wait," he said, waving his hand in front of his face. "You really mean it? You're not going into those pods?"

His mom shook her head. "Nope. I'm staying right here." She lifted her foot off the brake and pressed down on the accelerator.

Jacob looked back out the rear window of the car. His house, with its front door still wide open, began to disappear into the horizon. But that made him wonder. *If Mom is staying right here, then why are we driving away from our house? Dare I even ask?*

As Jacob was about to turn back into his seat, he noticed the box Pin-bot was hovering over. It was the same box that his mom had with her when she entered his room earlier. He reached over and opened a flap to see what was inside. "Hey, my old limbs!" Also wedged between his old parts were the pictures from the staircase. "Where did you get them?"

"The school. I stopped by there while you were recharging."

"Oh! How's the professor? Did you tell him I said, thanks?"

His mom suddenly fell silent. She looked away.

"Mom? What's wrong?"

"Nothing," she replied, barely opening her mouth.

"Is the professor okay?"

Grace lowered her head slightly. The smile on her face became a horizontal line. "He was happy to see you again, Jacob. I know he would be proud of what you're about to do." Grace glanced back at the box. Jacob could clearly see that the glow in her eyes had dimmed. He wasn't sure why.

Hope nothing happened to the professor.

"Didn't want to throw them away," Grace said. "It'll be nice to have them in case I needed to recollect." That finally allowed the ends of her faded smile to lift. The glows in her eyes were slowly returning.

"Recollect? About what?"

"Just a reminder of the time when you were still a first generation. My hard-drive isn't what it used to be. Can't always pull up that data as quick as I once could. No harm in taking it with us."

Jacob shrugged. "First generation, second generation...it's just a number. It doesn't matter what you are. It's who you are that's important."

Grace clasped her hand over her chest. "Who told you that, Jacob? It's perfect."

Jacob stared out his window. "So was she," he whispered.

* * *

They had been driving for a quite a while now, but Jacob still didn't know why. He turned his head to face his mom. "So... If we're staying here then why are we...you know...still in the car?"

Grace smiled. "You'll see."

Jacob grabbed the door handle. "Not the pods! Because if that's where we're headed, I'm jumping. Don't think that I won't!"

"Beep-too!"

"See? Even Pin-bot says she'll jump out with me." Jacob paused and did the calculations. "Well, I guess she can't jump...Not with her turbines. But she'll follow me. Don't think she won't."

Even though he didn't want to go to the pods, Jacob knew he really didn't want to jump out of a moving car. At the speed they were traveling, that would not be a pleasant experience. To his relief, his mom reached over and removed his hand from the handle. She smiled at him, reassuringly. "Trust me, Jacob, we're not going into those pods. As to our destination... you'll just have to wait and see."

Jacob sighed. *Not this again*. "Okay... fine. But it better be good."

"It will be. I promise."

Suddenly, Pin-bot started flying erratically around the interior of the car, slamming into everything in her way.

"What's wrong with Pin-bot?" Grace cried, doing her best to keep control of the car, as it navigated the long stretch of empty road.

Jacob took a quick peek out from underneath his arm he had raised to ward off the frenzied helper-bot. "It's the longest she's ever been stuck inside like this. She doesn't like being trapped inside here." He sighed. "She's not the only one."

"I can't stop now," Grace said, anticipating another attack from Pin-bot. "We're almost there."

Jacob removed his arms from his head. "Almost where?" He received a swift butt to the head from Pin-bot, forcing him to dive back underneath his arms.

Grace also received a butt on the head from Pin-bot. "Please, make her to stop! She's going to make me crash into something. I just know it."

Pin-bot slammed into the front windshield of the car, bounced off and then spun away. Her constant beeping was annoying.

"Crash? Into what? Some dirt? We're the only ones out here."

"Just make her stop!"

"Okay-okay... I'll try." Jacob lowered his arms and glared at Pin-bot. "Hey! Remember what I told you back in my room?"

"Beep-beep, beep-beep-beep, beep..." She flew into the back.

Normally, Jacob understood Pin-bot's broken language, but she was making absolutely no sense at the moment.

"What's she saying, Jacob? Did she say she's going to stop? Make her stop!"

"Just keep driving, Mom. I'll deal with this." Jacob turned around in his seat and used the most threatening tone he could muster. "Pin-bot! I know you said you wanted to stay here with us, but if you keep this up, I'm going to throw you into one of those pods with the Mayor. Now...are you going to stop or should I tell Mom to head to the launch site?"

Pin-bot stopped. She hovered silently with large round eyes. Her tiny body trembled.

"Hey! It worked!" Jacob smiled at his mom. "See? Sometimes you just have to ask nicely to get someone to do what you want. Now we don't have to protect our heads from Pin-bot anymore."

The car came to a sudden and rather violent stop. Jacob was thrown forward, and his head slammed into the dash with a loud thud. He pushed himself back into his seat. "Mom! I was only joking."

"Sorry, Jacob. Just got excited."

Jacob was checking his head, making sure that his mom's excitement hadn't caused another dent. "Excited? That Pin-bot stopped attacking?"

Grace pointed out the car window. "No," she said, turning off the car. "Excited because we're here."

Jacob pulled himself up over the car's dash and looked out of the front windshield. What he saw silenced him. His eyes widened to their fullest capacity. His mouth opened, and their underlining gears locked it into place.

His mom let out a mild laugh. "Go on," she said, gesturing to the door. "There's no reason to stay in here."

Jacob did not even hesitate. He kicked open the car door and leaped out without even closing it behind him. He ran up close and then stopped to look at the fallen shutters, the door hanging on its hinges and flapping noisily in the breeze, the cracked windows neighbouring the vast amount of rusted holes in each wall. It was all there, exactly the way he remembered. It took a while for his mouth to finally close, and when it did, he looked back at his mom and said, "Our old house!"

Grace exited the car, finally letting Pin-bot out. The wound-up helper-bot took to the open air in an instant.

Grace walked up next to Jacob and stood beside him. For once, her hands rested against her hips for reasons that did not directly concern her. "It's just the way we left it."

She was trying to call up memories of when they had lived there, but Jacob interrupted.

"Can I?" he asked, his leg already coiled back and ready to spring forward.

Grace smiled. "Of course you can. This is what we came here for. It's still *our* house." She gestured over at the car. "Just help me with the box first. Then we can—"

Jacob lunged toward the house. He used his second generation limbs to clear all four of the rusty steps leading to porch. A thin door, kept upright by rusted hinges, did little to separate the outside from the house's dark interior. Jacob disappeared inside before the door could even close.

"Be careful!" his mom cried out, although there was no reason for her to be concerned. Jacob knew this house better than the one they had just left behind, so it wasn't like he would stumble in the darkness and fall.

"Mom! You coming?" Jacob yelled, from somewhere deep inside the house.

"Guess the box can wait." Grace went to the car, closed the doors and then made her way up the four steps leading into the house, allowing Pin-bot the chance to freely regain her composure on her own.

Jacob stood at the entrance to a room toward the back of the house, his hand bracing his weight against the door frame, empty cans of *Pure Blend* by feet. His face lit up with a smile. Other than a few slivers of light, caused by exposed seams in the walls, the room was dark. That didn't bother Jacob one bit. He could see everything he needed to see. He knew where everything was, and where everything should be. It was exactly the way he had left it. Trophies were scattered everywhere and experiments in all their stages concealed most of the floor. It was a mess—exactly the way he liked it. "My old room!"

Grace stepped up next to Jacob. She leaned against the door frame, her hand well above his. "Yes, your old room." She took a moment to survey the mess. "Didn't think I'd ever say this, but, I kind of miss this."

"Our house?"

"Yes, but also the mess you left in here."

Jacob looked up, only to see the distorted perspective of his mom standing over him. "I *would* have cleaned it up."

"I know, Jacob. It's not your fault. We were in a rush to get out of here." Grace waved her hand into the room. "Go on, then. It's your room, and your mess. I know you want to see it all again. No point in standing out here."

Jacob wrapped his arm around her leg and gave it a gentle nudge with the side of his face. "Thanks, Mom!" Jacob entered the room so completely overwhelmed by his past that he hardly knew where to begin. Trophies, old experiments, even empty cans of *Pure Blend* were given the same amount of attention—a quick scan and then a toss over his shoulder. He repeated the routine with most of the objects in his room until he finally reached the far wall. A covered window, too high for him to see out of, stared down at him. He turned and looked back at the path he had just taken. He didn't see Pin-bot anywhere, but his mom had followed and now stood next to him.

"Something wrong, Jacob? You've gone quiet all of a sudden. Miss your new room already?"

Jacob looked up. The expression on his face had lost all signs of excitement. While he was thrilled to see his old room and his things, there had been a reason why they left this house in the first place. Being back seemed like a contradiction. "Mom? Why did you bring me here? I know it wasn't for my trophies. We have enough of them back at our new place. And I know it wasn't for this mess. I can make one anywhere."

"You're right, Jacob. Although I did want us to see our old house one final time, this wasn't the real reason why we came." Grace pulled away the shutters over the lone window, allowing pale light to fill the dimly set room. Using her foot, she nudged a small, metal box up against the wall. "Go on. See for yourself."

It wasn't as if Jacob would be surprised at what he saw out there. He had been out there before. Many times. He knew their house was situated on a hill overlooking flat, barren land. He knew there was a distant mountain range that serrated the horizon with its peaks and valleys. *Why does she want me to see these again*? Jacob climbed up on the box, not concerned that even his second generation limbs still weren't adequate enough for some things. He clamped his fingers onto the window sill, pulled up, and looked out the window. His eyes grew wide at what they saw. "Pods!" he cried. "The launch site!"

"Yes, Jacob. It's the reason we left. I knew this area would be chosen as the launch site. That flat surface would be put to perfect use. I was hoping that maybe they would relocate, but, as you can see, that didn't happen. That's why I had to move us. I didn't want to be living so close." She sighed. "Didn't like having the Mayor being so close."

"I don't blame you." Jacob adjusted his vision so that he could see into the distance. The telephoto effect blurred the details, but Jacob could see the rows of pods settled neatly on their designated launching pads. He noticed faint movement all around which could only mean one thing. "They're still working out there."

Jacob didn't have to look up very high to see the moon looming large over the entire site. Its dull-grey surface never looked so uninviting. "Moon's almost here. Final preparations." He climbed down off of the box. There was something unsettling about what his mom had promised him while inside the car. She told him that they were not going to the launch site, but that's exactly where they were now. "You brought us back here just for this?"

Grace lazily pressed her back into the wall. "I remember you saying you wanted to visit our old house again. And seeing as how this *is* the launch site, I thought, why not?"

"Why not what? I didn't ask to come to the launch site."

"Since we *are* going to be the last ones here, I thought we might as well see them off. Wherever their journey takes them."

"A final goodbye?"

"Just to make it official."

Jacob did a quick calculation. "You know something, Mom? That's not a bad idea. We might not ever see them again." Jacob ignored the box and stood on the very tips of his feet. "But we're not going to see anything from this window. We need a better angle."

"What do you calculate?"

Jacob gestured toward the door. "I calculate that we should go outside and see them off. Maybe even wave at them if we feel like it."

"Outside it is. Not sure about the waving part though. Don't want to attract attention."

Jacob ran through the kitchen but stopped when he saw Pin-bot inside a box on one of the shelves. "Hey, let's go, Pin-bot! We're going outside. You coming with us?"

Not able to shift from side-to-side, Pin-bot simply let out an apologetic *beep*.

"Why not?"

"She's in her old charger," Grace said, catching up to Jacob. "Her batteries must be low. I knew they would be after all the flying she was doing inside the car."

"Too bad. She won't get to see them leave."

"She would probably shut down before we even made it outside. It's best that she recharges herself. Looks like it just you and me."

"Bye, Pin-bot. Charge well. I'll be sure to tell you everything that happens." *Probably nothing interesting.*

"Beep-beep," Pin-bot said, with crescent-shaped eyes followed by hearts.

* * *

Jacob and his mom found a convenient location situated on the hill overlooking the barren landscape—the perfect vantage point. Grace sat down almost immediately, while Jacob seemed poised to continue further down the hill. He scanned the horizon, absorbing everything in sight. He could see blurred outlines of the pods, the launch pads, the cannon, and even the straggling workers scrambling to find their own launch pads to secure themselves into.

"That's far enough," Grace called out. "We can see everything we need to see from here."

"Can't see everything. Where's the Mayor and Brute?" He went back and flopped down next to his mom. *Where's Hope?*

"I'm sure they're all down there. Might just be difficult to see everything underneath the moon's shadow. It's getting really close, isn't it?"

"It's almost here. Good thing we're over here, and not down there. I wouldn't want to be caught underneath the moon when it finally hits."

"I don't think anyone would." As Grace sat there, the moon's intensifying shadow was making her sensors uneasy. She turned to Jacob for reassurance. "This assignment of yours…how sure are you about it? I mean, once they leave, I don't think they're coming back, especially for us."

"I'm almost sure," Jacob replied, not sounding as confident as his mom had hoped. "I mean, I did the calculations. Everything should work out."

"Did one of your calculations include sitting here and watching something the size of the moon come crashing down on us?"

Jacob snickered. "It's not going to hit Earth the way you see it right now. Once the Mayor fires off the cannon, the moon will break into pieces."

"The cannon? What cannon?"

Jacob pointed at the second largest object in the distance, still aimed at its approaching target in the sky. "*That* cannon."

The glow in Grace's eyes turned to pinpoints of light. "Cannon..." she said "That...that's same one he used before?"

"Yes, it's the same one."

Grace practically lunged at Jacob who had to shift to one side so she wouldn't knock him over. "He attempted to do the same thing a long time ago...*It didn't work*!"

"Don't worry, Mom! Brute fixed it. He said it will work this time."

"Brute? You trust Brute?"

"He's not as bad as you think."

"But Jacob! What he did to Wheeler and Vision—"

"I know," Jacob lowered his head. "I know..."

"And you still trust him?"

"I trust that sooner or later, he'll find out that programs can be overridden, and that orders don't always need to be followed."

"I don't even know what that's supposed to mean, Jacob."

He squared off in front of his mom. "Just trust me on this. I did the calculations. I know what I'm doing."

Grace had to look beyond her jagged reflection in Jacob's eyes to see the sincerity behind them. The bright-blue glow had never been so dominate. "Okay..." she said, attempting to calm herself. "Okay...Let's just say it works this time. The cannon is able to destroy the moon...then what?"

"The pieces will fall from the sky and land on Earth. And then..." Jacob shrugged. "...we wait."

"We wait..."

"Yes. We wait."

Grace let out a nervous laugh. "We wait..."

"That's what I said."

"Okay, fine. We wait...For what, exactly?"

Jacob sighed. "Don't you see, Mom? The pieces will land and spread evenly across the surface of the planet. They will hit with just enough force to cause Earth to move. Earth *did* move at one time. You said so yourself. When it begins to move again, friction from within will cause the core, or the 'heart', as the professor would say, to warm. The warmth will rise, melting the frozen *Pure Blend* from deep inside the Earth. Then the *Pure Blend* will return to the surface."

Jacob's mom sat there waiting, hoping that Jacob's explanation would continue. It didn't. "And? What happens after that?"

"What do you mean?"

"I just want to know what happens after that."

"*Life*, that's what happens. Simple as that. All we have to do is sit back and wait."

"Okay...we wait. You said that already, and I believe you."

"So what's the problem?"

"The problem is, what if it doesn't work?" Grace turned her attention straight at the moon. "It's not like we have many options if this doesn't work."

Jacob reached over and grabbed his mom's arm. "You have to trust me on this, Mom. You trusted me with all of my experiments up to now, and every one of them brought home a trophy. You have to trust me one last time."

Jacob held her arm tight and continued to hold on while she took a moment of deep, sustained calculations. She finally nodded. "Okay…I trust you, Jacob. Always have."

"Wait and see."

"Yes…wait and see."

* * *

The last of the workers took their positions on the few remaining launch pads. They were cramped tightly together, shoulder-to-shoulder, with no room to even properly settle in. Arms hung awkwardly outside of the launch pad barriers, while limbs overlapped each other. Brute stood by the overcrowded launch pads and saw his comrades to the very end. He watched, as their eyes dimmed and their functions slowed, soon to enter a dormant state. Brute could not join them just yet, as his orders were still not completed.

A final pod stood next to a launch pad which was occupied by a single pod. Brute was the only one capable of making the lift which was the only reason he was still active. Pistons hissed, as he hoisted the last pod off of the ground and gently place it on the launch pad. He had to reposition it a few times in order to reserve enough room. When he was fully satisfied that all orders had been fulfilled, Brute stepped back and gave the site one final scanning. When his eyes met with the last launch pad in the distance, he stepped back. Something did not seem right. He restarted his scan. The results were exactly the same. Three launch pads and their contents were missing. Could they have been left back at the work site? "Impossible," Brute said out loud. He was meticulous about these sorts of things. There was absolutely no chance that he had forgotten any of them.

The Mayor suddenly appeared from behind the cannon that stood on a slight rise overlooking the launch pads. He was inspecting every last corner of its construction and examining the repairs made to it. He bent toward a complex arrangement of gears located at the base of the cannon and placed his massive hand between one of the gear's interlocking teeth, throwing his weight behind it. The gears bit into each other, slightly shifting the cannon's overall direction. The Mayor nodded.

"Sir! The launch pads are ready. But three of them seem to be—"

"What about this?" The Mayor tilted his head to the cannon. "Is it ready?"

Brute lowered one of the plates over his eyes. He didn't know why the Mayor would ask him again, knowing very well that the repairs had been made. "Yes, sir. It's aimed at the moon. The only thing left to do is load it."

The Mayor pulled his hand out from the gears, allowing the cannon to reposition itself back to its normal position. "Still adjustable?"

"Yes, sir."

"Good. The Mayor made his way to the launch pad that Brute had just finished loading. He stared at the two of pods taking up space on its surface. His face suddenly became rigid. "What is this?"

Brute scanned the launch pad but did not see anything out of place. He had arranged the pods efficiently enough that there was still room for at least three more occupants. "I…I don't understand, sir."

"This one has pods on it."

"Yes, sir. They all have pods on them."

"No," The Mayor said, before Brute had any chance to explain. "The one Hope and I will board will *not* have pods."

Brute took a moment to scan the rest of the launch pads. None of them were capable of taking the pair of pods. "But, sir, I…I don't know where else to put them."

The Mayor pointed to the ground next to the launch pad. "Leave them here."

"You mean…leave them here, on Earth?"

"Is that a problem?"

Brute shook his head. "I…I can't do that, sir. You promised them. You promised all of them."

The Mayor squared up in front of Brute. The glow of his eyes intensified, as he looked down at the concerned worker. "You seem to have trouble following orders lately. Hope is waiting for me. When I get back here, I expect my launch pad to be ready." The Mayor turned his back on Brute. "That's an order," he said, walking away.

Brute stood motionless until the Mayor was out of his sights. Frustrated, he slammed his hand against the launch pad, causing it to sway back and forth.

* * *

"Guess the Mayor and Brute were down there after all," Jacob said, staring off into the distance. "Looks like Brute just finished loading the last of the pods. They must be almost ready to go. Good thing too." He pointed up at the moon. "Look, Mom. Look how close it's getting. You can see all the craters from here."

Grace nodded, though she did not look up. She kept her head lowered and had both hands crossed over her lap. The look of concern on her face was easily noticeable. "Yes, it's getting close alright."

Jacob sighed. "I told you there's nothing to worry about. We should be safe here. There's no way fragments of the moon will come up this far. And even if a chunk does head this—"

"It's not that." Grace looked up, smiled and then patted the ground next to her. "Sit down. I need to talk to you."

"Now?"

"Yes, now."

Jacob made his way over, but he was hesitant about it. *What could she possibly need to talk to me about? Nothing could be more important than what is about to happen and she wants to talk?* He sat down next to his mom, leaving a slight gap between them.

"Do we still have time? I mean, before the moon gets here."

Jacob nodded. "We still have a bit of time, but not much. Did you forget something?"

"Yes." Grace shifted her body so that it angled sharply in Jacob's direction, closing the gap he had purposely created. "I need to tell you something before it's too late."

"Okay. I'm listening." Jacob slid slightly away from her intense gaze. "What do you need to tell me?"

"First of all, Jacob, I need to know something. The professor..." Grace had to pause. *If only I had stayed with him. He might be sitting next to us at this very moment.*

"What about the professor?"

Grace straightened a bit. "Did he ever get the chance to show you those pages?"

"Like the ones I found in the box in my room? Yes. I decoded every last page. The data is still on my hard-drive."

"Perfect."

"Well, no, not exactly. Even after I decoded them, I still don't know what they mean."

"That's because you probably missed a few."

"I know the Mayor had a few pages. I wasn't able to decode them. But the ones you had and the ones I found at Wheeler's place should have had enough information for me to make sense of them. But I still don't understand. And the ones from Professor Smith made everything even more confusing."

"Well, Jacob, you don't need to decode anymore. I think it's time I explained everything to you."

"You were able to decode the pages?"

Grace let out a brittle laugh. "No. Unlike you, I'm not capable of decoding. It wasn't a function that I needed when I was made."

Jacob shook his head in confusion. "How are you supposed to explain things to me when you're not able to decode those pages?"

"There was never a need to." Grace tapped her chest. "It's all on my hard-drive."

"Your...hard-drive? But...but how?"

"Simple. I was there when it happened."

Jacob felt his entire body shift. He had to brace himself otherwise he would be at the bottom of the hill at any moment. "I...I don't understand. What do you mean, you were there?"

"I know this might be difficult for you to understand, Jacob, but what you decoded from those pages, *actually* happened. Eve, her father—"

"Eve?"

"Yes, Jacob. Eve. She's the girl in those pages."

"I realize that, Mom. You met her?"

"Yes. I was there. So was the professor, the Mayor, Hope…" Grace paused. Her eyes locked firmly in place. "And most importantly…*you*."

Jacob's hard-drive whirled, as he threw his hand against his chest-plate. "Me?" he cried. "I was there? Me? Jacob?"

"We were all there."

Jacob waved his hands back and forth. "Wait-wait-wait…I don't understand how this is possible!"

Grace took hold of his hands and forced them down to his sides. "That's what I'm trying to tell you." She stared deep into Jacob's wondering eyes. "Just calm down, and let me explain everything. Please?"

Jacob forced his hands out from his mom's grasp and threw them out to his sides. "Okay…" he said unconvincingly. "Okay. I'm listening. Go on. I'm extremely curious to know what it all means."

"Good," Grace said, repositioning herself. "Just...Brace yourself, Jacob."

"Seems like that's all I've been doing lately."

Grace sighed, tapping her finger against her chin. "Where to begin, where to begin…"

"How about the very beginning? There's no point in leaving any of it out now."

"Ah, perfect. From the beginning, then." Grace sat back and rested her hands inside her lap. Her inner core began to hum. Her hard-drive spun violently in order to retrieve information that she had stored deep along its inner edges. Once they were made current, she finally began. "I was working with a patient when I heard my name being called.…

Chapter Ten

"Hey, Grace!" Jan, the nurse, called from the other end of the brightly-lit room.

Grace retracted the ratchet she had been using on her patient and glanced over. Jan pointed toward one of the many windows facing out to the waiting room.

"My visions a bit blurred, but it looks like it's him again," Jan said.

Grace looked over. She could barely see the top of his head because of the window sill. Behind him was a long, winding line. Many more were waiting for repairs. They were noisy and impatient, as expected. Grace was impressed. He already made it back to the front of the line. "Thanks, Jan."

"Do you want me to ask him to leave again?" Jan asked.

Jan was busy. It was her job to sort out parts, new and old, and have them ready for specialists such as Grace. It was a simple task made difficult due to Jan's poor vision. The lenses of her eyes weren't what they used to be, and she was too selfless to ask for an upgrade. Jan was a few generations older than Grace, as evident from the patches of rust already forming on her exterior, but they shared one thing in common. Even during times of great uncertainty, they were always smiling. It was something programmed into them. They could override this minor program at anytime but knew it was best to keep it enabled. It was the only way they would remain sane for the entire work day.

Grace wanted to make sure her patient was stabilized before she left. She took pride in everything she did. A quick clockwise turn of the ratchet here, a couple adjusted bolts there and she was fully satisfied that the leg was secured onto its new owner. "I'll be right back," she said, smiling as usual. She walked over to the window.

Jan was surprised to see Grace making her way back to her patient only a moment later. "Was I right? Or were my eyes seeing things?"

"Your eyes detected correctly. It was him again."

"What was it this time?"

"The same as usual. Dents, scratches, torn wiring." Grace smiled at Jan. "He wants upgrades. Same old story."

"What did you tell him?"

"Same as always."

"Another rejection."

"Unfortunately. All of our parts have to be reserved for major injuries and upgrades. He doesn't fall into any of those categories. I hate sending him off this way, but there's not much any of us can do for him at the moment."

"No need to explain to me, Grace. I work here, remember?" She smiled. "I'm sure he'll get what he needs...eventually."

"I hope so. Generations like him should be embraced at a time like this, not rejected." Grace sat her patient up and tested out the new leg she had just attached. Everything seemed to work perfectly so she sent him on his way. She crossed his name off her list. Another repair completed. The day had only recently begun, but her list of crossed out names was long and impressive.

Grace was a motivated worker, young and eager to learn. Ever since she had been built, she wanted nothing more than to fill her empty hard-drive with useful information. Only recently, she had been taught how to attach and reattach limbs, and there wasn't a shortage of patients for her to test her newly acquired skills. Repairs were her speciality, but complete upgrades were becoming more frequent.

"Ready for another one?" Jan asked. "I can bring in another patient for you while you set up."

"Human or one of us?"

Jan scanned the window. "There are more of us out there, but I should really bring in a human next. Might as well deal with them first. They're our priority after all."

"Sure, Jan. Bring them in."

"Probably won't shorten the line at all, unfortunately."

"But at least it'll keep it moving."

* * *

"Wait..." Jacob said, forcing his mom to pause, "you also fixed humans?"

Grace was hoping to answer all of Jacob's questions after she finished her story, as she was sure there would be many, but Jacob wasn't the type who would wait. "Yes, Jacob," she replied. "Well...sort of. I had just started learning how to do human repairs during that time. I never actually worked on a human before that day."

"When was this? How long before I was built?"

"Before the Earth no longer moved. Before the moon was nothing more than a subtle distraction in the sky, and before any mention of the future was restricted to what you could accomplish in a single day. It was a time when we co-existed as one. Humans and mechanical beings. Creators living side-by-side with their creations. We were in perfect harmony—meticulously balanced on opposite sides. We had been created from their design, born to aid them in their daily lives. We performed the most basic tasks for them, from cooking their food, to cleaning their homes. Eventually, we began doing the jobs that they found too *inhuman*, like fight their wars. We did so without question or remorse. That's when we became a constant reminder of their lethargy and inadequacy. They needed us more than we needed them at this point. Balance, as you may know, Jacob, is very delicate at times. One mere shift to either side can cause it to crumple.

Earth's resources were dwindling. They, the humans, had been using it up at a staggering rate, bleeding it dry. They did little to restore its health, and by the time they tried to reverse the damage they had done, it was already too late. The planet was on its last breaths, and the humans were the ones who ultimately suffered for their ways. With their evolution weakening, they did the only thing they knew how—they built more of us in order to help them lengthen their time here. Balance was shifting to our side.

I barely had enough parts installed on me to be even called a third generation at that time."

Jacob snickered. "You? A third generation?"

"Yes, Jacob. I was new once. Maybe not as advanced as you, but I still had a purpose. I was built to help others, mainly our kind. It was a small hospital that I worked in, but at the time, it was the busiest. I would watch them come in. Some needing new arms and legs in order to help their human owner perform tasks quicker. Others required new hard-drives so they could help their owners calculate complex tasks more efficiently. For me, my job was fairly simple. Pull off the old part and then replace it with a new one. Every now and then, I would keep them around a bit longer, just so I could help them get accustomed to their new parts." Grace shrugged. "You know, make sure they were comfortable with their new functions. But in the end, they were usually out the door, as soon as the part had been installed. Our kind was easy in this way, Jacob. Repairs and upgrades…it was just a matter of installing them. Humans, on the other hand, were much more complex. They required immediate attention, and a special kind of knowledge. This was something I wasn't built for. When it came to human patients, we relied on the best…"

* * *

The door with an inscribed *333* above its frame opened, temporarily exposing a long hallway. Like always, Grace and Jan immediately stopped working. Every time this particular door opened, it always managed to attract their attention. And why wouldn't it? This door was always used to admit a human patient, who would walk in accompanied by the lone male doctor of the hospital. A short while later, that same patient would exit the room…as a mechanical being—the same as Grace, Jan and the doctor.

This time was no different. The doctor took his patient to the far end of the room and put him on a long steel table where he worked for about an hour. When he was finished, he walked with his patient all the way back to the door and sent him on his way with a wave. A smile permeated his face, as his patient left the hospital.

The doctor stood tall and proud, not even bothered by the patches of rust forming on his exterior. Built by one of the largest manufactures of mechanical parts at the time, the doctor was unlike any other mechanical being. He was custom made—built solely for the purpose of fixing and repairing not his kind but humans. He knew the human anatomy even better than most humans, and because of this unique speciality, he was kept busy from the very moment he stepped off the assembly line.

"Another successful conversion, Doctor Smith?" Grace said.

"Absolutely," Doctor Smith said. "It's becoming routine now. My last patient was the quickest conversion I've ever completed." He glanced out the window into the waiting room. "A few more out there, I see."

"Adding our upgrades to them just isn't enough anymore. Most need to be completely converted."

"That's an understatement. Seems like all humans are sick or injured these days. Been seeing more of our kind than humans leaving the hospital lately."

"You're busying converting them, while I'm busying fixing and upgraded them."

"Wish I had many more of you, Grace. I've never met anyone so willing to learn. I just wished I had more time to teach you. Someone else will take my place sooner or later. These old limbs of mine will rust over, eventually."

* * *

"Doctor Smith?" Jacob said, confused. "Is he the same as—"

"Yes, Jacob. Professor Smith. Back then, he was known as 'Doctor'."

"When did he become the professor?"

"Let me explain..."

* * *

Between Grace, Jan and Doctor Smith, they had completely withered the waiting room's line down to nothing. The end of another day with only a few casualties.

Whenever door *333* would open, Grace and Jan would expect to see Doctor Smith standing with another newly converted patient. Throughout the day, however, there had been a few times when the doctor stood alone, silent and distraught. Humans were not like their creations. They were...different. Attaching a mechanical limb, such as an arm, was fairly routine now. In fact, most humans at this time had some sort of mechanical part attached to them due to injuries or sickness. It allowed for complete functionality and, at times, could even be life saving. But there were parts of the human anatomy that once damaged or severely ravaged by sickness could not be repaired using mechanical parts. Doctor Smith did everything he could save them, but in the end, even he could only watch, as they exhaled their final breath. He was always devastated to see one of them die within his hands. His main priority was to save them by any means necessary. That was why he had experimented with replacing human parts with mechanical parts a short while ago. Most humans were against this at first, but eventually, even they realized that it was the only way. Complete conversions, from humans to mechanical beings, were still new to Doctor Smith. Internal organs, such as the heart and brain, were complex and extremely fragile.

Still, having only a few human casualties for the entire work day was actually decent, considering the condition most of them arrived in.

Jan had already left for the day. She lived the furthest away from the hospital and would always leave before Grace and Doctor Smith.

Grace finished putting her tools away. She wanted to stay and learn more from Doctor Smith, as she did most days after work, but her battery was running low. It would need to be fully recharged if she wanted to make it through the next day. She walked over to door *333* and peeked inside. Down the long hallway, lined with display cases and closed doors, was one final room. It was the doctor's favourite room, and she knew she could always find him back there. Sometimes she wondered if he ever left. Light from the room seeped into the hallway. She could hear random tapping of metal from inside.

"Doctor Smith? Are you back there?"

The tapping stopped. "Yes, Grace. I'm here."

"I thought the last patient for the night left a while ago. What's all that noise coming from?"

Grace heard Doctor Smith laugh. "No one's back here with me. Just a broken chair I've been wanting to fix."

"Need any help? That's what I was built for."

"No. I'll be fine."

"Okay, then. I'm leaving."

"Wait. Do you need a ride home?"

"It's okay, Doctor. I have my car here."

Again, she heard Doctor Smith laugh. "The one with the wheels? How's she holding up?"

"Noisy, bumpy, rusty…but it still runs."

"Let me know when it finally dies. I can always use the spare parts."

"Of course, Doctor. It probably won't be long now. See you tomorrow."

"Take care, Grace."

Grace walked out into the waiting room. As expected, it was a complete mess. Chairs were tipped over, garbage was everywhere, and a long trail of dried mud stained the floor. Grace sighed. Her battery was too low for her to do anything about the mess. And there would just be more mess the following day. She walked over to the main panel on the wall and began switching off the lights one by one. The room became as dark as the night's sky. Grace barely had her hand wrapped around the door's single-sided handle when the door suddenly swung open, pushing her back. A man stumbled through and collapsed inside her arms. It was a human. A thick, red fluid, seeping out from the man's body, stained her arms.

He looked up at Grace. He had dark-brown eyes in a face that was stained with that red fluid. "Help…me...Don't…let me…die like this…"

Grace did an immediate scan of the man's body. His left arm was severely torn, and it appeared the bone was out of the socket. A deep gash in one leg exposed deep-red fibers that Grace was unfamiliar with. He had only taken a few steps inside the hospital but already, he added deep-red stains to the messy floor. "Everything's going to be fine." Grace wasn't sure if what she had told him was true or not. She had been programmed to be as helpful as she could, and any sort of reassurance would fall directly within those parameters. The man coughed and spit up some of the same red fluid that was seeping out of wounds on his entire body. Grace knew she was unable to help him. Humans were not her speciality. Thankfully, Doctor Smith was still here. She gently lowered the man onto the floor. "I'm going to go get help. Stay here."

The man grabbed her arm. "Wait!" He reached underneath his torn, stained shirt and pulled out a thick bundle of pages. Not surprisingly, they were tainted with streaks and blotches of the red fluid. "Take…these…Hold them for me…" The man forcefully shoved the bundle of pages into Grace's hand. "They're my...past…" he said, as his eyes closed.

Grace did not understand what he meant but did as she was told. She tucked the pages inside a seam behind her breast-plate and went for help.

Moments later, Grace returned with Doctor Smith. They hurried over to the man.

"He came through the door, Doctor. I don't know what's wrong with him, but it seems like he's about to shut down."

"Dying," Doctor Smith said. "Humans die." He picked the man up off of the floor and cradled him in his arms. Once he got a clear view of the man's face, Doctor Smith's eyes suddenly burst open. "Mr. Evans?" he cried.

"You know him, Doctor?"

"Yes, of course, Grace. His name is Michael Evans. He's my creator."

Grace stood back. She was lost for words. She knew that humans had created her kind, but she never thought she would meet one of her creators—directly.

"Severe damage to the deltoid region," Doctor Smith accessed, as he scanned his creator's body. "Trauma to the head and neck, deep lacerations to the arm and upper pectoral muscle." He looked up at Grace, who did not understand anything the Doctor was saying. "Predicting heavy internal bleeding in the chest cavity."

"What does that mean, Doctor?"

"It means he's dying."

The man's eyes opened, and he spoke in a bare whisper. "Smith? Is…is that you?"

"Yes, sir. Please…don't move. You've sustained many injuries."

"It…it was your kind," the man said. "They…attacked me. Is that what we built you for? To…destroy your very own creators?"

Grace reeled back. He was injured by his own creations, yet here he was, asking his creations for their help.

"Please…fix me," the man said. "Don't…let me die. I…have to get back to her."

"To who, sir?" Doctor Smith asked.

"Eve…"

"Who is Eve?" Grace asked the doctor in a whisper.

"His daughter."

"I have to…get back to her…" The man collapsed in Doctor Smith's arms.

"We need to try to save him, Grace. Prepare the table and ready the life-support."

"Life-support? But, Doctor, I've never—"

"It's the machine on top of the metal cart next to the table. We need to hook Mr. Evans to it. Now!"

"Yes, Doctor!" Grace exited the waiting room and made her way through door *333*.

"Everything is going to be fine, sir," Doctor Smith said. "I'll do everything I can to save you."

Following Grace, he carried the patient to the operating room. He hurried by the chair he been repairing before. It lay in pieces, with bent legs and an unattached backing plate.

Doctor Smith might not have been efficient at repairing things but he was unrivalled when it came to human anatomy. He put Mr. Evans on the table and began the work of trying to repair the damaged body.

A short time later, there was a quiet hum coming from the medium-sized machine that sat on top of a metal cart. Flowing from the back of it was a messy bundle of wiring and tubing. The ends were attached directly into the side of Mr. Evans.

Grace watched over the unconscious man, as Doctor Smith studied the monitor Mr. Evans was also hooked up to. She gently ran her hand across the newly attached arm. Like the table he was laying on, it felt cold, smooth and familiar. She could see her reflection in its surface.

"Be careful," Doctor Smith warned. "His new parts need time to heal."

"Just being curious, Doctor. It always fascinates me to see our limbs working on a human body. I think he should be happy with his new arm and leg."

Though it was subtle, Grace noticed Doctor Smith shaking his head, as if he was not pleased. "Something wrong, Doctor?"

"You pick up on things so easily, don't you, Grace?"

"I've known you for a while now, Doctor. I notice things." She glanced at the monitor. There was a simple green outline displayed depicting Mr. Evans anatomy. Green around the arm and leg had been replaced by a red outline, exactly where human parts had now become mechanical. Grace saw random patches of yellow inside the green outline, and she wasn't sure if they were normal or not. "How is he?"

Doctor Smith shook his head. "It doesn't look good."

"But you've attached new limbs. He seems stable."

"Yes…for now. But he's still dying. Those yellow patches you see there," he pointed at the monitor, "that is a sickness. Some sort of—"

A green line on the monitor suddenly spiked, as the patient shifted his body to one side and faced the doctor and Grace. "Where...where am I?"

Doctor Smith turned the monitor away. Mr. Evans did not need to see what was on it. "Just relax, sir," he said, gently holding him down. "Try not to move. Your new parts still have not healed. Your body needs time to adjust to them."

"My...my new...parts?" Mr. Evans brought his hand to his face. It rattled and creaked.

"We still need to inject lubrication," Grace said. "That won't occur until you're fully healed."

Mr. Evans saw his reflection in his hand's surface, something that was impossible only moments ago. The green line on the monitor spiked wildly. "No...*No*! What...what have you done? What...what the hell have you done to me?!"

"Please, sir," Grace said. "Be still. You will do more damage to yourself."

After a moment, he relaxed and was absolutely motionless on the table. Maybe it was shock.

"We had no choice," Doctor Smith explained. "This was the only way. Your body had sustained near fatal injuries."

"We restored complete functionality," Grace said, easing herself away from the table and the unhappy patient.

Raising his new arm, Mr. Evans twisted and turned his hand. It clicked with every one of his movements.

"That will all go away eventually," Doctor Smith said. "It's normal."

Mr. Evans brought up his other arm and compared it to his mechanical one. The difference was undeniable. Everything on his new arm moved so much more fluidly—it felt completely solid. He made a fist and noticed how strong his grip was, even with little effort being exerted. Finally, he twisted his hand, and it went all the way around, turning a full 360 degrees. He was shocked. This was something he could have never done before.

"You'll be able to do much more than you're used to."

"And no more pain," Grace added.

Mr. Evans sighed. "Didn't think I'd be a recipient of the very parts that I helped create and design."

Doctor Smith patted him on the shoulder. "And I must say, sir, you did a fine job."

The man lowered his arms. His left hand clanged off the table, while his right hand landed with a soft thud. He looked up at the ceiling. In the steel sheeting, he saw his entire body reflected there. There was wiring and tubing attached to the side of body being fed by a strange-looking machine. "I guess everything's okay, then? I survived?"

No one spoke. He saw the doctor and the one who had helped him exchange a nervous glance, before she stepped even further away. "Doctor? Is...is there something wrong with me?" Mr. Evans grabbed the doctor's arm with his new hand. It clamped down with such force, it made Doctor Smith wince. "I...I'm okay, right? You fixed me. I'm okay, now?"

Doctor Smith shook his head.

"What's wrong with me? Tell me. Damn it, I have the right to know!"

"Yes, sir, you do..." Doctor Smith braced himself. "During our scans of your internal structure, we found a virus...Cancer..."

Grace turned the monitor around so that Mr. Evans could see for himself. The yellow patches were dimly reflected in his soft, delicate eyes. His hand slipped off of the doctor's arm and clanged off the table. He looked away. A tear rolled down the side of his face.

"I'm sorry, sir," Doctor Smith said. "It's something I've seen many times before. Most do not survive."

"Eve...I have to get back to Eve..." Mr. Evans' voice trailed off. "I can't die like this...Not when Eve still needs me."

"There is a way, sir. I've been successful a few times."

Mr. Evans immediately grabbed the doctor. "How? Tell me! I'll do anything!"

Doctor Smith reached out and tapped the hard surface of the newly attached arm.

"No!" Mr. Evans cried, falling back against the table. "No! Absolutely not!"

"A full body conversion would be the only way to completely rid your body of the cancer."

The room filled with a dreadful silence. Mr. Evans reached over and touched the tubing that he was attached to. He felt it pulsating. "When I created you, I never thought I would ever become one of you." He shook head, shoving the tubing to one side. "I… I can't. I can't do this."

Grace walked around the table and rearranged the tubing, making sure it was still properly attached. "What choice do you have, sir?"

"I would rather die."

Doctor Smith stepped forward. He had heard enough. It took a lot to rattle Doctor Smith's sensors, and Mr. Evans had just done a good job of it. "Your daughter...Will she be able to survive without her father? I know she means a lot to you, sir. Your life is directly linked to hers and will always be."

After a moment, Mr. Evans sighed. "I...I can't die. I can't leave her alone."

"You know your options." Doctor Smith backed away, allowing Mr. Evans a chance to decide on his fate.

The painful image of his daughter that he left behind still burned inside Mr. Evans' head. Her emerald greens never faded, even when he handed her the revolver. She was brave enough to take it. Brave enough to watch he father leave her. *I had to leave her. I had no choice. I saved her. She's still alive. I have to get back to her. No matter what it takes...or what form I become.*

"I'll do it," he finally said. He grabbed Grace by the arm. "But first, I need you to do something for me...Those pages…"

Grace retrieved the pages from the seam inside her breast-plate and held them out to him, but he refused to take them. She looked at the bundle and noted that the red stains had blackened, rendering many of the inscriptions useless.

"I want everything I wrote on them to be stored in my new memory," he said. "I don't want to forget about my past."

Doctor Smith took the pages from Grace. "I'll do my best to integrate as much as I can, sir."

"Thank you, Doctor. I knew someday that I would benefit from creating you."

"I was created to help your kind. Now please, relax, sir." The doctor turned the dial on the life-support machine a full turn clockwise. The tubing attached to Mr. Evans expanded. "When you awake, sir, you'll be strong once again."

Grace waited for Mr. Evans' eyes to close before whispering to the doctor, "Are you sure about this? Are we doing the right thing?"

"He's human, Grace...my creator. It's in my program to save them. I have no choice." Doctor Smith bustled around the table. "You go on, Grace. This is what *I* was built for."

"Good luck, Doctor."

* * *

Doctor Smith pushed the metal cart back into the corner of the room. The machine sitting on top of it was now quiet. Its wires and tubing were coiled in a neat bundle and stowed away underneath the cart. He took one final glance over at the monitor and was satisfied to see the entire outline of the figure was red. "Another conversion successfully completed."

As the new mechanical being came to life, shutters retracted from its eyes, allowing a deep-red glow to blend with the spotlight overhead. Lenses twisted and turned in their sockets, letting off a resounding buzz with each movement. He saw his reflection on the ceiling, but he looked nothing like he had before.

"Sir?" Doctor Smith said, leaning over his patient and breaking the monotony of the spotlight. "How are we?"

Mr. Evans took his time in replying. He scanned his entire reflection on the ceiling, not wanting to miss a single detail of his shiny, metal finish. Every part of him came together with a linear quality that had never been seen or felt before. Seams were everywhere, some even overlapping themselves. He could see the underlying structure between the gaps of the harden plating that constructed his body. He understood what he was looking at. He was now one of them.

"Alive," Mr. Evans said and seemed startled by his deep, metallic voice.

"My apologies, sir. It's the only voice we had on file."

"It's perfect...I'm perfect." Mr. Evans sat up. Gears and pistons in his body hissed and crackled.

"Wait, sir! Please rest. You're not fully functional yet. You need a few adjustments."

Mr. Evans pushed off of the table. "What more do I need?"

Both of this feet collided with the floor with such force it made the floor tremble. Doctor Smith staggered back to nearly the end of the room. Mr. Evans stood up, straightening the massive twin pistons in his back.

"Sir, we still need to tighten a few things and adjust the displacement in your upper body."

Mr. Evans rotated his arms, shifting his weight from one side to the next, testing his new body. "Why? Everything seems perfect. I feel perfect...Strong!" He glanced down at Doctor Smith, the glow in his eyes becoming stronger, automatically sharpened their halos within. "I feel reborn!"

"There's a problem with weight distribution, sir. With a few adjustments, we can realign some of your weight so you're not so top heavy."

With each step the giant mass took to walk toward Doctor Smith, the floor groaned and shifted. Doctor Smith backed up until he was against the far wall. Mr. Evans leaned toward the doctor. "You saved me. You gave me strength. But more importantly, you gave me new life. "

"That...that's what you created me for, sir."

Mr. Evans smiled and then back away. "This is a new day, Smith." He walked over to a door in the room and threw it open. Natural light surged inside. He looked out at the endless sky, painted over by soft, repetitive clouds. His new body shimmered in the sunlight, with streaks of highlights racing up and down the edges of each seam. "I am no longer weak." Mr. Evans glanced over his shoulder. He was being back-lit by the light from outside, making the glows in his eyes even more daunting. "Now I know why your kind was created," he said with a clenched jaw. "You are strong...We are strong." He turn his attention back outside. "The ones out there...they are weak. Just like I used to be."

"Please, sir. If you can just return to the table, I can begin adding—"

"This is the only way forward, Doctor. Our past is what's keeping us from growing...It's what's keeping us from evolving."

"I'm not sure what you mean by that, sir."

"Humans! They're the cancer of this Earth. And we need to extinguish them from our future, just like you extinguished me of my past."

Doctor Smith's hard-drive began to stutter. He could not process what Mr. Evans was telling him. Doctor's Smith's primary orders had been to save humans, not destroy them. Clearly, this wasn't the same man who had collapsed in his arms only a short while ago. How could someone who had been human suddenly turn on his own kind? It was more than Doctor Smith could comprehend.

"Let it be known, Doctor, that from this day forth, weakness will no longer influence our future."

"Sir?"

"We are the future. And I vow to rid Earth of its past—its weakness!" Mr. Evans lowered himself through the door frame and exited the room. His heavy strides buckled the ground beneath his feet.

Doctor Smith was left silenced. He stood motionless, as the door noisily rattled against its framing. The monitor that Mr. Evans had been hooked up to shifted to idle mode, but the doctor was able to catch a quick glimpse of the red outline just before the screen faded to black. He slid down the wall and sat down on the disassembled chair in the corner of the room. He buried his face inside his hands. "What...what have I done?"

* * *

Jacob stood up. "The Mayor!" he cried, throwing his arms out to the side. "He…he was Mr. Evans! A…*human*!"

Jacob's mom reached over and grabbed Jacob's arm, attempting to drag him back down to her side.

"How could he have been a human? After all he's said—after all he's done!"

"Jacob! Sit down, and let me explain!" She tugged on his arm a few more times.

He slowly lowered himself. "But…but…human…the Mayor…"

"Yes, Jacob. He was once a human." She paused, making sure that Jacob was calm. "You okay? Should I stop?"

Jacob shook his head. "No…no, Mom! I'm okay. Keep going. This is getting interesting."

You have no idea. "You see, Jacob," Grace continued, "once Mr. Evans became one of us, he vowed to keep us strong. He wanted to rid us of our past. Rid us of our weakness. Many of us agreed with him at first, and because he had support, he appointed himself as *Mayor*. He quickly gained more and more support and power until his followers always did as he ordered, even if that meant destroying their past."

"Humans…"

"Yes, Jacob. Humans. He thought that their weaknesses would spread to us, and that it was their presence here that was delaying our own evolution. The Mayor ordered all of the humans destroyed. And the easiest way he knew how was to eradicate their home. He built his army of workers and ordered them to do something unimaginable."

"Project Redemption...Stop Earth's rotation."

"Yes, Jacob. Earth died that day. Balance had now shifted completely to our side. But victory was still out of his hands. He thought he had destroyed them all, but one remained..."

* * *

"Sir," Brute said, "we're here."

Brute had been built to lead Project Redemption, and while many with the same model number had permanently shut down after that, he was still functional. He remained loyal to his creator. With the Mayor's guidance, Brute led his team to a large abandoned house just shy of a single mountain which cut into the horizon. While his team waited out front, Brute and the Mayor proceeded inside.

"In the basement," the Mayor said. "Last floor. That's where you'll find her."

Access to the last floor in the house was blocked by a massive, metal door. Brute clamped his enormous hand on the door's edge and awaited further orders.

"She's in there. You know what to do."

"Yes, sir." Brute ripped the door from its hinges with little effort. He directed his shoulder-mounted light deep inside the cold, damp room. In the corner, trembling with fear, was the last human on Earth. Brute walked over and picked her frail body off the floor. She struggled, but she was tiny inside his hand. "Awaiting orders, sir."

"Give her to me," the Mayor commanded. "I will have the honour of ridding us of this last one."

"Yes, sir." Brute extended his arm toward the Mayor who took his offering with one single sweep of his hand.

The Mayor brought her up to his face. "To our future," he said.

Just as the Mayor retracted his other hand, ready to end her life, he suddenly caught a glimpse of the girl's vivid-green eyes. They lit up the dim, drab room. The Mayor pulled back. His hard-drive began to stutter, filling the room with a deep, rumbling sound that echoed off the walls. The data he had ordered the doctor to load into his hard-drive, those many years ago, was made current.

He suddenly remembered her. He remembered who she was. He remembered who he was to her. With her still in his grasp, he dropped to his knees. The tremor that caused was powerful enough to stagger Brute back a few steps. The Mayor scanned her body. She was frail, thin and most of all...weak. Her internal structure was poking out through her outer layers in places. This wasn't how he had left her. "Eve..."

Eve looked deep into the eyes staring at her. It was difficult to see beyond the daunting-red glows, but something about the Mayor reminded her of someone—someone she once loved, someone who once promised her that he would never leave her side. "D-Dad..." she said, a pitch below a whisper. "Is...is that you, Daddy?"

The Mayor began to tremble. "Yes, Eve. It's me. Daddy..."

He relaxed his hold, and she was able to pry herself out of his hands. Even with the Mayor down on his knees, Eve stood no higher than his chest. She stared at the man—the thing—in front of her. This was not the one who had been lying next to her while they stared up at the stars. He wasn't the one who left her side in order to protect her from his own creations. He was no longer her kind—no longer human.

"Daddy? What...what have they done to you?" Eve backed away. "What...what have you become?"

"Strong. I've become strong."

"They...they killed you. You're no longer one of us."

"No, Eve. I'm alive. They saved me...*Just like they're going to save you.*"

Eve latched herself to the wall next to the room's only exit. "No..." she whimpered.

"Please, Eve. You have to come with me. You're weak. We have to save you before it's too late."

"No! I'll never become one of you!" Eve escaped out of the room.

"I'll get her, sir," Brute said.

"Stop!" the Mayor yelled. "No one is to touch her!" he ordered. "She's still a part of me."

"Sir, she's a human. She must be destroyed."

"She is not to be harmed. It's the only way we can carry out the conversion. Bring her back to me, *alive*! Your new order is to keep her safe. You are to protect her."

Brute looked hesitant. Up until now, he had been ordered to destroy every human that he had encountered. Keeping one safe would completely override one of his primary objectives.

"That's an order!" the Mayor yelled.

Loyalty was something Brute did not lack. "Yes, sir," he said, setting his new order to priority.

* * *

Grace walked away from the waiting room's window.

"Had to turn him away again, huh, Grace?" Jan said.

Jan's eyes had deteriorated over the years, but she could still detect subtle movements.

"Yes. He sure is persistent. He shows up three times a day now, instead of his usual two. More scratches and dents than ever, but they're still not enough to warrant an upgrade."

"Eventually, Grace. I know I've said this for years, but eventually, he'll get the upgrades he's looking for."

"I hope so." Grace glanced over at door *333*. "How's Doctor Smith doing? I hardly see him come out here anymore."

"Why should he? After Project Redemption, there are no more humans left for him to fix."

"I hear him doing something back there."

"He's doing some mechanical repairs. He was happy the way his chair turned out and now wants to repair everything he can get a hold of. Watch it, Grace," Jan joked. "He might take over your job one of these days."

Grace smiled. "I welcome it. My body is beginning to wear down from all this work. I might have to upgrade myself if I want to continue doing this."

A loud commotion suddenly sounded from the waiting room, as the door was violently pushed open and loud footsteps sounded. Grace ran to the window to see the Mayor charging through the waiting room, cradling something in his massive arms.

"Where is he? Where is Doctor Smith?"

"Sir, please calm down," Grace said.

"Where is he? Tell me where he is!"

"What is the problem, sir?" Grace asked.

"My daughter. She…she's dying!"

A human! But how? "This way, sir!"

It had been a long time since Doctor Smith had used the metal table at the back of the room. He had been contemplating on whether to remove it in order to free up more space for his future projects. The first of which, was pushed into the corner. It was a clumsily constructed base, with suspensions of some kind, sitting next to his fully assembled chair. He was happy to be putting the table to use one final time.

Eve was motionless on the table. Her body was mangled, but unbelievably, she was still alive.

"What happened to her?" Doctor Smith asked, applying pressure to one of her wounds.

"My workers found her at the bottom of a mountain. She...she must have fallen." The Mayor was standing in the corner of the room to be out of the way.

Grace turned the monitor toward the doctor. The green outline, which would normally signal stability within the body, was nearly nonexistent.

"How is she?" the Mayor asked. "Is she going to be okay? You have to save her! Please save her!"

"Please, sir," Grace said, attempting to calm the Mayor. She stood as high as the Mayor's chest, so all she could really do was raise her voice.

"Multiple lacerations," Doctor Smith said, "some of her skeletal structure is shattered, massive loss of blood..." He turned to the Mayor with a grim expression. "She's beyond repair."

The Mayor braced himself against the wall, nearly taking down the entire shelf. "No! Please! Doctor, you have to save her."

Doctor Smith removed his hand from one of Eve's wounds. Red fluid seeped out. "She's sustained too much damage, sir. There's only one way to save her now. But she won't be the same."

"Do it!" the Mayor said. "I don't care what it takes. Make her strong. Make her one of us!"

"But she...she's the last human. Converting her will completely—"

"Conversion will rid her of any weakness. Proceed with it. That's an order!"

Doctor Smith silently looked at Grace. They both knew what Eve represented. She was last human to ever walk the Earth. Converting her would completely destroy their past. Neither of them had been built to see this day.

Grace left and went back into the waiting room to take care of her other patients, leaving Doctor Smith alone to proceed with the Mayor's orders. One by one, he began removing Eve's damaged parts and replacing them with mechanical ones. The Mayor had gone out of the room, as well. He could not bear the sight of his daughter being disassembled.

Doctor Smith took advantage of being alone and set aside some of Eve's former parts. By keeping them inside a container full of clear fluid, he was able to keep them alive. He needed to. Eve was far too important to let die. She represented his past, and although the Mayor would not agree with him, she was strong—she had survived this long on her own. Eve, as a whole, might have died but her parts—her human parts, would always remain...as long as the Mayor did not find out.

The Mayor could not wait any longer. He shoved open door, drenching the room in natural light. "Doctor? How is she?"

Doctor Smith finished coiling the wires next to the life-support machine and placed them underneath the metal cart. "See for yourself."

The Mayor walked into the room, leaving the door open. He stopped next to the table and leaned down, drowning the tiny figure in his shadow. He was pleased to see that Eve's entire body was constructed out of the most flawless parts he had ever seen. Not a single seam was evident. Her glossy-white complexion reminded him more of stars than metal. "Is she complete?"

"As complete as I can get her."

"What does that mean? I wanted a completed conversion." The Mayor reached over and swivelled the monitor in his direction. The outline of the figure on the screen was entirely red, except for a small section within the upper left chest area. "What is this? Why is this still part of her?"

Doctor Smith had left one human part in Eve, her heart, but he didn't want the Mayor to know it had been on purpose. It was one of the most significant parts—the one part that humans could not survive without. By leaving it there, encased inside a metal enclosure, it meant that the Mayor could never completely rid Earth of its past. "I'm sorry, sir. I wasn't able to remove it."

"You were ordered to make her one of us. You were ordered to take weakness out of her."

"I can't, sir. She'll die if I remove it. I no longer have the replacement parts. It has been so—"

"She…she'll die? I...I can't let her die. I won't let her die!" He glanced at the doctor. "When can you make this part?"

"I'm not sure, sir. It'll take me some time. I'll have to find my design notes. And those heart replicas were very complicated."

"I don't care what it takes. Just complete it!" The Mayor closed his eyes. "My hope is that one day, she'll finally be one of us. Project New Hope..."

"Excuse me, sir?"

"Project New Hope. Eve was her past. Hope is for her future. It's a perfect name for her." The Mayor suddenly felt Eve's hand shift underneath his. "Is she functioning?"

"She should be."

Eve's entire body began to shift.

"Will she remember who I am?"

"She'll remember everything you tell her from this point on. Her past is no more."

"Exactly how it should be." The Mayor leaned in closer to Eve. "Hope, it's me. Your dad."

"D-Dad?" Hope whispered, in a soft, fragile voice. Her eyes slowly opened, exposing the most vivid-green eyes the Mayor had ever seen. She reminded him so much of Eve.

Grace entered the room but stood well back from the others. The green glow was the first thing she saw. "Is…is that Eve?"

"No, Grace," Doctor Smith said. "She's Hope, now."

"Can she walk?" Grace asked. "I'll need to adjust a few things on her."

The Mayor took Hope by the waist and brought her down off of the table. "Go on, Hope. Everything will be fine. I'll come and get you soon."

With her usual smile, Grace extended her hand to Hope. Hope mimicked Grace's smile and stored it into her hard-drive. Together, they exited the room and made their way down the hallway.

The Mayor kept a keen eye on them until door *333* closed behind them. With has back facing Doctor Smith, the Mayor quietly said, "Thank you…for saving her."

Doctor Smith sighed. "That's the last of them, sir. My job is officially complete. I'm not entirely sure what I will do now. Maybe I'll take some time off. Temporary shut down."

The Mayor turned and faced the doctor. "Your knowledge is invaluable. When it comes to humans, you're services are no longer necessary, but that does not mean that your knowledge should go to waste. We must prepare for our future. And I want you to be a part of this. You will remain here, and I will turn this hospital into a place of knowledge."

"A school?"

"Precisely. You will teach our kind, and I expect you to prepare them well. You will be known as 'Professor' from this day forward."

"Professor?"

"Is there a problem?"

Doctor Smith backed away. "No...sir. Knowledge is something I certainly do not lack."

"In the mean time, Project New Hope is your priority." The Mayor began making his way down the hallway. "I expect to see results soon."

Not if I can help it. The newly assigned professor sat down in his chair and waited. He knew Grace would come back once the Mayor left with Hope. He stared at the small, metal container that he had stowed away underneath the table—hidden away from the Mayor. Things of great significance were concealed inside that container. He hoped he had done right by keeping them alive.

Grace walked into the room and stopped next to the doctor. "It's a sad day. I never thought I would see the last of them."

"She may have been the last but she's far from being completely gone."

"What do you mean?"

Professor Smith walked quickly to the doorway leading to the hall and looked out. "Are they gone? Is the Mayor gone?"

"Yes. He left with Hope. Why?"

Professor Smith pulled out the container from underneath the table and set it down on its flat surface. He removed the covering from the container and allowed Grace to look inside. She wasn't exactly sure of what she was looking at. A pair of strange, green orbs and a much larger, heavily texture object were soaking in clear fluid. They looked so unfamiliar to her...so dissimilar to everything around her.

"I know it may be confusing," Professor Smith said. "But I managed to save parts of Eve. What you see here are her eyes and her human version of a CPU. I managed to keep them alive in this fluid."

Grace staggered back. She clasped her hands over her mouth. "You... you kept them alive?"

"Yes, but they might not stay this way for long. Not if they are here. They need to be kept alive and hidden, somewhere where the Mayor will never know about them."

Grace allowed her hands to fall to her sides. "How? I mean...is it even possible?"

"The same way we were able to attach our parts onto humans. I will just reverse the process."

"You mean—"

"Yes, Grace. I think I can integrate them into one of us. Know anyone out there who might need an upgrade or hoping to get any upgrade soon?"

Grace paced for a moment and then asked, "Can it be anyone?"

"As long as it is someone willing to accept these parts. Do you know anyone?"

Grace stopped in front of the container. "All I know is, he wants an upgrade, and he's been asking me forever about it."

"Desperation might be useful. Bring him to me."

"Yes, Doctor. I'll go and look for him."

"Please, hurry, Grace. I don't know how long I can keep Eve's parts alive."

Grace exited the room. As she fled down the hallway, she bumped into Jan. "Sorry, Jan. Can't talk now. There's someone I need to find."

Jan yelled back, "Need any help—"

Door *333* closed in front of her. Jan walked into the room at the end of the hallway and stood next to the table. "Where's she going in such a hurry?"

"She's looking for someone. Someone important, I hope."

"Oh... I finished sorting all of the parts in the boxes up front, Doctor. You might have to double check their contents. My eyes are having trouble detecting the finer instruments."

"I'll be out there in a minute. Thanks, Jan."

"Anything I can help you with back here before I leave?"

Doctor Smith stared into Jan's cloudy eyes. "Actually... there just might be..."

* * *

When Grace finally returned, she noticed Doctor Smith cleaning some of the tools that he had scattered all across the table top.

"Grace, what took you so long?"

"Sorry, Doctor. That damn car of mine finally broke down, but not to worry, I managed to find him." She pulled a timid looking first generation out from behind her.

The doctor stowed the tools underneath the metal cart and made his way over. "Who do we have here?" he said, kneeling down and smiling.

"Go on," Grace said, coaxing the mechanical boy forward. "Tell him your name."

"Please to meet you, sir," the boy said with a soft, delicate voice. "My name is Jake."

"Why, hello, Jake. I'm Professor Smith."

Grace placed both of her hands on her hips, something she had never done before. "*Professor* Smith?"

"I'll tell you later," Professor Smith whispered to Grace. He offered his hand to Jake, and they shook. Professor Smith relaxed the motors in his arm, making it seem as if Jake had a strong grip. "My-my, quite a bit of torque for a first generation."

Jake giggled.

As their hands separated, Professor Smith took a moment to scan Jake's exterior. Scrapes, scratches, and dents were unusual for a first generation, and Jake was full of these blemishes. There was also a generous encrusting of mud on his feet that travelled all the way up to his knees. "What happened to you, Jake?"

"Just doing what first generations do," Grace said, "I'm sure of it."

The professor laughed. "Indeed, it looks that way."

"Go on, Jake. Tell the professor what you're always asking me for."

Jake suddenly shied away.

"He's been coming in here three times a day, every day, asking me for the exact same thing," Grace whispered to the professor.

"Well, we won't be able to get him what he wants, if we don't know what that is," the professor said, smiling at Jake. "Go ahead. Nothing to be afraid of. I'm listening."

Jake shrugged. "Well, sir, I was hoping to get an upgrade. I've wanted one for so long now."

"Any upgrade?" Professor Smith looked up at Grace. He had yet to relinquish the smile he had on his face. "Well, young one...I think we can arrange that."

* * *

A few hours later, the indicator light on Grace's breast-plate was now at yellow. Fortunately, her job had come to an end. She placed the ratchet down on the cart and took a single step back, allowing her the chance to marvel at her accomplishment. "My first complete build."

"And a fine looking first generation, if I do say so myself," Professor Smith said, coiling up the wire and tubing from the machine on top of the metal cart. "You did good, Grace."

Grace pushed the monitor back into the corner. A red outline of a small figure, with green highlights around the head, flickered on the screen briefly before Grace turned the monitor off. "I couldn't have done it without you."

"You did the hard part. I was merely there for support."

Grace returned to the table that was engulfed by the spotlight overhead. She placed her hand deep within Jake's chest-plate. "Should we?"

Professor Smith stepped to her side. "By all means, Grace. But I'll let you have the honours. He's yours. You should the first one to switch him on."

"I'm so excited."

"I'm sure he'll make you proud."

"I already know he will."

Grace flicked the small switch located deep inside Jake's chest-plate. Nothing happened. Grace glanced over at Professor Smith who shrugged. "You know something, Professor, I think he was on this entire time."

"What? He couldn't have been, could he?" Professor Smith began scanning Jake's exterior, attempting to detect any sign that would indicate he was not in a dormant state. Grace placed the side of her head against the front of Jake's chest-plate.

"Yes. He's on. I hear his hard-drive spinning."

Professor Smith crossed his arms over his chest, slightly embarrassed. "Huh…must have forgotten to switch him off. Well, not to worry, Grace. He shouldn't remember anything beyond the point when we integrated Eve's part into him."

"His memory was erased?"

"It's best this way. If he or anyone else knew about this, his well-being could very well be forfeited. We certainly wouldn't want that."

"No, absolutely not. Especially now that he has brand new limbs. Look at how shiny he is. I hope Jake likes his new body. He probably won't want another upgrade for a very long time."

"Oh...about the name, Grace. Now that his past has been erased, I think it's best that we give him a new one. Don't want the name to accidentally trigger a memory."

"Would that be possible?"

"With that human part of his? It could. It's a complex piece of non-machinery."

A soft-blue glow suddenly filled the room.

"He's switching over from idle mode. Hurry, Professor, what should we call him?"

"That's completely up to you, Grace."

Jake began looking around. Distortion was restricting his vision, but it wasn't difficult for him to see Grace standing over him. "Where…where am I?" he moaned. "Who…who am I?"

Grace thought for a moment. Although Jake's past was now gone, she didn't want to completely ignore it. The future may always be obtainable, but the past is what shapes one's future. "Jacob," she said. "How are you feeling, Jacob?"

Jacob smiled. "Fine…"

A red light on his chest-plate began to flicker.

"Professor? What's going on?"

"Turned him on a bit too early," Professor Smith said. "We will need to turn him off for now."

Jacob was looking around, quietly observing his surroundings. Grace leaned close and whispered, "Sorry to have to do this, Jacob. But I need to switch you back off for now. We still need to make a few minor adjustments."

"Okay...but wait. Who are you?"

Grace glanced over at the professor. The plates over her eyes rose to their absolute peak.

"Your call, Grace."

"Grace?" Jacob said.

She looked down at Jacob. Every part of him was metal. She wanted to embrace his human part, a part that he would probably never know existed inside of him. "No, Jacob," she replied. "Please...call me...Mom."

Jacob smiled. "Okay. See you later, Mom."

The professor flicked the switch inside Jacob's chest-plate. The glow in Jacob's eyes subsided until it was no more.

"Mom?" Professor Smith said.

Grace shrugged. "I just...well...you know, I just figured—"

Professor Smith smiled. "No need to explain, Grace." He reached under the table and retrieved two metal cans. "Here. Take these."

"What are they?"

"Inside is a liquid that Jacob will need to keep him running properly. It's something all humans require. It's similar to what *Artificial Blend* is for us."

Grace turned the cans in her hand and read the inscription. "*Pure Blend.* How much should I give him?"

"I don't know the exact amount, but try two cans a day for now. Just make sure he takes them."

"Okay. That shouldn't be a problem."

"And if you haven't already noticed, I've added a special light on his chest-plate. Try not to allow it to get to red. It monitors the human side of him."

"What happens if it gets to red?"

"His human part requires a few things in order for it to function properly. First thing is rather simple. Sunlight. Make sure he gets as much sunlight as he can. It will keep his human part strong and healthy. Next, rest. Make sure he gets a lot of rest. Otherwise his entire body won't function properly. The final thing, you don't really need to worry about. I added vents on his cheeks to allow a constant flow of circulation. They'll automatically open and close. If he gets everything he needs, he should be fine. Take care of him, Grace. Our past is a part of him now."

"I will, Professor." Grace began to pick up some of the tools still scattered across the table.

"No-no-no, Grace," Professor Smith said, taking the tools out of Grace's hands. "Go on. Take Jacob home with you. I can clean up this mess."

"Okay, let me grab a few things from out front."

"Wait, Grace! I almost forgot." The professor walked over to the nearby wall and picked up a box that had been resting on the shelf. He brought it over to Grace and handed it to her. "Here, take this."

Grace set the box down, opened it and pulled out a strange, metallic orb.

"The Mayor gave it to me as a *thank-you* for saving Hope. It's a helper-bot...or something along those lines. It's brand new, but very rare. First off of the line."

"A helper-bot?" Grace said, using her hand to examine the smooth, outer surface. She accidentally snagged a small switch at the very bottom of the orb causing its entire front side to light up with red LED lights. It let out a series of loud *beeps*. Startled, Grace immediately switched it back off. "Interesting..."

"Take it with you. It might prove to be useful one day."

"We'll have to wait and see." Grace placed the orb back into the box and sealed it closed. "I'll be going now. It's going to be a long walk."

"What do you mean?"

"My car broke down, remember?"

"Oh...that's right." The professor paused. An idea suddenly popped into his head. "Didn't you say I could have the car for parts when it stopped running?"

"Sure, Professor. But I have to tell you, the wheels are the only things on it that still work," she joked.

"Perfect." *I need someone to look after Jan.*

* * *

Grace looked over at Jacob, who had become eerily quiet. He was taking it pretty well, considering she left absolutely nothing out of her explanations. "Are you okay, Jacob?" she asked hesitantly.

Jacob continued to stare off into the distance.

Grace wanted to close the small gap between herself and Jacob, but with each of her attempts, Jacob simply retreated further and further away. Grace stopped, otherwise Jacob would have potentially retreated all the way down to the bottom of the hill. "You have every right to be upset with me, Jacob. It wasn't right of me to keep this from you." She lowered her head. "But it was the only way I knew I could keep you safe. I was afraid of the Mayor finding out who you were." She paused. "You saw what happened to Jan."

"*Vision,*" Jacob finally whispered. "I knew her as *Vision*." Jacob thought back to the times when he was inside the crater. "So that's why Vision tried to return her eyes to me. They *were* a part of me. The human part of me." Jacob glanced over at his mom. "That's why I connected so well with Hope. We're the same inside. We're both...Eve."

"Yes, Jacob. Eve will always be a part of you now."

Jacob's eyes began to wondering around in their sockets. "Mr. Evans was her dad..." Jacob quietly exclaimed. "And Mr. Evans became the

Mayor..." Jacob paused and did the calculations. His conclusion made him tremble. His eyes suddenly increased in size, overwhelming most of his face. "So wouldn't that mean that I...I'm the Mayor's—"

"No!" Jacob's mom promptly said.

"But he was Eve's father! Eve's now a part of me!"

"Yes, Jacob. You're right about Eve being a part of you, but not about the Mayor. The Mayor you see today is not the human that he once was. That human is gone...They are not, and will never be, the same—*ever*!"

Jacob's sensors eased. "Well, that's a bit of a relief...I guess." Jacob reached up and began feeling the back of his head. "But how? How's it possible that I have a human part inside of me? How was it able to survive all this time?"

"Don't you see, Jacob? *Pure Blend*, the sunlight," she pointed at his face, "the vents on your cheeks. Like Professor Smith explained to me, the vents on your cheeks allowed circulation to flow inside of you. I think there's something in the air that your human part requires. Then there's the sunlight. Professor Smith said you needed sunlight. That's why I was always trying to keep the window open in your room."

Jacob calculated. "That's why I felt so strange whenever I was over at Wheeler's house. There's no sunlight on that side of the Earth." Jacob now fully understood why Wheeler had to harness the sunlight inside the cave. It was to keep Vision's human parts alive.

"I probably don't have to tell you about *Pure Blend*."

"Two cans a day," Jacob recited.

"And you saw what happened when you didn't. That's why Professor Smith decided to integrate it inside of you. One less thing to worry about."

"I never realized how important all of these things actually were," Jacob admitted. "Had I known, I would have taken better care of myself."

"No need to worry yourself, Jacob. That's what I'm here for. To keep you safe—just like Wheeler tried to do with Jan."

There was a long pause, as Grace and Jacob reorganized their hard-drives. Jacob wasn't sure about his mom but he definitely needed a moment or two to himself.

From the day he first step foot inside of his new school, his existence completely changed. He met Wheeler, Vision, and Hope. Then he eventually lost them within the same day. He was challenged with the prospects of saving Earth and his kind and eventually solved it on his own. Now most importantly, his past had been finally revealed to him, and it was overwhelming to say the least.

"So I guess I was never upgraded, then. My CPU, I mean."

"It never needed to be. That's what makes you very special, Jacob. Your human part is the most unique part about you. It never needed upgrading. The Mayor says they were weak, but it was that part of you that remained strong. It was what won you all of those trophies, and it was what helped you finally solve Forever Jacob." Grace looked off into the distance. Her hard-drive humming so loud it made her tremble. "I...I'm sorry, Jacob. I'm sorry I kept all of this from you for so long. I didn't want you to get hurt. You're far too important to all of us—too important to me..."

Jacob sighed. He decided to close the ridiculous gap he had selfishly created between himself and his mom. "I'm sorry for what happened to Jan and the professor," he said, placing his arm around his mom's waist.

Grace placed her arm around Jacob's shoulder and smiled. "I am too, Jacob. But I know they would be happy knowing that you're still around."

Jacob smiled back at her. "Thank you, Mom...For everything."

Chapter Eleven

Hope walked hand-and-hand with the Mayor, impervious to Brute. To him, she was a harsh reminder of frail innocents lost by the hands of the Mayor, but she didn't know that. She also didn't know that his primary orders to protect her were still enabled.

The Mayor's shoulder grazed Brute's chin, as he stopped in front of his designated launch pad. It had been altered to his exact liking, but he still complained. "Where are they? Where are the pods I ordered you to leave back?"

Brute innocently pointed at one of the launch pads off to the side. The pods that the Mayor was referring to were now wedged deep inside the alternate launch pad.

"We couldn't just leave them behind, sir. They were all promised a new future."

"You disobeyed a direct order." The Mayor looked away in complete disgust. "Is my launch pad ready?"

"Objective complete, sir."

"Then it is time." The Mayor grabbed the metal barrier surrounding the launch pad's perimeter for support and pulled himself onto the main level. He straightened his massive frame and then scanned the entire launch pad. His was generous in size, unlike the others. The two pods he had ordered Brute to discard could have easily stated their claim on the empty surface. Off to one side, the Mayor noticed an array of buttons, controls and levers adorning the main panel box. That was all he needed to see. The Mayor turned back to the launch pad's single entryway and called out, "Time to go, Hope. Our new future awaits."

His arm extended down but failed to reach her. Even with Hope extending her arm up, they were still separated by a large gap. She was too far down, and the Mayor, who had selfishly pulled himself up first, was too far up. He shouted an order to Brute, "Bring her to me."

Brute stepped forward causing Hope to stumble back. She looked up at him with frightened eyes. It was never his intention to do her any harm. He proved this by gently wrapping his hands around her waist, picking her off of the ground and hoisting her up to the waiting hands of the Mayor. When he let go of her, he realized that might be the last time he would make contact with her.

With Hope now secured, Brute retreated. He stopped in front of a large, metal peg that anchored the launch pad to the ground. It needed to be removed in order for the launch pad to begin its ascent toward the sky. The Mayor's launch pad was the last to have these anchors removed.

Hope was now on the far side on the main level, allowing the Mayor to make his way to the control panel at the other end.

"These control the rockets *and* the cannon, I presume?" The Mayor asked Brute.

"Yes, sir. Main buttons start the initial lift off phase. The solid-state rocket boosters need to warm up before we can lift off. We'll slowly ascend until the boosters reach their maximum levels. Once this stage is complete, pulling down on the lever will aim the launch pads at a forty-five degree angle, just enough to clear the moon and get us out into space."

"I know about the lift sequence," the Mayor said. "I meant the cannon. How do the controls for it work?"

Brute twisted and pulled at the chain attached to the anchor. "All cannon functions can be remotely controlled from up there, sir. Just a press of the button and the cannon will start up. Once it has primed itself and warmed up, all three barrels will fire off automatically in sequence. But we should wait until we are at a safe distance before initiating their firing stage. We don't want sections of the moon crashing into us."

"And this other lever? What's its purpose?"

"The lever is already set, sir. I have the cannon in-line with the moon."

"It controls the alignment?"

Brute gave the anchor one last pull, finally setting the launch pad free from the ground. "Yes, sir. Everything is ready. We just need to load it."

The Mayor nodded and grinned. "We already have."

"We have?"

The Mayor pressed down on the button to begin the cannon's start up sequence. "You see, three barrels make up the cannon," the Mayor explained. "I had to sacrifice three launch pads and their pods."

Brute stumbled back, his eyes lit up. "You…you did what, sir?"

"They might be dormant at the moment but the energy stored inside of them is more than enough. They'll make the perfect ammo."

So that's what had happened to the missing launch pads. Brute's CPU may be simple but he was positive that he did not forget them. If Brute knew their fate would come to this, he probably would have left them back at the work site. "You…you can't do this, sir! You can't use them to destroy the moon. They were promised a future, like all of us."

"They made a sacrifice to me the moment they stepped inside their pods. It's a sacrifice that will not go to waste. I'll be sure of this. And besides, I never had any intentions of using them to destroy the moon."

The ground trembled deep beneath Brute's feet, as the cannon was prematurely awakened from its long slumber. It commenced as a loud rumble and creaking, and the lights on its base exploded into a blinding, chaotic display. Its gears whined atrociously, as they began to turn, violently intertwining their teeth and locking together with unbelievable force.

"The moon's harmless at this point. It is no longer the enemy. In fact, aiming the cannon at it was never my intention. No, the moon will help me do what needed to be done a long time ago." The Mayor reached over and pulled down on the final lever. A loud click locked it in place.

The ground shook even more, dropping Brute to his knees. There was nothing he could do. The cannon's three main barrels began to shift away from its current target. "What...what are you doing, sir?"

"Earth still harbours the weak! As long as Earth exists, weakness has the potential to grow from it. I will not allow this." The Mayor walked to the launch pad's outer barrier and leaned over. "The time has come. Our future begins now."

Brute looked away, shaking his head. "I…I can't let you do this, sir," he said, his voice almost lost in the horrific noise from the cannon behind him. "I can't let you destroy the Earth."

"Destroy? It's already dead. I'm just putting it out of its misery."

"I can't let you."

The Mayor pushed off of the barrier. The fiery-red glow in his eyes grew dark and narrow. "So your future is to stay here on Earth?" The Mayor slammed his closed fist against one of the buttons on the control panel. "As I expected."

Brute felt a dry wisp of heated air surge out from the launch pad's rocket boosters. Heat waves distorted the ground below. Brute braced himself but was overwhelmed by what happened next. The rocket boosters, running along each side of every one of the launch pads, burst into flames. Violent explosions erupted in unison, sending thick walls of flames billowing out in every direction. The Mayor had initiated the primary lift off stage. Brute was thrown clear and away from the launch pads, landing just shy of the cannon. He staggered back to his feet, only to watch in total dismay, as one-by-one, the launch pads began to slowly peel away from the Earth.

"The time for reconsideration is nearing an end," the Mayor yelled over the thunderous screams of crackling flames scorching the Earth. "You've been loyal to me in the past, and for that, I will give you one final chance to join us."

The choices offered to Brute were conflicting, but he knew what he needed to do. For the first time ever, he was allowed to come up with his own conclusion. His decision was final. He turned his back on the Mayor and threw himself into the cannon's gears.

* * *

"Damn, *331*. Look at all that smoke!" Jacob said, watching the activity on the horizon with his telephoto capability.

Grace sighed. "I know it might not matter any longer but please, Jacob, stop using that word. Where did you learn it from anyway, and why do you add a number at the end each time?"

"I heard you say it once, a long time ago. I think you stepped on one of my cans of *Pure Blend* I left on the floor. You nearly fell down, if I remember correctly."

"That would explain it. No better time to say that word."

"I've been using that word ever since. The first time you heard me, you asked, 'How many times are you going to say that?' To make sure I wouldn't forget, I began counting the number of times I say it."

Jacob's mom sat up straight. "Are you telling me you've used that word *331* more times since you first heard me use it?"

Jacob grinned. "Damn, that's a lot. *332*!"

"Jacob."

"What? I don't even know what it means."

"Good. Let's keep it this way."

"Okay-okay. I'm done. I won't use it again. Promise."

A series of ground-trembling explosions erupted in the distance, and a great roaring noise rolled over them.

"Damn!" Jacob yelled. "*333*!"

Not even taking the time to extend her lecture to discuss broken promises, Grace jumped to her feet. "What's going on down there? Are they finally leaving?"

The sound of the distant explosions made it seem as though the horizon was being ripped apart.

"Looks like they're lifting off..." Jacob paused after that, however. Something didn't seem right. "That can't be..." he whispered.

Grace scanned the entire site below, but she was never able to see as far as Jacob could. The best she could tell, it looked like the launch pads were lifting off the ground in a blinding display of smoke and fire, slowly ascending toward the sky. It's what they were both expecting to see. "What's wrong?"

"Brute's still on the ground. Why's he over by the cannon and not on the launch pad?"

"He is? That's weird. I thought he and Hope would be the first ones the Mayor would take with him." Grace focused her eyes, attempting to filter out the thick smoke which seemed to be everywhere. She adjusted her telephoto capability and was just able to make out a form over the cannon. "He's not moving much. Looks like he's stuck inside its gears."

It was then that Jacob realized what was happening. "Oh-uh," he cried, quietly at first. He did a few calculations. "Oh-uh!" he yelled, after coming up with a unanimous conclusion. "This…this can't be!"

"What?"

The glow in Jacob eyes lit up, as the blue hardened to an almost blinding white. "The Mayor! He's not planning to blow up the moon. He never was!" Jacob looked at his mom. "We have to stop him or this could be the end of Earth...The end of us!" Not giving the situation another thought, Jacob lunged forward. He charged down the hill, as quickly as his second generation limbs could take him.

"Jacob! No, stop, get back here!" She went after him.

"We have to try," Jacob yelled back. "The cannon has to be aligned with the moon. There's no other way."

The moon's shadow bit into Grace within a few strides. "There's nothing we can do. The moon's about to hit. It's not safe for us to be down there!"

Her pleas went unanswered. Jacob was at the bottom of the hill and was heading to the launch site. He calculated it was just less than a mile away. He could cover that distance in mere minutes with his new legs. As he ran, he noticed that the ground was becoming increasingly unstable. It felt as if the Earth was crumpling beneath his feet. Already more than half of the launch pads had been sent into the sky, never to be seen again. Their powerful rockets had blazed a red trail across the sky that seemed to never fade. They stained Jacob in an eerie-red glow. Their crackling explosions screamed out, drowning out any other sound, including his mom's desperate calls for him to stop.

When Jacob did finally stop, it wasn't because her. It was because he finally arrived at the launch site. The heat pouring down from the remaining launch pad's rocket boosters kept him at a distance. The Mayor was now high above the ground. His launch pad had yet to reach its maximum velocity, forcing him to hover, while the boosters whined and tore into the Earth. A surge of dark-red fire cut a nearly solid line all the way down to Jacob, before erupting into a dense blanket of smoke.

The Mayor leaned over the railing to look at Jacob. "What a surprise. Had I known you were coming, I might have reserved some space for you. In the corner, perhaps."

Jacob stretched his head way back and shouted over the screams from the rockets, "We're not going with you!"

"My...my. Such disrespect coming from an insignificant first generation."

"Second generation!" Jacob yelled, pumping his first into the smoke-swollen air.

Grace finally arrived by his side. Using her arms, she shielded her upper body and face from the intense heat.

"Grace... It's been a long time," the Mayor said.

"Not long enough," Grace countered.

The Mayor grinned. "I see that the years have been good to you, not even a hint of rust. It's unfortunate that you and your boy will never get the chance to succumb to rust. It just might have been a bit more pleasant than the fate you brought upon yourselves." He turned and pulled Hope over to the rail with him. "You must remember Hope. Especially you, Grace. Without you, neither Hope nor I would have come to realize this day."

Hope looked down without saying anything. Grace noticed that the girl's eyes were cold and empty. This was the first time she had seen Hope since her conversion—when she was Eve. She looked so different. There was hardly any resemblance to the Hope she had remembered. "What have you done to her?"

"Something I should have done a long time ago," the Mayor said. "I freed her from her weakness!" He gestured for Hope to go back to the end of the launch pad.

Grace turned to Jacob and pushed him gently toward Brute. "He needs your help. Go on! Don't worry about me."

"Stall him," Jacob said. "He can't fire the cannon if he's still here."

"I'll try my best. I don't think he cares either way." Grace waited until Jacob was at a distance before shouting at the Mayor, "You had no right to do what you did. You killed her—your own daughter."

"No, Grace, I gave her what you and Ted Smith gave me so many years ago. I gave her strength. I gave her life." He spread his arms out across the remaining pods. "I gave them all life!"

"She's dead. Humans are gone. You won," Grace said. "You destroyed them…all of them. You don't need to do this. Stop the cannon."

The Mayor clenched his jaw. "No, Grace. There's still one human left." His eyes drifted slowly over to Jacob and then back to Grace. "You honestly think I didn't know about him? You think I didn't know about the secret you and that creator of mine had been hiding from me?" He leaned over the barrier. "Tell me something, Grace, did you tell him about his past? Did you tell him who he really is? Did you tell him who I used to be?"

"He knows everything. He knows what you've become."

The Mayor pushed away from the barrier, enraged. "What I've become?" He slammed his hand into his chest. "What I've become? I've sacrificed. I've endured. I'm the one who realized that *we* are the future, not them. I was the one who promised an Earth that would no longer harbour the weak." His stance grew. "Destroying the Earth will finally end all weakness." He yelled over to Brute and Jacob, "You're only delaying the inevitable!"

Brute was immobile beside the cannon. His arms were locked tightly around the cannon's main gears, merely delaying their progress. Jacob could not only see the pistons in the worker's arms buckling under the enormous pressure, but he could hear the disgusting crackling and popping, as Brute's body was being torn by the gear's indomitable bite.

"What are you doing?" Jacob yelled.

Brute looked down at Jacob. His eyes were narrow slits. "Have…to stop this…" he moaned, clenching his jaw. "Can't…let it complete its turn."

"No, I mean, why didn't you go with him? Why didn't you leave with the Mayor?"

Brute looked away. His mouth tightened. "All I've done during my existence is destroy. They were his orders. I can't let him keep doing this."

If the situation wasn't so dire, Jacob would have celebrated the fact that Brute had taken his advice, but there were more important things to deal with—like stopping the cannon. The gears were ripping into Brute's hard shell, as if it had been heated and the metal softened.

"I…can't stop this thing for much longer," Brute said. "He…he's using the cannon to destroy the Earth, not the moon!"

"I know. That's why I'm down here." Jacob lunged forward and wrapped his arms around one of the gear's teeth, the biggest one of all. He immediately understood why Brute was trapped in such an awkward position.

The gear bit down on Jacob's arms, causing him to wince. "How…are we going to stop this thing?"

Digging his feet into the Earth gave Brute a slight bit of leverage and allowed him to take some of the burden off of Jacob's diminutive hold. "I don't know. But we need to come up with something. The cannon's going to fire...any moment now."

Even with Brute's assistance, Jacob felt the plating on his arms beginning to warp and then crack. "There's no way we can stop this thing with just force," Jacob calculated. "There has to be controls….something. There has to be some other way of...stopping this thing!"

"Controls!" Brute said. "They're…on the Mayor's launch pad!"

Jacob turned his head as far as it could go. He saw the Mayor's launch pad hovering high above the ground. Second generation limbs could not help him this time. "Impossible! There's no way either of us can reach it."

"I can..."

"What? Really?"

"Yes."

"Well...even if...you got up there, how are you going to...get through the Mayor?"

"We'll see what happens. I have to try. It's the least I can do for all the...damage I've caused during my existence. And I'm still in your debt for what I did to your friends."

The gears were relentless. Jacob's arm twisted, as their teeth sank in deeper. "Okay. Go. Just...be careful."

"I have nothing to lose."

Brute released his hold on the gears. The additional pressure immediately threw Jacob flat on his back. He jumped right back up, latching onto one of the gears. Grace finally came to his aid, grabbing one of the teeth in an attempt to prevent it from locking down. It bit down anyway, forcing her to readjust her hold. "I'm sorry, Jacob. I'm not as strong as Brute."

From his ascending vantage point, the Mayor scoffed at their pathetic attempts. "Earth gave up a long time ago. You should follow its pathetic lead."

The Mayor paused when he noticed Brute making his way toward the launch pad. He laughed. "And you think I'll let you back on? You had your chance. You'll remain here with them." The Mayor's laugh faded the instant Brute disappeared beneath the launch pad. "What…what are doing? Get away from here!"

Brute hesitated for just a moment and then walked straight into the intense fire billowing out from the boosters. Everywhere he looked, he was surrounded by a deep-red tinge and distortion. The pressure from the flames, driving themselves down on top of him, caused his knees to buckle. He felt his internal structure ripping apart from the excruciatingly heat. Tubing and underlying wires began to bubble and blister. His outer shell, which was harden and accustomed to dealing with extreme conditions, reached its tolerance, yet his determination could not be denied.

He lowered his massive frame, driving his feet deep into the scorched Earth. Then with everything he had left inside of him, he jumped to grab onto the railing of the launch pad. The Mayor backed away from the barrier and braced for the impact. Brute wrapped his massive hand onto the edge of the launch pad, and his enormous weight dipped the entire floating structure to one side. The Mayor and Hope fell to their knees but quickly recovered. He glanced back to make sure Hope was okay. She was holding the metal barrier tightly, keeping herself balanced.

"Stay there, Hope," the Mayor ordered.

Brute managed to pull himself onto the launch pad. Heat waves continued to erupt from every section of his now distorted body. Most of his surfaces were now blackened and warped, but that didn't deter him from his mission. He locked his sights onto the controls. Although most of Brute's joints had been damaged from the heat, he managed to stagger to the controls.

"Get away from there!" The Mayor ran toward Brute and tried to grab him.

Brute turned and gave the Mayor a mighty shove. "No more. I take orders from you no more." He gripped the control lever and pushed it back to its rightful position.

On the ground, Jacob and his mom felt the pressure from the gears immediately subside. All movement from the cannon suddenly stopped and then it reversed direction, slowly realigning itself with the moon.

"He did it!" Jacob said. "Brute did it!"

The Mayor charged at Brute, slamming his entire weight into him. The impact drove Brute into the control panel and knocked the lever back down. Once more, the cannon's gears reversed their direction.

Grace and Jacob quickly grabbed the gears and hung on in a futile attempt to keep the gears from fully engaging.

Brute reached for the lever again, but the Mayor seized his arm. Brute's sensors whined, and a thick gush of sparks burst forward, as the Mayor crushed his arm with his massive grip. Brute tried to relieve the pressure by shifting from side-to-side, but it was no use. The Mayor's immense weight pinned him to the wall.

"Stand down!" The Mayor ordered. "This is not your fight."

Brute pulled his other arm out from underneath the Mayor. He closed his fingers and drove his fist into the Mayor's head, forcing him to let go. The Mayor grabbed his face and stumbled back. Brute quickly scanned his arm. The damaged was severe. At least half of his fingers no longer functioned. Wires were torn, completely exposed and dangled freely from the seams. He reached over and did what was necessary. He ripped off the fingers that no longer worked and allowed them to clang off of the floor.

When the Mayor took his hand away from his face, a large dent was exposed. It dominated the side of his head, forcing pressure onto his right eye. He tried to readjust his vision. His eye buzzed around in its socket, attempting to realign itself with the other, but it would no longer function.

"After all I've done for you, you side with the weak?" Releasing an infuriated scream, he lunged at Brute and pounded him with all the strength in his massive arms. The worker crashed to the floor, and the Mayor swivelled his base nearly all the way around and turned back sharply. He let out a metal-rippling grunt and drove his foot down on the helpless worker. Brute innards let out a deafening whine. The pistons in his shoulders tried to push back into their chambers but could only let out a wretched scream, as they scraped the sides, eventually getting stuck halfway down. Nearly every gear within him now turned with irregularity, failing to achieve their most basic, primary functions.

The Mayor stood over Brute. His one working eye scanned the worker's broken body. "I trusted you at one time. But like the Earth, your loyalty has faded." The Mayor dropped his foot onto Brute's head, bouncing it off of the floor.

Dark fluid had burst out from inside of Brute's torn body, creating a dark, shallow pool beneath him. In its reflection, Brute could see the Mayor lift his foot once more. He had to move. Brute straightened his legs and pushed himself off of the floor. On his way up, he grabbed the Mayor's leg and pulled him in. Brute then retracted the covering over his arm, exposing his welding nozzle and shoved it into the Mayor's face. Then he reached over and clamped his freed hand onto the launch pad's barrier. A small spark between the metal surface of his hand and the barrier confirmed that he, as well as everything else on the launch pad, was grounded. "Loyalty is mutual…sir!"

The welding nozzle flashed a brilliant-white. Molten wire erupted out of the tip, sizzling and crackling, as it drenched the side of the Mayor's face. The Mayor stumbled back into the center of the launch pad, before dropping to his knees. His face was buried inside of his hands. Heat waves and a deep-orange glow seeped out from between his fingers.

Still clutching the barrier, Hope cried out, "Stop it! Stop it!"

The Mayor attempted to pull his hands away from his face, but it required some force. As the welding puddle cooled, his hands had fused with the surface of his face. He ripped his hands away, pulling parts of his face with it. He winced, rippling his jaw and glanced up. His vision was now completely disrupted. The entire left side of his face was melted and torn apart. Gears and underlining circuitry were completely exposed. His right eye had burst apart from the inside out.

Hope turned her face away. She could not stand to look at the horror that his face had become. His voice, however, was still familiar. She recognized who he was, and not what he had become.

"Just stay there, Hope," he said. "This will be over soon."

Brute attempted to stand, but his damaged legs could barely support his weight. He leaned into the control panel next to him, using it as a brace to stay upright. His shattered arm let out a showering of crisp sparks every time he tried to use it. It dangled down, secured to the rest of his body by a thin bundle of damaged wiring. He tried to ignore Hope's pleas. They tore into him more easily than any of the Mayor's attacks. Little did she know that all of his actions so far, had been defensive. She would never understand his true intentions. Not now, not ever.

Brute now used the screams from the canon as his main source of motivation. Its cries were more infectious to him. He went for the lever one more time, and the Mayor lunged at him. When their bodies collided, Brute was thrown into the control panel, and the lever shattered upon impact. "*No*!" He tried to move the lever, but it broke off in his hands.

The Mayor staggered back to his feet. The undamaged side of his face grinned. "Inevitability," he said. "Earth's fight is officially over. And soon, so will yours."

I now have nothing to lose. Brute tossed the lever aside and then turned around, throwing his functioning arm into the Mayor chest. The impact sent the Mayor reeling. Brute continued the attack, driving his broad shoulder into the Mayor, who went down. Metal shards erupted from the Mayor's head, as it clanged to the floor. The Mayor quickly recovered, and he wrapped his arms around Brute's legs, picked him up off the ground and then took him down. Now in Brute's half-guard, the Mayor began pounding his closed fist into Brute's head.

From the ground, Jacob and Grace heard Hope's cries, "Stop it! Stop it!" But they couldn't see what was happening.

"What's...going on up there?" Jacob said, watching the launch pad shift from side-to-side. "Why hasn't he stopped the cannon?"

"I don't know," Grace replied, adjusting her grip on one of the cannon's gears.

Jacob saw Hope step to the barrier at the very front of the launch pad, but she didn't look down at him. He had no choice but to hang on to the gears and hope that Brute would be able to get to the controls again.

Fluid poured from every corner of Brute's body. It leaked out from his eyes, forming beads that eventually trickled down, distorting his vision. There wasn't a single plate on his body that wasn't cracked, dented, or nearly falling off. But still, he was ready to fight until he could function no more. He dragged himself to his feet.

The Mayor slowly reached up and ran his hand ran down the side of his face. His fingers got caught in the sharp edges where his face-plate had been ripped apart, causing a wretched squeal. He held his hand out and looked at it. It was wet and glistened from the fluid that was now pouring out from every crack in his face. "How could you?" he snarled. "After all I've done for you. I built you! I created you!"

"Creation was...never your intent. You only built us to destroy Earth—destroy humans. They created me...They created *you*."

"So be it. I'll end your fate like I did the humans." He picked himself up and lunged at Brute one final time.

Brute had nothing left inside of him. All he could do was brace himself. On impact, the pair slammed into the barrier, bounced off and crashed to the floor. Their combined weight threw the launch pad into a frenzy, tipping it severely to one side.

Hope did all she could to keep herself balanced, but her body was too frail to stay upright. She fell on her back and slid helplessly over the edge of the launch pad.

"Hope!" Brute cried. He kicked the Mayor off of his leg and threw himself over the side without even the slightest bit of hesitation.

The Mayor fell back, stumbled to his feet and looked around. His distorted vision only saw an empty launch pad. "Hope?" he desperately cried. "Where is she!" In an instant, he realized what must have happened. "No!" he screamed. "Hope!" He staggered over to the edge of the launch pad. What he saw when he looked over the edge, caused him to collapse.

Brute dangled precariously over the launch pad's edge. The flames from the rocket boosters battered his already broken body. The unbelievable heat ripped open his external plating, their edges liquefying, blistering and popping. But still, he could not disregard his single most important command. Brute held onto Hope, doing all he could to keep his arm extended, not allowing the flames get to her. Hope was to be protected, at any cost.

Jacob and his mom watched in total dismay, as Brute and Hope dangled precariously. "They're going to fall!" Jacob let go of the gear, forcing his mom to do the same. "We have to help them!"

Jacob ran toward launch pad. Grace followed, but they could only get so far before the heat from the rocket boosters drove them back.

"We need to do something," Jacob pleaded. "The drop is too severe. They won't make it!"

Grace did her best to hold Jacob back. The heat was causing her outer layers to blister and then flake away. "There's nothing we can do."

Every time Jacob pushed away from her, and attempted to get closer, the heat drove him back. Helpless, they watched Brute and Hope sway, and it looked like Brute's damaged hand was giving way.

The Mayor leaned against the railing, extended his hand and yelled, "Give her to me!"

Brute slowly looked up, bypassing the Mayor's offering. His vision was nearly destroyed by distortion. His hand was barely gripping onto the edge of the launch pad. The only thing keeping him and Hope from dropping was the thin bundle of wires from his torso to his arm. He tried to pull up, but the exposed wires let out a dim showering of sparks. They whined and screamed every time Brute tried to pull them up. Hope struggled in his other hand, and he could feel what little strength he had waning. He was weakening with every passing moment, and his functioning arm could barely keep her away from the heat's terrifying calls. Flames lashed out at her, stinging her sensors, forcing her to cry out, "Daddy! Help me, Daddy!"

"Give her to me, and I'll pull you up," the Mayor said.

How could he be trusted?

Another wire in Brute's arm snapped, and they slid further down.

"Give her to me! Give her to me, and I'll help you!"

Brute felt his sensors switching off. He knew that he was moments away from permanent shut down. His entire body sagged, as plates melted and slowly dripped to the Earth. He had no choice. Hope's well-being had priority over his. This was something he could never override. She was better off in the hands of the Mayor instead of facing certain demise. With the last bit of energy he could bring forth, Brute raised his arm, hoisting Hope into the waiting arms of the Mayor.

Hope's outer shell was darkened from the heat but she had no serious damage. The Mayor gestured for her to go over to the far end of the launch pad. "Stay there. I have one last thing to take care of before we leave."

Brute was now dangling from a single wire. All he could do now was wait for the inevitable. He looked up at the Mayor, silent. There was nothing left for him to say. His entire face was nearly blown apart from the rocket booster's relentlessness. Regardless of what would happen next, Brute had no fight left in him. The Mayor stood over him.

"I promised that I would help you," the Mayor finally said. "You wanted to stay back here on Earth? As you wish."

The last Brute saw of the Mayor was his foot coming down over top of him. The final wire in his arm snapped. His massive body fell from the sky.

"*No!*" Jacob cried.

Grace reached out and pulled him back. As Brute's body slammed into the ground, it rippled the Earth in all directions, knocking them down. Jacob quickly got back to his feet and ran over to Brute. What he saw forced him to his knees. Brute's body had sunk into the ground from the impact. All of his limbs were broken. His outer plating was completely melted off, spilling his insides onto the ground. Smoke billowed and swirled around him. Jacob reached out, but the heat coming off of Brute forced him to retract his hand. "Brute..."

Brute slowly turned his head in Jacob's direction. His eyes no longer functioned, but he could detect Jacob's presence. His mouth slowly opened. "Hope...is she..."

"Hope's with her father," Jacob said "She's safe. You saved her."

Brute did his best to offer Jacob a smile, but all the sensors controlling his face had been destroyed. "Objective...complete..." Brute said, for the final time. His head shifted to one side, settling quietly against the ground. His body twitched, and he flattened out. His hard-drive completed its final rotation. Brute was no more.

Jacob slammed his hand into the ground. *If only I hadn't asked him about the controls.*

Grace walked over to Jacob and forcefully brought him back to his feet. She moved him away from the heat of the rocket boosters, pulling him behind her. Then she looked up at the Mayor. "You monster! He saved your Hope from falling!" she yelled. "He was completely loyal to you!"

The Mayor leaned over the barrier. He ripped Brute's arm from the edge and threw it over. It disintegrated in the flames. Then he reached up to his face, making sure the damage he had sustained was clearly visible. "This is loyalty? After all the sacrifices I've made. He was disloyal—like the rest of you." He pushed away from the barrier. "All of you want to be returned to your precious Earth? As you wish! You will soon join him."

Explosions from the rocket boosters erupted from every direction. The lift-off sequence of the remaining launch pads, including the Mayor's, was now complete. Flames ripped through the smoke-filled air with blinding intensity, forcing Jacob and his mom further back. Rocket boosters angled themselves at forty-five degrees and then ignited. The crackling of the flames, alone, caused the Earth to tremble. An immense light engulfed the entire launch site. All but the Mayor's launch pad, streaked across the sky, keeping under the moon, until they were out of its direct path. Once free, they accelerated, merging with the sky. Long-lasting trails of solid-white smoke were the only things they left behind.

Screams from the rocket boosters began to die down. Jacob and his mom were now able to lower the hands they had raised to protect themselves from the scorching heat. They were expecting to see an empty sky, but one last launch pad remained, and it was hovering high above them. The Mayor's.

"Project Retaliation!" The Mayor pointed to the cannon which was aimed directly at Earth. One of the three barrels glowed red-hot at the tip, preparing to fire. "Maybe I should rename it, 'Project Conclusion'."

"Damn, you!" Grace cried.

The Mayor smiled. "To our future!" he proclaimed.

Rocket boosters screamed out one final time. They angled the forty-five degrees needed to clear the moon and then erupted in a violent plume of flames. The Mayor and Hope ascended into the deep-black sky. Their eyes locked firmly with the pair below—it would be the last time they would exchange stares. The moon eventually overlapped them but it was the promise of an indomitable future that ultimately swallowed them whole.

Trails of smoke were rising, colliding with the moon and then dissipating.

"They're gone..." Grace said. "They're all gone..." She turned and looked down at Jacob. Her eyes were wide. "We...we're the last ones..." Her voice trailed off.

Jacob tugged firmly at her arm. "Calm down, Mom. It's what we expected." He pointed to the cannon. "But *this* isn't what we expected. We have to stop it!" One of the barrels, that was once red, now glowed white-hot. It retracted with a series of loud clicks.

"They're about to fire!" Grace reached out and smothered Jacob in her arms. "We need to get back to the house—our car!"

Jacob pulled free. "Mom! Calm down, I'm trying to think."

The cannons let out a horrible wail.

"Well, think faster!"

It was too late. They had been given enough chances to reconsider. It had been an impossible wait, and the cannon could no longer hold back for either for them. One of the three barrels erupted. Its hollow tip blew apart, sending forth a massive fireball. The Earth was defenceless, as a massive gash was ripped into its surface. The blast sent a soaring wave of debris straight into the sky, most of which collided violently against the moon. The moon didn't budge. It would eventually get its revenge.

The shockwave from the blast came fast and immediate. When it hit, Jacob and his mom were thrown off of their feet and were carried through the air. Brute's body trailed closely behind them but did not complete the journey. It disintegrated like loose sand and was swept away, never to be seen again.

They came crashing down a good distance away from the launch site. The violent landing wedged them deep into the Earth, forcing them to fight their way back out. It was no easy task. Rocks and other debris, from the blast, hit the peak of their trajectory and rained down on them, pelting their metal surfaces unmercifully.

Jacob managed to dig himself out of the massive trench that he had created and began wiping the loose debris from the lenses of his eyes. It didn't seem to help his vision much. Everything around him was a blur, and a high-pitched whining disrupted his hearing. "Mom..." he moaned. "Mom...w-where are you?" Jacob saw her lying in a deep mound of Earth which had been created when her body skimmed the surface and was dragged along for a short distance. "Mom!" Jacob cried. He ran over and immediately began digging her out.

Grace was covered in dirt and debris, and the small dent in her head had been replaced with an even larger one. Jacob wrapped her arm around his shoulder, allowing her to use him as a temporary brace. She laboured to get back to her feet, while Jacob brushed away the rocks wedged into the seams of her plating.

"I...I'm okay, Jacob," Grace moaned, backing Jacob away from her. "Just a bit of dirt. What about you?"

Jacob scanned himself from top to bottom. He had a lot more scratches than his first generation body had ever sustained but no internal damage. "Fine. Can't believe we're standing after that."

They surveyed the damage around them. The blown-apart barrel, from the cannon, had yet to cool, and the destruction it had caused was beyond anything Jacob and his mom could have imagined. The Earth was now scarred so deeply, it appeared as though the horizon had been pulled closer to them. The massive gash dragged across the Earth's surface and ended just shy of the hill that Jacob and his mom had been perched on earlier. A bit more torque and their house would no longer be standing. It was terrifying for them to realize that a single blast from the cannon had been able to achieve such an enormous scale of destruction. And there were two more to go.

"That's it, Jacob. We are leaving. The next time, we might not be as lucky." Grace attempted to wrap her hand around Jacob's arm, but he backed away. "Jacob!"

"Wait, mom!" Jacob was staring directly at the cannon and saw that it now stood at an angle. "The blast must have shifted it!"

Jacob ran a few yards, to get a closer look, and saw that the cannon's anchors had been severely weakened from the blast. They were now loose, and the gears were rotating with irregularity, even stuttering from time-to-time. "The blast must have weakened the gears. We might be able to turn them, now."

"Jacob! Are you crazy? We are not going over there. We're leaving. *Now*!"

The second barrel retracted, giving off its frightening and distinct clicks. If the first blast was any indication of the cannon's true potential, Grace did not want to be anywhere near its radius. She wrapped her hand around Jacob's arm.

"Come on, Jacob!" she pleaded. "It's too late for that. We have to leave!"

Jacob managed to wretched his arm free.

"Jacob!" *Damn, second generation limbs!*

"We have to realign it!" Jacob yelled back. "Now is our only chance."

"Damn it, Jacob!" Grace had no choice but to go after him...again.

Neither of them got very far. The tip of the second barrel glowed an intense white. It erupted with an incredible blast, easily eclipsing to the first. For a second time, they were thrown through the air before crashing back to the ground. Debris rained down on them, pounding every part of their body. Jacob pulled out from under the pile of rocks and dirt. His movements were much slower and rigid this time. A glance down at his left leg explained why. It had sustained major damage. Most of its protective plating was bent inward, although its internal structure was not exposed. He had to test it to be sure it was still stable. A quick push off of the ground, and he was back on his feet. He took a step back and then a step forward. A loud series of popping noises rang out from somewhere inside his leg, but at least it still worked. He immediately limped over to his mom. He lowered down and lifted her head off the ground. "Mom, are you okay?"

"Am…am I shut down?" she said.

Jacob couldn't help but smile. "No, Mom, you're not shut down."

Grace reached out and placed her hand on Jacob's face. "Are you?"

"Mom, get up. I'm fine." As Jacob began digging his mom out from the deep trench, he noticed that she had suffered major damage. Her leg was shattered. It was twisted all the way around with wires completely exposed. With the help of Jacob's shoulder, Grace managed to hoist herself off of the ground. She balanced on one leg.

"It…it's okay, Jacob. I can still move it." She turned her leg, only to have it squeal, as its internal gears snagged on one another. "Maybe not."

"Can you at least walk?"

Grace hopped back and forth, testing her functioning leg. Her motions might not have been graceful but at least she wasn't completely immobile. "I can still move. What about you?"

"My leg is damaged, but I can still walk."

"Good," Grace said, already swivelling her hips toward the hill, "because we are *leaving*!"

"Wait, Mom." Jacob pointed at the cannon again. "Look!"

The cannon was now overshadowing a massive crater the second blast had caused. A vast layer of peaks surrounded the crater, also formed by the blast. They could have been easily mistaken for mountaintops if it weren't for the mighty cannon standing next to them. All of the cannon's anchor points had been ruptured, leaving its stability uncertain. The shift in balance allowed the barrels to pivot skyward, nearly in-line with its original target.

"The cannon is almost realigned with the moon!"

"Okay, fine, I believe you, but we have to go, Jacob. I don't want to be here for the final blast." Grace pulled on Jacob's arm, but again, she wasn't even able to budge him.

"There's only one blast left," Jacob said. "We might be able to turn the gears just enough for the cannon to align itself directly with the moon. It's our last chance."

The cannon's final barrel retracted, letting out the series of clicks. Its tip glowed red with intensity.

"I have to try!" Jacob yelled, slipping around his mom for the consecutive time. "We're Earth's last hope!"

"Jacob, no! Stop! The cannon's unstable!" Grace had to bring him back. Not only was the cannon about to fire but the moon was now so close, she could see the foot prints from both her kind and humans on its surface. She winced and limped off after him. At her slow pace, the moon might actually beat her to him.

Jacob now stood at the very edge of the crater left by the second blast. It easily rivalled the crater that he and Wheeler used to journey down into. Whereas that crater was cold and motionless, the one left by the cannon was still active. Jacob felt the heat of scorched Earth rising from it. The orange glow of molten rock was still burning away from its edges. This was as close as Jacob wanted to get. Falling down into it and there would be no chance of returning to the surface. The ground pulsated beneath him. The cannon was ready to fire again. He needed to hurry.

Jacob ran to the cannon and saw that the gears no longer had any rhythm to their bite. Instead, they were grinding into each other with a wrenching squeal. Jacob grabbed one of the gear's teeth. Other than its hefty weight, there was barely any fight left in it. He straightened out his legs and arched his back. To his amazement, the gears began to reverse direction. Each time the gears interlocked, the entire cannon shifted. Its alignment was steadily returning to its original target. "It's working!" Jacob yelled. "Mom! It's working." His eyes followed the arc of the glowing-red tip of the third barrel until it finally came to a stop, completely in-line with the moon. "I did it! I did it!"

The final barrel clicked several more times and then rendered its tip a brilliant-white glow.

"Oh-uh…"

The cannon erupted with such force that all of its barrel tips ruptured and split down the center. A red fireball surged into the sky and collided with the moon. The sky disappeared behind a massive cloud formed by dust and debris. Jacob was thrown to the ground and flattened by the shockwave.

Grace had witnessed everything at a distance but still felt the impact from the blast and was thrown back. When she was finally able to raise her head from the ground, she immediately looked up. "Oh, no..." she moaned. She fought just to get back to her feet and limped her way toward the cannon—to Jacob.

The intensity of the final blast seemed to equal the last two combined, and because of this, the cannon could no longer support itself. The entire structure began tipping underneath its enormous weight. It finally settled at a precarious angle.

Tremors in the ground jolted Jacob's sensors back on. He pulled his head off of the ground. He looked to the sky, hoping to see it empty of the moon. At first, he could see nothing through the thick cloud lingering across the entire sky, but, as it began to dissipate, Jacob felt his sensors drop to the very soles of his feet. *It's still there.* The moon was still nearly fully intact and continuing to descend toward the Earth. "It...it didn't work..." Jacob's shoulders slumped so far down he heard a pop, as their joints locked in place. Some damage was evident on the moon's surface—it just wasn't nearly as overwhelming as it needed to be. Jacob struggled to his feet and stood silently, motionless—distraught. He didn't even care that the blast had taken a chunk out of the moon. The shattered pieces of the moon were now falling toward the Earth.

A small clump of rock landed just in front of Grace. It was the first of many. She looked up and nearly collapsed at what she saw. A section of the moon, which looked like a mountain from where she stood, was falling...toward the cannon—toward Jacob. "Jacob!" Grace screamed. "Jacob! Run!"

He didn't hear her cries. Even as pieces of the moon were colliding with the Earth, he was still motionless. His plans had withered away like the plant he had found behind his old house. A piece of the moon clanged off his plating, but it did little to distract him. "Now what?" he mumbled aimlessly. "Pods are gone. The cannon failed. Moon's still here."

A larger piece of the moon landed next to him, rippling the ground beneath his feet. Jacob finally snapped out of his depression. He glanced down at the piece of rock which still had its outer surface glowing orange. He looked over and saw his mom who was still at a distance. He heard her yell, "Cannon!" but he did not understand why. The canon was useless to him, now. Its purpose had failed for the consecutive time. Brute was not to be blamed for this, however. It was the Mayor who altered the cannon's intent. *It's always the Mayor.*

"The Cannon!" she yelled again.

What about the cannon? Jacob finally looked over. Sections of moon were colliding with the cannon, causing it to tip back and forth. It was unstable. It was going to fall, and he was standing right in its shadow. "Damn it! The *cannon*! 33—" He lost count.

Jacob took a step forward but immediately fell back. The sensors in his legs whined. He looked down and saw why. His leg was ripped open exposing its internal structure. Wiring had been severed, not allowing any sort of functionality. There was a pool of clear fluid beneath his leg where the wires had ruptured. Jacob looked up, and his eyes widened. A mountainous-sized piece of the moon struck the cannon. The once functional cannon started to fall.

With every ounce of strength he could muster, Jacob put his hands on the ground and pushed off. As he regained his feet, the sensors in his leg chimed uncontrollably. Jacob did want to hear it. "Shut up! Shut up!" He limped forward, but he wasn't moving fast enough. The cannon's shadow was strengthening, dimming the redness of the plates he was wearing. "Come on, Jacob! Come on…got to move…got to move!" He put forth one last effort, but his leg took him no further. He looked up. It was too late. Jacob reached up and covered his eyes. There was no point in watching.

Earth continued to convulse long after the cannon collided with the ground. The shockwaves were strong enough to physically tear into the Earth's surface, sending a mountainous wave well into the horizon.

Then it was over.

A deep and eerie silence swept across the entire launch site and did not think twice about overstaying its welcome.

This is strange. Jacob remembered being directly underneath the cannon, as it toppled to the ground. Nothing could have survived that impact. So how was it that he could feel the sensors in his body still functioning? He opened his eyes. Distortion was all around him in thick, random bands. A loud, high-pitch ringing erupted inside his head, and it felt like the inside of his head wanted to seep out from the two bolts on top of his crown. It made him wince. The shutters in his eyes suddenly closed. His vision went blank.

A moment went by. Jacob was able to open his eyes again. This time, he saw a grey haze floating over him. *Maybe this was what it was like to be permanently shut down.* He brought his hand up to his face and was surprised to actually see it. He wiggled his fingers. They moved exactly the way he wanted them to. Most of his sensors still felt intact. The ringing in his head was even subsiding, allowing his hearing sensors to switch back on. *If this was permanent shut down, it wasn't so bad.*

Jacob remained still, not exactly sure what to do next. Debris was still raining down on him, and a small rock struck his chest-plate, loosening a clump of dirt that had collected on him. A green light lit up the bottom half of his face. "My indicators lights are still working," he said. "I'm not shut down!"

"No, Jacob…you're not…" It was the shallow voice of his mom somewhere in the distance.

Jacob eyes widened. He lifted his upper body off of the ground. "Mom? Mom, is that you? Where are you?" He looked around. There was really only one thing that his eyes could detect, and it wasn't difficult to miss. The cannon had fallen from its mighty perch and was now grounded, relinquishing its once vertical stance. Even sideways, the cannon easily blocked out most of the sky. *That's odd. I was right underneath the cannon when it began to fall. How did it miss me?*

He heard his mom call again, and he staggered to his feet, ignoring the dirt that was encrusting most of his body. He scanned the area, but he still could not see her. "Mom! Where are you?"

There was a long pause before his mom replied, "Down…here…"

Jacob's eyes fell from the cannon all the way to the ground. What he saw made him wish that his eyes had never opened. There was a reason why he wasn't permanently shut down, a reason why he was still completely intact and now even standing. That reason was his mom, and she now lay nearly decimated beneath the cannon.

"Mom!" Jacob limped over as fast as he could. Without even considering that it might be impossible, he threw his weight against the cannon, attempting to push it off of her. "No!" he screamed, pressing himself against the indomitable mass. He dug his feet into the solid Earth. His joints began to pop, and his sensors whirled with a maddening whine. "No!" he screamed. "No…"

He swung his fist wildly at the cannon's hard surface again and again but got nothing for it except damaged fingers. The cannon did not budge, nor would it ever. Weak, he dropped to the ground but quickly forced himself to get back up. Grace reached out to try to stop him, but he brushed her hand aside. He threw his shoulders into the cannon, cracking his red plating. "Get…off of her! Get...off her!"

Again, he felt his mom's hand reach up, only this time, it held on.

"Jacob…Jacob…it…it's okay…"

He fell to his knees, helplessness overwhelming him. He scanned as much of his mom as he could, but only half of her was exposed. The rest of her had been taken away in an instant beneath the stubborn piece of machinery. He pulled her hand into his grip and held on tightly. "Mom…"

Grace looked up at Jacob. Her vision was nearly non-existent. She could detect the brilliant-blue glow of his eyes, the colour she had selected when he was being reassembled. She could see the red plating and knew that he had chosen it earlier today because it was her favourite. Despite his boyish pranks, he did always want to please her. She did her best to offer him a reassuring smile, the same one she would always offer him whenever optimism would leave his side, but everything was shutting down so quickly. Surges of energy would give her a moment or two of clear vision, and she used every single bit of it. She looked at Jacob for a long moment and then shifted her gaze around him. "You…you see that?" she whispered.

Jacob turned his head and looked up. The only thing as far as his eyes could see was the moon. It was so close now. Its shadow felt heavy and cold against his back.

"That's where your boot landed," Grace pointed out.

She was right. There it was in plain view. The perfect imprint of his first generation boot still completely unscathed on the moon's ravaged surface. Jacob remembered that day as if it had happened only recently. As usual, he'd forgot to enable the magnets on the boot, and it simply floated away. It landed on the moon, and he thought it was lost forever. A few days later, he found the boot anchored to the floor in front of his room. When asked, his mom told him that she had gathered the neighbours from their sector, and they had managed to retrieve it.

Such a petty thing to remember at a time like this...but also a noble one. His mom had been doing things like this for him for as long as he could remember. Saving him from the cannon would be the last.

"Magnets on," Grace said, her voice beginning to be replaced by static.

Jacob turned to his mom. "Please, Mom..." he cried, "don't move...You have to save your energy." He desperately scanned the immediate surroundings, trying to come up with something... anything that he could use to help her. All he could see was that damn cannon pinning her down.

Grace tugged on his hand, silently wishing that he would end his futile attempts to move the cannon. Fluid now poured out of from her mouth and created a deep pool beneath her. "I...didn't want to leave you here alone." Distortion and static now controlled her voice.

"Mom...No! I can help you...I just...I just need to—"

Grace tightened her grip on Jacob's hand. "Listen to me...Jacob. The moon's almost here. It...has to be stopped. You...know what you need to do." The glow in her eyes was fading.

Jacob could see the moon behind him through the refection in her eyes. "I don't know what to do." He squeezed his mom's hand even tighter. "Mom...what do I do?"

"It's all up to you, Jacob. I know you can do it."

"It's going to hit. I've calculated, but I don't know what I supposed to do!"

A sudden surge of energy finally allowed Grace to offer Jacob the smile she had been wanting to save until later. "No, Jacob. Don't calculate. Just *think*...You've been doing it your entire life." Her smile faded.

Jacob felt her hand slide out of his grip. "No...Mom! Mom...don't...please don't...please don't leave me here by myself!"

With the last reserve of energy Grace would ever need, she whispered for the final time, "I won't leave you completely, Jacob. Your...human side... will never forget me..." Her eyes became pale and empty. The low hum of her hard-drive completed its final rotation.

She was gone.

An eerie silence tore into Jacob, causing his sensors to feel cold. He needed to fend it off, even if all he could muster up was a mere whimper. "Mom?" He reached out and tugged at her shoulder. "Mom? Mom...please, don't leave me here! Mom!"

He tugged on both of her shoulders, but the result was the same. She was now returning to the Earth—her rightful birth place. Jacob fell into the embrace of the very same cannon that had taken his mom away from him. Debris from the moon was still falling down all around him. "What do I do?" He stared off into the horizon. As expected, it was empty. "I'm the last one here. They left me here...alone. All of them."

His eyes were staring off into the distance, but nothing was working behind them. No thoughts or recollections were taking place in that most significant part of him. He tucked his hands into his lap and curled up into a ball. Everything he had planned up to this point had failed. Every calculation he had made has been wrong. The very least he could have done was listen to her. Everything his mom had told him, more or less, had been the truth. *Should have listened to her.* At least they would have been far away from the moon's reach by now. Everything after that would be impossible to predict, but at least he wouldn't be where he was at the moment—sitting cowardly next to his mom's motionless body, as the moon frown down on him.

He sighed and then gave himself a moment to recollect. *They all wanted me to go through with this. Wheeler, Hope, Professor Smith...Mom. They wanted me to get to the end of Forever Jacob.*

Using the cannon as a brace, Jacob slowly returned to his feet. The glow in his eyes was beginning to solidify. He tilted his head as far back as it could go to stare directly at the moon. "They wanted me to do this," he said. Confidence eradicated his simple need for a plan. He dug his hands into the cannon and pulled himself up and finally onto its peak. He limped all the way to the very tip of one of the barrels which had been shredded into sections from the blast. It was a far as he could go. From the high vantage point, he could see everything. The darkened patches where the launch pads had burned the Earth, his old house atop the hill, the crater caused by the cannon, and, of course, the moon. All the foot markings from when both humans and mechanical beings had walked on its surface were incredibly detailed. Even the serrated lining from his very own boot-print was angled perfectly in-line with him. The detail was so crisp that he could count each and every one of the indentations. *Too bad my boot isn't still on the moon. I could reach up and—*

Jacob suddenly had a crazy, unorthodox thought. He placed his functioning leg behind and then threw his disabled leg out in front for balance. His hands reached up and over his head. He pushed upward on the back of his feet, and for the first time ever, his hands made contract with the moon's cold, dusty surface.

The moon's undisputed weight was immediately felt. Jacob tried to push back, but the moon had no give, it only took. His second generation upgrades stood no chance against the incredible weight of the moon. It pushed down on Jacob, securing him in place. His entire body began to tremble. The indicator light on his chest-plate flashed madly in all colours. All of his sensors rang out, chimed, beeped, and even snapped. He let out a scream, as his internal structure started to break apart. The pistons in his arms could no longer deal with the pressure. They burst from their chambers causing fluid to erupt and stain his body. His soft, metal body squealed, as it scraped against the moon's indomitable surface. Wires and cables were escaping from the seams all around his body. Fluid was now pouring out from his mouth and spilling onto the cannon's surface, forming a puddle at his feet.

He saw the refection in the puddle. It was detailed enough to reproduce the exact image of the impossible weight he was carrying on his shoulders. It was sharp enough for him to see the blues of his eyes fading to white. With every passing moment, he detected the puddle getting closer and closer to him. He soon realized that it was *he* who was actually descending toward his own reflection. He was being crushed beneath the moon's weight, pushed deeper and deeper toward his own feet.

The moon's shadow was darkening, and the sensors in his eyes were shutting down. Night had prematurely fallen.

Jacob's head was now pressed deep into his chest. His legs began to crumble. His feet flattened out, buckling both his knees. As a result, his already damaged leg began to bend in the opposite direction. His sensors were begging him to back down, but he couldn't. He let out a dreadful scream that not even the moon could silence. It did not go unheard.

Within the repulsive sounds of his own body being destroyed under the moon's relentlessness, Jacob heard a whirring noise approaching from the distance. It was a sound that he had never gone a day without hearing. The near-silent hum of twin turbine engines revved up beside him. Jacob's eyes opened, and he saw the warm-red glow of Pin-bot's eyes hampering the moon's shadow. He wasn't alone after all. She must have heard his cries and hurried to his side, as quickly as her turbine engines could carry her.

"Jacob!" She flew under his arms. "What are you doing?" she cried.

"Pin…Pin-bot? You-you can…speak?" Everything was now reversed. Pin-bot's voice was crisp, clear and distinctive, while Jacob's was distorted and full of static. Jacob did his best to smile. "Sorry for…modifying you."

"It's okay, Jacob. You were only trying to help. Now it's my turn." Pin-bot clamped her tiny hands around Jacob's arm and tugged. "We need to get away from here, Jacob!"

"Can't...Moon has me trapped. I…I can't move."

Pin-bot flew out from under Jacob's arms and went on the attack. She began butting the moon, leaving her round indentation on its rough surface.

Jacob found it amusing every time her tiny body slammed into the moon. *Did she really think she could do any damage?* After the cannon's failed attempts at destroying the moon, did Pin-bot actually think she would be the one who would eradicate it from the skyline? "It…it's no use," Jacob said. "We're...out of…options..."

Pin-bot levelled off and returned to Jacob's side. Her front side was clouded with a thin layer of dust from the moon, but the glow of her eyes was as vivid as always. "I remember, Jacob!"

Jacob was now down on one knee. The pistons within his legs were completely shattered and hung freely at the joint. "Re-remember?"

"Yes, Jacob. I remember my model number!"

Though it was only for a brief moment, the blue in Jacob's eyes flashed bright. "You…you do?" *Please be 800!*

"Model number *800,*" Pin-bot said.

Jacob's eyes burst open. "*800*? Are...are you sure? You...you have to be sure...Pin-bot..."

"Yes, Jacob. Model *800*. The first off the line."

"And…and I modified you…That…that means…" Jacob did his best to look up, but his chest-plate had crumpled against his knee. "We can still…destroy the moon!"

Pin-bot's eyes nearly filled the black screen of her face. "But how, Jacob?"

Jacob made sure Pin-bot was looking into his eyes. "*You*...Pin-bot. It…it's up to *you*. You have to do this…for all of us."

Pin-bot's CPU was simple, but she knew what this would involve. Neither of them would survive. She rotated from left to right. "No, Jacob! I can't do that. I can't harm you."

The moon was now completely smothering Jacob. The seam in his back ruptured and peeled apart from opposing sides. The two bolts on top of his head, the ones that Pin-bot had helped remove not too long ago, came loose and splashed into the pool beneath his feet. "Please…Pin-bot…You promised to always help…Keep your promise. I need you to...keep your promise..."

Pin-bot had no choice. She had been given a direct order, and it was not in her to disobey. Regardless of her decision, she could see that Jacob would not survive the moon's arrival. If Jacob was moments away from returning to the Earth, she was not going to let him begin his journey alone. Her sacrifice to him meant everything to her. She flew up and nudged her tiny body against the side of his face. Although Jacob could not see them, her eyes had formed into hearts. "Goodbye...Jacob." Pin-bot ended her final words with a familiar, "Beep-beep."

"Goodbye…Pin-bot…'Beep-beep' to you too…"

Pin-bot's entire front side, including her eyes, transformed into a grid of red circles. One by one, they began disappearing with a resounding *beep* each time. She had begun her countdown.

Jacob slumped forward. He let out a scream for the very last time. His entire upper body exploded from the pressure. The moon came crashing down on him.

* * *

It was Earth's selflessness that allowed its inhabitants to inflict unwarranted devastation to the moon. It was the Earth that watched in silence, as its creations tainted the moon's surface, leaving footprints and wounds that would never fade. The moon had no sympathy for the Earth. It drove itself deep into the Earth, hoping to inflict the same amount of damage that it had been forced to endure.

Already weakened, the Earth was unable to put up a valiant fight. It trembled under the moon's might, and the now inseparable masses began to shift. Earth was beginning to rotate. The movement, however, was not smooth as it had been in the past. The weight of the moon was inconsistent. Its balance was unorthodox causing the complete destruction of the Earth's central pivot point. The Earth could no longer maintain its integrity, and it staggered through space, dipping uncontrollably from side-to-side, even threatening to release itself from the sun's grasp.

Gravity was immediately restored but with aggressiveness never before felt. Mountains flatten out, buildings crumbled to the ground, and valley walls collided against each other, filling in their gaps, eradicating their very existence. Violent winds roared constantly even as day fell to night, night to day, in an endlessly, sped-up cycle. The stars no longer twinkled with subtly but streaked across the sky as solid-white lines. The Earth was being reborn, and, as predicted, it was unpleasant.

There was peace, however, in the most unexpected part of the Earth. Impervious to what was occurring all around it, the actual site where the moon had made contact with Earth...was quiet. If it wasn't for this tranquillity, Pin-bot's final cries would have gone completely unnoticed.

"Beep... Beep... Beep..." She sounded small, even innocent at first. Quickly, however, the silent gaps between her calls shortened. "Beep, beep, beep..." A weak light suddenly fought its way through the tiniest of gaps that separated the moon and the Earth. "Beep-beep... Beep-beep..." The light intensified. "Beep-beep-beep-beep..." In an instant, her calls strengthened. The gaps were no more. Once rhythmic and with a balanced tempo, Pin-bot's beeping turned into one solid, high-pitched scream. And then, as suddenly as her calls had erupted from beneath the moon... they stopped. The light became solid. It was the perfect warning for the moon to brace itself. This would be its final moments of dominance.

Her promise, and in the end, her sacrifice to Jacob, was entirely for this moment. Modifications that Jacob had made to her, allowed for her internal circuitry to become unstable. She exploded with a vengeance. She tore into the moon with admirable force. The initial blast sent a shockwave screaming all the way around Earth's perimeter, and it eventually collided with itself on the opposite end.

The moon sustained a fatal wound. A deep crack appeared and ran all the way up its length before branching out in every direction. Parts of it began to break away, crumbling back down toward the Earth. Light bled out heavily from all of its newly formed crevices. It dazzled briefly until growing strong enough to become a single, solid light source.

A second and final blast, made the first one seem timid. The parts that had been held together by the moon's last breath, violently came apart. The explosion tore the moon from the inside out, forcing it to finally release its hold on the Earth. Its pieces were sent back into the empty sky, only to come back down again. But this time, the debris was dispersed evenly and peacefully.

Earth's rotation was finally allowed to regain normality. Its central pivot point was restored. The sun was even able to reach out and bring the Earth back into its ambient embrace, realigning their relationship. Day and night cycles stabilized, giving the sun the chance to warm the Earth's surface during the day, while stars were allowed to dazzle each and every night. And for the first time since Project Redemption had dragged the Earth to a halt, balanced gravity was restored.

Finally, after a long and enduring slumber, Earth took in its first breath and exhaled a deep sigh of relief. Earth's core was beginning to warm.

* * *

Below the surface, Earth had taken on a fiery-red demeanour with each beat of its core. Molten rock surged through Earth's veins, rising higher and higher, warming everything it touched.

Soon, the liquefied rock reached the massive deposits of frozen water and bored into the dense, crystallized mass. Cracks began to form across the nearly opaque mass, only to disappear as quickly as they were created. The water was melting so rapidly that cracks and imperfections instantly fused.

Eventually, the water's solid state was no more. The molten rock serenaded the water back toward the Earth's surface. Life, in its liquid form, was about to make its glorious return.

Silence had swept across the Earth's wounded exterior. It had just won a battle in which it had never even mounted any sort of offense. For now, rest was all it needed. Wounds needed healing, and scars needed to be formed. Earth wasn't expecting to awaken so soon after it had claimed victory. The thick plates forming Earth's protective skin began to separate, allowing a deep, guttural rumble to surface. Earth staggered. Water erupted from its pores, rupturing all of the wounds that had yet to heal over. The water was thick, and nearly opaque-white. It swept angrily across the barren land, swallowing valleys whole and drowning collapsed mountains with one overwhelming gulp. Raging rivers poured into massive pools, forcing them to swell into one massive ocean. Earth was plunged into deep-blue tones—a distinct complexion that, at one time, defined Earth's appearance against the black, empty canvas of space.

Molten rock, still erupting from Earth's surface, warmed the massive ocean, creating a thick layer of mist. With the majority of Earth now buried in water, this mist had nowhere to go but up. Constantly feed by the warming ocean, the mist reached the sky, and once there, it rapidly cooled and solidified into dense cloud arrangements. These clouds grew so thick and strong that they broke apart, forming new, extravagant formations. It wasn't long before the sky was filled with clouds in all shapes and sizes. They loomed high over the Earth and watched, as the past resurrected itself down below.

Engorged with water, clouds soon became heavy and broke apart. From their soft, gentle seams, droplets of water were released. The first drop to return to the Earth, slashed down and broke apart against the very hand that had helped bring it back to the surface. That hand belonged to Jacob.

Epilogue

Light from above penetrated the calm surface of the ocean, creating ribbons that danced against her vertically angled spines. The water was warm against her scaly surface and provided rich nourishment each time it filtered through her complex arrangement of gills. She had spent most of the day in search of a place that would become her new home. No ordinary place would do. She needed a place that would protect her from what grew inside these life sustaining waters. Monsters, many times her size, roamed these seas, hunting down her kind in order to fulfil their most basics of needs—survival. She could not let this interfere with her own needs, one that was nearly at the end of its cycle.

Lowering herself so that her soft underbelly was flat against the ocean's floor, her search had come to an end. Her black eyes spotted a reflective object poking out from the soft, sandy floor. Its main surface was flat, with five multi-jointed protrusions curled over itself forming a protective arch. The rest of it was buried deep inside the ocean's floor. She swam closer, allowing cautiousness to linger. There was no telling what was hidden in the object's grasp. Shells and coral adorned nearly the entire surface but posed no threat. Odd looking strands, pushing out from cracks in the object, did not match the textures of the surrounding plant life. They flowed with an artificial rigidness against the water's constant current. She had never seen anything like those strands, but they appeared harmless.

She had found the perfect place. Happily, she swam around her new home, sweeping her broad tail back and forth, removing the sand that had collected inside of the object's palm with each pass. Once satisfied, she stopped in front of the arch and slowly backed her slender body into the awaiting gesture. Her new home held her comfortably in place and gave her protection for what she was about to do. A surge of water was pulled deep into her gills, as she laid her batch of eggs.

* * *

The ocean's plentiful bounty had nourished his basic needs up to this point. The water was now receding. Any chance of survival would have to be sustained on land. Fortunately, he had evolved for this moment. He climbed out of the dwindling ocean for the first time and did not hesitate. His gills were now lungs, and they gorged on their first taste of air. It was painful, but it was something he would have to get used to. Leaving the water's security meant that vulnerability was immediately heightened. The soft mud underneath his smooth, moist body was cooling, but the comfort would not last. His skin was delicate and was not immune to the scorching heat of the sun. He needed protection. He needed to stay out of reach from potential enemies that walked the earth—enemies that he knew nothing about.

Two beady little eyes, set high on his head, searched the open landscape. Dense foliage, something he had never seen before, was too far in the distance for him to reach with his insignificant strides. He would never make it. Closer to him was something he could easily get to. An odd looking structure rose out from the mud. Five multi-jointed protrusions set on top of a flat base were casting an alluring shadow on the ground. It made for a perfect shelter. He waggled his tail, freeing himself from the last few drops of the ocean's influence. Then using his tiny fins, he hopped across the ground. Once at the base of the structure, he buried himself in the mud, only allowing his eyes to poke out. For now, he'll just have to wait. Evolution was all about enduring different stages of life. He had just completed his very beginnings.

* * *

A dense barrier of tall grass concealed him from the vast open plains. A herd of four-legged herbivores stained the vivid-green scenery. They grazed mindlessly on the plentiful vegetation provided by the Earth.

He had been following them for three days and three nights. They temped his hunger, and motivated his offensive stance. An intimidating spear, punctuated by a jagged tip and carved from bone, was held tightly in his enormous hand. He advanced, dragging his knuckles across the hard ground. His forwardly angled eyes were set high on his large cranium and kept the herd within his immediate field of vision. His body was thick, rugged, and bulging with muscle, contradicting his methodical movements. Hair covered his entire body and flowed in unison with the tall grass. He needed to be quiet. This was the only practical way to hunt. Brute force, something he had relied on during his youthful and inexperience days, would have driven the herd into a frenzy, successfully ending his hunt. Hunting in that manner was no longer efficient, and the scars riddled all over his body were a constant reminder of past failures. He had evolved his ways. He had learned that to make a kill and to satisfying his hunger, he would have to use the most significant weapon he had. Intelligence. The spear he held close to his side was merely a tool to be used to bring about a successful conclusion.

He parted the tall grass down the center and saw a straggler weakened by the simple need to constantly feed. It was an enormous buck, many times his size. The base of its antlers resembled tree trucks, with branches for tips.

He had purposely kept downwind of the animal, as a buck of this size would not retreat, nor would it be easily intimated. He crept forward and had only taken a step when he saw a strange object protruding from the ground. It was much too shiny and far too complex to be a rock, but it might serve a purpose. He used his spear to dig it free from the ground. Once in his grasp, he examined it closely. Though its complexity bewildered him, it was the way the light was striking the object's surface, causing a distracting gleam that excited him.

The buck was slowly moving away. He needed to make his move. With spear in one hand and the strange object in the other, he stood up causing a loud rustle in the grass. The buck immediately turned and faced him. It snorted, whipping its massive head from side-to-side.

The man planted his feet and stood his ground. He angled the object in his hand with the sun, allowing the glare to strike the buck's eyes. The buck winced. It pawed at the ground with his front leg, ripping a deep gash into its surface. The man remained calm, turning the object in his hand to allow all five protrusions to absorb the light. It was working. The distracting light was confusing the buck, driving it into a frenzy. It let out a deep grunt, preparing to charge. The man grunted louder, coaxing it toward him. The buck threw its weight on its hind legs, preparing to charge, but then, it simply collapsed. It let out a guttural cry. Slender hooves buckled under its enormous weight. When the beast collapsed on its side, the man saw the spear that had been driven deep into the buck's flesh, shearing the heart in half. It let out a final cry as life drained from its body.

The man walked over to the buck and waited until it took its final breath. He grunted, and another man jumped out of the tall grass. His hunting partner. It was his spear that was stained in deep-red ochre. Their strategy had worked perfectly.

No longer needing the object, the man set it down on the ground and then stood over the kill. Together, they let out a victorious grunt. They had used their ever-evolving intelligence to ensure their survival.

* * *

"Hey, over here!" A shirtless man yelled out, ripping his shovel out of the ground. His skin was golden brown, baked by the midday sun.

His partner, who wore a thick-rimmed hat, was in mid-stride, about to sink her own shovel into the hard bedrock. She wedged the shovel's head into the dry Earth and then used its shaft to brace her weight. Beads of sweat trickled down the side of her face. It had been a day full of disappointments, spent in the intense sun. She brushed some of the sweat away with her forearm, but it didn't make much difference. More sweat concentrated almost instantly. "What is it this time?"

"Come over," the shirtless man said. "I think I found something."

"More worthless rocks?"

"Just get over here."

She sighed and let go of her shovel, allowing it to fall onto the ground. She made her way over expecting to be disappointed as usual.

"Only started digging here a moment ago," the man said. "Looks like I might have found something already."

"I sure hope so. An entire week of digging in this dried up ocean bed, and so far nothing." She frowned. "Give us something, damn it! Anything! Doesn't even have to be museum-worthy." She crouched over her partner who had already begun the tedious task of picking away the embedded dirt that had impregnated itself around the object. “Oh, you *did* find something.”

Little by little, the object was revealed, which, ironically, made it more and more mysterious. The last bit of dirt was blown away with a gratifying exhale. There was an awkward pause, as they stared at the object. They studied the mangled form, the rust eaten surface, the flat part, and the three protruding sections.

“Okay…so what is it?”

The man studied the object. “You know, it sort of looks like a hand.”

She laughed. “A what?”

“A hand.” He moved the object around. He even sized it against his own hand. Some of the fingers were obviously missing, but what was there—the palm, the thumb, the two other fingers, all lined up perfectly. “See? A hand.”

She shook her head. “Hands aren’t made from rusted pieces of junk.”

“I know that. I’m just saying. There are fingers, a palm, and most of the forearm. It looks like a hand to me.”

“Okay, so who…or what…does it belong to?”

“I don’t know.”

“Well, then, who created this hand?”

“I don’t know!” the man replied, becoming annoyed.

She stood up, not giving the object another look. “I knew it,” she said, tipping her hat forward and wiping the sweat from her forehead. “Another piece of junk. Why am I not surprised?” She simply walked away.

The man wasn’t as easily discouraged. “It *is* a hand,” he said to himself. “What else can it be?”

With her backpack slung over shoulder and shovel in hand, she yelled over at him, “Let’s go! Time to move to another site. Maybe we can salvage the rest of the day. This dried up ocean bed has given us nothing.”

The man stood up and held the object out in front of him. “But there’s more here! I know there is!”

“All I see is rock and a lot of dirt.” She began walking off. “Stay if you want, but I’m taking the horse and carriage with me.”

“Alright, alright. I’m coming. Just give me a moment, will you?” Clumsily, he shoved the strange object into his backpack.

“Hey!” she yelled back at him. “You’re not taking that with us? Just leave it here. It’s worthless.”

“Fine!” He waited until her back was turned and then closed his backpack. *Never know. It might be important to us…someday.* The man hoisted his backpack over his shoulder and ripped the shovel out from the rock. Dirt clung to the tip of the shovel, so he banged it against the ground. The rock he was hitting began to crumble. A dim-red light filtered through the messy seams of the ground, causing the man to stagger back. “Hey! Hey, look! I think I found something!”

* * *

He had seen the girl come in once before. The girl was no more than ten years old and was again unaccompanied by parents. She kept her hands hidden inside the deep pockets of her ragged pants that were shredded at the cuffs. Hair long and tangled overflowed her narrow shoulders. She stood on the very tips of her mud-caked boots, worn high enough to engulf most of her legs up to the knees. She didn't seem to acknowledge, or want to acknowledge, the messy trail she dragged in behind her that led all the way back to the doors. She stood in front of the main window, as she had done earlier. Peering over from time to time, from the corner of the pale lit waiting room, the man had watched the girl make her way across the room, hampered by an obvious limp. Getting to where she was now had been a major accomplishment. From where the man was sitting, he could not see who the girl was talking to behind the window. All he could see was a frown appearing over the girl's face and then a lowering of the head. It was a disappointing send off. The girl turned away and followed her muddy trail all the way outside and out of the man's sights.

Wonder what that was all about. The man sighed. He fell back into his chair, silently praying for his name to be called soon. He had been trapped inside the hospital's waiting room for what seemed like forever. It was an impossible wait, one that was severely testing his patience.

The injured, the sick, the ones hoping that their loved ones would return with good news, filled the inadequate room beyond its capacity. Fortunately, he didn't need one of the room's poorly conditioned chairs. He just needed a place to park his. A distinct metal smell roamed the air, making the already sterile room even more potent. It didn't bother him, however. He was used to it. Next to him sat a woman, thick on all sides and laden with perfume pungent enough to fend off the room's metal aroma from time-to-time. Neither sick nor injured, she was obviously waiting for someone. She was reading a magazine and suddenly dropped it in her lap. "Can you believe this?"

Being the only one within her range of torment, the man predicted that her vocal opinions were about to continue with him as the unfortunate recipient. He glanced over at her and was met by a pair of budging eyes, a double chin, and a magazine article practically shoved in his face. "Excuse me?"

The woman shifted her immense weight toward him, furthering baiting him into the magazine article. "This," she said, jerking the magazine back and forth.

Not having any idea to what she was referring to, he shrugged and turned away.

The woman shook her head, clearly angered. "They found more pieces from the crash site on planet Titan," she said. "I tell you, it's like some sort of graveyard up there."

The man's eyebrow twitched, not particularly surprised at what he was hearing.

"Wonder how those pieces got up there in the first place," the woman said, continuing with her one-sided conversation. She slapped the magazine closed and then focused her attention entirely on the man who did his best to ignore her. "I tell you," she said, leaning closer, "ever since they found that mechanical hand here on Earth, years ago, these damn scientists will stop at nothing to find out more about the past." She sighed. "And now they're even searching around on other planets. Pathetic if you ask me."

"Well... not exactly."

She leaned back quickly, as if surprised to hear him finally speak. "Oh? And why isn't it?"

"Knowing our past may help our future. We can only benefit from it."

"Ha! The only thing they're doing is destroying our future. All those damn parts they keep finding everywhere only feed their experiments. It's a damn shame what we're becoming."

"There aren't many options these days," the man countered.

"What? Are you serious?" She smacked the magazine into the side of her chair. "Mechanical parts and humans don't mix and shouldn't mix! Perfect way to kill off our race if you ask me."

The man reached down to pull the jacket from his lap over his right hand, but his attempt at concealment came too late. The overhead light reflected off his hand in a way that it wouldn't off a human hand.

"Oh..." she said, both shocked and embarrassed. "I didn't realize." She glanced around the room making sure no one was watching her, as she leaned in even closer. Now practically in his face, the woman whispered, "It's okay. My cousin had the same procedure done to him. I was totally against it at first, but it saved his life. Should be thankful." She pointed at the man's hand now completely hidden by the jacket. "Is that what you're in here for?"

"I'm sorry?"

"Your hand? Is that what you're in for?"

"Oh, uh... sort of. Just a check up."

"You sick?"

The man turned to her and gave a sad little laugh. "Aren't we all?"

She studied his face for a moment and then pointed her finger at him. "Wait just damn a minute." She opened the magazine and flipped a couple pages to the article she had been reading. "The President of Mechanical Lifestyle Corporation shares excitement over recent findings on planet Titan," she read. "And this is the quote from the president, 'Findings are an important step forward toward the growth of our future'."

The picture inserted with the story showed a man with the same chiselled jaw, the same deep sunk eyes, and the same receding hairline as the man sitting next to her. The magazine fell out of her hands. "It... it's you!"

The man instantly looked away. Mercifully, a nurse came out from behind the window and walked over to him, saving him from having to respond.

"We're ready for you," the nurse said. She had the biggest smile he had ever seen.

"About damn time," he said, under his breath.

The nurse placed a simple, white folder down onto the man's lap and unlocked the wheels of his chair so she could push him away.

"You don't realize what you're doing!" the woman cried out. "You're going to destroy us all…"

The nurse rolled the man out of the waiting room and into a quiet hallway where the lady could no longer bother him. "She a friend?"

"No. Just an annoyance."

They shared a laugh, as they proceeded down the sterile hallway. Every door the man saw was closed off. Through the thin glass adjacent to each door, he easily noticed that each room was occupied. "Busy?" he joked.

"Been this way ever since I started. One patient leaves, another one takes their place. It's an endless cycle."

The man sighed. "We're doing our best to provide the hospital with parts. The demands are just overwhelming, and more testing needs to be done."

"And no slowing down, as far as I can tell."

"Trust me, after waiting that long inside the waiting room, I believe you." Unexpectedly, the man looked back at the nurse. "Almost forgot. While I was waiting back there, I noticed a girl come in."

"Yes, I know who you're talking about. She's always coming in."

"Is there something wrong with her?"

The nurse smiled and gently coaxed the man's head back around. "You know I can't give out that sort of information…even to you, sir."

"Just feel bad for her is all."

"You're not the only one," the nurse admitted. "I feel the same way every time she comes in."

"So she *is* injured."

"Some minor injuries…Cuts, bumps, bruises, everything we all suffer from time-to-time. Just makes it more difficult to deal with on someone so young."

"You can't help her?"

"I wish I could, but like I said, they're minor. We all have priorities at the moment, and unfortunately, her injuries aren't. That's why I have to turn her away every single time she comes in. Maybe I'll let the other nurse deal with her the next time. All she does is sort medical supplies all day."

"What do you tell that girl whenever she comes in?"

The man could feel the warm breath against the back of his neck, as the nurse deeply sighed. "Oh…just to wait and see. Who knows, she might get lucky one day."

"I hope so."

They continued down a long stretch of hallway where there were no doors. All was quiet except for an annoying squeal coming from the rusted wheels of the man's chair. Before they reached the room at the end of the hall, the man noticed empty display cases and wondered what they were there for. "Something going in those?"

"Eventually," the nurse replied, wheeling the man into the room.

A brisk beam of sunlight was pouring into the room. A large, metal table was taking up most of the space, but it was plain enough not to attract the man's attention. "Since you're back there, do you mind taking me right to the end of the room?"

"Not a problem," the nurse said.

Diagrams lined nearly every wall of the room, with each one depicting a familiar part of the human anatomy in extraordinary detail. Each bone, each muscle…each gear was so familiar to him.

Soon, they found themselves at the very end of the room.

"Here we are." The nurse bent down and attempted to press down on the locking mechanism on the man's wheel chair. It snagged and pinched her finger. "Oh, damn it!"

"You shouldn't say that," he joked.

The nurse smiled. "Sorry. I think I've said that word over three hundred times in the past week."

The man laughed. "Wow, that's a lot." He waved at her. "Don't worry about the chair. It's only rust. I'm fine."

Window shutters were open tempting the man to look out. He did so with a cautious smile drenching most of his face.

The powerful sun was scorching the barren Earth, but there was a small area of refuge. A secluded shadow was draped over an insignificant section of the Earth, caused by a massive asteroid looming in the cloudless sky. The man stared at the dull-grey object, observed it, and even wondered about it. A cold shiver ran down his spine, as he pondered what could have happened if it hadn't been trapped inside Earth's orbit.

"Getting closer?" the nurse asked.

"I sure hope not. It would be unimaginable to think what would have happened if it hadn't slowed down. "

"It's best not to think about that sort of thing. I certainly don't."

"I agree."

The nurse offered to take the man's jacket, and he kindly surrendered it to her. She made her way to the door, and, as she placed the jacket inside a small compartment in the wall, a stack of pages fell out from inside the sleeve. "Oh, I'm so sorry," she said and bent down and retrieved the pages from the floor.

"It's not a problem, nurse."

"A book you're writing?"

"Not really. More of a journal."

The nurse wedged the corner of the journal between her fingers, preparing to flip through the entire stack. "May I?"

"I wish you could. Unfortunately, all the pages are blank at the moment."

The nurse tucked the empty journal inside the jacket's sleeve. "When were you planning on—"

"Soon. This injury hasn't allowed me to write much. Still getting used to my new arm." The man turned his arm in the sunlight, causing it to shimmer. "I'll start writing as soon as I'm healed." He smiled. "Need to start filling that journal soon. I want my new-born son to know what kind of man his father is turning out to be."

"I'm sure by the time he's old enough to read, your journal will be filled with interesting stories."

"I *hope* so."

"I should be getting back to the waiting room," the nurse said. "That line isn't getting shorter with me standing around."

"I completely understand." The man smiled. "How long before the doctor gets here?"

"The doctor will be with you shortly, sir. He's with a patient at the moment."

"Mechanical or human?"

The nursed smiled. "Sir, you know the doctor only works on one kind."

"His specialty..."

"You're right, sir...Humans..."

THE END

About the Author

Vo Tran was born in south Vietnam. He moved to Canada at a young age and has lived there ever since. He enjoys visual arts, technology, and nature. Forever Jacob is his first novel and it was inspired by his early character designs and illustrations. The first draft of Forever Jacob was completed during his lunch breaks while working as a welder.

To see Vo Tran's artworks, including Forever Jacob art, please visit his webpage
yawzway.com

Contact him
yawdraws@gmail.com

CPSIA information can be obtained at www.ICGtesting.com
Printed in the USA
LVOW101953160212

268925LV00002B/22/P

9 781614 342779